SING FOR THE RED DRESS

Smokey River Suspense Series

By Joseph M. Marshall III

LUCID
HOUSE
PUBLISHING

LU(CID
HOUSE
PUBLISHING

Published in Marietta, Georgia, United States of America by Lucid House Publishing, LLC
www.LucidHousePublishing.com.
©2024 by Joseph M. Marshall III
All rights reserved. First Edition.
This title is available in print and e-book formats.
Cover design: Troy King
Author photos: Kevin Garrett
Interior layout: Jan Sharrow, The Design Lab Atlanta

This novel is based on the author's heritage and knowledge as one of the leading Native American historians and writers. Lakota is his first language, and he was born into a traditional Lakota household on the Rosebud Reservation. The characters and events in this novel spring from the author's imagination, and any resemblance to a person living or dead is coincidental. Names of some places are fictionalized.

Library of Congress Cataloging-in-Publication Data:
Marshall III, Joseph M., 1946-
Sing for the Red Dress: Smokey River suspense series/ by Joseph M. Marshall III–1st ed.
Library of Congress Control Number:
Print ISBN: 9781950495542
E-book ISBN: 9781950495580
1. Lakota 2. Kidnapping 3. South Dakota
4. Missing and Murdered Indigenous Women and Girls 5. Sex trafficking
6. Family drama 7. Indigenous 8. BIA and FBI jurisdiction
9. Red dress and spirits 10. Native funerals 11. Romance
FIC030000, FIC059000, FIC022080

Acknowledgement

Lakota Woman's honoring song is provided by Jerome Kills Small, Oglala Lakota, and used with his permission.

Dedication

For all those still missing

And living in our hearts

CHARACTERS
[IN ORDER OF APPEARANCE]

Dr. Gavin Lone Wolf – Sicangu Lakota and Scottish, twin brother of Gerard Lone Wolf and brother of Loren (Lone Wolf) Hale, professor at Smokey River University, primitive archer, hunting guide, historian and anthropologist, PhD

Katherine Hill – Sicangu Lakota, fiancée of Gavin Lone Wolf, also called Soldier Woman, environmental attorney based in Washington DC, JD

Loren (Lone Wolf) Hale – Sicangu Lakota and Scottish, older sister of Gavin and Gerard, director of nursing at Smokey River Indian Health Service Hospital, RN, MS

Gerard Lone Wolf – Sicangu Lakota and Scottish, twin brother of Gavin and brother of Loren, retired Marine colonel, Iraq and Afghanistan combat veteran, owner and chief executive officer of Washington DC-based security firm, PhD

Andrew No Horn – Sicangu Lakota elder, uncle to Loren, Gerard, and Gavin, traditional healer (medicine man)

Amelia Old Lodge – Sicangu Lakota, Melvina Old Lodge's grandmother

Melvina Old Lodge – Sicangu Lakota girl who saved twelve other missing girls

Lieutenant Justin Primault – Mniconju Lakota, criminal investigator (CI) with Smokey River Tribal Police, BS

Ben Avery – Choctaw, chief of Smokey River Tribal Police, BA, MS

Morgan Hale – Winnebago, husband to Loren, father of Thomas and Theresa, principal of Kincaid County High School, BS, MS

Thomas Hale – Sicangu Lakota and Winnebago, son of Morgan and Loren Hale, university senior at Smokey River University

Dr. Clayton Lone Hawk – Sicangu Lakota, husband of Veronica Streeter (Lone Hawk), retired school administrator and president of Smokey River Sioux Tribe, PhD

Veronica (Streeter) Lone Wolf – Wife of Clayton Lone Hawk, foundation executive

Joby Bone – Sicangu Lakota, cousin to Lone Wolf family

Audrey Hinson – Sicangu Lakota, patrol officer, Smokey River Tribal Police

Madonna White Bear – Sicangu Lakota, patrol officer, Smokey River Tribal Police

Jason Singer – Sicangu Lakota, patrolman, Smokey River Tribal Police

Geoffrey Brousseaux – Sicangu Lakota, patrolman, Smokey River Tribal Police

Ben Wilson – Surveillance specialist, Wolf Star Security

Arlo Kinsley – Sheriff, Leighton County, North Dakota

James Arnold – Sheriff, Benson County, North Dakota

ONE

Below the dark thunderheads towering into the sky over the endless plains, the distant undulating hills seemed familiar, connecting to hazy memory behind the brown eyes trying hard to focus.

I'm home—almost home, she thought.

Summoning every ounce of strength and willpower she still had, she lifted her head and then rolled painfully onto her left side. Jumping from that eighteen-wheeler when it slowed for the sharp curve was necessary. She had to or she likely would have ended up somewhere in west central Nebraska. But now she had a broken ankle to add to her other injuries.

That broken ankle wasn't her main concern. Inside her abdomen was a persistent ache that flared into excruciating pain that was impossible to ignore. That was from the beating at the hands of Tulo after he had retaliated when she had slapped him. Nevertheless, she had somehow gotten away from the seemingly endless rows of camping trailers. How long ago that had happened, she couldn't remember no matter how hard she tried. The days since then blurred from light to dark, warm to cold, trails, gravel roads, rain and sun, hiding in culverts and trash bins, in snake infested thickets.

Abdominal pain was the only constant, even more than shivering and hunger and thirst. Because of it she hadn't been able to walk fast, moving at a steady hobble at best. But movement was her savior, no matter how slow, no matter how painful. She was beyond grateful for the sneakers she wore.

Pulling herself onto her left side, she propped herself on her left elbow and slowly looked around, squinting to bring objects into focus. The fence she had crawled under last night was some yards away, and beyond that was the gravel road to the little town of Hestor. She turned her head slowly to the left in the direction she was fairly certain was north. Home and Grandma were somewhere in that direction. All she needed was just enough strength to make it.

Sitting up drained her energy. Pain she could tolerate, had learned to tolerate, but her waning strength worried her. She could feel her strength leaving, seeping out of her battered body with each movement, and there was no way to replace it. Her last meal had been days ago, perhaps two weeks, and that had been the last piece of an energy bar she had stolen from an unlocked car.

Once away from her captors she was overwhelmed with guilt because she had left everyone else behind. Their names were on the folded paper in her right shoe, twelve names. The face that went with each was in her head. They were her companions through the pain. She still cried for them, mourned for them.

When she noticed the plumbing truck parked next to the camp kitchen, she slipped out while the man in the trailer had nodded off to sleep. That was it. No thought, just impulse and action. She had spent the evening in a parking lot in some small town, taking the baggy grey coveralls the driver had left in the van, a half-full bottle of water, and a banana. Her plan was simple, to walk during the night and hide during the day.

Walking was not easy. The pain in her abdomen made it impossible to take a long stride with her left leg. She finally found a slight sideways movement that helped maintain a steady pace without aggravating the injury inside. She knew internal injuries were not a good thing and getting help was what she needed. Standing in the way, however, was the issue of trust. Who would help her, a Native girl in baggy coveralls? Who would believe her? Probably not a white person. Most of all she wanted to stay away from men.

A breeze caressed her face. She tried to pull herself into a sitting position. That slight movement sent sharp stabs of pain through her stomach and chest, taking her breath away. But not a moan escaped her lips. Reluctantly, she lowered herself back down, her breath coming in gasps until the pain subsided to bearable.

The activity had spent much of her precious energy. Shifting her left hip a bit to stretch out the right side of her abdomen always helped. She was so tired and her breath was labored, her lungs seeming to want more air.

A new feeling, a new grain of awareness came from some part of her being, prompting her to move yet again. This time she slowly tilted her head to the right and her fingers touched the bare ground next to her hip. Her visual perception and the movement of her fingers seemed somehow strangely disconnected. Slowly she brushed the dirt and created a flat area.

Lifting her head, she focused on her fingers and began to scratch the first letter into the dirt, digging down as much as she could. Onto the second letter. Controlling her breathing kept the worst pain at bay. Onto the next letter.

Urgency kept her finger moving as her neck trembled from the strain. Finally, she finished her task. Her head dropped to the ground and she stared up at the sky. The sun was to the west behind the clouds. Cool breezes flowed across her body. Rest, she needed to rest.

Then she would go home.

TWO

Time in Paris passed too quickly for Gavin Lone Wolf and Katherine Hill. Pleasant late July weather added to the ambiance of the City of Lights. It was the second trip to France for Gavin. As an environmental lawyer for a Washington DC based firm, Katherine Hill's job had taken her all over the world, with Paris a frequent destination. The reason for this trip was an international conference on global warming on the campus of *Ecole Normale Superieure*, near the city's center and west of the Seine River. Gavin watched and listened as Katherine kept an audience of nearly two thousand riveted with her presentation. He fell in love all over again.

During the noon break Gavin diplomatically rescued Katherine from a steady crush of audience members who wanted to talk to her. Among the variety of striking and colorful conference attendees from all over the world, the two of them stood out in the crowd. Gavin attributed the curious and admiring glances to the fact that Katherine was, hands down, the epitome of Lakota woman beauty both inside and out. Though she had trimmed her raven hair it still hung nearly to her waist, a striking contrast to the white blouse and skirt she wore. He never once considered that his six foot four inch stature and long black hair were any kind of a factor. They managed to find a bit of solitude and privacy at a sidewalk café nearby.

After the afternoon presentations, they went to an early dinner with an acquaintance of Katherine's from South Africa. The gathering of seven included five climatologists so the conversation, though informative, was highly technical.

In the taxi on the way home, Katherine decided on a change of plans. With her presentation done, she opted to skip the last day of the conference—since a video of all the presentations as well as a transcript would be provided for a small fee.

"We can catch the train to Saint-Malo after a late breakfast," she said. "That way we'll have nearly two full days on the coast."

They arrived at the train station several miles from Saint-Malo just after noon the next day and boarded a shuttle bus to their hotel, which was two blocks from the wall that surrounded the oldest part of the town. They could see it from their room.

"This is a citadel town, with walls around the older part," Katherine said, turning tour guide. "The story is that pirates holed up here. Now the walls are a way to walk around the city and get a view of the channel. Up for an adventure before dinner?"

"Lead the way," Gavin said. "I go where you go."

She turned from the view and grabbed the lapels of his jacket. "I've been here twice, in this very hotel," she told him. "Both times I imagined you were here with me, and now you are. It doesn't get any better than this."

"It certainly doesn't," he agreed, pulling her into his arms for a long, intense kiss.

Views of the town and the channel were stunning, from sailboats in the harbor to the castle in the bay, the beaches, and the dark blue waters.

Gulls and other water birds wheeled in the air and a breeze followed them as they walked leisurely along a brick path guarded by a low stone wall with an iron rail, and old cannons posted every few yards.

With Katherine by his side, Gavin hardly noticed the other people enjoying the view. She was wearing denim jeans with a matching jacket, and her hair was loose, cascading over her shoulders. Her only jewelry was a necklace of black pearls and the jade ring on her finger he had given her long ago. Her deep brown eyes were luminous in the midst of her flawless brown face.

Gavin squeezed Katherine's hand and gently pulled her to him. "Hey," he said, softly. "I can't think of a better place to ask you something."

She squeezed back and smiled. "Sure," she said, "what's on your mind?"

"Us," he said, a bit nervously. "You still take my breath away," he told her. "Whether it's in my daydreams or in real life, like now."

The smile stayed on her face.

"You can't imagine how many times I've done this in my mind, in my dreams," he went on, trying to control his emotions. "You've always been with me, in my wishes and hopes. And, now, here you are. Here we are."

A slightly quizzical expression filled her eyes. She nodded. "I don't want to be anywhere else," she said.

He took a deep breath, reached into his left pocket, and took out a small, tanned hide pouch, pulling the string to open it. "I've kept this," he said, taking out a diamond ring. Her breath caught as she recognized it from Gavin's first proposal to her ten years ago. She had said no because she was set on joining a law firm in Washington DC and could not see Gavin enjoying the crush of big city living.

"I don't know what the proper etiquette is for using or not using an engagement ring that was returned," he said, "but as far as I'm concerned, this ring was meant for your finger."

She smiled as tears came to her eyes and nodded in anticipation.

When he made a move to kneel, she stopped him.

"No," she said tenderly, pulling him up. "No, you don't kneel to me. We start this life eye-to-eye and heart-to-heart. Now, please, ask me the question."

He took another deep breath and ignored the tear sliding down his face. "Katherine, you are the love of my life. I love you more than anything in this life. Will you marry me?"

She nodded, taking his hand in both of hers. "Gavin, you are the love of my life, and I love you more than anything in this life, and you don't know how many times I've wanted to hear that question again, and give you this answer—yes! Forever, this time."

His hand shook a bit as he waited while she switched the jade ring to her right hand. In its place he slid on the diamond.

They held each other as if it were the last thing they would ever do and watched the reddish glow of the sun setting behind the city. People on the wall couldn't help but gaze at the brown-skinned couple, the tall man with the air of an adventurer, a single braid to his waist, and the slender woman with even longer hair.

"Now I have a question," she said

"And that is?'

"When?"

"As soon as possible, but whenever you say."

"As soon as possible," she replied.

"Right. Let's talk about it over dinner. I'm anxious to tell Loren."

Walking slowly, they retraced their steps, oblivious to the other people on the stone walkway.

"There's something I'm curious about," he said.

"What is it?"

"When you came home after Grandma died, was that something spontaneous?"

She smiled up at him. "No. Grandma was one of three reasons."

"Three?"

"Yeah, Grandma, a friend of mine who died of ovarian cancer, and you. I had a very close friend. Her name was Karin, and she had hopes and dreams just like me."

"Was she a lawyer, too?"

"No, an interior decorator who knew what she wanted out of life, and who she wanted it with. She was only thirty. She gave up part ownership of a lucrative business to move to Atlanta to be near her fiancé. She had it all planned out. She put nothing ahead of her feelings for the man she loved and wanted to start her life with him immediately. And then came the diagnosis."

Gavin squeezed her hand as they walked slowly. "Life isn't fair," he said.

Katherine nodded slowly. "After her funeral her fiancé, Josh, gave me a card with a note she wrote to me that said "There is no guarantee of happiness, and no happiness without risk." She knew about you because I told her, and she was always encouraging me to get back together with you. I took it to heart, partly because her time with Josh was so brief. And I didn't want to have an 'if only' moment in my life."

"I would like to have known your friend."

"You would have liked her. She was special and taught me a lot."

Gavin waved back at an elderly couple who had waved at them. Eventually they made their way down to the street level and, yielding to the moment and the seductive, warm summer evening, took a table at a sidewalk café where candles on each table flickered in the breeze. Both ordered a roasted quail dish with wild rice, and of course, a bottle of wine.

Gavin snapped a photo of the ring on Katherine's hand and texted it to Loren, with a message:

She said "Yes!"

He followed it up with a photo of the street. Loren's reply to the first message came less than a minute later:

> ***Congratulations to both of you!***
> ***Call if you can.***

He placed the call and put it on speaker.

"You realize, little brother, that I am now the matriarch of our family and as such I am in charge of planning your wedding."

"We wouldn't have it any other way," Katherine assured her.

"Wonderful! My sense is that we have the ceremony at Grandma's place. I know she is smiling on the other side. Just let me know when you set the date."

Katherine nodded at Gavin. "That's, a wonderful idea, and soon, very soon," she said.

"Well, we'll have time to talk. Have a great time and stay safe. Where in France are you, by the way?"

"A little coastal town called Saint-Malo," Gavin said. "It's an old pirate haven, picturesque, and very romantic."

"That's so perfect. Is it okay for me to spread the word?"

"Of course," Gavin said. "Do me a favor and give Uncle Andrew a call."

Loren Lone Wolf Hale was Gavin and Gerard's older sister, and the director of nursing at the Smokey River reservation Indian Health Service hospital. Her husband Morgan Hale, a Winnebago from Nebraska, was the principal at Kincaid County High School, the largest public high school on the reservation.

Gavin disconnected the call and reached for her hand. "Well, here we are, straight out of Horse Creek," he said. "That cute little Lakota girl with the large, dark eyes and the gangly Lakota boy. We certainly have a European connection now. I'll never forget this place."

After dinner they strolled along a narrow cobblestone street, peering into shop windows and watching street performers. Gavin purchased a hand woven scarf for Katherine from a street vendor, and two more for Loren and her daughter, his niece Theresa. On the way back to the hotel, his phone chirped. It was Gerard.

"Hey, little brother," he said. He would never let Gavin forget that he, Gerard, was two minutes older. "I felt a disturbance in the force. What's happening?"

"Oh, I just took your advice. She's not getting away. Here," he said. Say 'hello' to your new sister-in-law." He passed the phone to Katherine.

"Hey, Gerard. How's your day been?" she said, smiling.

"Never mind my day, sounds like you all had a great one. Congratulations!"

"Thank you! See you soon." She handed the phone back.

"Hey, bro," Gavin said. "I remembered what you said that day we had lunch at the Gemini Restaurant. Thank you for that."

"Well, it's a damn good thing you're smarter than you look, bro. I'm happy for both of you, beyond words. I am the best man, right?"

"That goes without saying."

"I'm honored, bro. I'm honored. Dinner's on me when you get back here."

"Thanks, see you in a few days."

Gavin disconnected the call. He had heard a tiny bit of wistfulness in his brother's voice. Twelve years ago Gerard had lost his wife Marilyn to cancer.

"I'll never grow old with the woman I loved more than life," he had said to Gavin.

Gavin stopped in front of a pastry shop and tenderly took Katherine's hand. Lifting it, he bent forward, and kissed it softly.

"Oh, my. Thank you. What was that for if I may ask?"

Holding onto her hand he gazed around at the setting—cobblestone streets, narrow storefronts, and sidewalk cafés, and the people going about wherever duty, need, serendipity, or whim was taking them.

"For life," he said.

THREE

Gavin and Katherine were surprised and baffled when they checked in for their flight at Orly International Airport just outside Paris, two days later. They had been upgraded from business to first class. After settling in, he took out his cell phone and texted a message to Gerard in DC.

Hey, Bro. Thanks for the upgrade.

The reply came quickly:

You're very welcome. Enjoy the ride.

Gavin followed up:

I don't recall telling you our airline or flight number.

The reply was not surprising:

Bro, I'm in the finding out stuff business.

Gavin could only smile. Colonel Gerard Lone Wolf, USMC, retired, was the owner and CEO of Wolf Star, a security research and assessment company based in Washington DC.

Right! Thanks again.

He should have known.

A chirp showed Andrew No Horn's number.

> ***"Hau, Leksi. Tonitkuka hwo (Hello, Uncle. How are you)?"***
> ***"Hau, Tunska, matanyan yelo (Hello, Nephew, I'm good).***
> ***Your sister gave me the good news. I've been waiting a long***
> ***time for that to happen."***
> ***"Thanks, Uncle. We want you to do the ceremony."***
> ***"I will, I will."***

In spite of the happiness of the moment, Gavin could sense an underlying tone of sadness in his uncle's voice. Andrew No Horn was a traditional healer, a "medicine man" in white people parlance. He had stepped in as the father figure for Loren, Gerard, and Gavin when their parents—Gabriel and Molly McClean Lone Wolf—were killed in a car crash.

"We're on the airplane and a few minutes to taxiing," Gavin said.

"Good, good. Hang on to the good news because there's some tough news here."

"What happened?"

Gavin could hear his uncle's sigh. "Do you remember Amelia Old Lodge, who lives in the Fast Creek District?"

"I do."

"Well, her granddaughter was found yesterday, just north of the state line."

"Dead?"

"Yeah, in a pasture by a ranch hand moving some cows. But the thing is she was missing for almost a year. She was fifteen."

A chill went through Gavin as he politely waved off the offer of a glass of champagne from the flight attendant.

"*Leksi*, are you saying that a girl who's been missing for a year was found dead in a pasture? Was she there the whole time?"

"No, that's the thing. She probably died there in that pasture a few hours or days before she was found, according to your friend, Lieutenant Primault, the criminal investigator."

"Oh, damn, why was she there?"

"Yeah, that's the question," Andrew said. "She was seven miles from home. And Lieutenant Primault wants to talk to you. I told him you'll be back in a few days."

"Right. I'll call him when we're in country."

"Okay, give my niece a hug for me."

Gavin disconnected the call and glanced at Katherine, who had been listening.

"Tell me," she said.

Gavin passed on the news. "Grandma Amelia Old Lodge is ninety," he said. "She's been a widow for nearly twenty years. Melvina was her oldest son's daughter, and he was killed in Iraq in 2004. I don't understand how life can be so tough on people like her."

Katherine squeezed his hand. "I think we should go see her. I've got to be in the office for a couple of days, but we can get you a flight out right away. I'll join you after that. Let's help her with all the expenses that are going to mount up."

He nodded. "Of course. I'm sorry for the sad news."

"No," she said. "No apology necessary. That's what life is, taking the good with the bad, right?"

He sighed. "It is, and I'm glad we're facing it together."

FOUR

Gavin followed Loren and Andrew to Amelia Old Lodge's small frame house three miles west of Hestor, a small town on the southern edge of the reservation. Her granddaughter Melvina had been found seven miles to the south, less than a hundred yards north of the Nebraska and Smokey River Reservation border. The body was still with the medical examiner in Rapid City.

Frail was the first word that came to mind when Gavin saw Amelia in a black dress that appeared two sizes too large. Her hair was totally gray and her face deeply lined. She reached out to shake their hands and smiled. The sadness in her old eyes was unmistakable, but with it was a spark of resilience.

"Sit down," she said, lifting small, gnarled hands and pointing toward a couch against a wall. "Bring some coffee for them," she instructed one of her granddaughters. It was apparent that everyone in the family was in deep shock.

"*Ake yupiyakel yahi* (It's really good of you to come again)," Amelia said to Andrew.

"*To, mitunjan na mitunska ob wahi* (Yes, I came with my niece and nephew)."

Amelia smiled at each of them. Doreen, one of the younger granddaughters, whom Gavin knew, brought coffee. Loren and Gavin stood to give her a hug. "Thanks," he said. She nodded and returned to the kitchen.

Cordelia Janis, Amelia's daughter, joined them. "The police just called," she told them after taking a seat. "The autopsy is done and they'll release my niece's body tomorrow. The funeral home will go up there and get her." She paused to glance at a calendar on the wall. "Mom wants two nights of wake, one night here and one night at St. Ignatius Church, so the funeral will be next Thursday."

Amelia listened with her head down, a white handkerchief in her hands, occasionally dabbing at her eyes with it. She lifted a hand and pointed to the south.

"They said she was just over there, seven miles," she said. "She almost made it home." She dabbed at her eyes as a soft sob shook her chest. "At least we have her back."

After Cordelia and Doreen served them lunch, Gavin said his goodby to Amelia and her family. Katherine was arriving in Sioux Falls on an eight o'clock flight and it was a four-hour drive. On the way he had a stop to make—in Agency Village, where the Bureau of Indian Affairs had been headquartered since 1896—a meeting with Lieutenant Justin Primault.

The only criminal investigator for the Smokey River Tribal Police greeted his friend warmly. "Maybe one day we'll have a cup of coffee just for the sake of having a cup of coffee," he said to Gavin.

"I second that," Gavin agreed.

In the small conference room of the building that housed the police and the jail, Chief of Police Ben Avery joined them. Primault immediately brought them up to date.

"According to the preliminary autopsy report, that poor girl lived through hell," Primault told them. "She was seriously dehydrated and severely malnourished. But that's not the half of it. She had a broken right ankle, and extensive internal injuries. Her abdomen was filled with blood. The Medical Examiner listed the internal injuries as the chief cause of death. And there was probably sexual abuse as well."

Gavin could only shake his head. "No idea how she got to where she was found?"

"No. We did find her footprints in the ditch along the road. She probably crawled under the fence. She was found beside some shrubs, on her back." Primault opened a file and passed two photos to Gavin. "This is why I wanted to talk to you. I want to give these to her family, and maybe I should have done that immediately."

Gavin looked down at the eight by ten photographs, and for a second his breath caught in his throat. He stared at them. One of them showed the girl's right hand and letters scratched into the dirt. The second was of the letters only.

Gramma I lov u

The letters were uneven and crooked, but the message was clear and obviously intended for Amelia.

Gavin gazed at the photographs for nearly a minute before he glanced up at the two officers.

Ben Avery shook his head. "Seven miles from home," he said. "She almost made it. But getting to Justin's question. I know they should have the pictures, but maybe through a close friend or relative. I would be happy to do it, but I'm a cop and they don't know me."

"I agree," Gavin said. "My sister Loren knows Grandma Amelia's daughter, Cordelia. I could ask her and I'll ask my uncle Andrew as well."

"Thanks," Primault said. "One more thing. I made a plaster cast of her note. But it's obviously the reverse. Do you think the art department at the university can, maybe, make an actual model of it?"

"I'm sure. I'll check. So, what's next, on this case?"

Primault glanced down at his file. "Melvina was reported missing by her family about a year ago. She went to Pierre with some friends and never came home. As far as I'm concerned, her case ties in with all the other cases of missing Native women and girls."

"Any idea where she might have been taken?"

"Not a clue at this point. I sent an officer to Rapid City to bring back her clothes. I'll take those to a lab in Minneapolis to be part of the analysis. Hopefully we'll get some indicators."

Gavin took copies of the photographs to Jon Daly, one of the instructors in the art department at Smokey River University. Daly taught a ceramics class. After looking at the photos and hearing the story, he wiped his eyes and nodded. "I'd be more than happy to make a life size model for Melvina's family," he said.

His last stop before the interstate to Sioux Falls was home, ten miles southwest of the small town of Cold River. As he filled the water tank in the corral adjacent to the barn behind his house, two horses ambled to the rails to have their ears scratched. Both of them were part Spanish Barb mustangs he had bought from a horse sanctuary in the Black Hills—Red Wing and Dancer, a gray and a bay.

The three-bladed fan to the wind generator atop the twenty-foot pole was a spinning blur. All the power to his log house and barn were provided by the batteries in the partial basement, charged by the wind generator and the bank of photovoltaic panels in the front yard. Every kilowatt of electricity was supplied by the sun and wind. He was totally off the grid. Not only that, every piece of lumber for the house and barn was recycled from old houses and buildings he had purchased. The logs for his house were cast-offs, blemishes, from a log mill in Minnesota. His brother-in-law and nephew, Morgan and Thomas Hale, had helped him size them and put up the walls. Only the electrical wiring and the pipes for plumbing and the bathroom and kitchen fixtures were brand new.

Furthermore, he had never purchased a new vehicle in his life. The four-wheel-drive Jeep Wrangler, lifted and equipped with special suspension for off-road use, was over ten years old. The half-ton Chevrolet pickup, also a four-wheel-drive was only slightly newer. He was a stickler for proper vehicle maintenance. Although he could more than afford new vehicles, he believed that being sensible and saving money was far more important than image. Especially since a brand new vehicle cost more than his house and depreciated the moment one drove it off the lot.

After a short conversation with the horses, he shut off the pump and climbed into the pickup, just as his phone chirped. It was Uncle Andrew.

"*Hau, Leksi.*"

"*Tunska,*" the old man said. "Are you on your way yet?"

"Just pulling out of my yard. What's up?"

"Ah, I have an idea that your sister and I were talking about, for that little girl's funeral."

Gavin stopped on the trail. "Okay, what is it?"

"Well, that poor girl almost made it home. Amelia brought that up several times. So, I think maybe she should be carried in her casket from where she was found to her grandma's house. What do you think?"

A chill coursed through Gavin's body, and a lump came to his throat. "*Leksi*, I think that's exactly what should happen. I'm sure there'll be all kinds of people willing to carry her."

"Oh, for sure. But your sister thinks only girls and women should carry her. They could take turns, sort of like a relay, you know. That way we could take her the last seven miles to her grandma's house. That way, she will make it home, because that's what she was trying to do."

Gavin blinked away the tears in his eyes. Uncle Andrew's idea was a fitting tribute for Melvina Old Lodge, and in a very real way she would accomplish what she surely wanted with every last ounce of will and effort.

"*Leksi*, let's make that happen. Let's make sure she finishes her journey on this side."

"Yeah. Yeah, we have to. I'm going back in the morning to see Amelia. That seven miles is her journey to peace," Andrew said.

FIVE

Katherine wiped away tears as Gavin filled her in on Uncle Andrew's idea. They had stopped at a restaurant near Interstate 90 for a bite. "We have to do that for her," she said. "She needs to finish her earthly journey, carried by women and girls."

"The funeral director is sending a hearse for her body tomorrow," he told her. "*Leksi* is going to talk to Amelia and her daughter."

Ten miles down the interstate Katherine shared her news. "I had a long meeting with my boss, Jared Snyder," she said. "And we came to an agreement. So, I have two new contracts in my briefcase, but before I sign either one, we need to talk."

"I'm all ears."

"Good. Well, here's the gist of it. He doesn't want me to leave the firm, so we came up with two options. One, the firm keeps me on half-time and pays me a straight salary, a regular paycheck every two weeks. Or, I work for them as the need arises and bill them for my time. In either situation, they cover expenses, such as phone and copying, and travel and lodging."

"Which would you prefer?"

"Well, half-time is more money but it means I'll have to set up an office, somewhere, with a separate phone and fax, and so on, and twenty hours of my week is blocked out. A case-by-case scenario gives me more free time. Either way there'll be some travel."

"I designed the house for just that—an additional room, for whatever purpose," said Gavin.

"Wonderful. Which of the two options would you prefer?"

"Given that I agreed to teach at least one class at SRU each semester, either option would work. But the case-by-case option is more appealing."

"Yeah, that was my initial thought. But Jared did give me a few days to decide, so we can talk about it again."

Though they pulled up in front of the log house around one thirty in the morning, Uncle Andrew's pickup was parked next to the Jeep and lights were on in the house.

"I wanted to be here when you arrived, my girl," he told Katherine. "You're already part of the family, but now as my nephew's wife, you're going to be my daughter-in-law."

"I'm so glad, *Leksi*," she admitted, enjoying the old man's welcoming hug. She glanced at the table where there were three cups and three bowls. "What's going on there?" she asked.

"Peppermint tea and *wasna*, made from chokecherries," he said. "I wanted our first meal together to be traditional."

In spite of the late night, Gavin was awake soon after dawn and slipped away for a shower.

Katherine was propped against two pillows and waiting with a smile when he returned. "Got any plans for this fine Saturday morning?" she asked.

"I do now," he said, pulling back the bed covers.

Afterwards they prepared and ate a leisurely breakfast of oatmeal, scrambled eggs, and black coffee.

"I watched the sun rise through the window of a remote hotel in Kenya," she told him. "A small herd of elephants walked by."

"No elephants here," he teased.

She chuckled softly. "That was a new and unforgettable experience, but so was this morning. I looked out the window and saw a familiar land-scape. I saw home, and for the first time in years, it felt like home."

He reached across the corner of the table and squeezed the tips of her fingers, marveling at how beautiful she was without make-up. But Katherine Kay Hill, or Soldier Woman as Grandma Annie had called her, was more than a beautiful exterior. That was a happenstance of genetics. The beauty on the inside was her real identity, a combination of kindness, grace, and emotional strength, among other things.

"Welcome home," he said. "Not all of us go back to where we belong, and this is where you have always belonged."

She raised her coffee cup. "I'll drink to that."

Deciding on a ride, they saddled the horses and headed for the river. Horses and riding were definitely ingrained in Lakota DNA, Gavin had always theorized. As far as he was concerned, Katherine proved his theory. Though she hadn't ridden in years, she quickly formed a bond with Red Wing, handling him as though she had ridden every day.

"I think this guy and I have made a real connection," Katherine said, stroking Red Wing's neck.

"Then, he's your new four-legged partner."

"Great. Can we get another Australian stock saddle like yours?"

"Sure. The Australian stock saddle store is just a click away."

Dismounting at the river, they led the horses and walked for nearly half a mile, startling several grouse and a small herd of Whitetail deer. A lone coyote watched them from a rise before melting into the thickets.

"Every time I was in a forest, I felt uneasy," she said. "They might have been beautiful and vibrant, but I still felt that uneasiness. The wide open grasslands of Kenya, on the other hand, struck a chord with me. And I knew why. A child of the plains connects with plains anywhere—the endless vistas and the open sky."

They rode up a long slope leading away from the river. At the top they turned north for two miles and then back east, riding along the north edge of Gavin's pasture. Katherine pointed to the three strands of light cable on the north fence.

"I've always favored cable for horse pastures," Gavin said. "No wire cuts that way. I've seen too many good horses with ankles, legs, and necks sliced by barbed wire. One of the worst inventions the *wasicus* ever came up with."

"That's a lot of work since the last time I was here," she pointed out.

"Yeah. Joby put it in for me, every last yard of it."

Back at the corral they brushed the horses after cooling them down. True to form, both horses immediately rolled in the dirt.

"I'd like to fix a meal for Uncle Andrew," she said. "He was so sweet to have tea and *wasna* waiting for us last night. What's in your freezer?"

"Buffalo steaks, burgers, and roasts. Might be some elk, too."

"Great. Feel like grilling?"

"Anytime."

"Wonderful, thanks. First let me call Uncle and see if he can fit us into his schedule."

As dusk yielded to night, Katherine, Gavin, and Andrew were seated around the fire pit in the backyard. The fire was more for atmosphere because the evening air was warm. Katherine had just explained her work situation to Andrew.

"I know you'll make it work," he said. "I'm just glad you're home."

Gavin's cell phone chimed in his trouser pocket, indicating an incoming text.

He read the message from Lieutenant Justin Primault.

> *Believe I have first solid clue*
> *regarding Melvina Old Lodge*
> *case. Brand of sneakers she*
> *wore is manufactured in*
> *Canada and sold in only two*
> *U.S. states-Minnesota and*
> *North Dakota.*

Gavin glanced up at the old man. "This is about Melvina," he said. "From the police?"

"Right. Justin Primault says that the sneakers she wore were made in Canada and sold in this country only in Minnesota and North Dakota."

The news immediately caught everyone's attention.

"So that raises the possibility that she was there, in either state," Katherine deduced. "But the obvious question is where, and why."

Gavin nodded. "You know as well as I do that where there are oil fields, there are 'man camps,' with workers who have nothing to do with the outrageous sums of money they earn but spend it on alcohol and women. Alcohol is plentiful even in remote areas, but not women. Native teenage girls are often lured or kidnapped in order to serve the men's undisciplined appetite for sex. I don't think there are any man camps in Minnesota.

But there are at least two in western North Dakota, so I think that's where she was."

"So, that poor girl somehow got away and traveled hundreds of miles trying to get home," Katherine said, shaking her head. "How did she do it?"

Andrew leaned forward, looking into the undulating flames of the fire in the pit. "I think she walked," he said.

Katherine put a hand to her mouth in both sadness and horror.

"Ask him about the soles of those shoes," suggested Andrew. "I'll bet they're worn."

Gavin nodded and typed out a text to Primault:

What is condition of the soles of those sneakers?

The reply came quickly:

Worn, with cuts and gouges.
Sides are torn and stained.

"He says they were gouged and cut and the sides were torn and stained," Gavin reported. On an impulse he dialed Primault's number.

"Justin," he said, when the CI answered. "You obviously have those sneakers in your possession. Will you still take them up to the lab in Minnesota?"

"Of course. Plastic bags with her clothes and shoes were brought back just today. I haven't opened them. I'll leave that to the lab. I was able to see them through the plastic."

"Right, Uncle Andrew thinks she walked."

"Given the condition of the shoes, I'd have to agree with him."

"And I'm just putting this out there. Maybe we can borrow one of those assault vehicles the state used against the protestors at Standing Rock to clean out the man-camps near the oil fields in western North Dakota."

"That's an interesting thought," Primault agreed.

"Right, anyway, thanks for staying in touch."

Gavin clicked off the call and glanced at the old man, who was looking back with a contemplative gaze. He suddenly realized that Katherine was looking at him as well.

"I'm sorry I said that," he told them.

"Sorry for what?" the old man asked. "From what I hear, cops know about our missing women. I mean the FBI, the North Dakota police, and county sheriffs. And they know about those man camps and they know about sex trafficking. What are they doing about it?"

"What about the Bureau of Indian Affairs and tribal police? What's stopping them?" Katherine asked.

Andrew's expression was grim. "I don't know about BIA and tribal cops, but the reason the feds and any white police don't care is because those are brown-skinned women and girls. If a cop in Winslow, Arizona, can shoot and kill a Native woman holding scissors—instead of talking her down or taking steps to disarm her—then why should society at large care about some missing Native girls?"

That was at the heart of the situation, the heated core, as it were. It was the reason law enforcement in general was doing nothing and why the perpetrators who were abducting and trafficking young Native women were getting away with it. That was the secret to success for the traffickers, pick on the one group that no one cares about.

"That's for damn sure," Gavin agreed. "And, I'm not excusing the BIA and tribal police departments, but a big part of the problem for them is jurisdiction. Without meaningful cooperation from the feds and county and state law enforcement, their hands are effectively tied."

"What about the tribes themselves?" Katherine wondered.

Gavin shrugged. "I don't know. It took a while for most of the tribes to get fully behind stopping the oil pipelines. The issue of missing Native women and girls has been happening far longer so it isn't as if their disappearance is immediate and compelling. Tribal councils don't work well with other tribal councils. Someone is always afraid someone else will get all the credit."

"That's a heck of a condemnation," Katherine said.

"Well, Native politicians are like any other color or ilk. They'll do what's necessary to keep their jobs, and that doesn't necessarily mean actually doing their jobs. There's only one exception that I know of."

"Really? Only one?" she asked, incredulous.

"Yeah, our neighbor has a first-hand perspective, unfortunately, about this issue of Native girls and women being abducted."

Andrew nodded emphatically. "He sure does."

"Well, tell me," Katherine commanded, wide-eyed.

Gavin took a deep breath. "I'm talking about our tribal president, Clayton Lone Hawk, and his wife Veronica. And I think we should have them over for dinner soon. The reason they met and eventually got married is because his daughter was abducted and raped."

"That's heartbreaking!" Katherine said. "I'm almost dreading hearing it."

Gavin nodded slowly. "It is, but it's also heartwarming."

"Okay, I'm listening."

"Well, short version," Gavin began, reaching for his tea. "Six years ago, Clayton's wife Celia died of cervical cancer. Almost four years ago, their only child, Autumn, was abducted by a white out-of-state pheasant hunter and raped. She managed to get away, but weeks later found out she was pregnant."

Katherine could only shake her head.

"Instead of telling her dad, she talked a family friend, a counselor, into arranging an abortion out of state. Something went wrong during the procedure and the doctor couldn't stop the bleeding, and she died."

"Oh, my god!"

"Meanwhile, the Redoubt County sheriff at the time was inept and racist, and didn't investigate the rape, which happened in Cold River. Turns out he helped to cover it up because one of his deputies was bribed by the rapist to destroy evidence.

"So when there was no other remedy, Clayton went after the rapist himself. He followed him to South America, to Patagonia, where he was hunting—the guy's name was George McKenzie. Clayton intended to kill him. Instead, he collected DNA evidence and brought it back, and somehow the FBI analyzed it, and matched it to the semen taken from Autumn and the sheets in the motel room, where she was raped."

"Please tell me that son-of-a-bitch is in jail."

"He is in federal prison. Twenty-five years with no parole. Turns out he was being investigated for being part of a ring that abducted Native girls."

"So how was Veronica part of it?"

"She was McKenzie's wife."

"No!"

"Yeah. She and her daughters were so horrified, angry, and hurt by what happened, that they came to apologize to Clayton. Both of them, Clayton and Veronica, said it was love at first sight."

Katherine dabbed at a tear.

"Three years ago they were married not far from here, along the river. And get this, Veronica's daughters proudly took Clayton's name—Dominique Lone Hawk and Pascal Lone Hawk."

"Even Hollywood couldn't come up with a story that gut-wrenching and powerful," Katherine said. "And I think you're right. Mr. Lone Hawk has a perspective only a few have."

"Right. So, after Melvina's funeral, I think we should invite them over, and the five of us have a conversation. There has to be an answer."

Andrew nodded and poked at the fire. "There always is, but sometimes it's not the one we expect," he said.

SIX

For two days the announcement of the wake and funeral for Melvina Old Lodge appeared on every smart phone, laptop, desktop computer, and just about every other contrivance of electronic communication connected to the Internet; not to mention it was sent over the airwaves by the three radio stations on the Smokey River Reservation. Melvina's family had readily agreed to Andrew No Horn's idea for her casket to be carried the final seven miles. On the designated day, family members were astounded to see dozens and dozens of vehicles arriving at the pasture where Melvina's battered body had been found. Even more astonishing, over two hundred women and girls, some from other reservations, were lined up to carry the cedar casket, and that number was growing.

In addition, just about every female, from toddler to elderly grandmother, wore a red dress or skirt. Originating on the First Nations reserves in Canada, the red dress had become the symbol for missing and murdered indigenous women. And on this cool midsummer morning, they were everywhere. Red was the only color that the Spirits could see when they met anyone passing over on the Spirit Trail, otherwise known as the Milky Way.

A white hearse with Melvina's casket drove into the pasture and backed toward the spot where her body had been found. Before the first six pallbearers lifted the casket to begin the journey home, Andrew No Horn presented the plaster cast of Melvina's final message to her grandmother: *Gramma I lov u.*

Those near enough to hear the story and glimpse the plaster replica were swept away with emotion. The story flowed through the crowd like a sighing breeze, tugging at every heart. No one who saw would ever forget the image of Amelia Old Lodge holding the message to her chest, sobbing softly from the depths of her soul.

Because Amelia's family were Catholic, Father Durbin from St. Ignatius Church in Hestor offered a prayer, after Andrew No Horn outlined a general plan for transporting Melvina. Every able-bodied female sixteen and older would have a turn at being one of six at a time to carry the casket. After fifty yards or so the next set of pallbearers would take over, and the casket was not to touch the ground.

Chief Ben Avery had arranged for the BIA roads department to close the highway from the state line to Hestor. He assigned four patrolmen in their cruisers to accompany the procession, one leading the way with lights flashing and one at the rear. Three units from the tribal ambulance service with six EMTs were also in the procession. Also accompanying the procession were three tribal social service department vans filled with cases of water. And approximately every mile, the tribal natural resources department had erected tent canopies for anyone who might need to rest in the shade, although a mostly cloudy sky kept the air temperature bearable.

Amelia insisted on leading the way but gave in to her family's insistence that she ride in an all-terrain-vehicle just ahead of the casket, although she did walk the first fifty yards. A female EMT walked near Amelia's vehicle.

Immediately behind the casket and pallbearers was the long procession of women and girls, even those who were too young or not physically able to be pallbearers. A column of red dresses covered the highway for nearly a hundred yards. Bringing up the rear were dozens and dozens of vehicles. No one could recall such a thing ever happening on this reservation. Smart phones and cameras were recording it for posterity.

Loren, Thomas, Andrew, Gavin, and Katherine walked in a group near Amelia, accompanied by Chief Avery and Lieutenant Primault. Morgan had driven ahead to the Old Lodge residence in the family Suburban.

After the second and third change of pallbearers, the process became smoother and those who were relieved went to the back of the column. There was very little conversation among the women and girls in the column; rather a somber and respectful quiet.

Gavin estimated progress was something over two miles an hour, a comfortable pace not difficult to maintain. The prevailing sound was hundreds of soles walking on the pavement.

Thomas joined the line in front of one of the tribal water vans and brought back an armload of bottles. Katherine, along with Loren and other women near Amelia, kept an eye on the old woman, looking for any sign of distress. So far, however, the ninety year-old was holding up well.

Katherine lost track of the number of times pallbearers changed, but the switch off was easily heard behind them—whispered instructions and words of thanks and encouragement. She wondered if all the red dresses in the long column behind would have the opportunity to carry the casket. Glancing at her watch she was surprised that two hours had passed.

At the halfway point, President and Mrs. Lone Hawk were waiting and joined the group walking with Amelia. No one in that group, or anyone in the column, for that matter, heard the slight hum of a drone flying ninety feet over their heads. Standing in an open box of a pickup moving slowly in the ditch along the highway, Patrolman Jason Singer was flying the drone and filming the procession.

From the halfway point, vehicles and people filled the ditches. Young and old, girls and boys, and women and men of all ages stood respectfully as Melvina's casket passed.

At three and a half hours, the procession turned west at Hestor and onto the gravel road for the last mile to the Old Lodge residence. There, at Cordelia Janis's suggestion, the procession paused while two female police officers identified any women and girls who had not yet carried the casket, to ensure that no one was denied the opportunity. Katherine, Veronica Lone Hawk, and Loren took a turn together after the procession resumed.

When the procession turned west onto the road leading to the residence, the last six pallbearers—Melvina's aunts and female cousins—were in place and carried the casket the final thirty yards to a gurney waiting under an elm tree. Melvina finished her journey home near the tire swing she had played on as a small girl. Father Durbin offered another prayer and several medicine men, including Andrew No Horn, burned sweet grass and smudged the casket. A star quilt in various shades of blue, Melvina's favorite color, was placed over the casket.

From all appearances, Amelia Old Lodge's yard had been turned into a temporary encampment. Not only were there dozens of large dome tents, and even a few conical Lakota lodges, for the relatives and friends that would spend the night, there were rows upon rows of folding chairs. The tents and lodges were southeast of the house in the large and freshly mowed yard. All the folding chairs were in semi-circles emanating from the casket and the elm tree, nearly three hundred of them.

Behind the house were nearly half a dozen propane cook stoves, each under its own canopy and each with a twenty-gallon propane tank. Also under each canopy was a large refrigerator stocked with food. Nearly two dozen cooks and their helpers were already at work preparing food.

The first night of Melvina's wake was to be here, under the stars in the yard where she had played as a little girl. Andrew No Horn, Morgan and Loren Hale, and Gavin and Gerard Lone Wolf had rented all of the kitchen equipment and canopies, as well as purchased the supplies, food, and water. They had also purchased most of the dome tents, which were to be given away after the funeral feast. Wakes and funerals were a huge cost outlay that most families couldn't afford, so the Lone Wolf family, including Andrew No Horn, had borne the cost anonymously, enabled by a windfall related to a family member who fought at the Battle of the Little Bighorn.

In the front lawn against the house, tables had been set up with coffee, tea, and water and stacks of paper cups. The yard filled fast and Smokey River Tribal Police officers directed parking so that an orderly egress would occur as the evening and night wore on.

The influx of people was steady with many bringing their own lawn chairs. By sundown the front yard was full and cars were parked along the gravel road on either side for at least a hundred yards in either direction. Yet, in spite of this constant movement of people, all was done quietly with a minimum of noise. Conversations were in low voices or whispers.

At sundown Amelia, her daughter Cordelia, and all the female cousins emerged from the house and opened Melvina's casket. She lay on a white silk star quilt and wore a red jingle dress because she had been a jingle dancer. Her hair was in two braids behind her back, signifying her status as a young unmarried woman. In her right hand was a large sprig of gray prairie sage and in her left was an eagle feather fan. On her feet were beaded moccasins. The part in her hair on top of her head was painted red, to signify a woman greatly loved.

One by one they stepped to the casket and reached in to touch her hand and leaned down to place a loving kiss on her forehead or cheek, and then quietly took seats in the first row of unoccupied chairs. As if on cue other women and girls out of the crowd came to the casket in an orderly line, each stopping momentarily to gaze lovingly or touch Melvina's hand, and then move on. It was not unlike a flowing ribbon of red. Nearly an hour passed by the time all the women who wanted to said their final good-byes. By then the dusk was deepening and night was falling.

SEVEN

The day after Melvina Old Lodge's funeral was bright and warm. Katherine and Gavin sat quietly at breakfast over plates of scrambled eggs and elk backstrap. A carafe of coffee stood on the table.

"So, I assume Loren is picking you up and then you're on your way to Pierre?"

Katherine glanced at her watch. "Yes. She should be here in about an hour."

"What's the plan for you two?"

"Well, she's taking her matriarch role very seriously. I told her I wasn't sure what kind of dress—*wasicu* traditional or Lakota traditional—I want for the wedding, so she thought it was a good idea to get some ideas at least. She likes a wedding specialty store in Pierre. What's on your agenda today?"

"Great, I'm sure you'll have a good time. I have a meeting with the new head of the Lakota Studies Department. Usual administrative and academic stuff, I think, but I know she'll try to talk me into teaching full time."

"You think so?"

"Yeah, but I'll have to disappoint her. I like the way things are, especially now."

Katherine reached and squeezed his hand. "Me, too." After a small sigh she turned and looked out the window. "I've never seen so many people at a young person's funeral," she said quietly. "I don't know if anyone bothered to count, but I have a feeling it was close to five hundred."

"Probably," agreed Gavin. "That poor girl's heroic effort to get home touched a lot of people. It shook up a lot of people, broke a lot of hearts."

"I hope people stay in touch with her family, especially for Grandma Amelia's sake. It seems to be the hardest right after a funeral."

"They have a large extended family and most of them have always been close," Gavin pointed out. "I know they won't leave Grandma Amelia alone."

After a long pensive pause and sips of coffee, Katherine spoke again. "Hopefully, all of those people will help to keep the issue of missing Native girls and women in the forefront of people's thinking, especially tribal governments and law enforcement."

"I hope so, too," Gavin replied. "After something like Melvina's situation occurs, we're all filled with resolve and good intentions, and then it usually falls by the wayside after a few days. Except for our own radio stations and newspapers here and on a couple of other reservations, Melvina's story barely received any notice statewide."

Gavin's ringing cell phone interrupted further conversation. "*Hau Leksi*," he said, and listened for a few seconds. "Sure, of course. Come on over. There's coffee and we can cook you up something if you haven't had breakfast…Okay, sure, we can do that, too. See you in a bit."

He glanced across the table. "Uncle Andrew and Joby are stopping by. Joby's going to help him hook up a generator."

"Great. Have they had breakfast?"

"He said they did in town. I think he just wants to go through with the idea of buying a car for Joby. He wanted us to do that together. Nothing fancy, a mid-size four-wheel-drive pickup."

"You think Joby will be okay with that?"

"We might have to talk him into it. He's a bit proud, so sometimes it's hard for him to accept help. He's been looking out for himself since his parents died when he was sixteen. But he's not getting any younger and I'm worried about him walking all over, especially when the weather's bad."

Andrew No Horn and Joby Bone—one of Andrew's grandsons and Gavin's cousin—arrived twenty minutes later. No sooner had they sat down for coffee than Gavin's phone rang again.

"Hello, this is Gavin,"

"Good morning, Justin Primault here. I have some interesting news. The coroner found a slip of paper folded inside of one of Melvina Old Lodge's shoes."

"A slip of paper?"

"Yes, with a list of names, twelve of them, and I think it's girls or women that Melvina saw or came in contact with while she was wherever she was."

Gavin looked at Katherine and nodded. "Damn. A list. Do you have the names?"

"I sure do, and some are young women we know to be missing from our Rez, reported by their families," Primault replied.

"That's incredible."

"For sure, and it means we haven't done enough to find those girls," Primault pointed out angrily. "And this list is current, I mean, right now. These girls are out there somewhere. It's frustrating as hell."

"It sure is. What will happen next?"

"Well, Chief Avery and I are going to talk in a few minutes. I just thought you should know, especially since you and your uncle know Melvina's family."

"Of course. Keep us in the loop if you can."

"I will."

Gavin put the phone aside and looked at Katherine again, somewhat disturbed by the call.

"Anything you can share with us?" wondered Andrew.

"Yeah, sure. Justin said the coroner found a piece of paper in Melvina's shoe. A list of names of women, girls. Some of the names are girls from here, our Rez."

"Oh my," Katherine said. "That means she was with them or at least knew of them. It had to have been recent. How long did it take for her to get home?"

"Days, a couple of weeks maybe. Hard to tell," Gavin guessed. "But you're right. She very likely knew them, might have been with them."

"What is Lieutenant Primault planning on doing?" Katherine persisted.

"He wants to do something. He's meeting with Chief Avery in a bit. I know this is a critical issue for both of them. I wish that were the case with every police department."

Katherine shook her head slowly. "I hate to be a cynic at a time like this, but if those girls were white and blond, the stories would be hitting the airwaves big time."

"You are right," Andrew declared somberly.

With a sigh, Gavin turned to Uncle Andrew and Joby. "So, you're hooking up a generator. Does that mean you're going off-grid?"

"I'd like to," Andrew said, grinning. "I cook and run my hot water heater with propane. The only thing I use electricity for are lights and the refrigerator. I don't have too much food that will spoil quickly, so maybe it's possible to get by with just a generator."

"I think there's a way you can charge up storage batteries with a generator. That way you can use some lights and keep your refrigerator going," suggested Gavin.

"Sounds good," Andrew said. "Today we'll start by hooking up the generator. A technician from the electric co-op is supposed to come out later."

"Just don't let him talk you out of the generator," Gavin warned.

"No chance. Joby's hooked up generators before, so we're good."

Gavin glanced at his cousin. "Hey, *Tahansi* (Cousin), we're thinking of putting another room on the house. Think maybe you can give us a hand with that, too?"

"Sure, anytime," Joby replied. "Thinking of expanding the family?" he said, grinning and teasing Gavin and Katherine.

Katherine smiled coyly. "It's not off the table, but first I need extra space for my own office."

Joby kept his smile. "Well, whatever you want it for, we need a set of plans first. I can help with that, too."

"Thanks, *Tahansi*," Gavin said. "Tell you what. You can start on that after you help *Leksi* today." He glanced at Uncle Andrew, who nodded at the unspoken question. "So, along those lines, we need to talk about how we're going to pay you."

"Okay," Joby said, offhandedly. "Straight cash always works. However much you think it's worth to you."

Andrew leaned toward his nephew. "*Tunska*," he said, "we—your cousin and me—want to get you a truck."

Joby looked first at his cousin, then his uncle. "What? You want to do what?"

"Get you a truck," Gavin affirmed.

"Whoa! That's a lot of money. I mean, I —."

"No worries," Gavin assured him. "We've always been able to depend on you, so we just want to pay you what that's worth to us."

Joby pondered for a moment, aware that all eyes were on him and seeming to be on the verge of crying. "Ah," he said, hoarsely. "Well, it's a damn good thing I have a driver's license then. Okay—damn, *wopila* (thanks)!" He reached out to shake Andrew's hand first, and then Gavin's.

"You're welcome, *Tahansi*," Gavin replied.

"*Tokasni yelo* (It's all okay)," Andrew said.

"I have a meeting today on campus," Gavin went on, "and you two are going to hook up that generator. How about tomorrow all of us go to Rapid City and find you a truck?"

"Sounds good to me," Joby said, still not quite believing the news.

An hour later the conversation around the table was still going strong after Loren arrived. The day's obligations, chores, and adventures were delayed in favor of an unexpected opportunity to visit over cups of coffee. Words and laughter hung in the air. Andrew and Joby were the first to peel off and leave. After clearing the table and filling the dishwasher, Loren and Katherine were ready to go out the door.

"You ladies have a safe trip," Gavin said, as he walked them out to Loren's car. "I'll probably be home before you. Let me know when you leave Pierre, and if you get here around supper time, maybe I can throw something together."

"You're on, little brother," Loren said cheerfully, as she hugged him.

Gavin returned Katherine's hug and kissed her. "Is there anything you want from Pierre?" she asked.

He smiled and squeezed her hand. "Just you."

EIGHT

At the table in the small conference room, Lieutenant Justin Primault stared at the list of names on the sheet of paper in front of him—sadness, frustration, and anger swirling in his chest. Chief Ben Avery had made two copies from the photograph faxed to them by the coroner from Minneapolis.

"Twelve young women, twelve human beings," the Chief said. "I can't help but think of how these names represent a hell of a lot of worry and heartache for their families. I can't begin to imagine how that feels."

"That's for damn sure," agreed Primault. He slid his finger slowly down the list, reading each name to himself, and underlined the three names he knew were from the Smokey River Reservation. "Three of them are ours, they're from here." He tapped the three file folders on the table. "I pulled their files."

> Julia Lake
> Carrie Little Wolf
> Neva Baxter
> Jenny Two Bird

Millie Rousseaux
Anna Yellow Hand
Maggie Henry
Ann No Horse
Winnifred St. John
Billie Andrews
Elizabeth Claremont
Sarah Hail

"Okay. I'm assuming the contact information we have in those files is current," Avery ventured.

Primault nodded. "I know for a fact that these young ladies have been missing for no more than a year. So, yeah, contact information is as current as that."

"Any thoughts about contacting those families?"

"I think we should," Primault pointed to the list of names. "This is very recent activity. The handwriting looks the same, so I think one person wrote that list—probably Melvina—likely within the past few weeks. Their families are entitled to know."

"I agree."

"My thought was to send two of our female officers, Audrey Hinson and Madonna White Bear, to inform them of this development," said Primault. "To me, it's an indication that as of whenever this list was made, those young women were still alive."

"That would be encouraging news for their families. What about the other names, beyond our three. Do we know where they're from?"

"I can check the list of missing that I have, and I can send that list out to the other BIA and tribal departments. I'll do that today."

Thirty minutes later two officers quietly perused the list of names printed on the sheet they each had. "As you can see," Lieutenant Primault said, "three are underlined. They are from here. Those are the families I'd like you to find."

"What do we tell them?" Madonna White Bear wanted to know.

"That this list indicates they were still alive as of recently, perhaps a few weeks ago."

"Forgive me, sir," Audrey Hinson said, hesitantly. "But isn't this like throwing straw out to a drowning man? Are we in danger of raising false hopes?"

Primault considered the question for a few seconds. "I've thought of that. The one thing I can tell you is that each of these families have been hoping for some good news, as opposed to hearing and knowing nothing for months."

Hinson, a tall, slender woman with short black hair, nodded. "I see your point, sir."

"I know they'll probably ask what we're doing, or have been doing, about these missing girls," White Bear pointed out. She was the older of the two officers, her hair in one long braid. "What can we tell them?"

"You know as well as I do that we're not doing enough," Primault said. "But that doesn't mean we've totally neglected this issue. We make inquiries constantly. I'm trying to put together a plan for the Chief. But what I hope you can do is reassure those girls' families that we haven't quit."

The two officers both nodded.

"Let me know how it goes. And by the way, if the Chief approves my plan, you two will be part of it. I'll let you know."

"Okay," Hinson responded, as they both stood. "We'll get to it."

Two hours later Hinson and White Bear lost count of the cups of coffee they had consumed while listening to stories about Anna Yellow Hand. They were drawn subtly into a gathering of memories which were the only connection to someone who was not there. Now, her name on a hastily written list brought a tiny spark of hope.

Anna was a senior at St. Ignatius High School when she had disappeared, a volleyball player and track star. At least a half dozen photographs were brought out and placed on the coffee table in front of the two officers. The slender girl in them was very pretty, a fact that was more than likely the reason she was missing.

The Yellow Hand residence was in the Gray Grass housing section, in the western part of the reservation, just north of Highway 33. It was a small, gray house near the end of the northern row of houses, twelve in each row. Most of the lawns around the houses were thin or bare, even at this time of the year. A few abandoned car bodies sat in some of the lawns or driveways. Several curious onlookers asked each other why a Smokey River Tribal Police cruiser was parked in front of the Yellow Hand house.

Anna's grandmother, Adelia, sat in a big soft chair opposite the officers, her gnarled hands twisting a small handkerchief. "She said she wanted to go to Chadron State College to play volleyball, because they offered her a partial scholarship," she told them. "She would be there now, if —." The old woman's voice trailed off. Anna's mother, Margaret, sitting next to her nodded somberly in agreement. Two small, pre-school age girls watched with wide eyes, listening to the conversation about their older sister.

"I had her when I was still in high school," Margaret said. "We got married, my husband and me, after he got out of the army." She pointed at the two small girls. "That's why she was so much older than these two."

Audrey Hinson nodded, while gazing at the photograph she was holding—Anna's senior picture.

"So, since her name was on that list," Margaret said, "prob'ly that's a good thing."

Madonna White Bear nodded. "It is, Mrs. Yellow Hand. We don't know exactly when that list was written, but we think within a month."

"Okay. And that list was from that girl that was found a couple weeks ago?"

"Yes. Melvina Old Lodge. It was inside her shoe. She was probably the one who wrote the names."

"That means she got away somehow, Melvina, I mean," Margaret ventured.

"Yes, it does," Audrey Hinson affirmed.

"So, Anna was still alive then?"

"Yes, we think so," Madonna White Bear said.

Adelia emitted a deep sigh. "I told her not to go that day," she said. "She was helping me cut pieces, the diamonds, for a quilt when those girls stopped in and asked her to go with them to Pierre. I told her 'no,' I just had a feeling."

"So, her friends didn't see her leaving with anyone, or get into another car?" Audrey Hinson asked.

"They said she went out of the store ahead of them, and that's the last time they saw her. They looked for her all over in that big parking lot, and back inside the store and around the store on the outside."

"What are you people doing, police, I mean?" Adelia asked.

"Well, after we put out missing person reports to the other police departments, we keep checking. That's all we can do," Madonna White Bear said, half apologizing.

"So, no one is out there looking?" Adelia persisted.

After a moment, Audrey Hinson slowly shook her head. "No. I mean, yes, no one is actively looking."

"Why?"

Hinson glanced nervously at Madonna White Bear. "Well, there's no system in place to actively look for missing persons. The BIA and tribal police departments don't do that. And—and we should, I know we should."

The old woman nodded, a flash of anger in her old eyes quickly replaced by one of sadness.

"Well, thanks for telling us this news," Margaret said. "It gives me hope."

A few minutes later the two officers silently sat in their cruiser for a minute before Madonna White Bear started the engine and backed out of the driveway. "Nothing like half-assed good news to pour salt in a wound," she said, cynically.

Audrey Hinson grimly nodded in agreement.

The interaction with the other two families was the same in one sense—a flash of hope that was quickly overwhelmed by heartbreaking reality. Though for the mother of Winnifred St. John, there was a different kind of heartache. Lilian St. John—a petite woman with a wary, haunted expression in her eyes—was a single mother and a triage nurse at the IHS hospital. Though the two officers were not surprised at the emotional strength they saw and felt, for her there was a definite sense of guilt.

"Winnie and I had a bad argument that day," she revealed sadly. "It was a late Saturday afternoon by the time we got to Rapid City. We'd been arguing over the way she dressed that day. I thought it was too grown up for her; she was only fourteen. She liked an older boy who was eighteen, and she wanted to look older for him. I thought it was because she had grown up without a father and she wanted some kind of male attention. Well, it got out of hand and when we got to the mall she went her own way."

Lilian paused to pull a tissue out of a pocket and wipe her eyes. "That's the last time I saw her. I looked all over. Called her friends to see if they'd heard from her. Then I went to the Rapid City police. All they did was take the report. It's been eight months now."

"Well, we think that Winnie is still out there," Officer Hinson said.

"Because of this list?"

"Yes. As far as we can tell it's recent."

Lilian wiped away more tears and looked down at the list in her hands. "Can I keep this?" she said, touching her daughter's name with the tip of her finger.

"Of course."

Two hours later at their last visit for the day, Audrey Hinson and Madonna White Bear watched Henrietta Two Bird light her second cigarette. "I quit smoking for a lot of years. I started again, after—. Well, my husband won't be home for a while yet, if you want to talk to him, too. I can tell him, about this," she gestured toward the list sitting on her table.

"We just wanted you to know this latest development," Madonna White Bear said.

"Thanks. Here's what I think," Henrietta said. "Whatever has happened to her, I want her to come home, one way or another. I want her to walk in the door, I want to see her face and touch her. But even if she comes home to be buried, at least she'll be home, where she belongs."

It was late when the two officers returned to the parking lot at the police station. There was very little conversation for the last few miles to Agency Village, both of them deeply affected by their visits with the three families of the missing girls.

Madonna White Bear pulled the key from the ignition and looked at Audrey

Hinson. "You have a younger sister," she said, "I have two. It would tear my guts out if one of my sisters turned up missing. Something has to be done, damn it."

"Oh, I totally agree," replied Hinson. "But somewhere along the line the system has to care about us brown-skinned women just as much as it does budgets, regulations, male egos, or anything else that has a higher priority than sadness and families torn apart."

NINE

The truck stop at the junction of I-90 and U.S. Highway 83 was busy as usual. Loren was about to exit the main store when she saw a dark-skinned man standing in front of the row of parked cars next to the main entrance. A second later she noticed that he was staring at Katherine, who was at the gas pumps waiting for the tank to fill. Loren stopped to watch him. He was tall, likely around six feet, dressed in denims and a dark green sweatshirt with a hood. After nearly ten seconds he pulled out a phone and quickly took a photograph, and Loren could only assume it was of Katherine from the direction he was pointing the phone. In the next second the man turned and walked toward another entrance to the building.

Loren took the coffees she had purchased to the car, looking back into the store but the man was lost in the crowd. "You won't believe what I just saw," she said to Katherine.

Katherine returned the nozzle to the pump. "What? What did you see?"

"A man taking your picture," Loren said. "He was right over there by those cars and then he went inside."

"Really? That's kind of odd."

"I thought so. It may be nothing but how about we wait for a bit and see if he comes out and what car he gets into."

After a couple of minutes, they had to give way for a pickup wanting to pull up to the pump. In that time the man had not exited the building.

"Did you get a good look at him? Is it anyone you know, maybe?"

"Yeah, I did. He's tall, dark hair, brown skin. Not Native, at least not from here I don't think. I probably should have taken a picture of him, but my phone was here in the car."

"Well," Katherine concluded. "As you said, maybe it's nothing."

"I suppose," Loren half-heartedly agreed. "I'm guessing more than one man along the line has given in to the urge to take your picture. On the other hand, the first thought in my head was Melvina Old Lodge."

"That's a bit scary."

No more was said until twenty minutes later. Katherine who was driving glanced in the mirror. "There's a white van that's been behind us for a few minutes," she said. "It's not catching up; it's been the same distance."

Loren turned to look out the back window. "Yes, I see it." Taking her phone, she set it to camera mode and tried zooming in the focus. "Darn. I can't see the license plate in enough detail for numbers."

"I don't know, maybe I'm suddenly paranoid," Katherine admitted. "But what if I pull us over and let it pass?"

"Yes, let's do."

She slowed gradually and turned onto the wide, paved shoulder and stopped. Nearly a minute later the van sped by without slowing down. It was a utility type vehicle with no side windows, except on the two doors. The only other windows were on the two back doors. But they were able to see that there was only one driver—a dark-haired man.

"Is that the man you saw?" Katherine asked.

"Hard to say," Loren replied.

Nearly half an hour later they arrived in Fort Pierre. Just across the Missouri River bridge they stopped at an Italian restaurant for lunch. After a leisurely meal and pleasant conversation, which was mostly about the impending wedding and nothing more about the picture-taking man or a white van, they left to find a shop on the main street. Loren stopped suddenly, but only for a split second, on the way back to their car. In the car she motioned back outside.

"Look at the row of cars on that side of the parking lot," she said, pointing north. "There's a white van there. It looks like the one that passed us."

Katherine turned and looked for several long seconds. "You're right! It is! What shall we do?"

"Let's wait," Loren suggested.

Just over twenty minutes later they were still waiting.

"You know, maybe it's nothing," Loren said. "Or he's in there and watching us. Just for grins. How about we pull out and drive by the van and take a picture of the license plates?"

"Okay, let's do it."

The van had Nebraska plates. Loren, since it was on her side, took several close-ups. "Just to put our minds at rest we can have Lieutenant Primault check on these plates. Then we can be sure and can feel silly for being paranoid."

"Better to be safe and silly," was Katherine's comment.

Andrew No Horn was pouring a cup of coffee for Joby Bone at the kitchen table. The technician from the rural electric cooperative had just left, after the diesel generator had been successfully hooked up. Suddenly a series of vivid images flashed through Andrew's mind so clearly it took his breath away.

The perspective was low, in the grass at first and then rising. There was frenzied movement, flashes of white in the dark grass. Then the image sharpened. Flashes of color turned into the narrow, undulating body of a white snake he immediately recognized, but the color was wrong. The snake he was seeing was something called "Blue Racer," usually pale blue, not white. It was doing what blue racers do, moving very fast, faster than other snakes. Then, in a flash, it totally disappeared down a hole.

Andrew finished pouring coffee for both he and Joby and took a seat at the table, staring for a few seconds into his cup.

"*Leksi*," Joby said, after a few seconds. "You okay?"

"Yeah, yeah, I'm good."

"You got a strange look on your face."

"Yeah, it's okay. I was just—just thinking about something."

"Oh, okay."

Andrew loosed a small sigh, unable to let go of the images that were now floating in his memory. He felt an undercurrent of sadness well up in his chest.

At precisely that moment, Officer Jason Singer knocked on Lieutenant Primault's door and walked in with a sheet of paper in his hand. "Sir, this is about the license plate Katherine Hill asked us to check on."

Primault looked away from his computer screen. "Good. What do we know?"

"The vehicle is registered to a delivery company based in Lincoln, Sherholt Transportation. It's been in business for five years. They haul anything but mail or food. Would you like me to dig into the company itself? You know, ownership and so on?"

"Yes, go ahead. See what you can find about number of employees. Names and photos would be great."

"Will do."

Lieutenant Primault glanced at his watch. There was time for a phone call. He scrolled to find Katherine Hill's number.

"This is Katherine Hill."

"Katherine, this is Justin Primault. I have some information from the license plate number you gave me."

"Well, I appreciate you doing that for me. What do you have?"

"My pleasure. The number is registered to a delivery company in Lincoln, Nebraska. Which in and of itself is nothing unusual."

"Glad to hear it."

"I'm having one of my officers do more follow-up, to find out more about that company. We'll keep it on our radar until we can cross them off the list as definitely harmless."

"Thanks again. My sister-in-law thought it was strange that someone would be snapping photographs that way."

"She's right to be suspicious," Primault agreed. "Better safe than sorry."

After the call he picked up the file folder sitting next to the keyboard. He was not a fan of storing information digitally, preferring paper files instead though he knew he was fighting a losing battle. With the file in hand, he walked across the narrow hall to Chief Avery's office and knocked on the door.

"Come in, Justin," the Chief said, gesturing toward the small conference table in a corner. "Let's sit there." Ten minutes later Ben Avery finished explaining his plan, which was simple. "Anything with fewer moving parts tends to run smoother," he concluded.

Primault nodded. "Yeah, I see your point. With this plan we can still make sure we're patrolling the Rez the way we should, the way we need to, and have man hours we can devote to the MMIW (Missing and Murdered Indigenous Women) situation."

"Right. Of course, it depends on enough officers volunteering to take part," Avery cautioned. "But if five officers can give us four hours a week, that's twenty hours of effort that we aren't making now."

"I'm pretty sure Jason Singer will buy in," Primault said. "And I'm hoping Audrey Hinson and Madonna White Bear will, too. I'll encourage them."

"Logistically, we can turn the conference room into a workstation just for MMIW business," Avery pointed out. "I can tap into my limited contingency fund and purchase a fax machine, or maybe two, and five cell phones just for those officers to use. We can use one of those month to month plans with unlimited calls and texting."

Primault was taking notes. "Okay. How are we going to put out the word, since it's hard for us to bring in all our officers for one meeting?"

"Initially, I was thinking an email. I'll explain our stance on the issue, throw in some stats, and ask for volunteers. And if you want to talk to Singer, Hinson, and White Bear before I write the email, go right ahead."

"I will. So, my question is, after we start compiling information about our missing women and girls, and especially if it's actionable information, then what do we do?"

Avery nodded thoughtfully. "Well, overall, one reservation police department taking on this issue is maybe like a sparrow trying to fly in a tornado. But it's a start. I'll reach out to other departments if our plan works. But before that I plan on having a meeting with our President."

"You mean Dr. Lone Hawk?"

"Exactly. He has a personal connection, as you know, to this whole sordid mess of human trafficking, so he'll understand what we're trying to do. But what I plan on asking from him is funding, so we can do the all-important and necessary follow-up work."

"Okay. Do we need to develop a budget?"

"Eventually, yes. But I have a good idea of what we can do with any funds we do manage to acquire." Avery shook his head and sighed. "The bigger problem is with the upper echelons of the Bureau of Indian Affairs, and federal and state law enforcement. We have to convince them that this is a problem that's bigger than regulations or attitudes that prevent us all from working on this together."

"Well, pardon me for being a pessimist, but sounds like a 'snowball's chance in hell' sort of scenario. Maybe what we need to do is convince the tribes to work together on this issue. That probably won't be easy either, but it might be something for President Lone Hawk to consider doing."

Avery nodded slowly. "Yeah. I can sure put the idea in front of him. Maybe we can turn that snowball into a stone."

TEN

A hundred miles north of Agency Village, a white van drove away from a furniture store in Pierre after unloading a dining table and four matching chairs. Making sure no other vehicles were near, the driver removed the black wig and placed it inside the center console, along with the can of tanning cream. Without it his head was shaved completely bald. A few blocks later he turned into a fast food restaurant and placed an order in the drive through lane. Picking up his bag of food and a drink he drove a couple of miles to the large parking lot of a big box store and parked. To anyone who might notice him, he was simply a guy eating his lunch, which he did leisurely.

From his parking spot he could see both entrances to the huge store. On this pleasant afternoon no one was bundled in coats or sweaters, which was to his liking. He paid no attention to older people or couples. His focus was on young, slender Native females, alone or in groups of two or three, ranging in age from the middle teens to early twenties. Age was a judgment call on his part, but he was adept at guessing.

The side windows, both driver and passenger, were tinted dark so that anyone who happened to look would only see an obscure image. This location was not new to him. He'd been here many times before, to the point where he recognized a few likely candidates. His memory for such things was good, better than most people. He could remember faces easily. The camera function on his phone was for those faces that were especially appealing, such as the one he had seen at the truck stop, although she seemed to be a bit older than most of the likely ones.

Nevertheless, she had been a looker, a downright beautiful woman, the one-in-a-million kind. The kind that was hard to get out of your mind.

ELEVEN

Lieutenant Primault arrived at Amelia Old Lodge's house just before noon. He had called and asked to see if the family had anything that had Melvina's writing or printing on it. If the handwriting matched that of the list of names from the girl's shoe, it would be affirmation that Melvina had written it and probably had seen or heard of the girls.

After twenty minutes of closely comparing the writing on the list to a card she had written to her grandmother, Primault was convinced that Melvina had indeed made the list. But when and where?

He had put in a call to the coroner's office in Minneapolis to send him the note itself, since all he had was a faxed copy. The paper it was written on might provide some clue. In any case that was his hope.

On the twenty-minute drive back to Agency Village, he considered the subject that had been part of his reality since taking the job as criminal investigator on the Smokey River Rez: how to effectively deal with the heartbreaking issue of missing Native women and girls. Primault knew that every reservation in the state had a list of missing women and girls. Many had been missing for years, and a few bodies had been found in different parts of the region. Nevertheless, no law enforcement agency—tribal, state, or federal—was putting forth any credible and sustained effort to address the problem.

Back at the police station Primault poured himself a cup of coffee from the break room on the way back to his office. Waiting on his desk were the three, now very familiar, paper files he kept there, each with a name printed on the tab:

Winnifred St. John

Jenny Two Bird

Anna Yellow Hand

There were other issues, other problems that needed his attention and would take his time, each a vignette of the darker side of life on a reservation: child, spouse, and elderly abuse, stolen cars, drug and alcohol fueled assaults—the list was long. Probing into each and every case was time consuming and often emotionally draining. Common to almost every case was the basic issue of Lakota people struggling to live in a white dominated society. American culture had tried various ways of dealing with the land's indigenous people—isolating them on reservations and forcing Native children into boarding schools to be "Americanized." It was clear that America did not care about quality of life for marginalized cultures, and did not give a damn that Native women and girls were being abducted at an alarming rate.

The flat envelope from Minneapolis arrived in the last delivery of the day. Primault quickly pulled the tab to open the top of the envelope and took out a smaller manila envelope. Inside it was a square of slightly soiled white paper, roughly six by eight inches, and a folded, sandwich size plastic bag. Primault assumed that someone—likely Melvina herself—had placed the list inside the bag to protect it. He slipped on rubber gloves and picked up the soiled paper with a pair of tweezers, immediately noticing a slightly waxy texture on the paper. The upper and left edges appeared to have been nearly torn, hinting that it had been part of a larger piece. And it apparently had been folded a few times, judging from the creases on it.

Primault opened his notebook and quickly jotted down his initial observations. Objectivity wasn't easy. His emotions were pushing hard against his training. At his fingertips was the physical manifestation of an act of hope. Several weeks ago, when Melvina Old Lodge had written the names of twelve girls in neat block printing, hopefully, each of them was still alive. Primault hoped they still were.

What were the exact circumstances that enabled or prompted Melvina to make the list? Obviously there had been a pen and a scrap of paper. The formation of the letters indicated to him that Melvina had carefully and deliberately printed each name. There was no ambiguity, every letter was unmistakable.

After writing the names she had somehow procured the small plastic bag, folded the list, and placed it in the bag, which had been found in the toe of her right shoe. What did she want to do with the list? What was her hope? For Primault her intent was obvious: she wanted someone to know. Melvina wanted to tell someone that those girls were being held against their will.

Some of the ink had faded. Primault initially assumed that was due to pressure, heat, moisture, and whatever other circumstances Melvina had traversed and endured on her journey home. He did notice however that the ink in the last three names was fainter than the others. Picking up a magnifying glass he leaned down for a closer look. With the glass the waxy appearance of the paper was easier to discern, and the paper was thick enough for the point of a pen to make depressions as each letter had been printed. Further indication that Melvina had taken time and care to make the list.

He was about to turn away when he noticed an ever so tiny detail below the last name—more depressions on the paper. As he angled the magnifying glass for a closer look, his cheeks grew warm when he saw that the depressions were distinct imprints of letters that formed the word PINNACLE.

Primault sat back and took a deep breath. An unusual name. Was it someone's first name? It was a simple noun, meaning the "top" or the "culmination." He had never heard it as a patronymic, at least not in this part of the country. Maybe it was a place, or a business. From the credenza behind him he found a spiral bound road atlas and quickly turned the pages to North Dakota, because Melvina's sneakers were sold only in Minnesota and North Dakota.

A cursory visional sweep of town names in large print on the state map did not find the word "Pinnacle." Taking a more methodical approach he started in the northeast corner and worked his way south, concentrating on the smaller towns indicated by smaller printing. From the southeast corner he moved slowly across the page to the west. Finally in the upper part of the northwest quadrant he saw it: Pinnacle—a blue dot on the prairie.

According to the Legend at the top of the map page, the town's population was five hundred or less. Primault's face grew hot as he recognized that region of the state was in the middle of one of the biggest oil booms in the country. There were at least two man camps that he knew of in that area. In all probability Melvina Old Lodge had been there. She had to have known where she was in order to write the name.

Primault looked at the map again. The Ft. Berthold Reservation was east of Pinnacle, so that meant the town was in the middle of white-owned land; probably a farming community, now either cursed or blessed by the oil boom, or both. Whatever the town was now, Primault knew it was the place to look for the girls on the list. He drew a line with his finger from the Smokey River Rez to Pinnacle and estimated it to be four hundred miles—a six to eight hour drive.

There was no way to officially justify a trip to Pinnacle. But the cruel reality was that Melvina Old Lodge had probably started her journey home from there, and that was the only reason he needed. It was only a question of when he would go. As soon as possible as far as he was concerned.

TWELVE

Gavin Lone Wolf added wood to the fire in the pit in the backyard. In addition to the security yard light, the fire was the only source of illumination on this dark evening. Around the fire with him were Uncle Andrew, Katherine, Clayton and Veronica Lone Hawk, and Ben Avery.

Gavin glanced at his neighbors, the Lone Hawks, as he sat back. "So, am I to assume that you're into glamping now, with that big motor home parked in your yard?"

Veronica Lone Hawk chuckled while her husband grinned. "Well, not by choice, necessarily," he said. "George Whirlwind Horse and his son are about halfway into remodeling our house, so we rented that motor home to be out of their way, essentially, while they work."

"I wanted to put up the tipi," Veronica added. "But apparently a few of the poles need to be replaced."

"That would have been my choice," Katherine said. "Not that I would have known how to put one up." She tossed a smile at Gavin. "Can we do that one of these days, before too long?"

"Of course."

"My grandma and her sister won money every year, in the early days of the Frontier Days Rodeo in Cold River," Andrew recalled.

"That was an event?" Avery wondered.

"Oh, yeah," Andrew went on. "There were usually half a dozen teams of two women each. All Lakota women, of course, and they drove horse-drawn wagons into the arena loaded with tipi covers and poles. Whoever could unload and put up the tipi first was the winner. But the door pins had to be securely in place and all the tent pegs in the right place. There were judges, older Lakota women. A blue flag, a streamer, was given to the pair who finished first, a yellow one to the second place, and green for third. And each tipi had to pass inspection, and then the winner was declared."

"You say your grandma won?" Katherine asked.

"Yeah, she and her cousin Susie won for five years in a row. Fifty dollars each time. Lot of money back then."

"I would so love to have seen that," Katherine said. "I'm sure there are still women who know how to do that."

"There are," Clayton Lone Hawk said. "I've seen tipis up in yards here and there across our Rez. And each year at the annual fair and celebration there are more and more of them."

"Whose job was it, in the old days, to erect the lodge and take it down?" Avery asked.

"The women," Andrew replied. "They tanned the buffalo hides, cut them to size, and then sewed the covering together. Groups of women would work together. So, the lodge, the house, belonged to the women in the family. It was their domain."

"I like that approach," Veronica asserted.

"It was a system that worked well," Clayton affirmed. "It was the man's responsibility to provide for the household and the woman's to run it."

"I'm assuming women were not considered less than men," Veronica stated.

"That's right," Andrew said. "Women were the first teachers of children, and as mothers, grandmothers, and aunts they were the focal point of family, of the *tiyospaye*, the extended family, so the whole community really. Those first years of influence from moms and grandmas stayed with boys all their lives. The men provided for and protected the family, and the women were the glue that held it together."

"Sadly, that's not the case now," Clayton lamented. "The European mindset of men in control took over. Consequently, on the grand scale of social status, Native women are now at the bottom."

After a momentary pause, Gavin leaned forward. "Which does bring us to the reason Katherine and I invited you all to come. Something, sadly, we all know about was brought into the spotlight in the past couple of weeks—the issue of missing and murdered Native women and girls."

"Indeed," intoned Clayton. "Indeed." He glanced at Ben Avery. "Chief, any more word on the Melvina Old Lodge situation?"

Avery cleared his throat. "As a matter of fact, yes. The reason I was late getting here, and my apologies for that, was an interesting meeting with Lieutenant Primault. He is relatively certain that Melvina was in or near a town up in North Dakota. A place called Pinnacle."

"Oh, my," Katherine reacted. "How did he learn that?"

"It was written, more or less, at the bottom of the list of names that was in her shoe," Avery revealed. "Pinnacle is a small town, probably smaller than Cold River. As far as I'm concerned Lieutenant Primault essentially confirmed that Melvina wrote that list. He compared her handwriting to a card she wrote to her grandmother. It matched. So, that tells us two facts, and one probability: that she was in or near Pinnacle and in the company of those girls she listed, and likely they are in or near Pinnacle. Furthermore, there are two man camps within a fifty-mile radius of Pinnacle, in the middle of a booming oil field."

"A ready-made market for trafficking women," Katherine declared.

"So, what's to be done now?" Clayton asked.

Avery nodded toward President Lone Hawk. "Well, President Lone Hawk has granted seed money to help get the process started," he said. "I don't have an exact plan yet, but Lieutenant Primault and I want the means to investigate and create a comprehensive data base of the missing."

"You can't do that now?" Katherine asked.

"We can, but to a very limited extent, in the normal course of policing. But I want us to be able to focus on that issue. In order to do that specifically, we need the legislated authority and funding."

"And as Chief Avery pointed out to me," Clayton added, "we can't depend on the BIA or any federal agency right now. They may, at some point, come around to it, but as of now we—the tribes and Indian country—are on our own. I think I can talk the tribal council into writing and passing a resolution that brings attention to missing and murdered Native women and a directive to take action. In the meantime, while we're trying to make that happen, the situation continues every day."

"Exactly," affirmed Avery. "Tomorrow two of my officers, Lieutenant Primault and Patrolman Jeffrey Brousseaux will drive to Pinnacle and do a bit of fact-finding, a reconnaissance, if you will."

"You mean, sort of undercover?" Katherine asked.

"For all intents and purposes," Avery said. "They will drive an impounded car with altered license plates, carry fake IDs, dress appropriately, and spend nothing but cash. Once there they'll be posing as two guys looking for work and try to learn as much as they can."

"Is it risky to any extent, even dangerous?" Katherine asked.

"The only risk would be if someone were to recognize either of them," Avery admitted. "But neither of them have been in that part of the country. I suppose there is a slight chance that someone from this Rez is working up there. I gave them two days, no more and no less."

"Whatever they learn will be useful, I'm sure," Clayton said.

Gavin glanced sideways to catch his uncle Andrew's attention. "I think we can scratch up some funds to match the grant you provided," he said to Clayton.

Andrew nodded.

"Thank you," Clayton said. "My office has a contingency line item. It's where the initial funds were drawn from."

"And my department has a Support Services line item," Avery said. "Those funds will go there and withdrawn or expended within the parameters we've established; which for now are any and all efforts to enable the investigation and relevant activities to deal with the issue of missing Native women. As time goes on I'm sure we'll refine the process, and the bookkeeping."

"Wonderful," Clayton asserted. "As you all know, this issue is critically important to me. The whole sad and tragic issue of trafficking should be of higher concern to everyone, especially to legislatures and law enforcement at all levels. As people, and as Lakota people in particular, we need to get past the mindset that this 'happens to other people,' or that 'it can't happen to us.' We have to realize it's the future of our Lakota nation that is being stolen from us. Those missing girls and women were to be the teachers and influencers of the children yet to be born. That's what we're losing as a community."

Veronica Lone Hawk reached out and took her husband's hand, a gesture seen by everyone. His words came from the perspective of one who had lost part of his own future, his lineage, when twenty-one year-old Autumn Lone Hawk had been raped by a sex trafficker and died from unexpected complications from an abortion because she didn't want to carry the rapist's child.

"You speak the truth, my friend," Gavin said. "This issue of missing and murdered Native girls and women touches all of us, and we all need to put our minds to it in order to stop it."

Andrew No Horn had been quietly listening. It was his way to listen carefully to others, a habit that served him well as a medicine man, as the healer. He looked across at Clayton and Veronica. "*Tunska*, what you say is true and your words should be heard by everyone. That's why we elected you as our leader. But as with most things that matter, the answers usually start out small or slow. If those two police officers can find out what might have happened to Melvina Old Lodge, then we will have the truth. That's good because truth is a powerful weapon to have. Now the states, South and North Dakota, may not care about our missing women, and the feds certainly don't. But we have to start somewhere. And it starts with one bit of truth, no matter how small, and we keep it going, we keep uncovering more truth. That's how we will solve this crappy situation. Eventually we will have too much truth for them to ignore."

Lone Hawk nodded and squeezed his wife's hand. "You are absolutely right, *Leksi*," he said. "And I can also testify to one other truth. That even from the worst of circumstances come good things, wonderful things." He glanced lovingly at his wife. "I lost my daughter, but out of that tragedy I was gifted another family. So, I learned that one reaction to heartbreak has to be hope. If we lose hope in any situation, no matter how bad it is, then we can't find the will to go on."

"Truth will lead us to hope," Katherine said. "That's a powerful lesson."

For several moments only the crackling of the fire could be heard as the yellow-orange flames cast hues of color on the faces of the people sitting around the fire pit. The mournful howling of coyotes rang out in the darkness beneath the star-filled sky. One especially strident voice came from the north with high, piercing barks. It persisted for several long seconds.

"They are crying for the young women," Andrew No Horn said softly. "Something is in the north. They are telling us to look in the north."

THIRTEEN

New construction was everywhere in Pinnacle, North Dakota. In a corner booth in the Flat Earth Cafe, Justin Primault and Jeff Brousseaux slowly worked on their meal while observing the comings and goings on the streets outside. They had counted at least three motels that were being built, in addition to new builds and renovations on the town's main street. In the cafe itself the tables, booths, and counter were brand new, and the smell of new paint was still fresh. New money everywhere.

"Where there's a boom there's usually a bust, sooner or later," observed Brousseaux.

"Yeah, the wonderful workings of capitalism," Primault responded.

As with most small towns in the Dakotas, the layout of the town was simple, only a few blocks on a square grid. But it was bustling like a big city. People, mostly men, were everywhere and traffic was frenetically constant. Whatever atmosphere the town had before was gone now, obscured by movement and noise. Pinnacle was no longer a quiet village. If anything, it reeked of confusion.

As they had assumed there would be, most of the other patrons in the restaurant were young men, sitting in groups apparently dictated by race. Most were white, but there were several tables of Spanish speakers and at the far end three Blacks were huddled over a table apart from everyone else. There were no Natives that they could discern.

The waitress, a young plain-looking white woman came to refresh their coffee. "You two are new around here," she stated. "You here to look for work?"

Brousseaux smiled affably and nodded. "Yeah, we are. Since you asked, do you know where we can go? Is there an office, or whatever?"

"Yeah, there is. There's a white building at the end of the street where the company does the hiring. You can't miss it, there's going to be a line of guys waiting."

"Thanks," Primault said. "What's the company's name?"

"High Plains Oil," the girl said. "You might have to stand in line but the good news is they're still hiring."

"Great. Thanks."

"Yeah. Probably won't be as easy to find a place to stay," the girl went on. "Every room in town is gone, I hear. If you work long enough you can move into the camp. It's got trailers."

"Camp?" Primault asked, innocently.

"Yeah, about twenty miles north. A shit load of camping trailers. After you stick it out on the job then you might get one of those. Anyway, that's what I heard."

"Okay, thanks again," Brousseaux said.

"Uh, you got any dessert?" Primault asked.

"Just pie. Apple, blueberry, and pumpkin. Want a slice?"

"Yeah, with ice cream for me."

"Same for me," Brousseaux added.

After she was out of earshot, Primault turned to look out and spoke softly. "I'm not that hungry but I just wanted us to have more time to see and hear what we can."

"Roger that."

The main road in town, which the restaurant faced, was constantly busy with truck traffic. There was a school bus painted white with the name of the company on the side—High Plains Oil. It was apparently used to haul workers to and from the job site.

"Where do we start after this?" Brousseaux asked.

"Well, I think we try to get a room, then take a drive around town, unobtrusively as we can, and then maybe drive north out of town and see if we can see where that camp is."

A few seconds later the server returned with their slices of pie, each topped with a generous helping of vanilla ice cream. As they ate, Primault leaned forward. "And from now on, anytime we talk about why we're here, we should do it in the car where no one can hear."

Brousseaux nodded. "Yup."

Twenty minutes later, Brousseaux was snapping photos with his phone while Primault drove. After criss-crossing the town using the eight east-west streets, they turned north onto the highway out of town.

The best they heard from the desk clerk at the third and last motel was a "maybe" and Primault left his phone number with him. In the trunk were sleeping bags and camping supplies, just in case. Their vehicle was an older light blue Ford Taurus sedan that had been in the impound lot, unclaimed for years. After a bit of refurbishment and a matched set of used tires were mounted, it was declared road worthy. Both of them had purchased used clothes from the rummage store in Agency Village, run by one of the local churches. Brousseaux wore a gray hoodie and Primault had on a faded denim jacket. In spite of Chief Avery's misgivings, Primault insisted on not carrying any weapons, reasoning that in white jurisdiction two Native men might be subject to stop and search. As a safeguard they had hidden their badges and identification under the spare tire in the trunk.

Truck traffic indicated they were headed in the direction of the oil fields, and before too long they saw a few drilling rigs on either side of the road in the middle of pastures and one newly planted wheat field. There were more pumping rigs, looking like giant forearms and hands monotonously dipping and lifting. Just past fifteen miles they noticed that a new road had been cut across a pasture, apparently not graveled since two vehicles driving on it raised a long dust trail. Owing to the flatness of the prairie, rows of light colored structures could be seen.

"Those have to be the camps," Brousseaux observed. "That's a lot of damn trailers."

Primault slowed the car for the approach onto the new dirt road but sped back up when he noticed the closed metal gate and what were probably cameras on posts. To one side was a small, square structure.

"I think I saw cameras," Primault said. "We shouldn't take the chance they aren't."

"Right," Brousseaux agreed. "But at least we know where the camp is. From everything I've learned about them, I would bet a month's pay they bring girls here, somehow."

Primault hit the steering wheel with a clenched fist. "Damn! So goddamn close. Wish there was some way we could get in there to have a look."

"If they have cameras at the gate, there's probably more in the camp."

"Or not," Primault suggested. "Maybe they think keeping track of people randomly driving in is enough security."

"It looks to be about a quarter mile from this road. I'm guessing they chose this location because this is the only road for miles around. No other way to get close in a vehicle."

"I have an idea."

Brousseaux turned away to look back at the road as the camp passed out of their view. "Okay. We sneak in at night?"

"Yup." Primault glanced around at the surrounding landscape. "It's damn flat around here. I think we find a place to pull over and look at the road atlas. There has to be some secondary roads. If there was something to the east we could use it."

"You mean go into the camp from another direction?"

"Yeah. But first I need to call the chief and let him know what we're thinking."

A few minutes later they came to a nearly overgrown road on the right side of the highway which led to a slight rise a hundred yards or so. They stopped beyond the rise once they were out of sight of the highway and turned the car around to face back to the west.

"Doesn't look like this road has been used lately," observed Brousseaux.

"Good, it's what we need at the moment. How about you look in that atlas and see if there are any other roads that connect to this highway. I'll give Chief Avery a call."

They both stepped out of the car. Primault placed his call while Brousseaux opened the atlas on the hood of the car.

"Hey, Chief, it's Primault,"

"Justin. How is it going?"

"Well, Pinnacle is a boom town right now. The motels are full. There are hundreds of people here, mostly men. It's what we thought it would be. A damn busy place. There's at least one man camp here. That's why I'm calling."

"Oh, what do you know about it?"

"Not much at the moment. We know where it is and there's front gate security. We could see rows of what are probably camping trailers. Chances are cameras record access, so we have sort of a plan."

"Sort of?"

Primault kept an eye on the road as he talked. "Yeah. We intend to go in after dark and check it out. At least get close enough to see what we can, get its layout."

"You think there's more security, other than the front gate?"

"Can't say for sure. Jeff is checking the atlas now to see if there's a secondary road from the east. We can hide the vehicle and hike in and leave before the sun comes up."

"I can have one of the techs access some satellite maps from the internet and send them to your email. Sometimes those paper atlases don't have enough detail."

"Great idea, Ben. Thanks."

"Sure, I'll get them on it right away. Anything else?"

"No, I'll check with you later."

What they intended to do didn't need any extensive or detailed planning. If they found another road to the east, they would walk in starting at dusk. And if there was no heavy security, such as patrolling guards and dogs, they would sneak into the camp.

"Once we're there and we can get in," Primault said, "we observe and then maybe go in and poke around. Just in case, be sure to take the spare ignition key out of the glovebox."

"And silence our phones."

"Oh, hell, yeah."

Primault glanced at his watch and then took a large thermos and a small box from the back seat, along with two plastic cups. From the thermos he poured coffee and from the box he grabbed energy bars. As they sipped coffee and snacked, he took a moment to glass the surrounding area with a pair of binoculars.

"Not much charm to the landscape, but the land is an economic windfall for the oil companies," noted Brousseaux.

"And for sex traffickers," Primault added. "Before it all goes bust they will make all the money they can."

"What about the local cops, don't they care?" asked Brousseaux. "I mean, they have to know."

Primault nodded somberly. "Here's the real issue as far as I can figure. This is a male-dominated world. Men—white men—are corporate CEOs, they're governors, senators, county commissioners, and county sheriffs. It's what they brought over from Europe, and in that white male mindset is that women are here for their use and pleasure. Even white women couldn't own property back in the day—hell, they were property—and they couldn't vote. So that adds up to Native, Black, and Asian women on the lowest end of the scale. As the Chief keeps saying, white America doesn't care about brown-skinned women."

"Makes me want to bust some heads."

"Me, too."

Emails with satellite maps of the area came an hour later. After several minutes of studying them carefully they could find only one indication of what was probably an old section road that ran north and south three miles east of Pinnacle. There was a connecting road to the south of the town.

"I think that's our best chance, if we can find it now while there's still plenty of light," Primault pointed out. "We can replenish our water and get some snacks in town. It might be a long night."

Forty-five minutes later they found a north-south, ungraveled road three miles east of Pinnacle. It was overgrown with no sign of vehicle tracks.

"I think this is our road," Primault decided. "We follow it north for nineteen miles and that should put us directly east of the camp."

"Works for me."

There was little choice but to drive slowly since they didn't know the overall condition of the road. Except for a few rain washouts, it was traversable. When the trip odometer turned over to nineteen, they pulled over. The sun was still about an hour over the horizon.

"What would you guess, about three miles to the camp from here?" Brousseaux asked.

"Yeah, according to the map. Maybe two hours to walk it in the dark. Sun will go down about eight. So, if we get there by ten or eleven, there's plenty of darkness for us to do our thing and get out. There's no moon."

"Right. Probably a barbed wire fence or two before we get there."

At dusk they checked their fanny packs containing bottles of water and snacks. Each of them carried a compass as well. In another moment they crossed the fence.

"There's sure to be lights once we get close," Primault said. "We'll take a straight westerly heading from here, at 270 degrees. If we keep track of any deviation from that when we see the camp's lights, we just take the opposite heading back."

"Right. Should be okay, other than the fences."

"Yup. And flat cactus and snakes."

"Snakes? I forgot about that."

Primault took a compass heading and pointed west. "That way."

Turning, they took the first tentative steps toward the black sky.

FOURTEEN

After the fire reduced to nothing but coals, Andrew No Horn's two helpers began carrying the hot stones out of the fire pit and into the small center pit in the sweat lodge. Each of them used a long handled pitchfork. They had to duck down to enter the four by twelve foot structure, which was dome shaped and covered with heavy canvas, its door flap facing west.

Waiting to one side in lawn chairs were five people: Andrew, Gavin Lone Wolf, Katherine Hill, and Clayton and Veronica Lone Hawk. They were in front of Andrew's sweat lodge behind the round ceremony house about thirty yards behind his residence.

"How many stones?" Lone Hawk asked.

"Only thirty-six tonight," Andrew told him. "We don't need piles and piles of stones. I don't want anyone to suffer from the heat. It's the act of purification that's important, not how hot you can stand it."

"That's what I always thought," Lone Hawk affirmed. "I was in a sweat so hot it formed blisters on my shoulders. I definitely suffered that time."

Andrew chuckled. "That's too much."

It was a warm evening and the two women wore loose cotton dresses specifically designed for sweat ceremonies. They had followed Andrew's advice and put their hair into one long braid, as did he and Gavin Lone Wolf. For Clayton Lone Hawk it was not an issue since his hair was short. The men wore thin cotton t-shirts and loose swim trunks. In the old days men and women did separate ceremonies and were usually nude, but as old traditions died out men and women participated together.

"Thanks for inviting us, *Leksi*," said Lone Hawk. "I was feeling the need for a good sweat."

"Glad to. I know you've sweated with Henry Two Crow," Andrew said, turning to Veronica. "So, this isn't your first."

"No. I'm looking forward to it. About a month ago my daughters did their first sweat with Henry. They can't wait to do more. They were very nervous, as I was before my first time, but they did well."

"*Leksi*," Katherine said, "when did men and women begin sweating together?"

"I'm not sure. Maybe in the sixties. When I was young it was still done separately."

"I guess it was natural and sensible to evolve," Katherine went on.

"I think it was a way to do the ceremony and not get caught," Andrew replied, "since the government and the Catholics were still against it."

"It's simply amazing to me," Lone Hawk said, shaking his head, "that it took an act of Congress to give us the right to practice our spirituality. This in a nation that was supposedly founded partially on freedom of religion. To me the American Indian Religious Freedom Act of 1978 surprised a lot of white Americans, mainly because most of them thought we were all Christianized. They couldn't understand why it was necessary."

"The bad side is that I hear about people putting on ceremonies who shouldn't be," Andrew said. "Like that white man in Arizona who had something like fifty people in one sweat, and at least one person died from the intense heat."

"Sadly extreme, and stupid," Lone Hawk agreed. "And people fall for their pitch and actually pay to participate, as if our ceremonies are pay-for-play social events.

What's to be done?"

Andrew shrugged. "I sure don't know. It don't matter how much we Natives protest or try to explain what is real and what is not, the whites usually have some Native involved and that makes it real in the eyes of other whites."

"I think that's the worst kind of selling out," Katherine said. "The worst kind of cultural appropriation. Sadly, it happens all over the world and most people don't realize it. A case in point is yoga. How many commercials do we see on television featuring a white woman yoga instructor? That obscures the fact that yoga had its origin in India."

"Same goes for the martial arts," Gavin added. "All of the instructors I had in Judo were Japanese, and they all taught the original forms and they were willing to teach any serious student. Most of them, however, thought non-Japanese, or at least non-Asians, shouldn't be allowed to teach it, and I agree."

Katherine turned to Veronica. "I hope you don't think this is unmitigated white-bashing," she said.

"I totally understand where you all are coming from," Veronica assured her. "The more I learn about Lakota culture, especially spirituality, I'm amazed by how unique it is. I think the downfall of any society or culture is to forget its origins, to forget how it all started. The old ways are usually the best ways. If we don't forget them they'll usually stand the test of time."

"I couldn't agree more," Gavin said. "My sinew-back hunting bow made from ash wood can propel an arrow over two hundred feet per second.

That's comparable to any style modern bow. I use the same materials and follow the same methods of crafting the bow that my grandfathers did. Old ways can fit in our modern world."

One of Andrew's helpers paused after taking another red hot stone into the sweat lodge. "That's the last of the first batch, Grandpa," he said to Andrew.

"*Ohan, waste yelo* (Yes, that's good)," the medicine man said. "Thanks, *Takoja* (Grandson)."

"Yup, we'll watch the door for you after you go in."

Andrew nodded and stood. "*Mitakuyepi*" (my relatives), he said, glancing around at everyone, "it's time to go in." Turning to Gavin and Katherine, he said, "*Tunska*, if you and *Tunjan* (Niece) can lead us in."

"Be glad to."

Gavin and Katherine picked up their towels and went to the door, with Gavin entering first, crouching down and crawling on hands and knees into the lodge, turning to the left as he entered. "*Mitakuye Oyasin* (All my relatives)," he said., circling to the right side of the door. Katherine said the same as she entered, as did Clayton and Veronica. Andrew was the last to enter and he turned to the right, taking his place on that side of the door. Sitting down cross-legged, he leaned forward and spoke to Jerome and the other helper waiting just outside. "You can pass in the bucket and then close the door." Everyone was sitting quietly. Gavin was next to Andrew, then Katherine, Clayton, and Veronica nearest to the door on the left side.

After Jerome passed in the galvanized metal bucket, with a dipper in it, to Andrew, he pulled down the flap, leaving the interior in near total darkness.

"Let us begin," Andrew said.

FIFTEEN

As Justin Primault had assumed, they had to walk around occasional patches of flat cactus, but their progress was steady. Once they heard snorting just to the north and movements they suspected were cattle, affirmed by the smell of fresh droppings. Fortunately, the night was not pitch dark so it was possible to discern objects such as thickets. Twice they scooted under the lowest strands of barbed wire fences.

It was not long before they saw a wide swath of soft light glowing just over the horizon slightly to the west northwest. They adjusted their heading. Half an hour later the lights were brighter, and soon they could discern at least two rows of security lights atop tall poles. They saw at least three sets of headlights as vehicles turned and approached from the highway to the west, a few minutes apart.

At about two hundred yards out they stopped at a water tank they assumed was abandoned since it held no water and they could discern no water source in the immediate area. They sat to rest while Primault glassed the camp with binoculars. Brousseaux illuminated his watch to check the time.

"Took us about two and a half hours," he reported. "It's almost eleven."

"Great," Primault said. "I say we stay out at this distance and go along the perimeter. We can get a good look that way."

"I think we have time to circle the whole camp. What do you see so far?"

"Uh, four rows of camping trailers, vehicles next to some of them. No fence at all, which is surprising. There's a quonset type building on the east side with a minivan parked in front of it. Not many people moving around. The good news is I don't see anyone doing sentry duty."

"Any dogs?"

He handed the binoculars to Brousseaux. "Didn't see any, but you might check for that."

"Roger." After several minutes Brousseaux happily reported, "Can't see any dogs, at least not roaming about. That doesn't mean one or two couldn't be in a pen or something."

"How about we move to the north?"

They cautiously closed the distance from the camp to about a hundred yards as they arrived at a point north of the eastern end of the camp. They estimated the spaces between the east–west rows of trailers to be wide enough for vehicles to drive in and out. Some vehicles were parked adjacent to the trailers. A few men walked from the trailers to the quonset building and a few walked out, returning to trailers. Some of them carried what appeared to be towels.

"I'm guessing there's showers in that building," Primault said, in a loud whisper. "Or maybe a mess hall."

"Or both."

"That's more likely. I wonder if it's ever closed for the night." Primault silently pointed north. "Let's head that way."

At approximately a hundred yards from the camp they were just beyond the reach of the security lights. Both of them had changed into dull colored clothing in order to blend in easier in the darkness. Reaching a point even with the northwest corner of the camp, they sat to scrutinize it with the binoculars. A car drove from the entrance gate near the highway and eventually parked next to a trailer in the second row from the south.

"Nothing much happening at this hour," Brousseaux pointed out, glancing at the luminous dial of his analog watch. "What's our next move?"

"Get close-up and look and listen," Primault said, "and here's how I think we should do that. You go back to the southeast corner. Send me a text when you're there, then I'll go in. I want to reduce the odds of both of us being spotted at the same time."

"Okay," Brousseaux reluctantly agreed. "Makes sense. But I think you should limit your time in the camp. As you say, don't tempt the odds. Fifteen minutes?"

"Right. Once you're back there and in place and I get your text, I'll go in. You keep the glasses and keep an eye out. If you see anything, call my phone. I'll feel it vibrating in my shirt pocket."

"Okay. Uh, you ever done this sort of thing before?"

"No. This is a first for me."

Brousseaux loosed a deep sigh. "Yeah, me too. Good luck."

"Thanks. See you later." He removed his fanny pack and handed it to Brousseaux.

With a nod Brousseaux stood and headed east, carefully staying in the dark beyond the reach of the security lights. Primault watched him until he disappeared into the darkness, suddenly noticing that his own heart was pounding.

A long twenty-two minutes later his phone lit up with the incoming text:

In place.

Primault texted his response:

Ok. Going in now.

He stood just as headlights came down the access road to the camp from the highway entrance, but waited until the small dark van turned and parked beside a trailer on the northern row. A man got out and went into a darkened trailer. Primault waited a minute more and decided that running or hurrying would probably attract attention if anyone in the northern row of trailers happened to look out, so he affected his best nonchalant walk with hands in his pockets. His heart still pounding, Primault headed for two darkened trailers. Darkened likely meant unoccupied or the occupants were already asleep, and in between them would be a safe zone, more or less. It seemed to take a long time to reach the trailers. With relief, he finally crouched down behind the back end of the slightly oval-shaped trailer. It was about eight feet long with the tongue or front end facing south.

The back end where he crouched was still in the light, and he knew he would likely arouse suspicion if someone spotted him. Smoking a cigarette or holding a canned drink of some kind would be perfect cover. "Should have thought about that an hour ago," he whispered to himself.

Hiding in plain sight might work, he thought. Taking a deep breath, he stood and walked to the other end of the trailer. To his left were three trailers and to the right were about ten more. A few vehicles, mostly sedans, were parked beside some, and some windows showed light. Two facts were in his favor; no dogs and no guards. This camp was no more than a makeshift motel or dormitory, likely with few or no rules imposed. There was one other thing he hoped was true, that the number of men living here meant no one knew everybody.

A simple plan formed in his mind. He would walk west to the end of the row of trailers and then cross over to the south side of the camp and walk east. After another deep breath he put his plan into action.

With considerable willpower, he walked slowly. Hands in his pockets and with his head down, he moved along the line of trailers. Music reached his ears; disco, he thought. Skirting around the trunk end of a sedan, he heard someone talking in the second trailer after the music, likely on a phone since he could hear only one voice. In the next trailer every window was ablaze with light. A male face appeared in a back window and looked out. Primault involuntarily held his breath and kept walking, expecting a door to come open. Nothing happened.

So far, so good. But the real test would be if he happened to encounter someone unexpectedly. On the road into the camp, more headlights approached. At the west edge of the rows of trailers the car turned right and went on the other side of the last row. Another sigh of relief. Two trailers from him he saw the back end of the minivan that had parked minutes before. He kept walking, glancing left and right without turning his head, his ears straining to pick up every sound. The unmistakable sound of a door opening made him pause, and then the sound of soft footsteps, and a hurried forceful whisper. As he took another step the side of the vehicle came into view just as he heard a van door sliding open. In the shadowy interior of the van, he glimpsed two figures.

Even in the partial light from the row of security lights, he immediately noticed two details that triggered a warning in his head; one of the figures was smaller and slender, obviously a female. Her hands appeared to be bound behind her and a bag over her head. As yet the other figure, a man, had not noticed him. In the next instant a realization popped into his mind as the man whispered harshly and shoved the smaller one into the van.

Primault heard the words clearly. "Get in and be quiet!"

Though the van's interior was in shadow, what he saw was unmistakable. There was another person, also small, in the van, also with a bag over her head. Primault knew it was another female, and both were barefoot. In the next few moments Primault acted purely out of instinct. He stepped toward the man and whispered loudly: "Hey!"

The man turned, not seeming surprised. Primault had already drawn back his clenched fist and swung from below his waist in a wicked uppercut and connected solidly with the man's jaw. THWACK! The man crumpled in a heap. Primault grabbed the front of his shirt and pushed him into the van.

"Girls!" he whispered, "I'm a cop! Come on! I'm here to help you!" He reached up and pulled the dark hoods off, revealing disheveled dark hair and frightened eyes.

They didn't move. He could see their wide eyes staring in fear and disbelief.

"Come with me! I'm a cop! Let's get out of here before someone sees us!"

He heard one of them reply, a faint, furtive "Okay."

Primault shoved the unconscious man farther into the van and held out his hands. Almost hesitantly both girls scooted toward the door. He helped them to stand, put a hand to his lips to signify silence, and slowly closed the door. He pointed toward the north and leaned in to whisper. "We're going to walk slowly that way until we're in the dark. Okay?"

They nodded. Both had their hair tied back in ponytails and looked very young, and wore thin hoodies and sweatpants and were barefoot.

His own heart pounding, Primault gently took each by the arm and guided them away from the trailer. "We're going to walk slowly," he whispered. "And don't look back."

They each gave him a wide-eyed, frightened nod.

It was the most nerve wracking two minutes of his life, but it seemed far longer than that before they reached the darkness beyond the reach of the security lights. When he was sure they were well hidden, he stopped.

"Okay," he said, speaking normally but in a low voice. "Let me untie your hands. My name is Justin Primault. I'm a cop from Smokey River. My partner is waiting out there in the dark. You're safe now."

They both nodded. He could still sense their apprehension. With his pocket knife he sliced through the duct tape binding their wrists.

"Okay. Sit down, please. While we figure out what to do next. First, can you tell me your names?"

"Julia Lake."

"Maggie Henry."

Pimault's heart skipped a beat. They were on Melvina Old Lodge's list.

After they sat down, he knelt in front of them. Even in the dark he could see they were very young. He took out his phone and dialed Jeff Brousseaux.

"Hey," Brousseaux answered. "What's going on?"

"Something totally unexpected," Primault said. "I have two girls here with me."

"What?"

"I have two girls here with me on the north side of the camp. Can you come around to us."

"Ah, damn! Okay! I'm on my way!"

He had a thousand questions but he decided to wait until Brousseaux arrived.

"How did you find us?" Julia Lake timidly asked.

"Just by accident. My partner and I were here just to check this place out. I happened to see you by that van."

"Can you take us home?" Maggie Henry asked plaintively.

"Yes. You'll be going home. As soon as we get away from here, we'll call your families."

For the first time, he heard a soft sob.

"You're safe now," he assured them. He looked back toward the camp but could see no activity. Apparently no one had seen them leaving. The man he had cold cocked was probably still unconscious. Primault kept an eye on the camp nonetheless.

"Where are you from?" he asked.

"Eagle Butte," Julia Lake said.

"Pierre," Maggie Henry replied.

"My partner's name is Jeff Brousseaux. We're on the Smokey River Tribal Police force. As soon as he gets here we'll figure out the best way to get you out of here as fast as we can."

"Okay."

"Are you okay? You're not injured, or anything?" He immediately felt foolish for asking considering why they had probably been in the camp.

"No, we're okay. I'm kinda hungry," Julia said.

"Yeah, me, too."

Primault pointed east. "We have a car out there, and food and water." He kept his gaze on the van, partially visible in the shadows between two trailers. He felt better with each passing moment. He thought about walking to meet Brousseaux but the two girls were barefoot, and there was flat cactus. Obstacles were hard to see in the dark. Impatiently he looked at his watch just as he heard footfalls. A few seconds later a breathless Brousseaux called out in a low voice.

"Justin!"

"Over here. Keep coming."

Brousseau materialized out of the darkness. Up close in the dark Primault could see the incredulous look on the man's face. "Damn! I didn't figure this would happen."

"Neither did I. I'll fill you in later. This is Julia and Maggie, and they have no shoes, and it's a hell of a long way back to the car."

"Yeah, I see your point. There's only one thing to do—carry them."

"Right." Primault leaned in toward the girls. "Listen, we've got a few miles to go and there's a lot of cactus, so Jeff is right. We'll have to carry you. Is that okay?"

They both nodded. "Yeah," Julia said. "Can we just leave?"

"Sure thing. Uh, we'll need to do this piggyback."

A few seconds later Brousseaux had Julia on his back and Primault stood up with Maggie on his. Surprisingly both were lighter than expected. Primault guessed their captors fed them just enough to keep them alive. The urge to bust more heads coursed through him as he started walking. Brousseaux followed.

"You're going home, ladies," Primault said.

SIXTEEN

The girls were thin but ninety to a hundred pounds was still a load. A slight lean forward helped both officers maintain a comfortable balance and keep a steady pace. Even so it was necessary to stop and rest. They did so after they crossed the first fence. Primault checked the heading on his compass in order to stay to an easterly course.

"Hey, ladies," Primault said. "Do you know Melvina Old Lodge?"

The girls looked at each other. "Yeah," said Julia. "She was with us, but she's gone. I think they took her away somewhere."

"She made it home to Smokey River," Primault told them.

"She did?"

"How did she do that?" Maggie asked.

"We don't know how exactly, but I'm guessing she walked mostly. She almost made it all the way to her house."

"Almost? What does that mean?" Maggie asked, with a fearful tone.

"She was found in a pasture a few miles from her house. She—she died there."

Both girls gasped softly. Julia covered her face with her hands and Maggie crossed her arms over her chest. They both wept softly, crying into their hands.

"I was scared for her," Maggie said, after a few moments. "She got beat up pretty bad. Carrie saw it happen."

"Who beat her up?" Primault asked.

"One of the guys who hauled us around in that van," Julia said. "I think his name is Tulo. Melvina slapped him after he shoved her down, so he beat her up."

"Was it the guy I hit?"

"No. His names is Riley; it wasn't him."

"Melvina had very severe injuries," Primault told them. "Probably from that beating. And she had a list of names on a piece of paper, twelve names. Your names were on that list. She also wrote the name of the town—Pinnacle. That's why we're here."

Both girls nodded as they sniffed and wiped away tears. Brousseaux took out his handkerchief and tore it in half, giving each girl a piece.

"Where are the other girls?" Primault asked.

The girls looked at each other. "They kept us in two places," Julia said.

"Yeah, basements," Maggie said. "Five or six of us. They kept switching us around so it was different girls, not the same all the time."

"Where were the houses they kept you in?"

"I don't know," Julia replied. "They put hoods over our heads when they took us out, so we couldn't see anything."

"Yeah, and it was always at night," Maggie affirmed.

At the next stop nearly an hour later Primault called Chief Avery. "Hey Chief, sorry for the late call," he said, after the man answered. "We have some news that will knock your socks off."

"Okay. I'm all ears."

"We managed to rescue two young women," Primault declared.

"Uh, say that again."

"We have two young women with us. We're about two miles from the man camp and headed back to our car. To make a long story short, we infiltrated the camp, and by an amazing stroke of luck, I came across a guy with two girls in a van. I took the guy out and the girls and I snuck out of the camp. Brousseaux and I have them with us now."

"Damn! I didn't expect to hear that kind of news!"

"As I said, it was totally unexpected. It's about another mile before we reach our car. But, uh, I would like to have these girls examined by a doctor, somewhere, and then we should let their families know we have them."

"Right, I completely agree. I'll get in gear here and see where you can take them. How are they, the girls, I mean? And who are they, what are their names?" Primault could hear Avery scrambling around.

"They're okay, considering. Julia Lake and Maggie Henry. Julia is from Eagle Butte, and Maggie is from Pierre."

"Great! Get phone numbers of their families. And I'll see if I can get ahold of the nearest IHS facility to where you are. Will that work?"

"Yeah, of course. They were both on Melvina's list. And I'd like to get a motel room so they can rest and clean up. Some place away from Pinnacle."

Avery paused momentarily to write down information. "Right. I'm at home but I'll get on it. I'll get Sergeant West to lend a hand. Hopefully we'll have something to tell you by the time you get back to your car. Are you walking?"

"Yeah, we are, but making good progress. I know that's a lot to ask—."

"Hey, it's okay! Ah, call me back later, maybe in an hour or so?"

"Yeah. I can do that. I'll talk to you in a bit."

Primault disconnected the call and took a deep breath. After switching on the light function on his phone he could see their faces. Julia and Maggie were sitting with knees drawn up, listening intently. Brousseaux was gazing off to the west and had been listening closely as well.

"That was our boss, a chief of police," Primault explained, gesturing toward Brousseaux. "We're going to get some help. Do you ladies remember your parents' phone numbers?"

They both nodded.

"Good." Primault turned on the Notes function on his phone. "How about you first, Julia?"

She nodded, looking like she was about to cry. "I live with my dad and my brother. My dad's name is Conrad."

Primault typed in the number and turned to Maggie.

"My folks are Adell and Lincoln Henry."

"Okay, thanks." Primault entered that number and then looked closely at his watch. "Damn, it's after midnight," he said. "Almost one-thirty in the morning." He looked toward Brousseau. "Any guess as to how far we are from the vehicle?"

"Well, I think I heard those cattle to the north of us as we passed earlier. So, maybe, less than a mile."

Brousseaux's guess was good. About forty minutes later they came to the third fence and beyond it was a shallow ditch to the dirt highway. But no vehicle in sight.

"We can't be off by too much," Primault hoped.

Brousseaux pointed north. "I'll go that way a bit and see." Six minutes later he was back. "It's about forty yards from here," he reported.

Fifteen minutes later the two girls were sitting in the back seat of the sedan with bottles of water and snacks in hand. They made short work of several nutrition bars. Primault's phone chirped a few seconds after he switched it off silent mode.

"Primault," he answered, then listened for nearly a minute. "Right, thanks, Chief. Yeah, we're back at our ride and we'll head for that motel. And I'll look for the text from Sergeant West. I'll ask the young ladies that question and I'll call you back in a few."

Primault disconnected the call. "Ladies, that was our boss again. He's arranged for motel rooms for us. One for you two and one for Jeff and me, in Blaine, about 40 minutes from here. After that we'd like to take you to the hospital at Fort Yates and have you checked over. Chief Avery is sending up two women police officers to escort you home in a couple of days. Are you with me, so far?"

They both nodded.

"Okay. Here's the next part. Because we are the police, we need to ask you questions about what you've been through these past few months. We want to do that mainly because there are other girls that are still missing. Whatever you can tell us, whatever you can remember, might help us find them. What we're asking you to do won't be easy for you, but I think it's necessary. Do you suppose you can do that for us?"

The girls glanced briefly at each other and then turned to Primault, who was kneeling by the open back door. Even in the dim dome light from the car, he could see fear in their eyes.

"Yeah," Julia said softly. "I'll answer questions."

"Me, too," Maggie said.

"That's very brave of both of you," Brousseaux quickly asserted.

"It sure is," affirmed Primault. "Thanks."

He could understand their apprehension but what struck him was the freshness of their young faces, in spite of what he could only imagine

Julia and Maggie must have endured for several long months. Part of him prayed that all the ugliness they had been subjected to did not extinguish their youthful exuberance for life. If that was gone, they would be defeated by the selfish sins of others.

Julia put her hands to mouth. "I can't believe we're here," she whispered.

Maggie nodded and put her arm around Julia's shoulders and pulled her close. They both sobbed, but managed to suppress the unbridled cry that was waiting to burst. They stifled sobs and wiped their eyes.

"In a couple of days, you'll be home," Primault assured them.

Julia nodded. "Thanks."

"Yeah, thanks. Thanks for saving us," Maggie added.

Primault nodded and glanced at Brousseaux, who looked as though he were about to cry. In the next few seconds Primault realized his right wrist was sore and he should probably soak it in some ice water.

SEVENTEEN

Gavin Lone Wolf sat at the table over his breakfast with the phone to his ear and took a sip of coffee, gazing absently out the east kitchen window as he listened. Katherine watched him, her curiosity rising as he nodded and muttered. All she could discern was that the call was from Chief Ben Avery. A few seconds later he disconnected the call and looked at Katherine.

"Well," she said, "judging from your expression, I'd say that was an interesting conversation."

"It sure the heck was. Ben just told me about Primault and Brousseaux's recon trip up north."

"I didn't think they had gone yet."

Gavin nodded. "Yes, they did, and with an astonishing report. They sneaked into a man camp near Pinnacle, a small town west of the Fort Berthold Rez, and they rescued two Lakota girls that were on Melvina Old Lodge's list."

"That's amazing! How did they manage to do that?"

"Sounded like an unexpected circumstance. Primault was in the camp and saw two girls in a minivan. A man had them tied up with hoods over their heads. So, he knocks the man out cold and walks out of the camp with the two girls, and he and Brousseaux carried the girls on their backs til they got to their car. Now they're in a motel in a little town called Blaine waiting for two female Smokey River Police officers to arrive, to help them. Ben arranged for them to be transported to the IHS hospital at Fort Yates to be checked over. Then they'll interview the girls and take them home."

"God bless Justin Primault," she said. "It's so astonishing those girls were on Melvina's list. Then she definitely was with them."

"Undeniably. But the sad part is the girls reported that Melvina had been severely beaten by a man who was probably a handler. So, the injuries revealed by her autopsy are not all from her journey home."

"Someone needs to have his testicles removed," Katherine said emphatically.

"My thoughts exactly," said Gavin as he poured coffee from the carafe to refill their cups and glanced at his watch. "I have a staff meeting with the Lakota Studies department in two hours," he said. "What's on your agenda today?"

"A face time call with Jarrod Snyder," she replied. "That long email last night was from him. He wants me to review some EPA regulations. Several congressmen and women think they need to be revised to adjust for the effects of global warming. So, they've approached our firm, and other environmental groups, to make recommendations. Totally a partisan issue politically, so it may be next to impossible for any to be adopted. But we must try nonetheless."

"Sounds like a lot of reading in your future."

"Right. Goes with the territory. But I get to do it here in sweats and sneakers. That's my kind of lawyering."

"Which reminds me. We can probably turn the spare bedroom into an office."

"Don't you think we'll ever have any overnight guests?"

"Well, since this house was built I've had four overnight guests in five years. My niece Theresa and her husband, a former friend, and you."

"Okay, but actually I don't need a lot of space. You saw my office in DC. It was a small cubicle. As long as there's room for a desktop, because I prefer the large screens, and a printer-scanner, I'm good."

"You don't need a file cabinet?"

"No. Flash drives don't take up much room."

Gavin nodded, gazing thoughtfully toward the spare bedroom. "Right. For now, maybe we can take out the bed and get a futon or hide-a-bed. That creates plenty of room for a desk and a chair and we can still accommodate a couple people overnight when we need to."

"I like that idea."

Katherine's phone chirped. She pulled it out of her pocket and glanced at the incoming number on the screen. "It's Loren," she said to Gavin, and then answered. "Good morning."

"Good morning. Hey, listen. I'm about to dash into a staff meeting, and I just got a call from that boutique shop in Pierre. They thought I was you. Anyway, your dress is ready."

"Oh, okay."

"They wanted to know if they should ship it, or if anyone would pick it up."

"Okay. Uh, I think I have their number. I'll give them a call."

"Great. I'll give you a call this evening. I've got some thoughts on the guest list."

Katherine put down the phone and reached for her cup. "My dress is ready. I'll drive up and get it. If I leave soon I can be back by the time you're done with your meeting. May I take the pick-up?"

"Of course. What about your call?"

"I can do it on my phone. I'll just pull over if I'm driving. I'm not in the fast lane anymore and my job—as much as I love it—will not dictate my life."

"I like that. Want to help me water the horses before you leave?"

She reached across the table and entwined her fingers in his. "Lead the way. Is there anything you need from Pierre, by any chance?"

He squeezed her fingers. "Just you."

A few hundred miles to the northwest, Justin Primault drove into the motel lot and parked in front of Room 6. He stepped out of the car and grabbed two large bags of fast food and a holder full of drinks from the front passenger seat. He tapped softly on the motel door with his foot.

Brousseaux opened the door and took one of the bags. Primault closed the door and glanced at Julia and Maggie sitting at the small table in the corner, their attention riveted on the television, as though seeing a long lost friend.

"Breakfast is served, ladies," he announced, still amazed at how young they looked and how vulnerable they seemed.

They both turned and smiled shyly. "Thanks," they said in unison.

Breakfast sandwiches and juice drinks were the morning's fare. Primault handed out the styrofoam containers, plastic cups, and napkins. "There's three of everything in there for you," he told them. "I'm hungry so I know you are, too."

The girls smiled and nodded, wasting no time arranging their food on the table. Primault was guessing it was probably the first real meal they had seen in a long time. In spite of that they still had dainty table manners. He caught Brousseaux's attention and gestured toward the door. "Hey, ladies," he said, "Jeff and I will be right outside. Take your time, there's no hurry about anything."

They both nodded.

Primault and Brousseaux took their food outside and sat on the lawn chairs in front of the window. The motel was a mom and pop operation on the east edge of town. Fortunately, there was a chain fast food drive-through next door. Primault took a sip of coffee before unwrapping his sandwich.

"I think I passed a second-hand store of some kind," he said. "Maybe we can get some fresh clothes for them." He glanced at his watch. "White Bear and Hinson should be here by noon. Maybe after they finish eating, they can call their families."

"Yeah, they asked about that, so I promised they could later this morning."

"Okay. I'm damn glad we did bring badges and ID. The motel owner was a bit squirrelly last night. I'm surprised he hasn't been around."

"Yeah, I guess two Native guys paying for two rooms with cash is unusual to him."

"Or just two Native guys in this town. It seems like a typical farming-ranching, white conservative place. Maybe not many people from the Rez come here."

Brousseaux took a bite and chewed for a while. "Uh, what's the plan after White Bear and Hinson get here?"

"Take Julia and Maggie to the hospital in Fort Yates and have them checked out thoroughly. After that, we see how willing they are to talk about what they went through. I think that's an interview where no males are allowed. I don't want them to feel scared about it. If they reveal any kind of details we can sink our teeth into, that would be great. Mainly I want them to be okay and there's probably a lot of counseling ahead for them."

"Right. All I can think of is my younger sister," Brousseaux said. "I guess we take a lot for granted until something happens. Like you said, I feel like busting some heads."

"Damn straight. If I was thinking more clearly, I would have grabbed that guy at the van, too. He knows things, like where the girls were kept and who's running the operation."

"Yeah, but you did good, you did what you had to. You rescued two girls. That's not nothing. I'm sure we'll learn something from them."

They ate in silence for a few minutes, until a man emerged from the motel office at the end of the row of rooms. "Heads up," Primault cautioned.

A sixty-ish man in a blue jeans, a plaid shirt, and a baseball cap approached and stopped a few feet away, clearly nervous. He cleared his throat. "Uh, gentlemen, how are you fellas this morning?"

"We're good," Primault replied.

"That's good, that's good. Just reminding you that check-out time is noon."

"Thanks, but we might need to be here after that. We'll be glad to pay for another day."

The man adjusted his glasses and looked nervously up the street. "Well, the problem is, uh, the rooms are booked for tonight."

Primault looked up and down the row. Theirs was the only vehicle in front of any of the rooms. He reached into his pocket and pulled out his identification and badge. 'Sir," he said carefully, "the two of us are tribal police officers. Around noon we're expecting two more officers to arrive to help us finish our task." He held up his badge and ID.

The man nodded. "Oh, I didn't know you guys were cops."

"It was our boss, our chief of police who made the room reservations last night. I'm sure he gave you his name."

The man nodded again, trying to remember the phone call, his expression somewhere between annoyance and apprehension. "Yeah, Avery, I think he said."

"Right," Primault said, maintaining a cordial tone. "Chief Ben Avery."

Brousseaux held up his own badge and ID for the man to see.

"We will be leaving after our fellow officers arrive," Primault went on. "We won't be here another night, but we'll be glad to pay you for using the room past check out." He stood up and took cash out of his pocket.

"Well, no, that's—that's okay," the man stammered. He spun on his heel and walked back toward the office.

Primault sighed, sipped his coffee and nodded toward the office. "I don't think he's going to let it go," he surmised. "I wouldn't be surprised if he gets on the phone and calls the local cops." He reached for his phone. "I think we try to beat him to the punch." He dialed Chief Avery's number.

"Ben Avery," the Chief answered.

"It's Justin, Chief," Primault began. "There might be some trouble here. The motel owner is nervous about us being here. He doesn't know we have the girls with us, and I'm guessing he's calling the cops as we speak."

"Okay. What do you want to do?"

"Well, I don't want the girls to be scared any more than they are, and just as importantly, I don't want any word that we were in that camp to get out. I think we need to keep a lid on that. Maybe a call to the county sheriff here, whoever that is, would help before this goes south."

"Right. I agree with your reasons. I'll get on the phone and talk to someone. What do you want me to tell him?"

"Just tell him we're on an assignment. We have badges and ID. I just don't want cops pulling up here and scaring the girls."

"All right. I'll get on it. I'll get back to you as quick as I can."

"Okay. I need White Bear and Hinson's cell numbers before you hang up."

"Right, here they are."

Primault wrote the numbers on the sandwich wrapping, then tore off the corner of it. Turning to Brousseaux he said, "The Chief is going to call the county sheriff and tell him we're here on an assignment. Meanwhile, we need to tell the girls something, just in case."

"That would be wise."

Primault took another sip of coffee and then stood. Knocking on the door, he waited a moment before he opened it. "Hey, ladies," he said, cautiously. "How are you doing?"

"Okay," came a reply. Both were still at the table, finishing their meal.

He stepped inside. "Great. Ah, listen, some cops may be coming here," he said, gently. "No one knows that you're here. So, if a cop does show up, Jeff and I will talk to them and I want you, the two of you, to just hang tight, and don't open the curtains."

"Is everything okay?" Maggie asked. Both immediately looked wary.

"Yeah, we're good. Two of our lady officers are on their way and should be here soon. After that, as I said earlier, they'll take you to the hospital and then home."

"Can we still talk to our folks?"

"Of course. But I want to make sure no one interrupts us. Then we'll make your calls home. Would that be okay?"

They nodded.

Primault closed the door and sat in the chair, reasoning that sitting would be better than standing for any passer-by to see. After a moment he dialed Madonna White Bear's number and waited.

"This is Madonna White Bear," she answered.

"Justin Primault here," he said. "Just checking to see where you are."

"Okay, I think we're about thirty minutes out, if the GPS is right."

"Good," he went on. "The motel is on the east side of town, easy enough to find. But there's sort of a development here, so you might roll up and find cops around."

"What's happening?"

"Oh, the motel owner is a bit nervous about us being here. I wouldn't be surprised if he calls a cop."

"Roger that. Well, I tell you what. There's really no traffic on this highway so I think we can step it up a bit. We're bringing two cruisers, as you asked, and we're in uniform."

"Great. See you in a bit."

Now there was nothing to do but wait. Brousseaux had been looking around at the buildings in the area of the motel, a few of them apparently unoccupied. The whole town looked drab. "This little burg obviously isn't reaping the rewards of the oil boom the way Pinnacle is," he commented.

"I noticed," Primault said. "Probably because it's not on a main highway. Frankly I thought it would be bustling. So goes the whims of capitalism."

"There'll be cheap real estate when it all goes bust," Brousseaux commented. "What tribes were here before all the Europeans got here?"

"I think the Arikara, but I'm not sure. There had to be others, maybe the Crow."

"Yeah? Well, whoever they were, I think they had a good thing going, according to a couple of old guys I heard talking. I remember someone saying the Crow would spend the summers in the mountains, where it was cool, and then winter along the rivers. Sounds good to me."

"It does. Native people did what was logical and within the limits of the natural environment," Primault asserted. "They adapted to it. That's why there's different kinds of dwellings all over the continent. Not all the same. I saw a photograph of two small towns, one was in the early 1920s in Massachusetts and the other was in England in the 1700s, I think. I couldn't tell which was which. They just brought their way of life with them and plunked it down here even if it didn't fit or make sense."

"Pisses me off," Brousseaux admitted. "I used to have arguments with my old man about what the French did. He was mostly French. He said the French intermarried more with Native people than other Europeans. And that was supposed to make all the bad things they did not as bad, I guess."

"The arrogance of Manifest Destiny," Primault said drily.

A dark sedan turned the corner from a side street next to the motel office and parked. The logo on the front door and a light bar on the roof was immediately noticeable. A man in blue jeans, white shirt, and tan straw hat stepped out and walked into the office.

"Well, your hunch was right," Brousseaux said.

"Yeah. This could be interesting." Primault clipped his badge to his belt and Brousseaux did the same. There was nothing to do but wait.

Ten minutes later the man in the hat emerged from the office and walked toward them. They both noticed immediately that he carried a weapon in a holster on his right hip. He walked with the gait of an older man. Not wanting to appear in any way reactionary, they sat until he arrived. The expression on his face was friendly. He had a slight paunch and thin arms, lacking the usual thick build common to most farmers and ranchers.

"Hey, fellas," he said, in an affable but raspy voice. "How you all doing?"

"We're good," Primault replied. "How are you?"

"I'm good. Thanks." He pushed his hat back a bit. "Ah, say, listen. Mel at the office had a question. So, he called me. I'm the town marshal. Tim Nicks is my name."

"Well, Marshal Nicks. We'll be glad to answer any questions," Primault said, as he carefully rose to his feet. He offered his identification as Brousseaux stood and did the same.

Nicks took both and looked at them for a few seconds before he handed them back. "Smokey River, huh? You're a bit out of your usual jurisdiction."

"For sure, on an assignment."

"I see. What sort of an assignment?"

"Up on the reservation, at Fort Berthold," Primault said, trying to be vague. "Couldn't find a motel room there, or anywhere. So, we came here. We're waiting for couple of officers who are on their way here to join us, and then we're going up to the reservation."

Nicks nodded, apparently accepting that explanation. Primault and Brousseaux saw the motel owner exit the office and turn in their direction. Nicks noticed their reaction and turned to look. "Looks like Mel's got something on his mind," he allowed.

Twenty seconds later the owner arrived, no less nervous than he was earlier, glancing a bit sheepishly at Nicks.

"What's up, Mel?" Nicks asked.

"Uh, the sheriff just called," Mel said. "He just talked to their boss." He pointed at Primault and Brousseax. "I guess these fellas are here on a special job."

"So, Sheriff Arnold vouched for them?"

"Yeah, yeah, he did," Mel affirmed, somewhat perplexed.

"Yeah? Well, that fits with what these gentlemen told me," Nicks said. "I figured there was nothing to be concerned about. Are you okay with that, Mel?"

Before Mel could reply, a black and white cruiser with Smokey River Tribal Police markings turned right on the street to the west, followed by an unmarked dark blue cruiser. Less than ten seconds later they rolled to a quiet stop in front of the small knot of men. Two uniformed female officers stepped out of the vehicles.

"Well," said Nicks. "I guess that ties a knot." He stared for a few seconds at the shiny cruisers and the two Native female officers with sidearms and turned to nod at Primault and Brousseaux. "You gentlemen have a great day."

"Thank you, sir."

"Come on, Mel." Nicks said, taking the man by the arm. "I hope you got some good coffee on in your office."

Primault and Brousseaux turned to meet the new arrivals.

"What was that all about?" Madonna White Bear asked.

Primault shrugged. "Somebody got nervous about two Native guys in a motel room, apparently. Maybe the light in the office was too dim last night, I don't know."

The women chuckled.

Primault nodded toward the door. "The girls are in there, having breakfast. All we could find was fast food."

"How are they?"

"They look okay. They took a shower. It's hard to tell how they're really feeling."

"I'm sure they're damn glad to be here, and away from wherever they were," Audrey Hinson observed. "What do you want us to do?"

"Just reiterate what I told them. That we're taking them to the hospital to get checked, and then home after that. I promised they could call their families, so maybe you can help with that. And I'd like to get them some fresh clothes, and whatever personal things they need. They're expecting you. After the hospital, I'd like you to interview them. I thought they'd be more willing to answer questions from women cops."

Both women nodded as they took notes.

"It's amazing you were able to find them." White Bear said.

"Yeah, I couldn't believe it when Justin told me he had two girls with him, after he had gone into the camp," Brousseaux recalled.

"A case of being at the right place at exactly the right moment," Primault said.

"And lucky for those two young ladies," White Bear declared. "I wish to god we could find them all."

Primault glanced at Brousseaux and nodded. "My thoughts, exactly. But we'll take our victories when we can. I'm going to call Chief Avery while you're with the girls."

Nodding, White Bear and Hinson stepped to the door and knocked softly.

EIGHTEEN

At the truck stop on I-25, the man in the white van was casually sipping his coffee when he nearly choked at the sight of the same incredibly beautiful Native woman he had seen the last time he had stopped here. He sat motionless and watched her step down from the dark blue Chevrolet half-ton crew cab truck and walk toward the west entrance of the truck stop. She was dressed in a gray shirt, blue jeans, and designer sneakers. Her hair in a long ponytail swayed tantalizingly as she walked.

The second the door closed behind her he stepped out and went to the back of his vehicle, opening the double doors. His heart pounding, he opened a small black case next to an orderly stack of boxes, his deliveries for the day. He took out a small voice activated recorder and turned it on. As he worked feverishly he looked frontward through the windshield of the van, at the door the woman had used. He found the recording he wanted and played it, and then reset the recorder. And waited.

His mind whirled as he restacked the boxes, wanting to appear busy on the off chance someone was watching him. He was thrilled he had backed into the parking spot and that the back of the van pointed west.

These truck stops usually had security cameras aimed at the parking lots, but the back of the van was out of sight.

He took deep breaths to calm himself. What he intended to do was a risk, but so far he had successfully taken fifteen girls and had the process down cold. The bigger issue was what Piano's reaction would be to this particular female. She was not a teenager and his reason for wanting to take her was purely selfish. He wanted her for himself. She was the most beautiful women he had ever seen. Taking her would be easy. Where to hide her would be the problem. But he was reasonably certain Tulo would help. In fact, he was counting on it.

Seconds passed, and then minutes. He looked at his watch. Another seven minutes crawled by. Cars and trucks were arriving at the gas pumps in the three islands south of the store. Semi-trucks were pulling into the entrance and around to the diesel islands on the north side. Two cars pulled out of the parking spots in front of the store, another pulled in and a family got out and hurried into the building. He looked at this watch again and decided to wait another two minutes.

His heart pounded harder when he saw her exit the convenience store entrance, carrying a go-cup of coffee, he guessed. She waited for a car to pass and then walked toward the blue pickup. A few feet from the back bumper she pointed the remote with keys and unlocked the door. He saw her through the van's driver window, and quickly looked south at the line of vehicles parked in the last row, where his van was. He saw no one in any of them. His luck was holding.

There was nothing to do but guess when she would reach the pickup door. He waited another second and then clicked on the recorder and pushed the volume high.

Katherine was reaching for the door handle of the pickup when she heard a voice call out, obviously in some distress. She glanced around but saw no one in the immediate vicinity. She heard it again—

"No! What are you doing? Leave me alone! No!"

It was unmistakably a girl. Given what she and Gavin had been talking about before she left, she felt the hairs on the back of her neck stiffen. She spun around looking and heard the plaintive voice again.

"No! Get your hands off me!" It definitely was a girl.

She noticed the van next to her and what appeared to be an open back door. Without a further thought she stepped toward it and peeked around the door. By the time she saw the man dressed in denims reaching for her, it was too late. In the next split second, she felt pressure on her mouth and jaw, and everything turned black.

Her hair was soft against his face and the scent of her perfume filled his nostrils as he pulled her against his chest. Her hand against his chest stopped pushing. His right hand and the cloth were still clamped over her mouth. Though she was slender the sudden downward shift of her weight as she lost consciousness caught him off guard. He quickly moved his left hand from the back of her head to her back and lifted her up into the open van and into the space between the stacked boxes. Reaching down he grabbed her ankles and folded her legs into the van, stepped back, and closed the doors.

With his heart thudding in his chest, he stepped around the van and saw the go-cup where she had placed it on the hood of the blue pickup. Opening the van's driver's door, he got in calmly. Knowing that a security camera would catch his movements, unhurried motion was his best safeguard. Without glancing back, he turned the ignition, starting the engine. She would be unconscious for at least another twenty minutes. Putting the transmission in gear, he eased slowly out of the parking spot and turned north onto the highway.

NINETEEN

avin was calling Katherine's phone for the third time when he heard a vehicle pull up outside the house. Relieved, he went to the front door to meet her, but instead saw Andrew No Horn's pickup. The old man stepped down and hurried up the front steps.

"I came over because I've had this feeling something is not quite right," he said as he stepped through the door Gavin held open.

A chill went through Gavin. "Well," he said, "the only thing is I haven't been able to reach Katherine on her cell phone. I've tried to call her three times."

"Yeah? Where is she?"

"She went to Pierre, but she should have been home hours ago."

"What do you want to do?"

"Ah, I'm not sure. Maybe it's something simple like her phone lost its charge. What do you think?"

Andrew went to the kitchen cupboard, took down a cup, and poured himself coffee from the carafe on the counter. "I think you should call the cops."

The cold feeling intensified. "You had a feeling something wasn't quite right?"

The old man nodded. "Yeah, all afternoon."

Gavin's phone chirped. Glancing down he saw the incoming number and let out a sigh of relief. "It's her," he said. "Hi, hon. I've been wondering where you are."

There was a pause, and then a deep male voice. "Uh, sir, is this Gavin Lone Wolf?"

After a second or two of confused silence, he responded "Yes, this is Gavin Lone Wolf. Who is this?"

"This is Deputy Sheriff Dan Jensen, and I'm calling on a phone that was found on the console of a dark blue Chevrolet pickup. Your name is under Call in the Case of Emergency, on this phone."

The chill went down to his toes. He glanced at Andrew before he replied. "I see. What—what else can you tell me?"

"Well, Mr. Lone Wolf, there is also a small purse with a wallet, and other things. The identification is a driver's license from Washington DC."

"Okay, and the name on the license is Katherine Kay Hill."

"That's correct, sir. Do you know that person?"

"Yes, she is my fiancée. And she is obviously nowhere around?"

"That's right. A clerk here at the truck stop says this truck, which is registered to you, has been parked here for a while. He noticed it hadn't moved for a couple hours and no one's been near it. The key to the truck was found on the ground near it, and a cup of coffee on the hood. Can you tell me why Katherine, your fiancée would have been here?"

"Yes, she was on her way to Pierre to pick up a dress. She left here about nine this morning."

"I see. Where is here, sir?"

"We live near Cold River."

"I see, and was nine o'clock the last time you saw her?"

"Yes. I was expecting her home by mid-afternoon. Deputy Jensen, what's going to happen now?"

"Well, sir, the state DCI people are here. At the moment they're dusting for prints on the truck. We've finished talking to two of the employees who saw your fiancée. She apparently went to the ladies room and then purchased a cup of coffee."

"Okay, what about security cameras? I know that place has them. Did you check those?"

A second or two of silence on the other end. The chill settled like a rock in the middle of his chest. The deputy spoke again.

"Yes, we looked at the footage for today. Your fiancée entered and exited, walked to her truck, paused by the truck, placed the to-go cup on the hood, and went around to the back of a white van. She did not reappear. A minute later a male with dark hair and wearing sunglasses appeared from the back of the van, got in and drove away. My guess, Mr. Lone Wolf, is that your fiancée Katherine was lured into that van."

Now Gavin felt his cheeks turning hot. "Did the cameras pick up the license number of the van?"

"Yes, it was Nebraska plates."

His legs turning to jelly, Gavin grabbed the arm of the recliner and sat. "Anything else?"

"That's the extent of information we've been able to gather, in addition to what you told me. Anybody other than you and Katherine Hill ever drive this truck?"

"No. I mostly do."

"Okay, so we probably won't find any prints other than Katherine's and yours. That won't tell us anything. You can come up and get your truck, and then stop by our office. We need to know whatever else you can tell us."

"Alright. I'm leaving now."

Gavin watched the highway roll by, inexorably slow it seemed, and the memory of him hearing that his parents were killed kept playing in his head. It had felt like someone had knocked the wind out of him emotionally. He and Gerard were thirteen and Loren was sixteen. The bottom of his world had fallen out then, as it had now.

He and Andrew rode mostly in silence.

"*Leksi,* you can just turn around and bring the Jeep home," he said to his uncle.

"Well, if it's okay I want to go with you to the sheriff's office. I want to hear for myself what they have to say.'

"Yeah, it's okay with me."

"She's okay, *Tunska.* I don't feel that she's been hurt. Something about her is, ah, is closed."

"Closed?"

"Yeah, shut down for a while. My niece is smart. She'll take care of herself."

"So, you're saying she's alive?"

"Yeah, and confused. But after that she's going to get pissed, really angry."

Gavin sighed and nodded. "I waited a long time, *Leksi,* to get her back. I don't want to lose her again. Not this way."

"We'll find her."

As encouraged as he was by his uncle's assertion, Gavin also knew the sobering statistics when it came to the chances of finding missing Native women. The odds weren't good. Most of them were never found.

An hour later they pulled into the truck stop and immediately spotted the pickup cordoned off behind a barricade of yellow police tape. Four sawhorses were around it to hold the tape. Gavin parked and went into the store and approached the nearest cashier.

"Can I help you?" the young man asked.

Gavin gestured toward the window. "I came to get my truck, the blue one out there. I talked to a Deputy Dan Jensen."

"Oh, right." The cashier reached for a phone and punched a number. "Yeah, Hank? A man's here to get his truck…yeah, that's the one… okay." He glanced at Gavin. "Hank—that's our manager—will bring you out the key."

A slightly balding middle-aged man emerged from a hallway and approached, handing the remote with a key attached to Gavin. "I'm so sorry about the circumstances concerning your truck," he said.

Gavin took the key. "Thanks. I appreciate all the help you gave to the deputy."

"Wish we could have done more," Hank said.

A thought popped into Gavin's head just as he was about to leave. He paused. "I don't suppose you still have the video you showed the deputy."

Hank nodded. "Yeah, we sure do. It's all digital these days. We burned a copy for him, as they say."

"Do you suppose you could show it to me?"

Hank didn't hesitate. "Of course! Sure. Come with me."

In the small office Hank played the video, and it was exactly as the deputy had described. Katherine parked, stepped out of the truck, entered the store, and twelve minutes later exited with a tall paper cup in her hand. She reached in her pocket and pulled out the remote and paused. For a few seconds she looked around, as if listening for something. Then she took a tentative step forward, placed the cup on the hood of the pickup and walked toward the front of the truck, then leaned forward and looked to the left, obviously trying to see behind a white van parked in the adjacent spot. Then she disappeared behind the van. After about thirty seconds a man dressed in denims, with dark hair and sunglasses covering his eyes, walked out from behind the van, got into the driver's side, and drove away a few seconds later.

"I don't suppose I could trouble you for a copy of that?" Gavin asked. "Be glad to pay you for it."

"No trouble at all. Just takes a minute or so to copy it."

Gavin left the store with flash drive in his hand and rejoined Andrew who was waiting at the truck. "I think we take the pickup," he said. "It's faster."

After bundling up the police tape and carrying the sawhorses to the grass, they got up into the cab. A soft hint of perfume still hung in the air. Gavin felt a sudden heaviness inside of him, a mixture of loneliness and fear.

Thirty minutes later they pulled into the parking lot of the Lehigh County courthouse. Inside they looked at a directory on the wall and went up to the second floor. Deputy Dan Jensen's appearance matched his deep voice. He was tall and lean and broad shouldered, with close-set blue eyes in a narrow face under a thatch of dark brown hair. He projected an air of no-nonsense. Gavin introduced himself and Andrew.

Jensen led them into an office where a man in a dark blue suit stood to meet them. "This is Sergeant Steve Winron with the state DCI," Jensen announced. "Please, everyone have a seat."

Winron wasted no time. "Dan tells me the missing person is your fian-cée, Mr. Lone Wolf. Is that correct?"

"Yes."

`"Did you know she was going to Pierre?"

"Yes. She was going there to pick up a dress. I expected her to be home around mid-afternoon. When I felt she was late, I called her. There was no answer, of course."

"Right. Do you have a photograph of her, other than the driver's license?"

"Yes, I do." Gavin took out his wallet, which had a small color head shot of Katherine that he handed to Winron. "You can keep that if you need to."

"Thank you. Does Katherine have any serious allergies, does she take medication? Is there any kind of health situation that we should be aware of?"

"No, no allergies that I know of. She takes no medication. She's very healthy and fit."

"What is her occupation?"

"She's a lawyer. Graduated from Arizona State University in environ-mental law and works for a firm in Washington DC."

Winron finished writing and looked up again. "Mr. Lone Wolf, do you feel in any way that this abduction is related to her work?"

"I don't think so, but that's just speculation on my part."

The investigator nodded. "As far as you know, has she made any ene-mies in the course of her work?"

"I doubt it. She's not the type."

The questions continued for another fifteen minutes. Gavin was impressed with Winron's copious note taking. When he finished he handed a business card to Gavin. "If you happen to think of anything else, please don't hesitate to call me." He also gave Gavin Katherine's clutch purse.

The only other stop they made was to top off the gas tank at the truck stop. Andrew took the Jeep key from Gavin but didn't immediately get out of the truck.

"I've been trying to get a feeling for her state of mind, because she was driving this truck," he said. "I don't sense anything bad, I mean like she was angry or feeling bad."

"You said earlier she might have been confused, or closed up What do you suppose that was, or could be?"

The old man shook his head. "I'm not sure. But I think you should put up a ceremony to ask for help, and for her protection. We should go talk to Henry Two Crow."

"You don't want to do a ceremony?"

"No, better if Henry did it. I'm too close to the situation, and I'm angry. I'll give Henry a call tonight."

Gavin watched an eighteen wheeler pulling back onto the highway. "Okay. Thanks, *Leksi*. I don't know what I would do if I lost her."

"No, don't think that way. We'll ask the Spirits for help and we'll get her back. Meanwhile, it might not hurt to bring your friend Chief Avery into this."

Gavin opened the console and looked down at Katherine's clutch purse containing her phone and wallet and a few other items. He touched it gently.

This can't be all I will ever have left of her.

He felt empty, and helpless, and willing to grab at straws. "Okay," he said. "I'll give Ben a call."

TWENTY

Fighting her way out of a dark haze, Katherine noted a slightly sweet metallic taste on her tongue. She slowly figured out that her ankles were bound tightly together, as were her wrists. And there was tape over her mouth.

Second by second more awareness crept in. There was a slight noise of some kind, and a steady vibration, and she was curled up on her right side. Something soft was under her head. She slowly flexed her leg muscles, then her arms and shoulders. A sense of dread mixed with the thought not to make any large movements.

Instinctively she knew where she was; inside a van. Her last concrete memory was a flashing glimpse of a man with something in his hand, and then boxes. Then, nothing until now. Apprehension instantly turned into fear with the realization she was a captive, a prisoner.

The conversation about Primault rescuing two girls popped into her mind, as did the whole sordid reality of missing Native girls. But she was far from a teenage girl, the usual victim profile. The distinction did not alter the reality of her predicament, obviously, and the reason she was abducted terrified her. She strained against the bindings until her wrists hurt. Whatever was around her ankles was no less yielding. Physically there was no way to alter her predicament. But there had to be something she could do. Thinking was her only hope for effecting some change, no matter how slight. As well as emotional toughness. She couldn't allow this to beat her down. At the moment her physical strength was negated, but she couldn't allow her emotional strength to be as well. She couldn't give up, she couldn't allow herself to quit, and she had to think.

TWENTY-ONE

Relentless thoughts and images plagued Gavin Lone Wolf as he drove on the interstate. The immediate consequence was a feeling of disconnection, disassociation. Nothing seemed real. He was alone in the cab of his pickup, and now alone again in his life. She was gone and he was trying not to give in to the worst possibilities flying at him like arrows he had to dodge. Unable to push the thoughts and images aside, he clumsily worked the cell phone with one hand and called Chief Ben Avery.

"Avery," the man answered.

"Ben, Gavin Lone Wolf. Hope you have a couple minutes to talk."

Avery's tone immediately turned cautious. "Sure. What's on your mind."

Gavin took a deep breath and exhaled. "My fiancée's been abducted, probably sometime this morning."

"Oh, shit! From where? How?"

"From the truck stop on I-25 on the cut-off to Pierre. A man took her and drove away in a white van. There's a video, I have a copy."

"Do the cops know?"

"Yeah. State DCI and Lehigh County sheriff. I talked to them."

"Good, good! Tell me what you know."

Gavin told Avery about Katherine's reason for going to Pierre and described the video tape, move by painful move.

"That's all good, my friend. Did anyone happen to get the license number of that van?" Gavin could hear Avery's fingers clicking across a computer keyboard.

"Yeah, I think so. The man from the DCI or the deputy sheriff would know, I think. I have their phone numbers. Ah, just a minute." He put down the phone and reached into his shirt pocket. "Okay, Ben, here it is: 605-555-4083. The guy's name is Winron."

"What was Katherine wearing?"

"Blue jeans, gray shirt, and white sneakers."

"Did she have her phone with her?"

"It was still in the truck, with her wallet, driver's license, credit cards. The key to the truck was on the ground, where she apparently dropped it."

More clicking faintly over the phone. "Okay. I'm going to call that DCI number and the deputy. What is his name, or hers?"

"Dan Jensen. He was the one who called me first to let me know."

"Okay. I'm going to make that call, and some others, and I'm going to see what I can put in motion here. Then I'm coming over to your place. Is that alright?"

"Yeah, of course. I'll see you later."

Gavin put down the phone and opened the console and reached in. He took out the clutch purse and held it. It was all the could think of to do. He held it all the way home.

Woodenly he walked into the empty house. Andrew closed the door behind him. The landline phone rang. After three rings Gavin walked to the desk in the corner and looked down at the small screen, He knew the number.

"Hey, bro," he answered, his voice raspy.

"Little brother, what's up?" A trace of anxiety tinged Gerard's voice.

Gavin glanced at Andrew and sat down in the recliner. "Nothing good," he said, the tension obvious in his voice.

"Tell me."

"Katherine's *gone*. She was taken, abducted earlier today."

"Jesus, bro! What do you know if anything?"

"I know where it happened, and when. I saw a video; I have a copy of it. It happened at the truck stop on the interstate, at the junction to Pierre."

"Okay. Are the cops involved?"

"Yeah, state DCI and Lehigh County sheriff."

"Good, that's good. Listen, give me phone numbers, and tell me what you can. I'm going to put one of my people on this, then I'm getting on a plane as soon as I can, to Sioux Falls. I'll rent a car from there."

"Thanks, brother. I sure appreciate that."

"Of course, of course. And don't be alone, get someone to stay with you."

"*Leksi* is here now."

"Good! What format is the video on?"

Gavin reached in his pocket and pulled out the flash drive. "It's on a thumb drive."

"Great. Can you email it to me?"

"Yeah, sure."

Five minutes later he finished the call. Andrew handed him a cup of fresh coffee. "I know you're probably not hungry, but this wouldn't hurt."

"Thanks." He took the cup. "Gerard's coming."

"Yeah. That's good. You call your sister yet?"

Gavin slowly shook his head. "I'll do that in a minute."

"I'm going to stay with you. Maybe I'll call Joby, too. I want him to get some stuff from my house for me."

"Yeah, okay. Thanks." A small sip of hot coffee was strangely reassuring. He dreaded the call he had to make to Loren. But it had to be done. Andrew's presence was more reassuring than the coffee, and now he needed a hug from his big sister. He reached for his phone, doing his best to stifle the sob building up in his throat.

A little more than an hour later the house was full. Loren and her husband Morgan were preparing a meal in the kitchen. They had arrived with bags and boxes of food. Their son Thomas was setting the table. His mother had instructed him to set a place for Katherine. Joby and Andrew had just finished checking on the horses and watering them, and Gavin was wrapping up another conversation with Gerard.

When the food was ready Loren placed small portions of food on a small plate, the Spirit Plate, and brought it to Andrew, who called everyone to the table, and offered a prayer.

"*Taku skanskan wakan* (All that moves and is sacred)," he began. "We gather here, this family, to offer our prayers to strengthen us in this difficult time. Protect my niece, our loved one, Katherine. Keep her safe from harm. Give my nephew Gavin strength of mind and the will to see clearly and help us all to bring her back home. *Mitakuye Oyasin.*"

"*Mitakuye Oyasin,*" they all said, with one voice.

Andrew placed the Spirt Plate at Katherine's place setting and invited everyone to take a seat. Loren, as the matriarch of the family, chose to put the food on the table in serving bowls, rather than have it dished out cafeteria style. She preferred the old fashioned way when people took an individual helping and passed the bowl to the next person. To her it was an appropriate symbol of giving and sharing, especially at this particular moment. The simple act of passing food, as far as Loren was concerned, also strengthened the bonds of family. It was what her brother needed.

Conversation was about anything but the tragedy that had brought them together. Horses, the weather, *wasicu* politics—which was always good for eliciting groans and laughter—and Joby's new truck filled the air. The empty chair next to Gavin was in everyone's margin of awareness, a subtle reminder of loss, and hope, and family ties.

"Hey, Uncle, I like your new truck," Thomas said to Joby.

"Oh, yeah, thanks. I do, too."

"It's a five-speed, stick shift," Gavin pointed out.

"You're kidding!" Morgan blurted. "I didn't think they made them anymore. How did you find it?"

Joby shrugged, a bit embarrassed at being the center of attention. "We were just looking," he said, nodding at Gavin. "It was there on the lot. I always liked straight sticks. It just seemed right to have a truck like that."

"Better gas mileage" Morgan said. "I had one some years ago. Is it a four-wheel-drive?"

"Oh, yeah," Joby said. "They don't always plow the streets when it snows, down in the housing project. Figured a four-wheel-drive was the way to go. Also good for hunting and hauling wood. Been a while since I went deer hunting."

"Well," Thomas offered, "we'll have to do that this fall. If we can draw tags."

"You can always get doe licenses, can't you?" Morgan wondered.

A phone chirped somewhere, faintly, just loud enough to catch everyone's attention. A quizzical look washed over Gavin's face. Glancing at Loren he stood. "It's Katherine's phone. I forgot I brought it in." He went to the master bedroom. Silence fell, except for the phone. Everyone heard him answer. Silence prevailed and Gavin's muffled voice could be heard.

"Hello," he answered,

"Yes, uh, I am calling for Katherine Hill. Is she there, please?"

"I'm sorry, no she's not. This is Gavin Lone Wolf. Who's calling?"

"My name is Jarrod Snyder, Dr. Lone Wolf. Katherine works for our firm, here in Washington DC."

"Yes, of course, Mr. Snyder."

"I'm calling because, uh, earlier today I was expecting a follow-up call from her. We had spoken earlier. My subsequent calls went unanswered."

"Yes, she did tell me, this morning, that the two of you were going to speak. Ah, Mr. Snyder—."

"Jarrod. Please call me Jarrod."

"Of course, Jarrod. I'm afraid I have some bad news."

"Really? Please, do tell me."

Gavin squeezed his eyes shut and sat on the edge of the bed. "Katherine is missing, I'm afraid." He saw the video in his mind's eye again. "She was abducted earlier today."

A pause for several seconds. "I'm so sorry. What is the situation now, if I may ask?"

"Of course. The police are aware. There is video footage of the abduction and the abductor."

Another pause. "Is there anything I can do to help? Anything at all?"

"Well, at the moment, I don't know. The state department of criminal investigation is on the case, and the tribal police. I guess we let them do what they do for the moment."

"Yes, course. And if there is any way I can be of help, please let me know."

"Yes, I will. Thanks."

Gavin disconnected the call and then shut off the phone. That was the third time in four hours he had described the incident. He could still see the white van driving away. He sat for a moment on the edge of the large bed where he would sleep alone tonight, and who knew for how many nights to come. He heard footsteps and looked up as Loren entered. He stood as she reached out and pulled him into a long hug.

"It will be alright, little brother," she said softly. "It will be alright."

Her voice broke loose the tears he had been holding back.

Ben Avery arrived sometime after nine-thirty and was immediately immersed into the closeness of the family gathering. After he watched the video on Gavin's laptop three times, he and Gavin joined everyone in the sitting area. Avery accepted a cup of coffee and shared a bit of news that was a shock to everyone and offered a ray of hope. He motioned to Loren.

"You and Katherine went to Pierre together some days ago, and you reported that a dark-haired man snapped photographs of Katherine."

"Yes. He was in a white van and we took his license plate number. Don't tell me there is a connection to what happened today."

Avery nodded. "As far-fetched as it may seem, there is. The van in the photos you sent us and in the video are the same. Same front grill, same license plate. One of our officers ran down the license number. It belongs to a delivery company from Lincoln, Nebraska. We have a list of the names of all their employees."

Loren was incredulous. "So does that mean the man who took her was stalking her?"

"Possibly," Avery allowed. "But that does seem far-fetched. I think he was at the right place at the right time and recognized her. He is obviously in the van when she pulls in, then he gets out and goes behind the van, and he has dark hair. My guess is he saw his opportunity and took it. The video is not very sharp. What do you remember about the man?"

Loren cupped a fist to her mouth. "He had dark, thick, curly hair, and I think he had a hoodie or some kind of sweatshirt on. He was a bit dark, certainly not white."

"Was he Black?"

"No, brown, like a deep tan."

"Any guesses on his age, approximately?"

She shook her head. "Wasn't close enough. But he moved like a young man, athletic. He was probably around six feet tall."

Avery finished jotting in his notebook. "Anything else you can remember?"

Loren shook her head. "He walked into the store, the truck stop. We waited for him to come out, intending to get a better look. But he didn't. Maybe he noticed us watching and waited us out."

Avery nodded. "Anything's possible." He looked at Gavin. "We have a lot to go on. Lieutenant Primault is on his way back from North Dakota right now. I talked to him a couple of hours ago. I told him what you told me earlier, and I'm sure he'll draw the same conclusions I did after he sees the video. He promised to hit the ground running on this one."

"Thanks. What's the situation with those two girls he rescued?"

"They're spending the night at the hospital at Fort Yates. Two of our officers—Madonna White Bear and Audrey Hinson—are with them. They've been in touch with their families and they will be home sometime tomorrow."

Loren reached and grabbed her brother's hand. "Good news, and there will be more, don't ever doubt that."

Avery nodded as he put away his notebook. "Amen to that."

Avery left an hour later and sometime after midnight Morgan and Thomas went home. Andrew put sheets on the couch and took spare pillows and a blanket from the closet. Gavin helped Joby inflate an air mattress and arranged it next to the fireplace. After a quick shower, he towel-dried his hair and put on sweats, then came out and stood at the foot of the bed. It seemed larger somehow.

Loren knocked softly on the door, already in her pajamas.

"I remember a few nights I had to tuck you and Gerard in because you were afraid of the thunder and lightning."

"Yeah, I remember that."

"We're going to get her back, safe and sound."

He nodded and motioned for her to sit on the stuffed chair. He sat on a corner of the bed. "Yeah. I wish I could snap my fingers and make it happen."

"Well, how about we start with the ceremony tomorrow evening, and ask the Spirits for their help?"

"Works for me."

"Look at it this way. We've got two medicine people, two wise elders—Uncle Andrew and Grandpa Henry Two Crow. They've got powerful connections. Remember what Dad used to say? 'All you have to do is believe.'"

"Yeah."

She took the hairbrush from him and pointed to the foot stool. "Sit," she said.

After he moved over she began brushing out his hair.

"You used to do that when I was first growing it out. I think I was seven or eight," he recalled fondly.

"Mainly because you didn't care if it was all a tangled mess. You used to fuss at Mom when she brushed it. My god, it's down to your waist."

"Probably needs trimming. I haven't done that for a while."

"Well, the good news is that I don't see any gray, yet."

He chuckled, and closed his eyes as she brushed, and remembered all the times his mother had brushed his hair, and how she had patiently taught him how to braid it. "Mom would say it wouldn't be so bad if she didn't have to do it twice. First with Gerard, then me."

"You know what else she used to say? 'I never dreamed that a Scottish lass like me would bring two Lakota warriors into the world, at once.'"

"Really? Well, one warrior, anyway. More to the point, a U.S. Marine."

"You're a warrior, too. Don't ever forget it."

"You sound like Mom."

"Oh, I don't know about that. She might have died young, but she was wise beyond her years. I'm not wise, yet."

"Well, yeah but I meant your voice. The sound of your voice, it's like Mom's."

She stopped brushing for a few seconds, "Thanks. That's quite a compliment."

"Truth be told, you look like her, too."

"Wait. How is this about me? I came in here to cheer you up."

"And you did."

"Well, okay, and you try and get some sleep tonight. You're going to need all the positive stuff you can muster. I know you're going to think and worry. But shut it down if you can, destress. Have you been running?"

"Yeah, a couple of times a week."

She finished brushing. "Okay, I think you should leave your hair loose and let it dry while you sleep. In the morning, wouldn't hurt to go for a short jog. Destress."

"Good idea, and thanks for being here."

"Hey, it's in the big sister job description. We stick together when times get rough, and we get through them together."

He remembered glancing at the digital clock on his nightstand at 2:19, and the next time he opened his eyes, gray light was in the east window. But he didn't feel rested. He glanced over at the left side of the bed. The bed covers were undisturbed and flat, the first jarring reminder of the reality that hadn't gone away. After a scant moment of quiet bliss, the thoughts and images that had been torturing him the previous; day attacked with renewed force. The smell of freshly brewed coffee wafted from the kitchen through his open bedroom door, and he heard muffled voices, someone speaking softly, then remembered that Loren, Andrew, and Joby had spent the night. After washing his face and putting his hair in a long ponytail, he joined them.

"*Hihanni lahci, Tunska* (Good morning, Nephew)," called out Andrew, already at the table. Loren was at the counter.

"Good morning," he replied.

"This is going to be a good day," the old man said, lifting his coffee cup.

Gavin reached for and took the cup Loren was holding out to him. "That's my prayer, *Leksi*," he said. "That's my prayer."

"*Waste yelo* (That's good)," Andrew replied. He nodded toward Joby who had emerged from the spare bathroom after a shower. "*Tunska* and me are going to go to *Tahansi* Henry's place and help him get things ready for tonight. He wants to do a sweat and then a singing ceremony, a *Lowanpi*."

"Good. What do you want me to do?"

"Put yourself in the right frame of mind. I think your sister has everything she needs for the feed afterwards."

Loren was putting out the fixings for breakfast. "I do. I'm going to do the cooking here and we'll take the food over. Morgan and Thomas will be here to help me."

Gavin looked toward the east window as the first swaths of bright sunrise washed over a few wispy clouds and nodded. In spite of his best efforts, the stress held at bay by the closeness of family broke past with a roar, overwhelming any hope for a peaceful day. Getting into the right frame of mind would be a struggle.

TWENTY-TWO

Lieutenant Justin Primault stumbled out of his bedroom and into the living room and crossed to the kitchen, squinting up at the clock on the wall. 10:37. He had managed to get just over three hours of sleep.

"I was hoping to see you this afternoon," his wife Sandra called out from the utility room after she saw him standing in the kitchen looking a bit confused. "I think you need more sleep."

"Sure feels like it," he groused. "Wouldn't mind some coffee, though."

Sandra put down the laundry basket and went to the cupboard. "Sit down," she instructed. "I'll get it for you."

She was already awake when he had arrived, a few minutes before seven. He took a seat at the table and then the cup of coffee she offered,

"Is it absolutely necessary for you to go to work today?" she asked. "You still look pretty wrung out."

"I guess I can do something here. Chief told me to take the day off."

"Then why the burr under your saddle?" She joined him at the table.

He took a sip and shook his head. "Katherine, Gavin Lone Wolf's fian-cée was abducted. She's missing."

"What? Are you kidding? When?"

"Yesterday."

"That's a shocker. I can't believe it!"

He nodded, deliberating. After a moment he looked up at his wife. "Hey, listen, hon. I've got to say this. I want you to be careful, from now on. I don't think you should go out of town alone."

She gazed at him thoughtfully, over her cup. "Is that what happened to Gavin's fiancée? Was she alone?"

"Yeah. She's smart and pretty, like you. Made her a target. A guy took pictures of her at the truck stop where she was taken. Same guy probably. I don't want you to be anyone's target. You've got to be careful. Native women are the prey. Those that are pretty and young."

"I'm not exactly young."

His gaze into her eyes hardened. "You know what I mean."

"Yeah, I know what you mean. But it also means you need to find the time to go with me to Rapid City, or Pierre, or anywhere out of town."

"Right. I can do that. I will."

She sighed and reached across the table and took his hand in hers. "Are you going to help look for her—Katherine?"

He nodded. "Yeah. We do have good information to go on. Can't waste any time though. The trail has a way of going cold the more time passes."

"What about the girls you rescued? What's happened with them?"

"White Bear and Hinson are still with them, up in Fort Yates. Brousseaux is with them, too. They'll finish interviewing them today and take them home."

"How are they, the girls?"

"Physically they seem okay. Sexually abused, obviously. I listened to recordings of the first interview. They're brave girls, they didn't hold back. What they described will scare the shit out of you, then piss you off. It did me."

"Really? Is that why you said what you did? That you don't want me to go anywhere alone?"

"Yeah. I don't want anything to happen to you."

She squeezed his fingers. The expression on his face matched the tone of his voice. He sounded as though he were about to cry. "Okay, okay," she said gently "I hear you. I'll be careful. I'll remember what you have told me a few times. Situational awareness—look around the car, see who's around, have the remote already in hand, and lock the door as soon as you get in."

He nodded, his lips pressed in a line thin.

"There should be a class for Native girls, to teach them that, to show them—step by step —how to do that," she suggested.

"Great idea."

"Maybe we can do that together, you and I."

"Well, I think I know two women cops who would be better at it than me, if you're serious about it."

"I am, this is real shit that's going down."

Primault took a deep breath and exhaled forcefully. "I'm going to do everything I can to find Katherine. Gavin's my friend, and I know he's hurting. He'd do everything he could if the tables were turned. I can't let him down, or her."

"So does that mean you're done sleeping?"

"Yup. Bring on the coffee."

"Okay, how about you tell me how you rescued those girls while I fix you some breakfast."

By one thirty Lieutenant Primault had returned the Taurus to the impound yard and walked to the station. The first stop was Chief Avery's office.

"You look like you've been rode hard and put up wet," was the Chief's comment, by way of greeting.

"Don't I know it," Primault replied. "Thought I'd start with catching up on the Katherine Hill situation."

Five minutes later Primault, Avery, and Patrolman Jason Singer were in the small conference room. Singer, somewhat nervously, began to enlighten his superiors on the results of his investigation regarding the white van.

"It's owned by Sherholt Transportation Company, Inc., of Lincoln, Nebraska. It's a small company, does dry goods deliveries in a four-state area, mainly—Kansas, Nebraska, and the Dakotas."

"Dry goods? What does that mean?" the Chief wanted to know.

Singer consulted his printed notes. "Nothing liquid or chemical, or perishable. I guess it's an insurance thing. They specialize in unusual or odd cargo, as long as they can fit it in their vans."

"Do they have a fleet?" Primault asked.

"Yes, sir, they do. About six vans, I believe."

Avery was nodding thoughtfully. "And is it safe to assume that each of those vans has its own regular route, and same drivers for each route?"

Singer looked at his notes again for a few seconds. "It seems more like each one covers a certain area and delivers within that area. And I don't know how the drivers are assigned."

"Stands to reason a driver would regularly cover one area, so he becomes familiar with it," Primault postulated. "Do we have names and photos?"

"We have the most recent photos they gave us," Singer reported. "About two years old, I think." He opened a paper file and pulled out two pages of black and white photos; four men and two women. One woman and one man were Black, the other woman was white, and there were three white men. Ages were hard to determine."

Avery carefully scrutinized the photos of the men and glanced at Primault. "I don't see any there that fits the description Katherine Hill and Loren Hale gave us."

"You're right," Primault reluctantly agreed. "Dark hair and brown skin."

"The man in the video, the one we damn sure know abducted Katherine Hill, has thick, dark hair," Avery pointed out. "Couldn't exactly determine skin color. We can rule out the Black guy here, and two of the white males are practically bald. The third one has light hair."

"That's a dead end I didn't expect," admitted Primault. He looked at Singer. "Has there been personnel turnover? Any new drivers recently?"

"That I don't know, sir."

"Okay. I can make a call," Primault decided.

"What about the possibility that the van in the photo doesn't belong to Sherholt Transportation?" Avery suggested. "What if the perp drives the same kind of van, same make and model, and is posing as a delivery driver." Avery paused and shook his head. "Well, but the license plate is real, it's what led us to that company."

"Unless, what you suggested is the case and the guy just copied any existing license plate," Primault followed up.

"Maybe we call the company and ask them where that particular van, with that license plate, was when Katherine Hill was abducted?" Singer asked.

Avery grinned. "That makes the most sense," he said.

Twenty minutes later Primault had some interesting answers. "Here's what I was told," he said, after he and Avery and Singer regrouped. "That van, with that license plate number, was doing their northern route yesterday., through South Dakota as far as Aberdeen. They're expecting it to return to base anytime. The driver's name is Todd Nomer, a white male, age thirty-two, he's divorced, and is six feet one inch tall, and weighs one hundred and eighty pounds."

Singer skimmed over the photos and found the one with the name Todd Nomer. "He's one of the bald ones," he said.

"Who did you talk to?" Avery asked Primault.

"The dispatcher. She's the one who takes the calls for parcel pickups and gives the drivers their routes and destinations."

"Where was the suspect van going to yesterday?"

"Mobridge was its farthest delivery yesterday, and it made all its deliveries."

"Damn!" Avery hissed. "At least now we know how far it went. How far is it from the truck stop to Mobridge?"

Singer found a road atlas and turned the pages to the map he wanted. After a few seconds he said, "About two hundred miles."

"According to the DCI person I talked to," Avery told them, "the people at the truck stop called about Katherine's truck a little after four o'clock. The time stamp on the video is just before eleven. So, conceivably, that driver could have made his deliveries, up to and including Mobridge, before the cops were called. More to the point, it wasn't until after six when the highway patrol put out any word about the van." Avery pointed out.

"That's a fairly smart guy," Singer said. "He made his deliveries so everything would seem normal. Then that would give him time to ditch the van."

"Right," agreed Primault. "Or hide it. It's out of sight somewhere."

"So that means he's got to find a new ride," said Singer.

"Or he already has one," Avery declared angrily. "In any case, he's gone underground."

Primault was pacing and thinking. "I'm willing to bet he's somewhere around the Mobridge area, hiding, probably. Makes sense to me, in a northerly direction. The man camps are northwest of there. We know—from what Maggie Henry and Julia Lake told us—they were kept in the basements of a couple of houses. So, if Nomer is taking Katherine Hill anywhere, it could be to that same area, to wherever those two houses are."

"Trouble is," Avery sighed. "All this is speculation."

"Based on good evidence, credible evidence," Primault stated.

"Tell you what," Avery said. "If that white van doesn't return to Lincoln, that would tell me we might be making the right conclusions."

"Good point," Primault agreed. "I say we give that dispatcher a call, say close of business tomorrow and ask. If it's missing, we're onto something."

"What do we do in the meantime?" Singer asked.

"Learn everything we can about Todd Nomer," Avery told him.

"Chief," said Primault, "do we have enough money in that contingency fund to charter an airplane? Like a two seater?"

"Ah, yeah, I think so. Hiring a pilot and an airplane might be pricey."

"Well, just the plane. I know a pilot, and I think he'd be willing to donate his time."

"Okay. You tell me what it costs, I'll find the money. Got a plan of some sort?"

"Yeah, I do. But first I want to talk to a friend of mine."

TWENTY-THREE

Gavin was finishing slicing carrots, dicing onions, and cutting up cabbage for the bison soup when Lieutenant Primault arrived. Loren met him at the door and invited him to take a seat at the kitchen table and followed up with a cup of coffee. Gavin wiped his hands and joined him.

"It's good to see you," Gavin said, shaking Primault's hand. "I'm anxious to hear about the plan you mentioned over the phone."

Primault gazed at his friend for a few seconds. The stress was evident in his eyes, hinting at the emotional turmoil that was surely swirling inside. "It's based on what we know so far, regarding Katherine's abductor, and what Maggie and Julia told us."

"Who are Maggie and Julia?" Loren asked from the kitchen.

"Oh, the two girls we were able to rescue," Primault explained. "They gave us a very detailed account of what happened to them."

"Oh, I see. Sorry, didn't meant to interrupt."

"Not at all. The most salient piece of information was that they, and other girls, were kept in the basements of at least two houses that have to be in isolated rural areas. They described being driven over what seemed like dirt roads and gravel roads. No paved roads, and always no more than about twenty minutes to a half hour away from where the houses were."

"So that, more or less, gives us a specific area," Gavin concluded.

"Exactly," Primault verified. "We know that the girls were being taken regularly to the man camp that Brousseaux and I were in. So, if we translate that half hour of travel into distance, then we can come up with an estimate. Since those were dirt and gravel roads, they likely weren't going faster than forty-five to fifty miles an hour; then we come up with about thirty miles. Then we extend a thirty mile line from the camp and draw a circle."

"And that becomes the search area," Gavin said. "So, you obviously think that Katherine might be taken to that same area."

"It's an educated guess," Primault asserted. "Her abductor knew what he was doing, which tells me he probably has done it before, many times. He might be part of a network. That van had a delivery route that extended into southern North Dakota. Yesterday it made a delivery in Mobridge. The highway patrol issued an all-points-alert just after six p.m. The van has not been reported. It should be returning to its home base sometime today, but I'm willing to bet it won't show up. If so, it's out of sight somewhere."

"Oh, damn, that all makes sense," Gavin concluded. "And that network you alluded to is likely trafficking girls to that man camp, or other places in that broad area."

"That's what I think. But like I said, it's an educated guess. I can't tell you with absolute certainty that Katherine is in that area, but it's a definite possibility."

"And so, you've come up with a plan based on everything you just told me, and that definite possibility?"

"I have."

Gavin leaned back in his chair. "Let's hear it." He caught Loren's attention and motioned for her to join them.

"Well," Primault began. "I like plans to be simple and uncomplicated. Fewer moving parts, less chance of things going awry. What I want to do is this: rent an airplane, one that can fly low and slow, and do an aerial search."

"And look for isolated houses, abandoned farms," Gavin said.

"Damn right. Chief Avery is going to find the money for us to rent an airplane, and I'm asking if you could fly it for us. It'll be you, me, and Jason Singer."

"I'll do better than that," Gavin said. "I'll rent the airplane myself."

"Ah, can you do that? I mean, it's probably expensive."

"Don't worry about it. We have to do it." Gavin insisted.

"And Morgan and I will help with the cost," Loren said emphatically. "We won't take no for an answer."

"Great, great," Primault said, smiling. "Now all we have to do is find where we can do that."

"There's a charter service in Bismarck at the regional airport," Gavin said. "Probably won't be difficult to rent a plane. When do we start?"

"As soon as we have an airplane to fly, and if it's from Bismarck, we get on the road as quick as we can," Primault said.

Gavin nodded thoughtfully. "Could be as early as tomorrow, if we're lucky."

"Alright. I will let Chief Avery know and beg my wife's forgiveness for having to be gone again," Primault said, sighing.

"And I'll get on the phone and see about an airplane," Gavin declared.

"I chatted with your wife at Melvina's funeral," Loren recalled. "If you think she wouldn't mind, maybe I can invite her for lunch," Loren suggested.

"I don't think she would mind at all. I'll tell her." He took out one of his business cards and wrote down a phone number. "This is her cell phone," he said, handing the card to Loren.

A few minutes later Primault was driving away, taking the back roads home, intending to turn in early and get a good night's sleep, after he called Chief Avery.

At about the moment Primault was snuggled up with his wife on their couch and had finished telling of his plan, and that it would mean having to be gone for several more days, the fire in the pit behind Henry Two Crow's house had burned down, and the rocks beneath the ashes were glowing red. That was the signal for the participants to enter the sweat lodge. Soon Gavin, Loren, Morgan, and Thomas Hale, Clayton and Veronica Lone Hawk, and Andrew No Horn were in the lodge waiting for Henry to pour the first dipper of water on the hot stones in the center pit. The other two participants were two young men whom Henry had asked, simply because they were traditional singers second to none. More importantly they knew all the ceremony songs. They would also participate as helpers in the *Lowanpi* that would occur later.

After four rounds of songs and prayers, the *Inipi* (sweat lodge purification ceremony) concluded. Each round ended with the two outside helpers pulling open the west facing door to allow a few minutes of fresh air. Each of the participants, except for the two singers, focused their prayers on the welfare and safety of Katherine Hill. And during the prayers and singing, the Spirits entered, blowing on eagle bone whistles and rattling the pumpkin gourds. To nonbelievers who happened to be present at such auspicious and holy moments, the whistles and gourds were nothing but noise—likely blown and shaken by the medicine man, as far as they were concerned. But to participants who knew better, it was always affirmation that the basis of their spiritually was manifested and present; that all things in the world were connected. And that connection was always invoked and acknowledged with the simple phrase, which was also a prayer—*Mitakuye Oyasin.*

Gavin felt energized as he exited the sweat lodge after the last round. He and the other men changed into their usual clothing while the women changed in the ceremony house, only yards away. When everyone was ready, Henry invited them into the small round house, and the second ceremony began.

To start it off, Gavin offered his pipe, loaded with red willow tobacco, four times to Henry. The old medicine man accepted the offering after the fourth time, lit the pipe and smoked it. Then he returned it to Gavin to hold during the songs and prayers to follow.

Henry took his place in the center of the room, atop an elk hide and in front of an altar prepared by his helpers. Looking around at the circle of people around him, he cleared his throat softly. "We are here because a loved one was taken from us, and we want to bring her home," he said. "We will offer prayers and ask the Spirits to help us. We know she is not the only one, there are others who are also missing, many of them for months and years. We will pray for them, too. We will also pray for clear minds and strong hearts so we can find the ways to protect our young women."

The lights were turned off, pitching everything and everyone into total darkness. The singers lifted their voices into the first of several invitation songs.

The Spirits came in force, once again blowing on the eagle bone whistles and rattling the gourds. Gavin bowed his head and humbled himself to ask them to protect the love of his life. He closed his eyes and visualized her in the center of a circle. And with her in the circle he placed other figures with brown skin and dark hair, as many as he could fit. In his mind he transposed the circle into a bubble, a protective sphere around them all. He held that image as he heard the others praying, taking in all that his senses perceived, adding his own prayer, and beseeching the swirl of powerful presences to give Katherine and the figures with her the strength to endure.

He let go of the image only after the last thanksgiving song was finished, after the last beat from the hand drum. When the Spirits departed and there was nothing but absolute silence and darkness, he lifted his head and waited for the lights to come back on.

A ceremony's power and relevance emanate from the connection formed between the participants—people in the physical realm and the Spirits from theirs. When the lights came back on Gavin felt with all his heart that he would see Katherine again, in this physical realm, but he also knew that he had to do what he could to make it happen. A jolt coursed through him when he immediately spotted the long, black prayer flag at his feet. It, along with the red, yellow, and red flags, had been at the corners of Henry's altar in the center of the room. Black was the color of victory.

Gavin felt Henry's gaze as soon as he picked up the flag and looked up.

"*Tunska,*" the medicine man said, pointing at the flag. "Carry it with you until you find her."

TWENTY-FOUR

A leering, swarthy face leaned in over Katherine when the trunk lid opened, a sickening image of the dark side of life. Standing next to her captor was a shorter man with narrow shoulders. His long, thin face was a caricature of villains she had seen in second rate movies. Down to the mustache.

"Two rules you busted, man," the thin face said, a whiny tinge to his voice. "From what I can see, she's too old and you didn't cover her head. She's seen my face, you shithead."

"This one ain't for the herd," Nomer said. "She's mine."

"Piano won't like it."

"He doesn't have to know."

Thin Face looked around, his eyes darting, his head twitching. "I don't know, man. You know the rules."

"I got five K if you help me hide her," Nomer offered. He pulled aside the hem of his hoodie and exposed the handle of an automatic pistol. "Or I can drive away and you'll never see me again."

"What do you mean?"

Nomer knew his impulsive abduction meant he was no longer useful as a lookout, so he was on thin ice. But he also knew that Tulo liked cold hard cash. "It's easy money. You don't have to do anything but keep your mouth shut."

"I—I don't know, man."

"Think of it," Nomer pressed, "it's an easy five K."

Tulo turned his mercenary gaze into the trunk, and his expression changed. Katherine could almost feel his carnal thoughts.

"Well, I gotta admit. She's damn good looking. A prime piece of meat."

"All I need is a place to hide her for a couple of days."

Tulo blinked his eyes, thinking. "Then what?"

"Then you don't have to worry about it anymore, and you'll have five K in your pocket."

"Okay, but I gotta have it now."

"Right. Sure."

Tulo grinned, revealing yellowed teeth and looked in the trunk again. His gaze lingering this time. "Okay, you got a deal. Damn. I only seen women this good looking in magazines, not in real life like this. This here's a real woman. Can't blame you for grabbing her for yourself. You wouldn't mind sharing, maybe?"

"Fuck no!"

The trunk lid slammed shut and Katherine loosed a sigh of relief even as her stomach churned. She thought she had seen the entire spectrum of men in her adult life, from worst to best. A little more than twenty-four hours ago she had been with her definition of what an ultimate good man was: the one she wanted to spend the rest of her life with. Now she had just seen the slimy end, one who made her skin crawl. She had never felt such instant revulsion, and hoped she would never see him again. But her instincts were telling her otherwise.

She had heard a name—Piano—someone who her captor and Thin Face apparently answered to, someone who preferred young girls. She burned it into her memory. And now she also knew she could look forward to more hours in the dark trunk and the musty smell. She was surprised when her captor had draped the camel back water pack over her shoulder. An unexpected show of compassion. Now all she had to do for a drink was suck on the tube.

The brief conversation she heard meant she was being taken to a hiding place. After switching from the van to the sedan, they had traveled about four hours. A rough guess at best. She had regained consciousness the night before, in total darkness, with her mouth taped shut, and her ankles and wrists bound with the same kind of tape. Strangely, she had been covered with a blanket and a soft backpack was under her head. Switching sides from laying on her right side to her left helped, but she had quickly turned over when the car stopped. She didn't want her back to the rear of the trunk. Either way she couldn't fully stretch her legs and the faint smell of feces lingered in the tight space.

She had felt around in the dark for any rough edge to file down the tape around her wrists and ankles. There was nothing. Fortunately, her captor had switched her hands from back to front before he had put her in the trunk. She started to twist the tape again, trying to tear or stretch it.

She heard the two men talking but it was unintelligible. A door opened and closed and the engine started, and they were moving again. As far as she could determine, it had been roughly twenty-four hours since she had heard the call for help from the white van at the truck stop. It was clearly a girl's voice. But there was no girl.

Gavin would have been worried when she didn't get home by mid-afternoon. He would have called her phone, and by now she hoped Gavin's pickup had been noticed. From what she generally knew about missing person situations, police put out basic information on hand. But how hard would they search? There was one undeniable fact: Gavin would search. She knew he would do everything he could to find her. That was her best hope. She thought about Melvina Old Lodge. She had escaped. Anything was possible.

TWENTY-FIVE

Lieutenant Primault stretched his patience until four o'clock before he placed the call to Sherholt Transportation. They had been on the road for nearly four hours and were already north of Pierre en route to Bismarck. A plane was waiting.

He asked the question and waited, then grimly disconnected the call. The van was missing and the driver could not be reached and his cell phone was no longer in service. He turned to Gavin, who was in the back seat of the cruiser..

"It's as I suspected it would be. The driver and the van are a no show."

Gavin nodded stoically. "I'm glad we didn't wait. I booked us rooms at a hotel close to the airport. There won't be time to fly before the sun goes down, but we'll have the whole evening to plot out a search pattern."

"Right," Primault pointed at the map tubes on the back seat. "We've got the latest satellite maps we could get our hands on."

After checking in and taking their bags to their rooms, they met for supper in the hotel restaurant, choosing a table in a far corner. Gavin picked at his food but downed nearly the whole carafe of coffee. The conversation and low noise in the room grated on his nerves. It was too normal. He felt lost and couldn't wait to get into the planning.

Primault and Singer had agreed not to bring up the issue at hand unless Gavin Lone Wolf did. The CI could sense the turmoil in his friend, who was more reserved than usual. He had finally met Katherine Hill at Melvina Old Lodge's wake and funeral. She had a vibrant personality and a dazzling smile, a truly beautiful woman. The love of my life is a drop dead gorgeous, raven-haired woman, Gavin had said. Indeed. She and Gavin were a striking couple.

"The plane I rented is a Cessna Skyhawk," Gavin volunteered. "It's a four passenger and will carry us comfortably."

"Great. You've flown them before?"

"Yeah. I learned to fly in a Cessna. Always liked them."

"How far can we go?"

"Well, it's got a range of about six hundred and fifty miles. So, when we look at your maps this evening, we'll figure out what the straight line distance is to the search area, and then that will give us an idea of how much time we have to search. I don't think it's more than two hundred miles, so that means we can work out a search pattern that encompasses two hundred miles. I think there's a municipal airport at Williston, so we should be able to refuel there. That will extend our time."

"Why did you decide to learn to fly?" Singer asked.

"I had an interesting adventure in Siberia, some years ago. After that I decided to acquire all the skills I could. That and I'm afraid of heights."

"Damn," said Primaut. "Therein are some stories, I'll bet. Is that why you're into martial arts?"

"Martial arts was a natural outgrowth of my dad teaching my brother and me some cool moves that Lakota warriors used when fighting with the lance," Gavin said.

"Really? They really did that?" Singer was astonished.

"Oh, yeah. There is a routine for fighting from the back of a horse and several for fighting on foot."

"Damn. I thought they just threw them," Singer said.

"No, that's an erroneous assumption, played up by bad movies. The lance was a thrusting weapon. One kind for combat and another for buffalo hunting."

"You know, I never heard that from anyone growing up," Singer lamented. "That's so damn cool."

"It is," Gavin affirmed. "The Lakota warrior not only had a code of conduct but he was a highly skilled war fighter who started training at the age of about six and never really stopped."

"Explains why our ancestors won at the Battle of the Little Bighorn," Primault said.

"Right. They just plain kicked ass because they knew how to fight," said Gavin.

"Wait!" Primault said. "But did you say you learned to fly because you were afraid of heights? Is that still an issue?"

Gavin chuckled. "Well, I still have trouble climbing up a ladder to a roof. But flying is different, at least for me."

"So, you'd rather fly a plane than climb a ladder?" Singer asked.

"Affirmative."

Both Primault and Singer shook their heads and grinned.

A few minutes later they adjourned to Gavin's room and spread out the satellite maps on a coffee table. Primault circled the small town of

Pinnacle and Gavin drew a straight line to it from Bismarck. Then plotting the distance from Pinnacle to the man camp, they drew a fifty mile circle around it. That was their initial search grid.

"What's the most sensible approach for us?" Primault asked.

"I'm not sure," Gavin admitted. "But I think I know someone who might have some suggestions. Let me make a phone call."

Half a minute later he was talking to Gerard. After a few moments of banter, he got down to the issue at hand. "Hey, bro, as I said, we laid out a grid, a circular grid a hundred miles across. We're looking for abandoned houses and farmsteads, likely along little used roads. We're searching from the air. How should we start?"

Gavin put his phone on speaker and put it down on the coffee table. Singer and Primault scooted close.

"Are you doing only a visual sweep or are you taking photographs and making videos?" Gerard asked. "A visual record is essential."

"We plan on doing both still photos and videos," Gavin replied.

"Well, if the circumstances allow, I advise doing a broad sweep first. By circumstances I mean distance, fuel, and daylight. After your broad sweep, or more than one if necessary, then review the data, put it on the biggest screen you can find, and go over it with a fine tooth comb, if you know what I mean."

"Right. Then what?"

"Then eliminate what does not fit your profile and zoom in on what does. After that you narrow it down with whatever criteria you've established."

"Makes a lot of sense. Thanks, bro."

"No worries. So, you think Katherine was taken to one of those abandoned farmsteads?" Gerard asked.

"Correct," Gavin replied. "Justin—Lieutenant Primault, who's here with me—rescued two girls from a man camp. They told him they were being kept in the basement of a house, no more than twenty or thirty minutes from the man camp."

"Damn! Then I think you're on the right trail. Well, you caught me in between flights. I'm in Kansas City on the way to Sioux Falls. I'll be there later tonight. Keep me posted. I'll help however I can."

"Will do."

Gavin disconnected the call. "My brother was a recon Marine," he said, and looked at Singer. "Is your camera high speed?"

"Yes, sir."

"What about the video? Would you be able to keep it fairly steady in the airplane?"

"Yeah, I think so. It's got a tripod. I can probably use that to keep it steady."

Primault leaned back, crossed his arms over his chest, and looked at Gavin. "Can you fly and spot at the same time? Because Jason can't operate both the still camera and video at the same time. I'll have to man the video."

"Oh, yeah, no problem. Do those things both have zoom, for close ups?"

Singer looked at the cases where the cameras still where. "I'm pretty sure they do, but I'll check."

"So, if I get what you're leading up to," Primault said, "once we find the places that fit our profile—as your brother said— we get close-ups, more detailed pictures."

"Right, but it's the initial sweep that's critical, too. Depending on the zoom capabilities of those cameras, I'd like to be over the area at two thousand feet above the deck, at an altitude of about four thousand. The higher we are the less noticeable we will be to anyone who might be looking, because they have something to hide."

"I got it. So, a lot depends on those cameras." Primault turned to Singer. "What are you finding out?"

Singer brought both cameras over and pointed to the window. "It's dark out, but we can point them out there and see how close we can pull something in." He handed the video camera to Primault. "The On button is the white button, and the zoom is that slide button, the yellow one."

At the window the officers worked the cameras, getting familiar with the zoom function on each. Singer attached a zoom lens on the still camera and pointed out at the city lights in the distance.

"I think this one's fairly good," Primault announced. "It might be better in the day with more light. How's the still camera?"

"I think it can probably spot something small from a half mile up," he said.

"Good and we'll just fly lower if we have to," Gavin said. "At some point we might have to throw caution to the winds."

"When do we start?" Primault asked.

"I think the charter service opens at eight, so we should be at the air-port by then."

They went back to the map to figure out the initial flight pattern once over the area around Pinnacle. "For the initial flyovers, for the broad sweep that my brother suggested we do, I think the video camera is the one we use." With his finger he traced a pattern back and forth over the northern half circle of the grid. "How wide an area that it can film clearly will determine the width of our pattern. It'll be like mowing a lawn, back and forth until we cover the entire half."

"How long do you think that will take?"

"I don't know. It'll take us just over an hour to just get there. At the widest point this grid is a hundred miles, so once across that is about forty-five minutes."

Primault nodded. "So, conceivably, it could take us half a day just for half that grid."

"Possibly. I think what you can do is use the flight out to see how broad an area, a swath, that video camera can cover and provide good detail. That will give us an estimate on how high we can fly, and that will further —"

"Give us an idea how many passes we need to make to cover half a grid," Primault concluded.

"Right. So tomorrow we see what we can do. It's the shakedown cruise, more or less. Then we come back, see what we have, and make adjustments for the next day."

The planning session broke up sometime after nine. Gavin sent a text to Gerard:

Give me a call when you arrive Sioux Falls.

He took a shower, but wasn't looking forward to turning in. He switched on the television and found a news channel, more for distraction than a need to know. The coffee in the to-go cup from the restaurant was still warm. Sipping it while absently staring at the television screen, he suddenly realized his phone was chirping. It was Gerard.

"Hey, bro. How's Sioux Falls?"

"Dark outside, and full of white people inside, at least the airport is. How are you?"

Gavin sighed. "Trying to keep a cool head. Finished with Primault and Singer about an hour ago."

"Okay. Tell me about your plan."

In less than five minutes Gavin outlined the plan for the initial search. "A lot of what we see or don't see depends on the cameras, how high the resolution is," he concluded.

"Sure does," agreed Gerard. Then after a pause. "I have an idea, and I should have thought of it earlier. One of my surveillance guys is an expert at that sort of thing. We recently invested in some ultra-high resolution equipment, and some for night-time surveillance. He's a young man, name's Ben Wilson. Say the word and I'll send him to you, with his equipment."

Gavin was momentarily taken aback. "Uh, sure. Damn, thanks bro! When can he be here? And can you come up as well?"

"I'll call my office manager first thing in the morning and get it moving. I'll have her email you the flight itinerary. Hopefully in two days. Do you have a big enough plane to take him and his gear?"

"Yeah, a Cessna 172."

"Great. Give me your hotel number and I'll have Denise reserve him a room And as far as my joining you, well, I did something to my left knee playing tennis the other day. Damn thing's swollen and it's slowing me down. I'm afraid I'd just be in your way."

"I thought I warned you about those white man games, didn't I? In the meantime, we'll start our initial searches. Maybe we'll have some areas narrowed down by the time your man gets here."

"Right, time is of the essence. Don't give up, don't stop thinking, and keep looking. We'll get her back, bro."

"Damn straight!"

In another minute he reluctantly disconnected the call, but he was encouraged. Ultra-high resolution cameras would definitely increase their chances of success.

He was glad to be in a different bed. It didn't feel empty like their bed at home. But he was still alone in it without Katherine. That was the darkest reality imaginable. But this situation wasn't about him; it was about Katherine.

She was somewhere, alone, probably locked up, caged, blindfolded, cold, hungry, maybe injured. From the recesses of his being came the impulse to hurt whoever had taken her. In a moment he pushed it aside— or tried. He needed to think clearly. Though rage was fuel for action, it was never a tool for discernment, never a way to think clearly.

He carried some guilt and shame beyond Katherine's situation. Though he always cared about the reality of Native girls disappearing, he could now identify with it. It had reached out and punched a hole in his life. He could understand the anguish and heartache, and the cruelty of not knowing. Yet he was fortunate.

All the heartbroken Native moms and dads and grandparents could do virtually nothing to rectify the situation. They did not have his resources and could only rely on the compassion and good graces of others, in most cases white authorities, who cared little, if at all. Nor did missing Native girls seem to be a priority with tribal authorities or the Bureau of Indian Affairs.

Gavin had the support of Justin, Ben Avery, his brother's connections, and the wisdom of Andrew No Horn. There was no guarantee that whatever he could do would bring success. But he would expend all his physical, mental, and spiritual energy to get Katherine back, and the other ten girls. Eleven precious souls.

Knowing he needed the rest, he got into bed. Like the night before he couldn't fall asleep, so he lay awake invoking images of their time in Saint-Malo, and the walk along the wall overlooking the harbor. He recalled vividly the moment he had proposed, accentuated by the screech of a gull. Startled, he sat up and realized it was the alarm he had set for 5 a.m.

He threw off the covers and sat up. An image of eleven figures bathed in a half-light popped into his mind, and nearly took his breath away. They were sitting in a circle with heads bowed. In a few seconds they faded away. Gavin looked at the light of a new day in the window. "*Takuskanskan wakan* (All that moves and is sacred)," he prayed. "*Iyuha awanwicayakapo* (Watch over them all)."

TWENTY-SIX

Gavin announced to Primault and Singer the shift in the overall objective in the search while they were waiting for breakfast.

"I think we need to broaden our focus," he said. "We should be searching for eleven people."

Primault mulled for a moment. "I think I know where you're coming from, and I agree, but maybe you can explain."

"In all probability, the man who abducted Katherine has done that more than once, so it's very possible that he's part of a system, a network, that has abducted Native girls over the years. That being the case, he is taking, or has already, my fiancée to wherever he has taken other girls."

"Makes all the sense in the world," Primault said. "So, when we find Katherine, we will in all likelihood find those other missing girls."

"Right. The girls on Melvina's list."

"It won't alter our plan or how we work our search pattern," Gavin pointed out.

"And my brother is sending out one of his people who is bringing ultra-high resolution cameras, with night vision capability. He might be here tomorrow. With that equipment we should be able to see a mouse scratching its ear."

"Outstanding."

After breakfast they loaded their equipment in the unmarked cruiser and arrived at the general aviation section of the airport just before eight. The woman at the counter of High Skies Charter Service greeted them warily. She was tall with a pleasant face behind a pair of glasses with round, dark frames. The name stitched above the right pocket of her shirt was Rona.

"Good morning. Is there something you want here?"

"Yes, I have a reservation for airplane rental. My name is Gavin Lone Wolf."

She pursed her lips and touched the computer keyboard and perused the large flat screen in front of her. "Yes, a 172, it seems. I need your ID, pilot's license, and a credit card if you please."

Gavin produced the required documents and waited.

"You, of course, want the insurance?" she asked, abruptly.

"Yes. And can we add another day to the contract?"

She replied without taking her eyes off the screen. "Yes, we can." She held up the credit card and glanced at Gavin for a split second. "This is contingent, of course, on your card being accepted for payment," she said icily.

Gavin nodded. "Of course."

Her lips compressed into a thinner line when the card cleared. Instead of handing the ticket to Gavin for his signature, she laid it on the counter. "There's a pen over there," she said, pointing to a cup of pens with the company logo. Turning to the printer she pulled out the printed pages, stapled them, turned it to the last page of both copies, and placed them on the counter. "Signature and date," she instructed.

After he finished she folded and inserted the pages in an envelope and tossed it on the counter. "For your records," she said.

"Thanks," Gavin said. "May we drive our vehicle to the back, onto the tarmac? We have some equipment to unload."

"Yes, but you need to park it in the front after you unload. It can't stay on the tarmac."

Back in the parking lot, as they were about to drive around, Singer shook his head. "What was that all about?"

Gavin grinned. "What do you think?"

"Well," Singer said, "either that woman doesn't think Natives can fly planes or have good credit, or both."

"To say the least," Primault added.

"Sadly," Gavin said, "I'll bet she wasn't the slightest bit aware of what she was doing, or how she was coming across. And society assures her over and over that it's okay."

"That's not right," Singer blurted.

"It isn't. But the reason we're here is bigger than her or her attitude. The first time I flew a plane to North Dakota, after I got my private pilot's license, I landed at an airstrip at a little town on the Fort Berthold reservation. While I was waiting for a ride the manager of that airport arrived, so I asked him to top off the tanks. He looked around and asked, 'Where is the pilot?'"

"Oh, shit. When does it end?" Primault asked.

"Well," Gavin said, "it won't end soon. As Native people we have to keep going, keep doing what we need to in the meantime, and keep hoping and praying that this society learns fairness and tolerance. What else is there to do?"

Primault shook his head. "Nothing, short of an outright revolution."

An employee of the charter service was waiting for them near one of three small aircraft parked on the tarmac. All of them were white high wing Cessnas with blue trim. The man greeted them with a smile and handed the key and the manual and flight log to Gavin. "I'm Brad. Rona should have given you these," he said. "We can do the walk around together, if you'd like."

"Thanks, Brad, I can do it."

"Great. It's practically brand new, and it's got all the bells and whistles."

"We'll be back more than likely around sundown, probably after you're closed."

"Right. Just park it and tie it down. We can refuel in the morning."

Primault and Singer unpacked the cameras and prepared them for use and loaded only the cases into the small cargo hold, while Gavin did the walk-around. A case of snacks and water was the last thing to be loaded onto the back seat.

While Primault was returning the car to the front parking lot, Gavin went back into the charter office and filed his flight plan. A few minutes later Gavin turned the key to the On position, and the digital panel came to life. They were ready to go.

After startup and taxi, the tower brought them up behind a regional commuter plane, a twin-engine nineteen passenger turbo-prop. Less than forty seconds after they were cleared for take-off, they were airborne and climbing into a bright sky. The power and tone of the nearly new, smoothly droning engine was reassuring to Gavin as his gaze swept over the instrument panel.

Singer watched Bismarck grow smaller behind and below them. "This is only the second time I've been in a small plane," he admitted.

"I'm sure there's a bag in the seat back ahead of you," Gavin told him.

"No, I'm good," Singer reassured him. "This is cool."

"You can check out your camera anytime," Primault suggested.

Both he and Singer proceeded to do just that. By the time the plane achieved cruise altitude and Gavin trimmed for level flight, Primault and Singer had the functioning of the cameras down cold. From two thousand feet above the deck, Singer aimed his still camera at a moving vehicle on a road below. "Damn," he exclaimed. "I can see that truck well enough to know it's probably an older Dodge," he said.

"Great!" Primault said; he glanced at Gavin. "If that camera is that good, that means the equipment your brother is sending out can get us in really close."

In order to conserve fuel Gavin opted not to cruise at the Skyhawk's maximum speed and made sure the fuel mixture was set as lean as possible. Forty seven minutes after take-off they were over their search area. After matching the map coordinates to markers on the ground, they established the imaginary middle line of the search grid and flew from one end to the other in just over forty-five minutes. Gavin concentrated on flying on the initial pass and let Primault and Singer test the capabilities of their cameras. He used the autopilot to follow the heading he wanted. After reaching the west end of the line, reversing course, and resetting the auto-pilot, he did some quick calculations and was able to project two estimates: overall time on target and probable fuel consumption.

"How is it looking so far?" he asked the officers.

"I was able to photograph every farm and ranch we passed," Singer said. "Most of them aren't abandoned."

"Well, the one factor I didn't consider is the amount of video we will have," pointed out Primault. "From just today, it'll be over three hours, I'm guessing."

"Do you have enough storage?" Gavin wondered.

"I think so. This camera has several memory disks, or whatever they're called. I'm just saying that all this video will mean long hours of reviewing. But it's all a part of what we need to do."

"We'll just need a lot of coffee," was Singer's solution.

"Well, we stretched the search grid twenty miles, from thirty to fifty outward from the man camp," Gavin said. "We're overreaching to make sure we cover the whole area. When we finish the northern half today, we'll see how much daylight we have left. From today we'll establish two factors; fuel consumption and the amount of visual evidence we will have collected. Both will help us project what we need to do, where we need to make adjustments for tomorrow, and so on. Also, before we hit the rack tonight, we will know how much time is necessary for review."

"Right," agreed Primault. "And I was wondering about overlap. I mean, that depends on how wide an area we're recording, you know. For instance, a farm or ranch could show up on the next pass as well."

"Just remember what we're looking for—abandoned places," Gavin reminded him. "A place that shows up more than once shouldn't be a problem."

"Good point," Primault replied. "I think when we get back to the hotel, we order up room service and get to work."

"They've got to be down there, somewhere," Singer said.

"They are," Primault asserted. "They're down there, in a basement with covered windows about thirty minutes from that man camp, and we're going to find them. We're their best hope."

After turning around at the end of the east leg, Gavin widened the next pass, although he maintained the same altitude. Relying on the autopilot, he divided his concentration from spotting on the ground to watching for other aircraft. Eventually they settled into a routine. Gavin could hear the cameras clicking and whirring, and conversation was down to a minimum. Just over three hours from the time they had arrived over the target area, they finished the last pass. It was just past one o'clock in the afternoon. Gavin had been watching the fuel gauge.

"We're going to land to refuel," he said, reaching for the radio microphone. "Williston Radio, Williston Radio, this is November 719 Jacob Michael requesting permission to land to take on fuel."

In a few seconds a voice replied, granting permission and announcing the weather and wind direction and speed and other pertinent conditions.

While the plane was being refueled they took a bathroom break and walked to the main terminal to grab a quick meal. Back at the airplane Gavin checked the time. "We have plenty of daylight to cover the other half of the grid. We'll do it at the same altitude but I'm going to expand the passes wider. This evening we'll see how all that comes out in the wash, you know, see what we see in the photos and videos."

Twenty minutes later they were back in the air.

At the western end of the first grid line, Primault recognized the town of Blaine, where he and Brousseaux had found rooms for them and the two girls. It looked bleaker from the air. He pointed it out to Gavin and Singer.

"Before this afternoon is over we will have passed over the places where those girls are being hidden. However long it takes us this evening, we pick out all the abandoned farms, ranches, and houses. Tomorrow, with the ultra-high definition cameras, we take a closer look at those."

"What's going to happen when we identify the places that fit our profile?" Singer asked.

"I've been thinking about that," Gavin said. "The air search is only the first phase. The next phase is on the ground."

"Exactly," Primault followed up. "We need to check out each place we identify, up close. That means we rack up miles on the ground, and it will take us a few days."

"So that becomes a rescue mission," Singer said.

"Right," Primault agreed.

"What happens if we encounter some type of resistance? Can we carry our sidearms?" asked Singer.

"North Dakota permits carrying handguns for licensed individuals," Primault said, "which you and I are, technically. We're not empowered to make arrests, but that doesn't mean we can't react, if the situation warrants, and subdue a threat. I guess we'll cross that bridge if and when we come to it."

"I just want to be clear about that," Singer said.

"Right. I know one thing; there is a guy out there who hauls girls around in a dark van. I knocked him out cold but I'm sure he's still doing that," he pointed toward the prairie sliding by beneath them, "somewhere down there. I'll damn sure be tempted to shoot that son-of-a-bitch if I see him again. But he's a part of some evil system that takes advantage of our young women in the worst possible way, and he knows things. So, if I do see him again—and I hope I do—I guess I'll just settle for kicking him in the balls."

They finished the second search grid at just after six and shut off the cameras. They arrived at the Bismarck airport just as the runway lights came on. After parking and tying down the plane, they carried their gear and equipment around the building to the parking lot. By 9 p.m. they were back in their rooms, ordering room service. They decided to review as a group, starting with the video, and settled in for a long evening, hardly pausing after the meal arrived, eating as they watched.

Dogged determination was the shared mindset as they slogged through the video. It was paused at the location of each likely house or farmstead or isolated structure, correlated to the satellite map, and marked with a red circle. At something past midnight, they finished the video, only because they sped up the playback as they watched. Singer counted the red circles on the map and announced there were twenty-seven. A lot of abandoned places.

After a moment of contemplation, Gavin had a thought. "My brother's technician will be here, at the earliest, sometime tomorrow. We've had a long day, a good day, and we need some rest. So, I say we hit the rack, have breakfast in the morning, and then look at the still photos. We look for those twenty-seven places in the still photos."

Gavin turned to Singer. "What do you think, Jason?"

"Sure. Let's do it that way."

Gavin left the maps on the coffee table and took a quick shower after Singer and Primault left the room. He adjusted the spray and let the water pummel the muscles around his neck. If at any time in his life he felt his age, it was now. He was not an old man, but neither was he young. It was more than physical fatigue, however. He was emotionally wrung out. A piece of his soul had been bitten off, just like the clouds would sometimes bite off a piece of the moon.

If this is how he felt, he couldn't imagine what Katherine was feeling, or those ten girls, for that matter. For them, he had to find a way. Melvina Old Lodge had given her life, her last ounce of energy. She left big shoes to fill. Fatigue was a small price to pay.

TWENTY-SEVEN

In spite of Katherine's best efforts, fatigue won. She awoke with a start, with the realization that she had fallen asleep. The car was still moving, judging from the motion and the noise. She straightened her legs as far as she could, flexing her leg muscles. After that she flexed her shoulder muscles, then down her arms with each muscle group.

From the sound she knew the car's tires were not on a paved roadbed. It was either gravel or dirt, a rough surface, with an occasional hole or depression that translated to a bump that tested the limits of the car's old shock absorbers. Before too long the noise changed to indicate a decrease in speed, and then a sudden turn. After that the speed slowed more and the road was rougher. After ten minutes, she estimated, it turned again and stopped.

It had been a long day and a long ride. Most of the morning had been stationary, parked, she guessed, in some out of the way place. Twice she had been allowed out of the trunk, once to relieve herself and once to eat a few snacks. The camel back water bag was still on her back. She was grateful that, for whatever reason, her captor had not mistreated her. She prayed that would continue. Yet the threat of the unknown was like a dark predator always ready to pounce.

There was a noticeable coolness in the air, telling her it was night. After the car stopped, a door opened and closed. A few minutes later she heard footsteps and mentally braced herself as she heard the key in the trunk lock.

It was the same two men, now dark outlines against the night sky.

"Come on, hon," her captor said, reaching in and grabbing her arm. "We have new accommodations for the night." The other man, the one she thought of as Thin Face, stood back, waiting.

"Shit man," Thin Face whined, "Put a bag over her head."

"Don't sweat it. There's nothing she can do to hurt you."

"You keep saying that but I ain't so sure."

A moment passed before she found her balance on the gravel. The night air was cool. Katherine immediately noticed there were no lights. Darkness prevailed. An outline of a building materialized as her eyes grew accustomed to the shadows. Her captor tugged on her arm. "Come on," he said.

She was nervous about Thin Face walking behind her. His footfalls were easy to hear on the gravel, a surface she surmised had been a driveway. The shadow of the building grew larger as they approached. Up close it was obviously a house, a darkened house. At one corner Thin Face stepped ahead and unlocked a padlock and opened the wooden door, squeaking slightly on its hinges. Old basement mustiness wafted upward, stinging her nostrils. Thin Face flipped a switch and dim light revealed narrow wooden steps leading down. Apprehension swelled like a cold balloon in her abdomen as she took the first tentative steps down. At the bottom was a narrow hallway with bare, plywood walls. Various sharp smells touched her nostrils, none pleasant.

A door was on each wooden wall. Thin Face pushed open the one on the left and reached in to flick a switch. The light was just as dim as the hallway, coming from a single bulb in the ceiling. Katherine thought she heard a soft cough, somewhere.

"Stand there," her captor directed.

Katherine watched as he went to peek into two cardboard boxes against the wall, checking their contents. Against the opposite wall was a mattress with a bare pillow and bed covers folded on top. Next to the boxes were bottles of water inside a small plastic tub. In a far corner was a blocky stool, which Katherine realized was a composting toilet. The floor was bare concrete.

Her captor stepped in front of her and spoke, almost apologetically. "I'll be back in a day or so, and get you out of here," he said. With a pocket knife he sliced the tape around her wrists.

Without another word, he and Thin Face left. She heard the door being locked.

Katherine took a deep breath as she peeled the tape off her wrists. A myriad of thoughts and perceptions whirled in her mind. She was glad to be out of the trunk, but she was still clearly a prisoner in every sense of the word. Turning to the door she instantly saw there was no door handle. She walked to the door and tapped on it. It was solid. There was no way to open it from the inside.

She turned to peruse the room again, shaking off a momentary indecisiveness. Hesitating no further she went to the boxes and looked in. There was food—snacks, a loaf of bread in plastic, packaged luncheon meat, and a bottle of orange juice, a new hairbrush in a plastic case, a box of tampons, rolls of toilet paper, and a box of facial tissues.

Against the wall was a large plastic tub, inside were folded towels. Two five gallon buckets were next to the tub. One had water in it.

There were two cases of small plastic bottles of water in the small plastic tub. It was all puzzling, though she was glad to have food and water. She opened the lid of the toilet stool and caught a scent of cleaning solution. Someone had obviously planned for her coming here. She looked again at the walls. One wall was cement, the other three were plywood. A small opening high on the cement wall had been covered over.

She opened a packet of luncheon meat and made a sandwich, drinking from a bottle of water. Maintaining her strength with whatever was at hand was necessary. The mattress was the only place to sit, and it was fairly firm. Surprisingly, the bed covers felt and even smelled clean.

She finished the sandwich quickly and made another, her mind racing the entire time. Obviously there had been preparations made, hence the food and water and other supplies. Then it dawned on her; all this wasn't specifically for her. It had to be a routine of some kind. A system that provided the bare minimum essentials necessary for survival and comfort.

Katherine searched her memory. Lieutenant Primault told Gavin that the two girls they had rescued had spoken of being kept in a basement. She looked around the room. Perhaps this basement. An icy chill coursed through her body. Standing, she went to the boxes and searched through the contents. As she suspected, there were no utensils of any sort. No sharp edges.

Back on the mattress she sat with her knees drawn up. She was here until her captor returned. She took slow deep breaths. At the very least she could rest, stretch out her legs. Outside it was night. In here it was impossible to know the exact hour, though she felt it was late evening, perhaps nine or ten. She fought down a rising sense of panic. Unfolding the sheet and blanket, she made the bed, and then dragged it to the other side of the room, as far from the door as possible.

Undressing to sleep was out of the question, someone could come through the door at any time. She removed her sneakers and socks but placed them next to the pillow. No way was she going anywhere without shoes.

On her side with her head on the pillow, she could see the door. It was the only defensive act she could do; watch the door. Weariness crept up on her, yet she fought sleep as long as she could. A thought slid through her mind as sleep overtook her: there has to be something I can do.

Like a cold slap, a realization jarred her awake. Piano! The name screamed from her memory. Someone Thin Face invoked, out of fear, someone of consequence. Someone the reprehensible low life was afraid of. Perhaps whoever Piano is, he was the one pulling the strings, and Thin Face and her captor were the puppets. Only one detail didn't fit. Her captor had apparently broken rules by abducting her. What did it all mean?

There was, of course, no way to know how long she had slept, but she had. Sitting up and pushing off the blanket, Katherine reached into the right pocket of her jeans and pulled out her engagement ring. It was the only thing she had with a sharp edge. Then looked up at the bare wood walls.

Hours later she finished. For now, time didn't matter. She had downed two bottles of water and another sandwich, and her fingers were sore from the effort, but she was finished. Standing back, she gazed at her handiwork.

Eye level, she deduced, was the most logical height, and in a conspicuous spot. So, she had selected to the left of the door. There, in six inch high letters, she had scratched the word into the wall. In smaller lettering beneath it she wrote her nickname and the date:

PIANO

Soldier Woman

Aug 22, 2018

She walked closer. It was, she realized, perhaps nothing more than an act of desperation. Frustration rose from her gut. She clenched her fists.

"Go to hell, Piano! Whoever the hell you are!" she blurted. Her voice was hoarse, but full of spite and determination. Raising her fists, she pounded the wall as hard she could, jarring her arms up to her shoulders.

Standing back, she suppressed a sob. Seconds passed, then she heard a faint thump.

TWENTY-EIGHT

Primault and Singer waited for the server to depart after he had refilled their coffee cups. Though it was early the hotel restaurant was half full and the clink of silverware and the soft buzz of conversations filled the air.

"Can I ask you something?" Singer said.

Primault nodded. "Sure."

"Did Gavin Lone Wolf ever live anywhere else, off the Rez?"

"No, I don't think so. Why do you ask?"

Singer leaned back and crossed his arms. "Well, for such an accomplished guy, I never heard of him until the Arlo High Crane case that we worked together. I mean, why isn't he tribal chairman, or something like that?"

"He's too smart for that. Who wants the crap that comes with that kind of a job? I wouldn't. The High Crane murder was the first time I met him, too. As far as I know, he's always lived on the Rez. He went away to school and traveled a bit. He's a big game guide for bow hunters. But he was born and raised on the Rez. I think he has a place on the Wind River reservation, either has relatives or friends there."

"I don't know too many Natives that can fly airplanes," Singer went on. "I mean, I'm sure there are, but he's the first I've ever met who does. And it still blows my mind that he jumped out of an airplane at night to capture the suspect on the High Crane murder case."

"Well, tell you what, I sure wouldn't want to meet him in a dark alley when he's pissed."

"Yeah. I feel sorry for whoever took his fiancée, if and when he gets his hands on him."

Primault grinned. "Yeah, I'm looking forward to that. That poor guy will get exactly what he deserves." He leaned forward, elbows on the table. "But keep this in mind, whatever I know about Gavin, I learned from someone else. I had to ask Chief Avery what he knew. Gavin never said anything about himself. He has a doctorate in history, makes his own bows and arrows and hunts with them, has a fifth degree black belt in judo, is a skydiver, a pilot, and a scuba diver. Lakota is his first language, and in high school and college he was a long distance runner."

"Damn!" Singer exclaimed.

"And you know what else? He has an identical twin brother, also with a PhD, a retired colonel in the Marine Corps, owns a security firm in DC. And don't forget his sister, she's the director of nursing at the hospital."

"Shit. Makes me feel lazy."

"You're still young, Jason. And what you do has nothing to do with how smart you are or aren't. It's about how willing you are to try, and not be afraid to fail. My wife is dyslexic, she struggled in school. She still has to deal with it, but because of it she became a teacher."

"I didn't know that."

"Sandra doesn't make a big deal out of it. When Gavin was in college and on his way to making the Olympic track team, he was in a car wreck.

Laid him up for months. Kept him out of the army, and he had to learn to walk all over again. After that came the judo and the skydiving, and so on. You know, white people look at us natives and they zero in on the worst they see; the alcoholics, drug addicts, abusive husbands and they see how tribes struggle with health issues, and they judge us as incapable or misfits They don't see the people among us, like my wife, and Gavin and his brother and sister. They don't see that we can be better than they are at things that matter. They're too quick pointing out how we're failing."

Singer shook his head. "I guess I never thought of it that way."

"Many of us don't. But here's what's just as important. When you know about people like, Gavin, and his brother and sister, or my wife, don't idolize them. The best thing you can do is follow them. You know what I mean?"

Footsteps caught their attention and they turned to see Gavin Lone Wolf approaching. "Good morning," he said, taking a chair and sliding up to the round table. "Didn't mean to be late. Had a long conversation with my brother."

"No problem," Primault replied. "We're just having coffee and waiting to order. Is the man with the cameras arriving today?"

"Affirmative, just after one this afternoon," Gavin replied. "So that fits in with our plan for the day. We can take the morning and scrutinize the stills. That might push back our search for a day, so I hope that fits in with whatever time you have."

"No problem," Primault assured him. "Chief Avery is treating our involvement as necessary off-reservation investigation. We're still on the clock."

After breakfast Singer took the yards of cable that came with the camera equipment and jerry-rigged a system that brought up the photos on the flat screen television in Gavin's room. He downloaded the photos from the camera disc onto a laptop, and then connected that to the television. Then they settled into a routine.

Fortunately, Singer had put a time stamp on each photo so it was not difficult to correlate that to the search lines they had flown. From that they could locate the places on the satellite maps. They identified the same twenty-seven abandoned places they had found in the video, and the still photos revealed more detail. By the time they finished, it was nearly noon.

"I don't know about you guys, but my eyes are bleary," Gavin said. "Now's as good a time as any for a break. I'm going to try to arrange for the hotel shuttle to pick up Ben Wilson. How about lunch? It's on me."

Primault glanced at his watch. "Right. We'll meet you downstairs in about twenty minutes. I need to have a conversation with the Chief and check in with my wife. I'm sure there's a batch of young ladies waiting breathlessly to hear from Jason."

"Don't I wish," Jason said, standing and slapping his thigh. "Gotta let my mom know I'm still alive."

After lunch Gavin rode the shuttle to the airport to meet Ben Wilson. The young man emerged from the concourse and immediately spotted Gavin waiting to one side. He broke out of the crowd and approached. "There's no doubt you are Dr. Gavin Lone Wolf," he said, holding out his hand. "I'm definitely seeing double. I'm Ben Wilson."

"Great to meet you, Ben. I'm glad you're helping us."

"My pleasure, sir," Wilson replied. He indicated the carry-on bag hanging by a strap over his shoulder. "One bag and two cases will be in baggage claim."

After hauling Wilson's one large roller bag and two even larger fiber-glass cases onto the shuttle, Gavin decided to rent an SUV, just in case. The vehicle was delivered while Wilson was unpacking and checking over the equipment in a small meeting room at the hotel. Gavin had lunch delivered for the new arrival as they began to plan.

On his laptop Singer showed the twenty-seven places to Wilson. "Those are damn good," Wilson observed. "But I'm here to tell you, we will do even better."

"Great," Gavin said. "I have a thought. Those photos are from two thousand feet above the ground. If we drop down to one thousand, how much detail will we pick up with your cameras?"

"Well, we can see which way a cat's tail is curling, if we see a cat."

"Okay, here's what I think," Gavin turned to the circle of faces standing around him. "We zero in on those twenty-seven. We look on our satellite map and plot out our course. Over the search area we fly at one thousand feet and at one hundred miles an hour. Will that work?"

"I don't see why not," Wilson said. "But I think we need to number each site, that way there's no confusion at which place we're looking at later."

"Right," said Primault. "And then we eliminate those that we can. Those that have absolutely no sign of use or occupation. Those that are promising, we take a closer look."

Gavin glanced at his watch, and then at Wilson. "We'll shove off when you're ready. In the meantime, I need to call and check the weather, although I think we're going to have great conditions."

Brad was waiting for them at the plane when they drove up in the SUV Gavin had rented, a full size Chevrolet Suburban. "I took the liberty of topping off the tanks," he told Gavin. "And I turned it around so you can taxi right off."

"Thank you," Gavin told him. "We had to alter our schedule. Slight change in plans."

"Not to worry. You gentlemen have a great day."

Soon they were climbing into a bright cloudless sky. In the back seat Jason Singer and Ben Wilson unfurled the map they had covered with clear plastic in order to pinpoint the abandoned houses and farmsteads, marked with a red grease pencil. Gavin finished filing his flight plan and turned to everyone, tapping his headset. "Put these on, all of you, so we can hear each other." He waited and then spoke again. "We should be on target in about forty minutes, over the first place." He glanced at the altimeter. "I'm holding at thirty-three hundred, that keeps us at a thousand feet above the deck. And I'll slow us down once we reach the area. After that, Ben, you're calling the shots—no pun intended."

"Got it," said Wilson. "Between here and there I'll take a few test shots. I think you'll see how amazing this camera is."

True to his word, after a few shots, Wilson showed them on the camera's small screen. He had snapped three photos of a mid-size Ford pickup, down to its license number.

"Holy shit!" was Singer's assessment. "The bad guys better look out."

"Well, they won't be," Wilson said. "Most of them aren't smart enough to look up."

Primault took the camera and showed the photo to Gavin. "This will definitely enable us to move faster," Primault concluded.

Singer functioned as the spotter. Because they didn't need to fly the entire length of each search grid, they were able to photograph each and every one of the twenty-seven abandoned farmsteads in two hours. In a few instances Wilson asked Gavin to circle back for additional angles. Since there was no need to land and refuel, they landed back in Bismarck at sundown. After dinner back at the hotel, they gathered in Gavin's room.

After several carafes of coffee and two pots of tea for Ben Wilson, they finished after ten, having eliminated eighteen of the abandoned places. The nine they marked as possibilities had indications of visitation. The obvious clues were tire tracks leading to and away from the structures. Footprints were also visible in four of the places. "Well, gentlemen, all we need now is a foolproof plan for the next phase."

"We need to eyeball each of those places," Primault pointed out. "They can't all have basements, and we search the ones that do."

"Won't that be trespassing?" Singer asked, cautiously.

"Absolutely" said Primault. "But how long do you think it would take to get search warrants? Those places are in at least three different counties, meaning non-Indian jurisdiction. And no country or circuit judge will give credence to a request for a search warrant from an outside agency."

"What about the FBI?" Singer pressed.

"Well, even if we did manage to convince them, somehow, it would still take some time."

"What are we going to do?" Singer asked. "We can't just quit now."

Primault rubbed his face and stood from his chair. "We're not. This may sound crazy, but I think we hide in plain sight. When Jeff Brousseaux and I reconned the man camp, the way I got in was to walk in like I owned the place. Pretty damn nerve wracking, but it worked."

Gavin nodded for a few seconds. "That's a good idea. So how do we do that, three Native guys and one white guy in the middle of a redneck, white conservative stronghold?"

Ben Wilson chuckled. "That's easy. We come up with a cover story. It's what police and detectives do sometimes when they're on a stake out or going undercover."

Primault grinned. "What's our story?"

A long thoughtful pause. Wilson looked around at the equipment scattered in the room. "Well, it's obvious to me," he said. "We can be a film crew doing a documentary on the oil boom, or something along those lines that won't seem too far-fetched to rednecks."

"There's one other fact in our favor," Gavin said. "Most roads are public highways, secondary roads, section roads, country roads. As long as it's a common causeway, the public has a right to use it."

"Right, good point," Primault said. "There's a lot of unused or little used roads out there. If it's on the map, we can drive on it."

"And most abandoned properties aren't posted," Gavin said.

"Alright, that works for me," Primault declared. "What's next? Maybe somehow getting the most up to date maps would be one step, I think."

"Right," Wilson agreed. "Counties and cities regularly update maps of roads and streets, and they're a matter of public record. But it might take time to get maps if those places are located in several countries."

"Well, we're in the state capital," Gavin pointed out. "There's got to be a state agency with those records."

"What about the department of transportation, or whatever passes for one at the state level?" Primault asked.

"Bingo!" Wilson exclaimed.

"It might set us back a few hours, but it would be immensely valuable to have reliable maps. I'm sure there's some type of fee for printing or copying. That's not a problem," Gavin said, "but this being North Dakota, I don't know how they would regard a long-haired Native guy asking for maps of ranching country."

"Hey," said Ben Wilson. "In that case, I'll do it. Just point me in the right direction."

Singer had a thought. "Gentlemen," he said. "I think I'll go down to the hotel's office center and get on the state transportation web site. Maybe I can print some maps."

"Good idea" Gavin said. "Pursue all the possibilities." He turned to Wilson. "State offices likely open at eight, I think straight from the source is our best bet."

"That's first on my agenda," Wilson said. "After an early breakfast."

Gavin paused and gazed at the map where the nine identified places were marked with red Xs. They were there, she was there. He was certain of it. He caught Justin Primault's attention. "I'm going to keep the airplane on stand-by in case we might need it after tomorrow. But since tomorrow is a ground search, I think we need to rent another SUV. Jason and I can do that while you take Ben to the Capitol. Two vehicles might be an advantage, and it would give credence to Ben's cover story. A film crew with two rented vehicles seems bona fide to me."

Primault nodded in agreement. "And we'll need to transport our missing girls when we find them," he said.

"Absolutely."

After rolling up maps and gathering up all the other material, everyone left. Gavin walked to the window and stared out at the city lights and buildings, only now becoming aware of traffic sounds.

"We're coming to get you, hon," he said gently into the night. "Live up to your name, Soldier Woman, and hang in there."

For the first time he felt truly confident. He was certain she was in one of those nine abandoned places.

He picked up his phone and called Gerard.

"Hey, bro. I was hoping you'd call."

"I hope I didn't wake you."

"No worries," Gerard said. "Joby and Uncle Andrew are here with me. Uncle Andrew was just about to go home. What's the situation?"

Gavin took a seat and summed up the day's activities and the plan for tomorrow. "Ben Wilson is giving us the edge we need," he concluded. "He knows what he's doing."

"Great. Glad to hear it. I don't doubt that you'll make some strides tomorrow. I damn sure hope you'll have some good news for us about those girls and Katherine. You've done everything to make that happen."

"We're going to bust down doors if we have to," Gavin said. "We'll find them, all of them."

"I don't doubt it. Uncle Andrew was just reminding me of the strong women in our family, like Grandma Annie and Loren. He was talking about how we were a matriarchal society, but not so much anymore because we've bought into European patriarchy because of Christianity. He thinks that's at the root of the Lakota people—especially men—not being more up in arms about missing women and girls."

"He's right," Gavin said.

"There's a bigger picture here, bro, and Uncle Andrew reminded me of that, too. He said, 'we can only be defeated when the hearts of our women are on the ground.' White society has been trying its utmost to beat us down. Now, for whatever reason—be it because of coincidence or bad juju—something is after our women, our source of strength."

Gavin nodded as he listened to his brother. "Yeah," he said, "you're right. And we can't let that happen. The system that's doing that isn't going to help us, so we have to do it ourselves. And it starts with those girls on Melvina Old Lodge's list. I'm not stopping until I find them or get some answers."

"I know you will, brother. I know you will. Let me know if there's any-thing else you need. I'm just a phone call away."

"I have a feeling that by the time the sun sets tomorrow, we will have some answers."

TWENTY-NINE

During breakfast Gavin ordered box lunches to go. He and Jason Singer returned to the hotel just minutes ahead of Ben Wilson, with his newly acquired batch of plat maps. An impromptu final planning session occurred as they gathered around the maps spread out on the hood of one of the SUVs. They were able to correlate the target locations with the small maps Singer had printed last night. Most importantly, the plat maps showed every road in the target area.

"How did you manage to get all these maps?" Primault asked.

"Well, I just flashed my company ID," Wilson said, sheepishly. "Gerard purposely designed it to resemble a government ID. I told the clerk my company was doing research and I hinted it had something to do with national security. A little bit of a white lie, but that's my story and I'm sticking to it."

"For which we are grateful," insisted Gavin. "It's about a four hour drive, gentlemen. Interstate 94 west to highway 85 north. We will probably need to spend a few nights there."

"I would recommend the little town of Blaine," said Primault.

"Good. I'll make sure the hotel here will hold our rooms. Nothing to do but get on the road."

Primault and Singer were in one SUV and Gavin and Ben Wilson in the other. It was definitely a feeling that they had gone from hawk to turtle mode as the miles rolled by slowly. At Dickinson they stopped to top off the tanks, since the SUVs were gas guzzlers, especially maintaining the speed limit. Primault's concern of lacking effective communication on the ground, other than cell phones, resulted in a quick side trip to a big box store specializing in electronics. From there they left with the best civilian walkie-talkies money could buy, with a range of three miles.

Nearly three hours later they arrived at Williston, a college town overwhelmed by the hustle and bustle of the oil boom. They topped off the tanks again, and an hour later pulled into Blaine, a ghost town compared to Williston. Primault arranged for rooms at the motel where he and Brousseaux had stayed. Mel, the proprietor, was friendlier, especially when he was selling four rooms for seventy-five dollars each for at least five nights.

Unable to hold back the anxiety they all felt, now that they were in the target area and practically on top of the place or places where Katherine Hill and ten girls were hidden, they all climbed into one SUV and drove to Pinnacle. As sundown approached they reached the entrance to the one man camp north of town. Wilson and Singer pinpointed the location on the map and verified the locations of the nine abandoned farmsteads that fit their profile. All, of course, were within the original fifty-mile limit estimate made early on.

Just over an hour later they convened in Gavin's room to plan the initial searches.

"None of the places we selected are south of Pinnacle," Primault pointed out on the map. "Most of them are northwest and a few to the east. The road that Brousseaux and I found and took to get east of the man camp was not used at all. If we're lucky that will be the case with some of these roads that take us to those places. Those are the places we should search first, where the roads are not used or not as much. And my reasoning is that we would be less apt to encounter anyone."

"Makes sense," agreed Gavin.

"Now," Primault continued, "we have a cover story if we meet anyone. If anyone does become too confrontational, we just pick up our marbles and leave. No matter how righteous our cause, this is white jurisdiction legally. Like it or not, we play nice, and find another way."

"I didn't realize that was such an issue," Wilson admitted. "Sort of sounds like the wild west."

"County sheriffs are the big dogs out here," Primault said. "White males. I wouldn't be surprised if one or two of them thought he was a reincarnation of Wyatt Earp. We can't afford to let anything interfere, so the most sensible thing to do is make sure no one else is around before we move into any one of those places."

"In other words, be as sneaky as shit," Wilson said.

"I couldn't have said it better myself," chuckled Gavin. He looked at Primault and Singer. "So, what about your sidearms? Will you carry those?"

Primault nodded as he took a sip of his soda. "I've been thinking about that," he said. "In the remote chance that we do run across Wyatt Earp and he wants to question us, he might want to search us as well, meaning our vehicles and equipment. Again, I don't want anything to derail us, so I think Jason and I will just leave our pistols here. I think that the most aggressive person we might run across is a farmer with an attitude. Unless he's got a bunch of guys with him, I think we'll be okay."

"If that happens, he could still call the county sheriff, if he's just a little suspicious," Singer pointed out.

"This still blows my mind ," Wilson said, perturbed. "I mean, there are laws, right, having to do with 'search and seizure' and 'probable cause'? And they apply to everyone."

Primault shook his head "Not necessarily out here. In any legal situation, a Native male has two strikes against him. Thirty some years ago a teenage Lakota boy stole a dollar can of Vienna sausages in a border town grocery store. He was sentenced to three years in prison. In that same town, a white rancher purposely opened his pickup door as he passed a line of Native people walking and struck a little Native girl and killed her. He never went to jail. People think the deep south is a hot bed of racism, well, they haven't been paying attention. Manifest Destiny is alive and well in the Dakotas. Nothing would stop some sheriff from slapping cuffs on us and hauling us off to jail, even on the flimsiest of reasons, because he knows, wrong or right, the system will see it his way."

"Fuck me!" Wilson blurted. "I did hear Gerard say once that he had grown up in one of the most racist states in the country. I guess that wasn't bullshit."

"Yup. Bottom line is we're walking on the razor's edge here," Primault cautioned. "We just need to be careful—and as you said—sneaky as shit."

"And we Natives have sneaky down cold," Gavin said, grinning. "I'm for breakfast at six. I think I saw a restaurant on the edge of town."

"You don't think three Native guys and a white guy together is not going to raise some eyebrows, given what you all just said?" Wilson wondered.

"I have a sneaking suspicion, thanks to Mel, who owns this motel, that the word is already out," Primault said. "Besides, four guys in two big blue

SUVs looks somehow 'official.' Nothing is more bona fide than looking 'official.' Especially if you carry a clipboard."

Wilson decided to cover his bets and carried a clipboard into the small restaurant. For twenty minutes they were the only customers, until what was probably a few regulars straggled in. The food was good and well prepared. They paid no attention to the curious side glances sent their way and talked about hunting and football while polishing off their meals. Leaving generous tips, they departed with to-go cups full of coffee.

With growing anticipation, they drove through Pinnacle and found the first county road they had marked. It was a few miles north of the entrance to the man camp, and, as they had hoped, showed no indication of recent use. Pulling in a few yards off the highway onto a rise, they helped Ben Wilson unload a tripod and camera onto which he screwed a long zoom lens.

Wilson worked quickly, scanning the area to the west. "Nothing but one roof top and a few cattle," he reported after a few minutes. "I think we move in another mile or two."

At the next stop Wilson did the same. They were relieved to see that the road was slightly overgrown with no discernible vehicle tracks of any kind. Primault and Singer glassed their back trail with binoculars.

"So far, so good," Primault said. "No movement of any kind."

Gavin consulted the map. "We're about five or six miles from our first location," he said. "I think our next move is to get as close as we can and check it out."

Proceeding slowly, they connected with another old road, more grown over with grass and weeds, and turned north. Their first marked house came into view. From a distance of half a mile, it looked dark and innocuous. West of it was a thinned outline of trees, an old shelter belt, common on many farms. Some yards east of the house were two outbuildings, one larger than the house.

"That has to be an old barn," Primault said.

A twenty minute scrutiny affirmed no activity of any kind around or near the old place.

"That place is just east of this road," Primault pointed out. "I think we park behind that shelter belt and check the place out."

Up close the condition of the old farmstead was more obvious. The barbed wire fence paralleling the road was virtually nonexistent. Only a few rusted strands hung stubbornly to the rotted wooden posts, and most of the trees in the forty-yard long shelter belt were dead and gray. Gavin pointed out there were no tracks of any kind to indicate that vehicles, livestock, or people had been in the area, at least not since the last heavy rain.

Weeds and tall grass filled the ground around the house itself. It was an old style frame house. Glass was still in the windows but the wood siding was shades of brown and gray and extremely weathered, and its roof was sagging, with most of the shingles gone.

"Unless that house has a basement, we can cross it off the list," Primault said.

It didn't take long to see that the small square house sat on a crumbling concrete foundation. Gavin marked the location with a red X on the map, and they plotted the route to the next location.

Disappointment was a pin prick. It was to be expected, given the process of elimination they were following. Driving away from the first place meant there were eight more to go, and the odds were slightly smaller. Of course, the positive spin was that the chances were increasing. But the next three locations were busts as well. One did not have a basement and the two that did were treacherously inaccessible.

Finding an east-west dirt road they eventually came back to the main highway north out of Pinnacle and paused for a break.

Gavin glanced at his watch. "It's after six. By the time we get to the next place, it'll be close to sundown. I don't know what we gain by running around in the dark."

"Outside of being hidden, nothing, really," Primault said. "Daylight lets us check out a place from a distance, and it's easier to find our way in the light. I think we call it a day and start again tomorrow. If we're lucky we can get to all of the remaining five places by this time tomorrow."

They arrived in Blaine just after sunset. As the last customers at the restaurant, the owner let them linger over their coffee while cleaning up. As they had at breakfast, they didn't talk at all about their day's activities until gathering in Gavin's room.

"We've definitely narrowed it down," Primault said. "I have a feeling tomorrow is the day we find some kind of an answer. I think tomorrow we take plenty of water and beverages and maybe some sandwiches from the restaurant, in the event we need to stay out longer."

"I wish there was way we could have watched the traffic into that man camp," Singer said. "If that man you caught was driving a van, we could have watched for vans. I think most of the people who live there drive sedans or pickups."

"Yeah, that would have been good," Primault allowed. "And it may be what we do if the remaining five places turn out to be dry holes."

"You think that's a possibility?" Wilson asked.

"Well, only slightly," Primault replied quickly. "I have a feeling one of those last places isn't a dry hole."

"What is a 'dry hole'?" Singer asked.

"It's a well driller's term," replied Primault. "When they drill and find no oil."

"I agree with your sense of it," Gavin said to Primault. "I think one of those five places is where we'll find those girls."

"And what's our plan when we do?" asked Wilson.

"I think that depends on the girls," Primault said. "Maggie Henry and Julia Lake were malnourished and, of course, abused. The others are likely in the same fix, and maybe ill or injured. I'll call Chief Avery and have him on standby and ready to call the IHS hospital at Fort Yates. They helped us with Julia and Maggie. So, it won't be a total surprise."

After the others left, Gavin considered calling Uncle Andrew. He wanted to hear a voice of encouragement but decided it was too late. Toweling his hair dry after the shower, he heard his phone chirping and recognized Uncle Andrew's land line number. "*Hau Leksi*, I was wondering if you were still awake."

"Yeah. I had supper with Gerard and Joby earlier," Andrew said. "I'm doing a sweat tomorrow with the Black Butte family. One of their boys, I think he's about twenty-six, just got the word. He's got full blown diabetes. So, before I got busy with that I thought I'd give you a call."

"I'm glad you did. How's everything at home?"

"Good. It's good. How's it going there?"

"Well, we narrowed our search down considerably. It's down to five places tomorrow."

"Yeah? I got a feeling you're going to find something. I don't know what it is exactly, something's going to happen tomorrow."

Gavin walked to the window and closed the curtain, shutting out the night. "I think you're right," he said.

"Good or bad, you should be ready."

"That sounds kind of ominous."

"Not all victories give us what we want. Sometimes we need to keep fighting."

THIRTY

Katherine awoke realizing she had lost all track of time. She had communicated with the thumps from the other side of the wall and there was no doubt in her mind that it was the missing girls, or some of them.

She had managed to break off a small corner of the concrete covering the only window in the basement. Using it as a hammer stone she pounded the wall. But that was the extent of the communication, only thumping. There was no way to convey any kind of information. But someone was there, alive and energetic enough to pound on the wall.

Frustration returned in a rush, and a growing sense of rage. This was real. She was a prisoner, a captive, and so were the girls locked in the other part of the basement. Men had brought her here, likely the same men who had taken those girls. There had to be a way to fix it. She looked at the door without a doorknob. Someone had built this room, had put up the walls of thick plywood. There was just enough here to maintain life and provide basic comforts, and someone would likely come to resupply. That would be her only opportunity. But to do what?

Katherine glanced down at the piece of concrete on the floor near the mattress. It was small, no more than three inches, but felt heavy, it had weight. It was the only weapon she had. She knew Gavin was looking for her and would not quit. But she had to do more than wait. There had to be something she could do to help herself, and whoever was in the room across the hall.

She picked up the piece of concrete. This was it. This was her chance. This piece of concrete and a surprise attack.

Leaning back against the wall, she visualized the two men who had brought her here, her captor—whose name she did not know—and the one she had dubbed Thin Face. Her captor was the bigger of the two, but something about Thin Face projected evil and aggression. He would be difficult to subdue.

Her eyes came open and she realized she had dozed off. Picking up a bottle near the end of the mattress, she took a drink and thought about making a sandwich. First she used the toilet and rinsed off her hands. As she knelt down to reach into the food box, she heard the door open. They were in the room before she could grab the concrete rock.

A flashlight snapped on and blinded her. Footsteps came across the floor and rough hands grabbed her arm and twisted. Before she could react her other arm was pulled back and handcuffs slid over her wrists.

"Take it easy!" her captor said. "No need to be so rough."

"You heard Sanders," Thin Face spat out. "We got orders. Piano's pissed and you're in deep shit. Get her in the car so we can get going. He's waiting for you."

Thin Face shoved her, catching her by surprise and causing her to stumble. Her captor grabbed her arm.

"Come on, Katherine," he said. "Better do as he says."

Katherine gasped slightly. "You know my name?"

"Yeah. Your picture's on the internet. Cops put out a bulletin," he rasped.

A spark of hope flashed. Someone knew. In the next split second the hope was extinguished with the knowledge she was being moved. Perhaps to where Piano was. That didn't feel good. A thump came from the other wall as Thin Face and her captor guided her out into the hall. Thin Face viciously kicked the door.

"QUIET!" he shouted.

That was all the affirmation Katherine needed that there were Native girls inside the other room. Now she had to figure out where this place was. But any further hope of that disappeared when the hood came down over her head.

Stumbling up the stairs she could feel the cool in the air. It was probably night.

"I can take it from here," Nomer said.

"Nice try, man. Sanders told me to ride shotgun and make damn sure you get to the ranch," Thin Face declared. In a swift motion he drew a snub-nosed pistol out of his waist band and pointed it at Nomer's chest. "Which reminds me, give me your gun, now."

Nomer handed over his semi-automatic, which Tulo promptly threw into the darkness.

"Now, put this bitch in the trunk. You're driving."

THIRTY-ONE

Justin Primault knocked on Jason Singer's door just before six and was not surprised to see that he was dressed and ready. "Just a few clouds in the west," he said, stepping into the room.

"Sounds like a good day for the good guys," Singer said.

"I think Gavin and Wilson are up, but I wanted to chat a bit before we go to breakfast."

"Sure, what's on your mind?"

Primault took a seat on the only chair in the room. "I had a talk with Chief Avery last night. He'll get in touch with the hospital at Fort Yates. But I wanted to share some numbers he gave me."

"Numbers?"

"Yeah, on missing Native girls and women. He sent me an email, too." Primault took a few seconds to pull up the email on his phone, and then read. "Going back twenty years the total number of missing girls and women from the reservations in the Dakotas and Wyoming is 142. Of that total, only 7 were found or returned, and 11 were found deceased."

Singer shook his head. "Damn. If that don't sober you up and piss you off, I don't know what will."

"Well, I never heard it put quite that way, but when we find those girls and Katherine Hill, which we will, that has to be some kind of leverage. We're going to find them for the sake of those girls, and then that will show anyone who cares it can be done."

"Totally agree. You going to share that information with Dr. Lone Wolf?"

"I don't think so. It's tough enough for him as it is."

They downed their breakfasts in a hurry at the restaurant and left as soon as the to-go lunches were ready. Their route for the morning took them south of Pinnacle and then north. Just before nine, after changing direction twice, they turned north again on a gravel section road. They saw little sign that it had been driven on recently, although they did pass a self-propelled combine in a corner of a pasture. The grass around it hinted it might have been years since it was last driven.

Their first stop of the day was at a lone cottonwood tree, a towering and aging giant standing in the shallow ditch against the fence. About a half mile to the northeast was an old farmstead. In the shade of the tree, they stepped down from the vehicles and began glassing the house and outbuildings in the distance. The barn, which was the biggest of the three structures, had been red but its paint was yielding to the ravages of time and the hot summer sun.

"Definitely abandoned," Primault said.

It took a moment for Ben Wilson to ready his camera and attach the zoom lens. "The house has a cellar or a basement," he announced, after only seconds of looking. "There's an outside storm door entrance."

"Damn, you can see that?" Singer said.

"Heck yeah."

"Well, let's not waste any time," suggested Primault. "There's got to be a road leading to that place."

Fifteen minutes later they drove into the yard, tall and thick with grass. The storm door Ben Wilson had seen was on the south side of the house. It squeaked as Singer pulled it up, revealing dust and debris covered wooden steps down to a door, which scraped against the cement floor when Singer pushed that open. Primault followed him in, turning on his flashlight.

"Nobody's been here in years," he said, stepping back out.

Less than five minutes later they were back in the vehicles and heading to the next site. "Four more," Wilson said, turning to check that his camera was riding safely in the back seat. "I have a feeling, sir, that this is the day,"

Gavin nodded. "Absolutely. And when we find them, I hope you take as many photographs as possible. There has to be a record."

"I will."

"People have to know," Gavin insisted. "Especially those who don't consider this a problem."

They backtracked to a north-south numbered county road and stopped, gathering around the tailgate of Gavin's SUV, on which they laid the map. After a minute of perusing, Primault pointed north. "About four miles from here, as the crow flies. A six-mile drive, more or less." He traced the roads leading to the place with his finger. "It's about three miles east of this county road, the one we're on. The road to the farm curves a couple of times, so I think it's a private road. Maybe just a pasture trail."

The tire tracks turning from the county road onto the secondary road were plain to see. Gavin pulled over, wanting a closer look. Like the tracker he was, he knelt on the road and bent to study the tracks. The road itself was narrow and only a dirt center bed. Gavin pointed to the marks.

"There's definitely more than one set of tracks," he told everyone as they gathered in the narrow ditch. "Going both ways, to and from." He looked east down the road. "Question is, where did they go, and how far?"

"Only one way to find out," Primault said. "It's about three miles to that place."

Singer pointed to a structure about a hundred yards to the east, on the north side of the road. "Maybe someone was going there," he said. "Looks like a grain bin."

"We'll see," Primault said.

They drove the hundred yards and parked. Up close the building was larger than it had first appeared and was indeed an old wooden grain bin. The east side of the roof was caved in. They turned their focus on the tire tracks and were mildly surprised to see that they went farther east.

"Let's keep going," Primault said.

"Hey, what's that?" Singer asked, pointing to the west.

All eyes turned and saw a dark truck approaching. After a few seconds of uneasy silence, Primault turned to Gavin. "The good news is it's not a cop," he said, as the truck stopped a few yards from them. A tall man with a wide face under a baseball cap stepped down from the cab. He didn't seem overly anxious to approach. He took a few steps and stopped. Ben Wilson took the initiative and walked up to the man.

"Good morning, sir. How are you?"

"Mornin', young fella. I'm doin' fine, how about yourself?"

"We're good," Wilson said, nodding toward the others behind him. "We're out here doing, ah, doing some testing. These gentlemen are my crew. And who might you be, if I may ask?"

"I'm Karl Young. My place is a bit more to the north," he said, gesturing with his thumb. "And where might you fellas be from?"

Wilson reached in his pocket for his wallet, and from it he pulled out a business card. "Name's Ben Wilson, I work for Wolf Star Security Assessment out of Washington DC. This is my card." He held it out to Young.

"Thank you," Young said, squinting at the card. "Whatcha testing for? You said you were doing tests. Whatcha testing for way out here?"

"Well, sir, I tell you, we—we are testing for…ionized radon."

Primault scratched his chin and glanced sideway at Gavin, who was working hard at keeping a straight face.

"I see. And just what is ionized radon. Don't think I ever heard of it."

"No, no, doesn't surprise me," Wilson went on. "It's a very rare gas. It's—it seeps up out of the ground, usually where there's oil."

"Oh, oh, I see. They been drilling for oil in these parts. I suppose that's why you fellas are here."

"That's exactly why we're here, Mr. Young. You see that old building over there, across the road? Those are the kinds of places we test. Structures like that."

Young lifted his cap, brushed back his thinning hair, and put it back on. "Well, I saw your vehicles and was just wondering who it might be. Don't see too many folks out here," he went on, affably.

"You are the first person we've seen," Wilson said.

Behind him, Gavin, Singer, and Primault were trying to maintain benign expressions.

"Well, I'll leave you to it, then. Pleased to meet you."

They watched Young as he backed his truck to the fence, then cranked his wheels hard right. He turned back onto the trail and drove west, and then south at the county road.

"Ben, what happened to our cover story?" Primault asked, grinning.

"Shoot, I don't know. I couldn't think of it, and I panicked. I had to tell him something."

"Well, ionized radon sounds genuine to me," Gavin said. "It did to Mr. Young, too. The important thing is, he believed you."

"Yeah?" Wilson said. "At least until he asks someone what ionized radon is."

"By then it may not matter," Primault said. "So, let's see if how far those tracks go."

The tracks continued to the turn-off leading to their target house and turned into the overgrown yard hiding an old gravel driveway. Two round aging metal grain bins stood side by side some forty yards from the house. Closer was a dilapidated wooden corral with sagging and fallen rails. Leaving the SUVs at the turn-off, they stepped down and approached through the grass. Primault pointed to the car trail.

"This is damn recent," he said. "Days, maybe. The grass is still matted down."

"And they turn toward the house," Singer said, pointing.

Gavin stopped and looked at the house, now less than twenty yards away. It was like all the others they had so far visited—old and neglected. Flat lumber siding and wooden shingles were dried and aging. Some of the siding sagged or was hanging, exposing rusting nails. Windows were narrow. Everything indicated the 1930s and 1940s era. The one detail that immediately caught their attention was the height of the concrete foundation, suggesting a basement beneath the structure.

Primault held up a hand. "The tracks go up to the house," he said. He turned to Ben Wilson. "We need photos of all this," he said.

Wilson removed the long lens and began snapping away, staying to the side of the tracks. They all moved to the side and slowly proceeded to the house, approaching the northeast corner where a narrow wooden door with faded white paint was obvious. Primault stopped and looked down, bending over. He motioned to the others. "There are footprints here," he said, pointing down. "I think they were very recent."

He stepped aside to let Wilson take close-ups as Singer and Gavin moved within a few feet. Very clearly the prints led to the door.

"There's more than one set of prints," Singer said, bending down to get closer. "These look really fresh." His hand hovered above several obvious smudges in the dust where the grass was sparse.

Primault walked around to avoid the prints and stopped a few feet from the door. "And look here," he said. "There's a padlock and the hasp on the door frame is new. I'll bet that door leads down into a basement."

The padlock was shiny and immediately became the focus of their attention. "The lock and the hasp are the only thing new about this house," Primault said. "I have a feeling someone is storing something here."

"Something they don't want anyone to bother," Singer reasoned.

"Or see," Gavin said.

Wilson took extreme closeups of the padlock and hasps. "Gentlemen," he said, "we have to break that lock. What do we have that can do that?"

"There's got to be a tire wrench of some kind in those vehicles," Gavin said.

While Singer and Primault hurried to the first SUV, Gavin noticed there were no cobwebs around the edges of the door. A detail that sent a small shock through him. Also noticeable was dust on the bottom door sill, suggesting someone had kicked dust going through the door. He could suddenly feel his pulse in his temples.

Singer and Primault returned with an L-shaped lug wrench. Stepping to the door Primault lifted the wrench and slid the flat end behind the hasp, wiggling it and forcing it down as much as he could. After gaining nearly three inches, he pulled on the wrench. The hasp bent slightly, allowing him to wiggle it down another inch. "Jason," he said, "help me. "With two of us pulling, we'll have more force."

They pulled together, straining their arms, shoulders, and backs. CRACK! The screws holding the base plate to the door frame gave way, yielding their tenuous hold on the dry, rotting wood.

Dropping the wrench, Primault grabbed the old doorknob, turned it, and pushed the door inward. The musty smell of old basement wafted out. Singer and Primault pulled out small flashlights and turned them on, aiming them into the darkness.

"Steps leading down," Primault announced. He probed the wooden steps with his light beam.

"Lead on," Gavin said.

Primault stepped across the threshold cautiously and immediately saw the floor of the basement in the circle of his flashlight beam. All heard the slight groan from the slats as he took tentative steps down. From the bottom he called over his shoulder. "It's good, stairs are solid."

He was sweeping his flashlight over the floor and walls of the small room. Without a word he pointed at a corner where the light revealed two cases of bottled water, one stacked on the other. A finger to his lips cautioned everyone to silence. In the opposite corner were two car batteries, with wires leading out from the terminals atop each. The wires were attached to a wall and disappeared around a corner. A shadowy opening was unmistakably the end of a narrow hallway.

Wilson had switched to the video camera. The light from it illuminated the floor and walls as he filmed. Primault held up a hand for silence, and then waved everyone to move down the hallway. Two doors opposite each other came into view, the left one was ajar. Wilson followed Primault as he pushed the door further open and stepped slowly into the room. A quick sweep of lights revealed a mattress, with sheets and a blanket and pillow, boxes in a corner, and a toilet in the other corner, and a large plastic container against a wall. A single bulb in the ceiling was not on. Gavin saw a switch to the right side of the door and flipped it. The bulb filled the room with low light.

Implications and conclusions whirled in their minds; most obvious, was that someone had been in the room, and probably very recently, perhaps no more than hours ago. Singer pointed to a half empty plastic water bottle next to the mattress.

"Let's not touch that," Primault said. "There's fingerprints on it."

Gavin stood over the cardboard boxes. There was no doubt in his mind. The contents of the boxes were food and supplies essential to survival. Food and water. Someone, perhaps more than one person, was in this room for extended periods of time. He spotted the small blue container of tampons. His heart rate increased. There was no doubt now that it was women or girls that had occupied this dank little room. A cold knot of heavy disappointment settled in his gut.

"Look," he said to Primault. "They were kept in here."

Primault stepped to the box and looked down. "Damn! Where did they go?"

"There's another door," Singer said. "On the other side."

With a nod Primault headed for the open door with Gavin and Singer on his heels. Wilson stayed and kept filming. The hallway was narrow, no more than three feet, and the door, like the other, was of thick plywood. A round doorknob looked fairly new and appeared to be brass, and below it was another hasp. But instead of a padlock there was a large metal rod wedged in the U-bolt.

Primault lifted the rod out of the U-bolt and turned the doorknob. With a click it opened as he pushed. A slight scuffling noise reached their ears as they saw another room with the same dim lighting as the other. The air in the room was warm and an indiscernible odor was detectable. Flashlight beams revealed what they had been hoping for, but shocked them, nonetheless.

Six figures were huddled on several mattresses, figures with dark hair, wide, frightened eyes, and brown skin. All the men were struck with how young the faces were. After a few seconds, Primault finally found his voice.

"Ladies," he said, "We're going to take you out of here. We're help to help you."

Silence.

"It's okay," Primault said. "Two of us are cops from the Smokey River Reservation. We're going to take you home."

A tiny, plaintive voice came from the corner. "Are you for real?"

Gavin's elation was shattered because Katherine was not in the group. There were twelve names on Melvina Old Lodge's list, and two had been rescued. Six were here, which meant that four were still elsewhere. And Katherine.

"We are," Primault assured them. "Can you all walk? Is anyone sick or hurt?"

"We're okay," said the same tiny voice. "We can walk."

"Good, good! Let's all go outside, into the light."

There was instantaneous but quiet movement. All six girls came to their feet and went for the door. Gavin and Singer stepped out of the way.

Wilson appeared in the opposite doorway, and his jaw dropped. "Holy shit!" he blurted.

Outside the girls gathered in a small group, collectively holding their hands up to shield their eyes from the bright morning sun. Some of them looked around at the building and the overgrown pastures. Some of them stared unabashedly at their rescuers, a few were smiling slightly. All of them were still on edge, and uncertain.

Primault and Gavin walked to the front of the group. "Ladies," Primault called out. "My name is Justin Primault. I'm a cop from Smokey River, and so is he, Jason Singer," he said, pointing at Singer. "The other gentlemen are Gavin Lone Wolf and Ben Wilson, the guy with the camera. We'll get your names in a minute, but I want to assure you, you're safe now. We're going to take you home."

Soft sobs came from the group, hands went up to mouths and a few embraced one another. And then they cried, softly, into their hands or holding each other. Singer turned away and dabbed at his eyes, and Primault felt the lump in his throat. Wilson didn't bother to raise his camera. This was their moment and he didn't want to intrude. Gavin waited, enjoying the moment. Later, he would have questions.

One of the smaller girls broke from the group and approached Primault, wiping her eyes. She was dressed like all the others in sweatpants, a hoodie top, and sneakers. "How did you find us?" she asked timidly.

"Do you know Melvina Old Lodge?"

She nodded. "Yeah. She was with us and then they took her away."

"She almost made it home, and she had a list of names in her shoe, twelve names. I'm sure it was you girls. What's your name?"

"Lizzie Claremont."

"Where you from, Lizzie?"

"Fort Thompson. Melvina made it home?"

"Ah, not quite." Primault took a deep breath. "She—she died, seven miles from home."

Lizzie brought her hands up, one to her chest and the other to her mouth. Soft sobs made her chest heave slightly. One of the other girls saw her and stepped up to put her arms around her friend's shoulders. "Liz, what's wrong?"

Lizzie wiped her eyes with the heels of her hands. "Melvina. She died."

The other girl turned a shocked expression to Primault, a questioning gaze.

"What's your name, hon?"

"Carrie Little Wolf. What happened to Melvina?"

Gavin, who had been watching and listening, leaned over and spoke softly to Primault. "I think it would be best to tell them all."

Primault nodded and loudly cleared his throat. "Ladies! Ladies!" he called out, raising his voice. The four standing together hurried over to join Lizzie and Carrie, and all turned expectant gazes to Primault. "Lizzie asked me how we found you," he said. "We were looking for you because your names were on a list that Melvina Old Lodge had."

Soft gasps.

"Melvina almost made it home to her Grandma's house. She died in a pasture seven miles from home. We found a list of names in her shoe. She wrote all your names. That's how we found you."

Primault let the news sink in. Within the space of a few minutes the six girls were confronting totally unexpected changes in their circumstances. One minute they were captives with no hope for freedom, and in the next they were walking out of their prison. Now they were learning one of them had died. They were entitled to whatever reaction that came. The four men stood by quietly, respectfully giving them the time and space.

After a minute, Carrie Little Wolf waved a hand at Primault. "Can I ask you something?"

"Sure."

"Where are we?"

Primault glanced at Gavin with an incredulous look on his face. "North Dakota, west of Fort Berthold." he told Carrie.

She nodded, processing the information. "When can we go home?"

"Very soon," he said. "First, we're going to take you to a hospital and have you all checked over. Then we have a few questions. Were the other four girls in the other room?"

Carrie shook her head. "No, there's another place, somewhere. Sometimes they took some of us there. But there was someone in that other room."

"Who?" Primault asked gently.

"I don't know, we couldn't see anyone."

"How do you know someone was there?"

"Someone was pounding on the wall, so we did, too."

Gavin reacted immediately and headed for the door to the basement. Bounding down the steps he rushed into the first room. He was willing to bet any amount of money that Katherine had been here, pounding on the walls.

Singer entered. "What are you looking for?" he asked.

"I don't know. Anything."

Gavin swept his gaze deliberately over the room. The sheet, pillow, and blanket atop the mattress, the half empty bottle of water. In the corner, two boxes of supplies and food. The toilet in the other corner. Newer concrete closed off the room's only window. There had to be something. Some indication. He lifted the mattress to look underneath and saw nothing but bare concrete. Two of the walls were concrete, two were plywood, the same thick, sturdy material as the door. He noticed the inside of the door had no handle.

Something caught his eye, causing his breath to catch in his throat. A word. Big letters on the wall. Smaller letters beneath it. He stepped closer and his face turned warm when he read the words.

PIANO

Soldier Woman

August 22 2018

A cold, heavy disappointment in his gut intensified as he stared at the words. Katherine had been here only two days ago. Her nickname and the date were obvious. But what was Piano?

"I think Wilson should take a picture of that," Singer said.

"Good idea."

Singer left and returned with Wilson while Gavin stood rooted to the floor, staring at the wall. She had been here, in this dank basement. That reality was a cruel tease. Where was she now? Where had she been taken?

Heart pounding, he stepped to one side to let Wilson photograph the wall. A last glance at the words and he hurried out, the letters seared into his mind. Outside Primault was huddled with the girls. Gavin joined them.

"What's the plan?"

"We take them to Fort Yates and come back and check out the last two places. What did you find down there?"

"Wilson's got pictures."

Primault looked at the photos on the camera's screen. "What does it mean?"

"Soldier Woman is Katherine's nickname, and she obviously added the date. What Piano means, I don't know."

"Damn. That means she was here two days ago. She was the one doing the pounding the girls heard." He paused and turned to the group of girls. "Hey, ladies," he said. "Did you ever hear the word Piano while you were here?"

They all shook their heads "no."

"Who brought you here? Do you know?"

They shook their heads or shrugged. "Two guy hauled us around," one of them said. "Tulo and Riley."

"Yeah," affirmed another of the girls. "He'd say 'Listen to Tulo,' or "Don't piss Tulo off. He was kinda mean and smelled bad."

"When was he here last?"

"A couple of days ago. It sounded like he took away whoever was in the other room. Tulo yelled and kicked the door."

"You said there was another place?" Primault asked the question of Carrie Little Wolf. "But you don't know where?"

"Yeah, there's another place, another basement. I don't know where it is."

"Can we leave now?" Lizzie Claremont asked imploringly.

"We can." Primault gestured toward the vehicles on the road and pulled out a notebook and a pen. "Give me your names and then go and climb into the first car," he said. "There's water in the back, if you're thirsty." He gestured at Singer. "Can you go and pull open the third seat?"

"On my way."

A thought worked into Gavin's head as he watched Ben Wilson filming the exterior of the old house. There were three more target sites, and it was reasonable to assume one of them was the other location where the other four girls were hidden, and perhaps Katherine as well. And according to the map they were all probably less than an hour's drive away. Too close to ignore.

"Justin," he said, "I think there's an opportunity here, while you take those girls to Fort Yates."

"You know, I was thinking along those lines, about those other places. You want to go and check them out?"

"Right. I don't think we should waste any time. I can take Ben with me."

"Go for it. Katherine and those other girls have to be at the other place."

Two minutes later both cars were heading back toward the county road. In Primault's SUV, the six girls seemed to be over the initial shock of the sudden, fortuitous sequence of events of the past hour. There was no excited chatter. Instead, every one of them was looking wide-eyed at the prairies that lay bright all around them. A cold realization hit Primault. It was very likely that none of them had seen daylight for a long time, perhaps months.

Twenty some minutes later they were near the county road. Primault, grabbing the walkie-talkie called to Gavin. "Hey, Gavin. Let's chat a minute before you peel off."

Two squawks came back over the walkie-talkie, an "Affirmative" response.

They pulled off to the shoulder of the county road. "Ladies, I'll be back," Primault said, stepping down.

He smiled at the waves and walked to meet Gavin and Wilson.

"Hey," said one of the girls to Singer. "Can you turn on some tunes?"

"Sure." He turned on the ignition and then the radio and turned the tuning knob until he found a radio station, then said. "How about one of you do it? I don't know what you like."

"Anything," said one of them, leaning forward between the front seats. In a few seconds she found rock and roll music.

"So, is this North Dakota?" came a question.

"Yeah," Singer replied. "Western North Dakota."

"Looks like home."

Gavin, Primault, and Wilson met in the ditch next to the first SUV, joined a few seconds later by Singer.

"How are they?" Gavin asked.

"They're listening to music on the radio," Singer said. "They're talking and acting like young girls. Almost as if nothing had happened."

"It's not even been an hour since we found them," Primault said. "There's a lot for them to absorb. I'm guessing there's a certain amount of denial. I'm afraid after a while all the crap they've been through, all they've been subjected to, might come crashing down on them. Just going home isn't going to negate all that."

"At least they're out of that goddamn room and out of the clutches of whoever the fuck put them there," Ben Wilson said angrily. The sudden show of emotion surprised his companions.

"We achieved a big win," Primault said, "but it isn't over." He turned to Gavin. "I have a feeling you'll find the other girls and Katherine."

'I think you're right," Gavin concurred. "Whatever happens I'll use the phone and call you. Service out here doesn't seem too bad. Have you thought about what exactly is going to happen after doctors check them out? There's six girls there, and probably more, if our luck holds. Might be a good idea to talk to a mental health counselor at that hospital, if there is one on staff."

"Yeah, there is one. A woman. She talked to Maggie Henry and Julia Lake. She sat in when Audrey Hinson and Madonna White Bear took their statements."

"Good, if and when we find the others, we'll take them there directly."

"We'll wait to hear from you. Good luck." Primault reached out and offered his hand to Gavin, then Ben Wilson. "My guess is it'll be the same kind of set up."

Gavin and Wilson waved back at the girls as Primault and Singer drove past. Moments later they had the map open on the hood. Since the next three sites were already marked, Gavin found their current location and then picked the roads that would take them to the nearest one.

"We go there first. If there's nothing there, then on to the next closest," he said.

"Of course. Doesn't look that far."

"Probably about fifteen miles," Gavin estimated.

"They've got to be there. When Gerard told me about this situation, he also told me about your fiancée and emailed me a photo of her. He was broken up about it, and I can't imagine how you're feeling. I'm glad I could lend a hand."

"I appreciate it, Ben. My brother and I have always been close, as twins usually are. Did he tell you his wife died, about twelve years ago?"

Wilson was surprised. "No. No, he didn't."

"Yeah, her name was Marilyn. She was an Oglala, from a little town called Kyle. Ovarian cancer. I know he still mourns."

"Damn. I wondered why he was single, I mean, a guy like him. Well, we just don't know which way life will take us, do we?"

"No, we don't."

"I'm really glad we found those girls, and we'll find the others and your fiancée." He looked down at the map and pointed to the three sites circled in read. "They're there, in one of those places."

Gavin nodded and swept a long gaze over the prairie stretching out in every direction. Occasional thickets or small stands of trees dotted the landscape. An ordinary day with a few clouds in the west and a soft breeze. Bird calls floated from several directions, punctuated by the strident bark of prairie dogs. Anticipation swelled in his chest as he rolled up the map. "Right," he said. "Let's get going."

THIRTY-TWO

Someone unlocked the cuffs and removed them from Kathleen's wrists, but the hood stayed over her head. A door closed with a click, and then silence. Katherine stood for a moment before she reached up and pulled off the hood. She was in a large comfortably furnished bedroom. Another basement, this one with a smooth cement block outer wall painted a pastel blue. She stood unmoving, listening for sounds. It was unnervingly quiet.

The accommodations had definitely improved but she knew the door was locked. After a moment she walked to it and slowly reached for the knob, carefully, cautiously wrapping her fingers around it. It turned but didn't open. There was no doubt in her mind that there was a significant impediment on the other side of the door.

She turned around and slowly scanned the room. A round, white convex light fixture was in the middle of the ceiling; on at the moment. Two narrow nightstands stood on either side of the double bed, which was covered in a dark blue comforter. A small blue ceramic lamp was atop each stand. Blue was definitely the color scheme. A narrow, vertical glass-block window was in the middle of the cement block wall. Too narrow for her to squeeze through. In the far corner opposite the bed was a narrow door, which had to be a closet. Another door was at the other corner, to the left of the entrance door. Katherine walked to it cautiously and peeked in. It was a bathroom with a commode, a sink, and a bathtub/shower combination, all decorated in blue. Even the towels. She turned the handle on the faucet on the sink and water came out.

Switching on the light, she glanced at herself in the mirror. She looked tired and lost. With a sigh she adjusted the water flow and waited until it was warm, then she leaned down and washed her face, squeezing soap from the dispenser on the sink. Patting her face dry with the hand towel, she reached up and opened the cabinet and was not surprised to see a hairbrush, a comb, a new tube of toothpaste, and a toothbrush still in a plastic case.

All the comforts of home. But she couldn't ignore her growing sense of apprehension that this was more like going from the frying pan into the fire.

Turning on the cold tap she cupped her hands and drank. Hunger gnawed slightly after more than ten hours or so of not eating. But hydration was more important. Back at the bed she sat at the foot. A sense of helplessness surged. She was a prisoner. There was nothing she could do, at least nothing came to mind. Waiting was all there was. Waiting to see who would come through the door. Waiting for whatever would happen next. She stood suddenly, walked to the bathroom and grabbed the hairbrush from the medicine cabinet. Back on the bed she removed the ties holding her hair and began to brush it.

For one thing she was grateful: she had not been abused. Except for being shoved and jerked, and folded into the trunk of two cars, nothing else had happened. But there was a constant fear. She couldn't fathom why her abductor had taken her, but lust and entitlement likely were factors. Whatever had prevented him from acting out on his impulse any further to coerce sex or physically abuse her was a mystery, and a blessing. She prayed her luck would hold.

Katherine was a realist, however. Perhaps it was merely a matter of time and opportunity. Self-defense courses had taught her a lot, but they were not an absolute deterrent. Men were bigger and stronger on the average. And every man who raped a woman was compelled more by anger, hate, revenge, or a sense of entitlement than by lust. At this moment, in this room, she was at the mercy of all of those factors. A shiver went up her back.

She had never faced anything remotely like this. Gavin had been the only serious relationship in her life. Over the past ten years love or sex had not been a priority, though she had dated. Her job and career and the cause she had dedicated herself to was extremely fulfilling, to the point that it overwhelmed everything in her life. And though it did dangerously weaken family and cultural ties, and repressed feelings for Gavin, her friend Karin had made her realize that she had been on the wrong path.

One thing was certain. Anyone who came through that door intending harm or to take anything she didn't want to give would face resistance. She would fight. That much she could control.

THIRTY-THREE

Alone hawk prowled the sky over the eastern horizon and a slow moving breeze teased the tall grass into a lazy dance on both sides of the narrow dirt road. The air was becoming warmer under the bright sun. Gavin only marginally noted these things as he stood in front of the SUV with the phone up to his ear.

"I'm on the way to the next two places," he said. "Primault and Singer are taking six girls to the hospital in Fort Yates."

"*He lila waste yelo!* (That is very good)," Andrew No Horn said, on the other end. "That leaves four from Melvina's list."

"And Katherine. And she was there, where we found the girls, but in a separate room."

"How do you know that?"

"She wrote her name and the date on the wall. She was there two days ago."

"Do you think she could be where the other girls are?"

Gavin watched the hawk soaring closer to the horizon, becoming a smaller and smaller speck. "No, I don't think so. I have a feeling she was taken elsewhere."

"Why?"

"She wrote a word on the wall above her name, Piano. It could be either a place or a person. Whatever it is, it means something. She had a reason to write it."

"Damn. Figure that out and you might know where to look. But I never heard of any place named Piano. I was up there on and around the reservation about forty years ago, surveying for the government when they were bringing in that dam," Andrew said. "I can't remember seeing that name on any map. No county or no town anyway."

"Then it might be a person's name."

"You're going to find her, *Tunska*. Maybe not today, but you will find her."

"Thanks, *Leksi*. I just wanted to let you know about those girls. I'll try to call you later, whatever we find. Tell Gerard."

"*Ohan, hecamu kte* (Yes, I will do that)."

Gavin put the phone in his pocket and looked down at the road. There was one sign that was hard to miss: tire tracks, more than one set. And the tracks were pointing in the direction of the next place on the map.

Anxiety and frustration pressed in as he stared at the tire tracks. They were very recent. Most of the tread marks had not yet been disturbed by the breeze, and they clearly hadn't been made by a farm implement such as a tractor. One set of tracks could be by someone lost or simply exploring. Two sets of tracks implied, perhaps, that someone was frequently using an all but abandoned road.

A memory flashed into his mind of a similar ancient road in the Gornoi-Altai Mountains of Siberia that led to a small village where an old girlfriend was held hostage. He had been determined to find her—Natalya Simmons—and pay the ransom for her release, a ransom put up by her husband, Charles Whitehead. Whitehead had played on Gavin's feelings for Natalya to induce him to help. Though he had been extremely concerned about Natalya's welfare, there was no emotional connection other than concern for her safety. Such was not the case here. Deep inside he was terrified. Although encouraged by his uncle's confidence, there was no guaranteed outcome. And he tried not to think of what abuse Kathrine might have suffered since she had been abducted. He prayed she was unharmed.

He was on the right trail and sensed she was close. But close wasn't the same as seeing her and touching her and knowing she was safe. He sighed deeply. There was only one thing to do. Follow the trail.

He rejoined Ben Wilson in the SUV. "We're close now," he said. "About two miles, maybe."

"Then let's do it," Wilson said, resolutely.

After two miles, the tire tracks on the old road bent right at an old gate flanked by two tall posts with a cross-member. The posts were gray and cracked and the cross- member sagged. Two parallel lines of flattened grass led to a perfectly square house with tan asphalt shingle siding. Like the other places, there were outbuildings—an old barn and two smaller sheds grayed by age, any paint long since obliterated by the elements. There were still segments of an old picket fence around the house, stubbornly resisting rot and gravity.

Immediately discernible were smudges in the dirt indicating footprints. Gavin and Wilson followed them to the south side of the house to a wooden storm door into the basement. A padlock was on the large metal hasp. Ben Wilson retrieved the tire iron from the SUV. Wedging it behind the hasp they pried upward until the screws were torn from the wood. Throwing open the doors revealed wooden steps down to another door in the wall of the basement, which didn't appear to be locked. Just to the left of it were two car batteries, with wires attached to the posts.

"Just like the other place," Wilson commented.

"Right. The storm door was padlocked so that means someone is in there," Gavin said. Carefully climbing down the steps, they noticed the doorknob was new. Turning it, Gavin pushed open the door, and heard softs gasps and furtive shuffling.

It took a moment for their eyes to adjust to the low light. "Ladies," he said, "it's okay, you're safe. We're here to take you out of here."

Silence.

Wilson stepped into the room, as four pairs of dark eyes stared back—wary, disbelieving eyes. Four figures were huddled together in the corner. Gavin's heart sank. Only four. He cleared his throat.

"My name is Gavin Lone Wolf. I'm from Smokey River. This is my friend Ben Wilson. We're here to take you home."

A small voice rose from the huddle. "For reals?"

"Yes, for reals. Come on. Let's go."

Apprehension still clearly on their faces, the girls stood and stepped forward, still clinging to one another as they crossed the room. Gavin and Wilson stepped aside to let them through. Once past the door they scrambled up the steps in mere seconds.

"I'm going up," Gavin said. "Can you take pictures?"

"I sure as hell will."

Gavin rushed up the steps to join the girls standing together and squinting from the bright sun. All of them with the "deer in the headlights" look.

"Listen, listen," he said, "it's okay, you're safe now, and I've got a lot to tell you."

Like the others, they were all dressed in sweatpants, hoodies, and sneakers, and looked utterly small and child-like.

"What are your names?" he asked.

The first reply came after a few moments. "Neva Baxter."

"Millie Rousseaux."

"Ann No Horse."

"Sarah Hall."

"Thanks. About two hours ago we found six other girls, about ten miles from here. They're okay."

"You did?"

"Yes, we did. Right now, they're on their way to the hospital in Fort Yates, and that's where we're going to take you, so doctors can have a look at you."

They all nodded, processing the news, still huddled together, casting furtive glances around.

"How did you find us?"

"All of your names were on a list found on Melvina Old Lodge."

A few gasps.

"Found? What does that mean?"

Gavin was pinned by the wide eyes gazing at him, puzzled eyes. "About three weeks ago Melvina made it home."

More gasps.

"She was found just a few miles from her grandma's place at Smokey River."

"Was she okay?"

"No, she died."

Louder gasps, all eyes now filling with tears, still fixed on Gavin.

"She had a list of all your names in her shoe, and the name of the town, Pinnacle. That's how we knew where to look."

Millie Rousseaux, the tallest of the group, wiped her eyes. "She saved us. Melvina saved us," she said, on the verge of sobbing.

"Yes, she did."

"Do our folks know you were looking for us," Sarah Hall asked.

"No, we don't know who your folks are."

"Can we tell them, now?" she said.

"Yes, you can do that, we'll help you do that as soon as we can." Gavin pointed at the SUV. "See that Suburban over there? Let's go over there, there's water and snacks. As soon as Ben finishes taking pictures and filming, we will leave."

They were close on his heels as he turned and walked toward the SUV, still keeping in a tight group. At the back of the car Gavin opened the window and tailgate and slid out the cases of water and small boxes of snacks and passed them all around. Then he climbed in through the rear passenger door and flipped up the third seat.

"Okay, ladies," he said. "Anytime you want to get in."

"Can we wait?" one of them asked. "It's nice here in the sun."

"Um, what did you say your name was again?" said another, with especially large eyes.

"Gavin Lone Wolf."

She stepped forward and hugged him around the waist. "Thanks," she said, softly. "Thanks for finding us."

As if on signal the other three stepped up and joined the embrace, to the side and one of them from behind. After a moment Gavin put his arms around as many as he could.

"You are welcome," he said, choking back a sob as the girls quietly wept.

He marveled at their courage. After being controlled and undoubtedly unspeakably abused by men, their innocence had won—at least for the moment—enabling them to push past fears. Gavin would never forget this moment, accepting it and allowing it to go on as long as they chose. One by one they pulled away.

"Thank you, ladies," he said.

Still in a tight group, they looked around at the landscape and up into the sky. The wariness in their eyes began to fade. "We knew it wasn't Tulo at the door," one of them said, squinting up at Gavin. It was the second time he had heard that name.

"How did you know?"

"He only comes at night."

"Oh. How did you know it was daytime?"

Another spoke up. "Daylight comes in through a crack in the door. We could tell when the sun is out."

"If it's not cloudy," another said.

"What about Piano? Did you hear that name?"

They shook their heads "no."

Gavin saw Ben Wilson approaching with the video camera up, apparently recording the moment. He stopped next to Gavin. "Hello," he said, "I'm Ben."

Still standing together, they smiled and waved politely.

"Okay," Gavin said. "Let's get on the road."

Every one of them was enthralled by the passing landscape, as if seeing it for the first time.

They eventually came back to a county road and Gavin pulled over to dial Primault's number.

"What's the news?" Primault answered.

"We have four very courageous young ladies, all anxious to go home," Gavin reported.

"Damn! Great news! I assume you're all on your way here?"

"Affirmative."

"What about Katherine?"

"No. She was obviously taken elsewhere. As soon as we have all the girls squared away, we'll get on that trail."

"Right," Primault agreed. "A lot to be thankful for. We found all the girls on Melvina's list."

"That's a miracle in itself."

Gavin's next call was to Gerard, and he reported the day's events for the second time, including the words scrawled on the wall by Katherine.

"Uncle Andrew told me," he said. "I think Piano is a person. We looked on the map of North Dakota and couldn't find a town by that name. Trouble is we don't know if it's a patronymic or a first name. Maybe it's a nickname."

"I'm considering all of that."

"Did you ask those girls?"

"Yes. None of them know that name."

"Well, tell you what, it might be a long shot, but I'll get one of my people back in DC to check into it. He has a friend who works for the FBI so maybe he can ask her to check for that name in their data bank of felons."

"Great. It's worth a shot."

Gavin drove in contemplative silence after he finished the call, suddenly aware that conversations were occurring in the rear seats. At first just comments, as lone trees and farm implements or stacks of baled hay were pointed out. Finally, someone from the rear most seat asked, "What day is it?"

"Thursday," Ben Wilson told her.

"I mean the date."

"Oh, August 28."

"Ahh!" A squeal erupted from the middle seat. "No way! It's my birthday!"

More squeals of delight erupted. "Happy birthday, Neva!"

Spontaneous applause followed the squeals, lasting for nearly a minute. Then a low, soft voice spoke clearly.

"It's all of our birthdays."

"What do you mean?"

"Because today we're born again to the rest of our lives."

Gavin glanced in the rear view mirror and caught thoughtful expressions on the faces he could see.

"I thought being born again was a Jesus thing," an especially youngish voice said.

"Nah. That's them preachers on TV. I mean—like—when I get home I'm never going to argue with my mom again."

"Oh, yeah. Yeah, I'm going to be nice to my big brother."

Gavin caught Ben Wilson's side glance and smiled as they both listened to the conversations growing more animated and cheerful.

"Yeah, but I'm sad about Melvina," one of them said.

Several "me, too's" followed, and then a heavy silence.

"And Julia and Mollie. They never came back. I wonder what happened to them."

Gavin cleared his throat. "Hey, not to worry," he said. "Julia and Mollie are at home with their families. They were found last week."

"Oh, my god! Really?"

"Absolutely!" Gavin assured them.

Murmurs of joy prevailed for nearly a minute, and as it faded, a voice from the far back added, "That means we all made it out. All of us, except for Melvina."

Silence descended as each of the girls retreated into their own thoughts. No one spoke for several minutes. Ben Wilson glanced back but Gavin caught his attention and shook his head "no." He felt they were working their way through the swirl of feelings coming at them from every direction. Sometimes no interference was a good thing.

Once on a paved road, Gavin stopped the car at a small convenience store gas station.

"Ladies," he said, "give me a minute and I'll be right back."

He saw the sign in the window—ATM Inside—and immediately looked for it as he stepped inside. Crossing to it he inserted his card and got out cash, all twenty dollar bills. He nodded at the clerk behind the counter and quickly decided that the store seemed well stocked enough for what he had in mind, including a Restrooms sign in a corner.

He opened the rear passenger door. "Ladies," he said, "I thought you might need to take a break. It's a few hours to Fort Yates. So, here's a little money to get whatever you might need or want." He handed out the bills to the girls as they stepped down from the car. "Take your time," he went on.

"Could you come in with us?" one of them said.

"Sure, sure. We'll be right behind you."

Gavin and Ben Wilson stood near the front counter, making sure they were in plain sight for the girls, who used the restroom one by one and then shopped. After a few minutes they lined up at the counter to pay. Water and a variety of snacks were the popular choices, with lip balm and tissue as well.

The clerk, a middle-aged white woman, was obviously curious about the carload of girls who suddenly appeared. Gavin was glad that she politely waited on them. "We're on our way to Fort Yates," he said.

Three girls waited at the door for the fourth to finish the transaction, and then all exited as a group. Outside, one of them held out the change from her purchase to Gavin.

"Oh, no," he said. "That's yours."

She smiled. "Thanks!"

As they began driving east on the paved road, one of them leaned forward and looked at Gavin. "Gavin," she said, "are you married?"

"No," he said. "I'm not."

"Do you have a girlfriend?" A stab of sadness caught him unawares.

"Yes, I do."

"What's her name? Where's she from?"

"Her name is Katherine Hill and she's from Smokey River, too."

"Are you going to marry her?"

"Yes."

"Good. That's good."

Gavin sighed, trying not to yield to the dark shadow of sadness looming over him.

"Can we come to your wedding?" came the question. Another stab of sadness.

He glanced in the mirror and caught a couple of girlish smiles. "Absolutely," he said. "You're all invited."

Soft giggles and then quiet, as they came up behind a slow moving fertilizer with its four over-sized tires. After passing it and getting up to the speed limit, Gavin considered what to do after he and Wilson delivered the girls to the hospital. That he would keep looking was a given but he was at a loss about the next step. There was the one clue—Piano.

Perhaps Gerard's assistant would come up with possibilities. Perhaps another clue or an answer was on or in a piano. He dismissed the thought immediately. He had a persistent sense was that it was a person.

Finding all twelve girls on Melvina Old Lodge's list was a miracle, against all odds. He would find Katherine, too, no matter how long it took or how far he had to go.

THIRTY-FOUR

Katherine awoke with a start, immediately alert. A scant two seconds later the awareness of her predicament came crashing back. Relief came with a glance at the door. The nightstand and lamp she had placed in front of it were still there, undisturbed. It was an alarm she had devised to warn of an intruder. Anyone pushing open the door would bump the table and topple the lamp, making enough noise to wake her—she hoped.

The light from the bathroom was on as she had left it, with the bathroom door slightly ajar. There was no way of knowing the time.

Rising, she sat for a minute before she switched on the lamp on the other nightstand. After another minute she went to the bathroom and washed her face. Hunger pangs twitched. Drinking from the faucet, she patted her face dry with the hand towel and went back to the bed. A shower would be nice but she was leery of someone barging in, and she slept fully clothed.

In spite of her anxiety, she felt rested. She found the switch next to the door and turned on the overhead light, bathing the room in brightness. Standing at the foot of the bed she once again visually surveyed the room, looking for any crack, any hole, anything that she could exploit to facilitate an escape. There had to be something, and yet she knew the chances were infinitesimally small. The weak spot was the door, though she guessed it had some type of substantial lock on the outside, or there was a guard.

She had to escape, or try. She knew Gavin was looking for her. That was a fact. She needed to contact him, somehow. A text message would be the best way. For that she obviously needed a cell phone. But if she had a phone in her hand now, what could she tell him? Nothing useful. She didn't know where she was. She had to somehow learn where she was, and then escape.

A tiny sound came from the ceiling, a little like a birdcall. It faded quickly, then came again. Rising slowly, she took careful steps to the door. The sound became a little louder, but not distinct. It seemed to be coming from the bathroom, continuing, a bit louder, as she eased into the bathroom. Turning her head from side to side, she tried to gauge the direction of the sound. It was coming from the ceiling from the vent in the wall above the shower. She leaned closer, and gasped. It was music. A waltz, played on a piano.

THIRTY-FIVE

Primault and Singer had arrived at the Fort Yates Indian Health Service Hospital two hours ahead of Gavin and Ben Wilson. The first dilemma was explaining to the hospital staff the sudden arrival of six teenage girls. After a long and intense conversation with the service unit director and a phone call from Chief Ben Avery, most of the confusion had been cleared up by the time Gavin arrived with four more girls. Luckily one of the doctors had examined Julia Lake and Maggie Henry the week before. Understandably, ten girls having been rescued from sex trafficking was a difficult story to hear. Once that was known and understood by the nurses and doctors attending to the girls, the process went fairly smoothly. Adding to the intrigue was Lieutenant Primault and Chief Avery's insistence that the news be kept under wraps.

The second dilemma was accommodations for ten girls after they had been seen by doctors. Gavin solved that issue by buying rooms at the casino hotel north of Ft. Yates. Although a few eyebrows were raised at the sight of ten girls chaperoned, apparently, by four men. After some skillful negotiating, Gavin arranged for the cafeteria to deliver meals to the girls to eat in their rooms. They did so while watching television, and all insisted that their rescuers eat with them. So, fourteen people were crowded into two adjoining rooms. Interestingly, however, there was not a lot of frivolous noise, only quiet conversations with a fair amount of channel surfing. Consequently, the hour was late by the time the young ladies turned in and the men were able to retire to their own rooms. Before calling it a night, they gathered in Gavin's room.

"This is a day I'll never forget," said Singer.

"Amen to that," chimed in Ben Wilson. "I can't imagine how their families feel. Ecstatic, probably."

"Yeah," Singer said. "I couldn't help but overhear some of the phone calls they made home, from the hospital. Those girls were comforting their moms and dads, and whoever else. It was amazing."

"Whatever doesn't kill you will make you stronger," Primault said. "They're all tough, they had to be. I think it's in the DNA of indigenous women.

"I listened to them talking," said Wilson. "The four girls in our vehicle. None of them said a word about what happened, about what they went through."

"That's understandable," Gavin said. "Talking about it is remembering."

"My instincts as a cop tell me to talk to them," Primault pointed out. "Get them to tell me what they want, what they can. That means they relive it all, to describe what happened. Julia Lake and Maggie Henry told horrific stories. Still, they couldn't name names or visually identify anyone. Obviously they saw the men they were forced to have sex with, but they didn't know their names. The only names they heard were Tulo and Riley. They were the ones who transported them from the houses to the camp. Their shoes were taken away and their heads covered each time. These girls won't be able to tell any more than that."

"What's the plan now?" Singer asked.

"The Chief is having our social service people contact their counterparts from other tribal social service programs. He's asking for counselors and transportation to come and take the girls home. As much as we need to investigate and prosecute, there are a few obstacles, jurisdiction among them. We think the best thing is to reunite them with their families and impress upon them that, at some point, we do need to talk to them."

"They're not liable to forget," Gavin said, "and at some point maybe they'll be ready to talk. But because they can't or won't be able to forget, they'll need help. They suffered physically, emotionally, and mentally, and some wounds may heal sooner but some will take longer. Some may never heal."

"Who did this to them?" Singer asked. "I mean, who's behind it? There has to be a mastermind of some kind, maybe more than one."

"We may never know," Primault concluded. "However, our job isn't done. Katherine Hill is still missing. That's what we concentrate our efforts on next. Does anyone have any thoughts?"

"I think she left us a clue," Gavin said. "Ben has a photo of it. She wrote her name, the date, and the word *Piano* on the wall of the room she was in."

Ben Wilson turned on his camera and brought up the photograph and showed it to Primault.

"I don't think it's a place name," Gavin went on. "My brother is having one of his people working on it to come up with probabilities. I think it is a person's name. If there is a place by that name in North Dakota, it's not on the road map."

"We should search for that name and assume it could be either a first or a last name," Primault said. "What do you want to do as far as further searching?"

"We need to have a good idea of what to do next, otherwise we'll just be spinning our wheels. I do need to get back to Bismarck and settle up on the airplane rental and return one of the SUVs. After that, I was thinking of going back to the house where I know Katherine was. There may be something else there that we missed."

"Okay. I'll call the chief later tonight or first thing tomorrow," Primault said. "Singer and I can join you once the transportation for the girls arrives."

Anxiety, frustration, and worry kept sleep at bay for Gavin. A shower failed to calm his nerves. In bed he tried to consciously relax, taking deep breaths for several minutes and letting his body rest, but he couldn't slow the onslaught of thoughts and images of Katherine imprisoned and at someone's mercy. Perhaps by someone named Piano. Sleep came eventually and mercifully calmed his mind.

He went down to the cafeteria as soon as it opened, not surprised to see Primault, Singer, and Wilson a minute behind him. All of the girls came down in a group. The men pulled several tables together and waited for the girls to go through the cafeteria line and joined them.

Other hotel guests straggled in, but for the most part they and the girls were the only diners for nearly an hour. At Primault's suggestion, the four men sat among the girls, and not at one end of the table. Conversation began sporadically, though it was light-hearted and mostly about what had been on television, and grew steadily as the hour wore on. Two women counselors who had arrived late the night before came and introduced themselves to the group. They were from different reservations, and obviously thrilled to see the girls.

Gavin invited the girls to shop in the hotel's small gift shop and arranged for their purchases to be charged to his credit card. Later, the girls gathered in a lounge with Ben Wilson who took the time to photograph each of them individually and took nearly half an hour of video film as well, while Gavin, Singer and Primault met with the counselors. Before the day was over, other resource and mental health professionals would arrive to transport the girls home. Word was received that two families were on the way.

Eventually the girls were informed of the plans. As anxious as he was to get on his way, Gavin decided to wait and make sure each girl had a secure and safe ride home. He and Primault, Singer, and Wilson passed the time mingling and visiting with them in the lounge area. A few other guests, and some hotel employees, were mildly curious about the ten girls. Someone asked if they were a softball team.

By mid-afternoon two families had arrived and were joyously and tearfully reunited with their daughters. Primault, Singer, and the counselors met with each family before they departed for home, advising them of counseling options and necessary interviews with police.

Lilian St. John and Eugene and Nadine Little Wolf met with Primault in a quiet room away from the lobby. He was about to spoil their happiness at reuniting with their daughters with a cold, hard dose of reality. But he owed it to the girls, and it was their welfare he cared about most.

"Three things I want to say, because your daughters are going to need you to help them learn to cope with the trauma they've experienced," he began. "First, please don't blame your daughters for what happened to them. Victims—and that's what they are—often feel guilty and blame themselves. Don't let them do that. Second, they were locked in a small room, and then taken with their hands tied and a hood over their heads and were forced into sex with strange men. Please take them to a doctor—preferably a woman doctor—and have them thoroughly examined for any injury or disease. Third, be patient with them. They will likely act out in ways they haven't before, and they'll probably have bad dreams. It's called post traumatic stress. Get counseling for them."

Their initial reaction was stunned silence. Then grief, shock, and anger. All of them dabbed at tears, nodding as they continued to absorb all that they had just heard.

Lilian St. John was the first to speak. "Thank you for rescuing my daughter, and all of them. I will do everything I can for my girl."

Eugene and Nadine Little Wolf nodded in agreement. "Yes, thank you," Eugene said. "I don't care what it takes, we're going to help our daughter. I never thought we'd see her again, ever. So, thank you."

Before the group said goodbye to Winnifred St. John and Carrie Little Wolf, Primault spoke to them.

"When you get home, take care of yourselves, help take care of your families. Teach your little sisters to be careful. Don't give up on anything, especially yourselves. Do your best to be happy because you're all beautiful when you smile. You'll always be special to me, to Jason, Gavin, and Ben. And if there is ever anything I can do for you, let me know."

Winnifred and Carrie hugged each of their rescuers, whispered a last tearful "Thank you," and waved back at everyone as they walked away with their families. By early afternoon all other transportation arrangements were in place, and the other eight girls said their goodbyes to the four men. After many long hugs and wistful smiles, they boarded two vans and were down the driveway and out of sight in a few seconds.

But not out of mind.

"I'm never going to forget them," Ben Wilson said. "I'm going to make it my business to send good thoughts their way."

"They're all going to need every bit of it," Primault said. "The first miracle was finding them. The next one we need is for them to all find peace. But, we have some unfinished business."

He turned to Gavin. "Chief Avery has given the green light for Jason and me to help you in any way we can."

"I appreciate that, Justin. As I said, I want to go back to the room Katherine was kept in. But first I think we should get a vehicle more conducive to back country driving. We turn in the Suburbans for a Jeep. For that we need to go back to Bismarck; also I need to settle up for the plane rental. Then we'll gear up and get whatever supplies we might need. All as quickly as we can. We're checked out here, so good to go."

As the two Suburbans came to the stop sign at the end of the hotel driveway, a large red-tail hawk swooped down and gracefully landed on a fence post on the other side of the road, and for a moment kept its wings outstretched.

"Damn. That's a beautiful bird," Wilson said. "Quite a wingspread."

"The females are usually larger than the males," Gavin said. "That one is as big as I've ever seen."

A moment later she lifted into the air, rising quickly on powerful wings. They watched for several moments as it flew to the northwest in a straight line from their visual vantage point.

THIRTY-SIX

Three and a half hours later, Gavin signed a new contract at the car rental agency and drove away in a Jeep Rubicon. Though not as roomy as the Suburban, it was ideally suited to rough back country terrain in the event their upcoming search for Katherine led them to unpaved roads or no roads at all. The police cruiser was waiting for Primault and Singer at the hotel parking lot, where it had been stored.

After dropping his three companions at the hotel, Gavin hurried to the air charter service at the airport before the front office closed. Rona had left for the day, but Brad Coleman was able to help Gavin. As he stood at the counter waiting for the contract to slide out of the printer, he idly perused the photographs on a wall to the left. Most of them were photographs of student pilots posing next to planes after their first solos, some were the obligatory shots of politicians or notables who had used their service. In the top row of photos, Gavin noticed one of a helicopter lifting a large, flat load encased in what appeared to be a wooden crate.

"You apparently have at least one helicopter," he commented, pointing at the photo.

Coleman glanced up. "Actually, we have two," he said. "Both six passenger models, but that one had to fill a unique request to haul a piano."

"A truck wasn't good enough for someone?"

"Several winters ago we retrieved it from a truck that had slid off the road and then flew it to a ranch."

Gavin nodded. "Really? You said it was a unique request, did you do that kind of transporting on other occasions?"

"No, just that baby grand piano."

As Gavin turned away from the wall of photographs, an image popped into his mind; the word that Katherine had written on the wall. Piano. He stared at the photograph. "Where did you take that piano?" he asked. "Do you remember?"

"I sure do," Coleman said. "Just north of Medora. I flew the chopper. We took the load to a ranch on the edge of the Badlands, north of Teddy Roosevelt National Park."

Something prodded at Gavin. "By any chance, do you remember the coordinates?"

"Not offhand, but it's probably on record somewhere in our documents."

"Uh, you may find this strange, but can you find them for me?"

Coleman took pages from the printer, looking amused at Gavin's request. "Ah, sure, just give me a couple minutes. Everything is on the computers now, and I'm not the most skillful when it comes to using one." He folded the pages, handed them to Gavin, and stepped to the keyboard. Mumbling under his breath as he typed, he finally smiled and nodded. "Okay, here are coordinates and a Google photograph." He turned the screen for Gavin to see.

A large log house with a fenced yard and an even larger barn nearby were the most obvious images in the photograph. Something in the upper right also caught Gavin's attention as he wrote down the coordinates on a sticky note. "What is that?" he asked, pointing to what looked like a road. "Is that an airstrip?"

"That's exactly what it is," Coleman said. "The best grass strip I've ever seen."

"Must be a profitable operation," Gavin commented.

"The previous owners ran a large cow-calf operation, and then sold off most of it. The current owner is some company out of Colorado."

"So, you don't know who paid for that charter?"

"As I recall it was charged to a corporate credit card. Hanrich Group."

"Can you print that screen for me?"

A quizzical look flashed over Coleman's face. "Sure," he said affably.

Twenty minutes later Gavin, Primault, Wilson, and Singer sat down to supper in the hotel restaurant. Gavin took out the printed photograph he had folded and placed in his back pocket. Up until that moment he had wrestled with himself over the astronomical odds that it might be connected to Katherine. He had not come to a conclusion, but neither was he ready to dismiss the possibility.

"I found an interesting bit of information, just totally out of the blue," he said to Primault. Unfolding the page, he handed it over.

Primault gazed at the photograph. "Looks like a satellite photo. A damn nice looking log house. Are you thinking of buying a property?"

A smile played on Gavin's face. "No. The air charter service airlifted a piano by helicopter to that place."

Primault, Singer, and Wilson wore blank expressions.

"Brad Coleman, the pilot, says it was west of here, which means it's south of where we found the girls."

Realization flashed into Primault's eyes. "A piano! The word on the wall. So, you're thinking there's some connection?"

"I'm not sure. The odds are probably against it, but my gut tells me not to dismiss it."

Primault nodded emphatically. "I agree with your gut. We should find out as soon as possible if there is. Why not? At least make damn sure there isn't. What is that place?"

"It was a ranch, but from what the pilot told me, it may not be any longer. May be just a weekender for some rich people from Colorado. That upper area in the photo is the end of an airstrip."

"Well," Primault said, "we should find out exactly where it is and check it out."

"Are those coordinates on the map?" Wilson asked. "If so, I can put them into on an app I have on my phone."

"Yeah, they are," Gavin said.

Less than a minute later, Wilson found it. "It is just north of Theodore Roosevelt National Park, south unit," he said. "The nearest town is Medora, to the south."

"I've been to Medora," Gavin said. "A tourist town, along Interstate 94. It's a few hours drive."

"I'll get online and see what's there," Wilson offered.

"We should head out first thing in the morning," Primault said.

Gavin stared down into his coffee. "Well, at the very least we should maybe sleep on it. When it comes down to it, there's no logic here. What possible connection could there be between a piano being flown to that ranch and a word scrawled on a wall? I'd hate to waste precious time chasing a foolish whim."

Primault glanced at Singer and Wilson and shook his head slowly. "Let's look at it this way. You want to go back to that room and see if we can find something there, a clue we missed. If we're still doing that, we'll be heading in that direction anyway. In that sense then we won't be wasting time."

"Good point," Singer said, turning to Gavin. "I agree with Lieutenant Primault."

"You got my vote, for what it's worth," chimed in Wilson.

"In any case," said Primault, pressing his viewpoint, "part of logical deduction is to eliminate all possibilities until we arrive at probability. Besides, it will bug the shit out of me if we don't see what's at that ranch."

"Thanks, gentlemen," Gavin said. "How early can we leave?"

"As long as I've got a cup of coffee in my hand, I'm good to go anytime," Singer said.

"Ditto for me," Wilson said.

"How about 5 a.m.," Primault suggested. Receiving nods of assent, he turned to Ben Wilson. "Think you can pinpoint that location for us?"

"Will do." Wilson brought the map back up on his phone and began to scroll, an intense expression knitting his brows. "This is interesting," he said. "Remember that hawk we saw earlier today?"

Gavin nodded. "Yeah, I do. Why?"

"Remember how it took off and went in a beeline away from us?"

"I sure do. It stayed in a straight line heading toward the horizon."

"Well, sir, from where we were, at the casino hotel, to the map coordinates of that ranch, it's a northwesterly heading, the direction that hawk flew until it was out of sight."

THIRTY-SEVEN

Katherine was startled as the door clicked open. Leaning forward from the pillow propped against the wall, she held her breath and waited. The door opened only far enough for a cardboard box to appear and slide forward on the carpet. In the next instant the door was shut. She waited nearly a minute before she moved.

Her anxiety had increased since she heard what had to have been a gunshot, around two hours ago. There had been no other obvious noises. Previous to that there had been someone playing a piano.

Enticing smells were suddenly noticeable; broiled steak and a green vegetable, and perhaps a baked potato. Pushing aside caution she stood and walked silently to the door and looked in the box. In the bottom was a plate with a T-bone steak, a baked potato, and broccoli, all still warm, four wrapped pats of butter, and two dinner rolls. Next to it was a cup of dark liquid and a glass of water. In one corner of the box was a folded cloth napkin below a fork and a butter knife.

The dark liquid turned out to be tea. Carrying the box to the bed, she pushed aside the lamp and arranged the plate, cup, and glass on the nightstand. With watchful glances at the door, she attacked the food. Her last meal had been hours and hours ago, well before she had been brought here. Not knowing when the next meal would come, she decided to eat it all. It was something of a chore to cut meat with a butter knife, but nearly half an hour later, all that was left was the bone. She rinsed off the utensils and plate in the bathroom sink and put them back in the box, which she placed near the door.

Perhaps it was the meal, because after she had arranged the pillows against the wall and leaned back, she found herself nodding off. Or maybe it was some inner clock signaling it was night and time to sleep. She hadn't the slightest inkling if it was night or day. Startling awake again she glanced toward the door. The box was gone. Someone had taken it while she was asleep. A cold sense of dread brought her fully awake. Pulling the pillows aside she slid back against the bare wall, sitting up straight and vowing to herself to stay awake.

THIRTY-EIGHT

With the requisite coffee in go-cups from the 24-hour coffee service in the lobby, everyone was checked out and through the front door of the hotel a few minutes after five. Fifteen minutes after that they were merging onto I-94 West and twenty minutes later they cleared the western city limits of Mandan.

"According to my trusty app, we're a little over two hours from Medora," Ben Wilson told Gavin.

"Great. Just in time for breakfast."

"According to your brother," Wilson said, "your fiancée is one in a million. He thinks highly of her."

"Thanks. You'll like her, most people do, almost immediately. She's one smart lady, a heck of a lot smarter than me."

"How long have you known her, if I may ask?"

"Since I was fifteen and she was five, thirty-five years."

"Wow! That's amazing. Did you always know she was the one?"

"Yes. I always looked out for her because it was just her and her mom. Her dad was sort of an absentee father. When she was fifteen and I was twenty-five she picked me for a lady's choice round dance at a pow-wow, and I've been in love with her since. But I had to keep my hormones in check until she was older."

"Oh, man. They make movies about stories like that."

Gavin chuckled. "Well, the other side of the story is that for a long time she just looked on me as sort of an older brother. I think because of our age difference. I was out of college by the time she had a change of heart."

"Well, that doesn't sound so bad."

"There were a couple of twists, here and there. We were engaged when she was in college, then she went to law school. After she finished she broke off the engagement and took a job in Washington DC with an environmental law firm. A dream job. It was only this past year that we got back together."

"Damn. And you waited all that time? I mean, was she the only one?"

"I did briefly date someone my last year in college, before grad school, but Katherine was always the one."

"Well, my friend, I admire that, I really do. My dad left my mom for another woman, a younger woman. Men and monogamy don't seem to be compatible."

Twenty yards behind, Primault's unmarked cruiser was easily keeping up with the Jeep Rubicon.

"I'm surprised that Jeep can cruise the speed limit," Singer said.

"I've had them pass me when I was doing 80 on I-90 in South Dakota," Primault said. "It's their off-road capabilities that set them apart."

"Yeah, wish I could afford one."

"Well, Gavin has an older Wrangler that he had lifted and modified for off-road use. I'm sure he takes it hunting."

"So, he's a bow hunter? What does he hunt?"

"Yeah, he's been hunting with a bow since he was a kid, mostly big game; deer and elk."

"Damn. Must have to get close. What's the range of a bow?"

Primault shrugged. "I'm not sure, forty yards and closer, I think. It's not easy to get that close to a deer, or an elk. A different set of skills, for sure."

"He's kind of an unusual guy, isn't he?"

"Like a slow moving stream, which is deep and you can't see everything underneath. He's well educated, has kick-ass martial art skills—I saw him take down a guy in three seconds. And beneath it all beats the heart of an old time Lakota warrior. If we find him, I feel sorry for the guy that took his fiancée."

Singer nodded thoughtfully. "Shit," he said softly, staring at the back of the Jeep. "I'd like to get my hands on him, too. Only the worse kind of scumbag would do that."

"There's a lot of scumbags," Primault asserted. "This issue of missing and murdered Native women and girls has been happening for decades. A very small percentage are actually runaways; most of them, I'm sure, were deliberately taken."

"Well," Singer said, "my dad used to say that as Indians we are at the bottom of the list. When a white kid or a blond, white girl is missing, it makes the national news. The only way a Native women makes the news on the Sioux Falls station is if she is arrested for assault, usually against a white person. But when one goes missing, there's nothing. That's racism, pure and simple."

"Oh, hell, yeah," Primault agreed. "What pisses me off is that people in the Bureau of Indian Affairs are doing virtually nothing to help. No one in regional law enforcement for sure. You'd think that, with more women getting on tribal councils, they would work hard to bring this problem to the forefront, where it belongs."

"Damn! What do you think it'll take to stop losing our women and girls?"

Primault watched a highway patrol cruiser in the rear view mirror as it approached behind them in the passing lane, and then passed. "Well, anytime anything involves politics, it gets messy," he said. "There's the jurisdictional issue between states and tribes, and, of course, tribal governments, state governments, and the federal government. Bureaucracy rears its head big time and grinds very slowly. So, I think tribes have to pay attention to the issue of missing and murdered Native girls and women, and work together to find solutions, even if it's without cooperation from the states and the feds. One part of it would be to educate and inform Native girls, teach them what to look for. Prevention is important."

The walkie-talkie on the console suddenly squawked to life, and Ben Wilson's voice came over the air. "Gentlemen," he said. "We are in favor of stopping in Dickinson for breakfast. What do you think?"

Singer picked up the walkie-talkie and glanced at Primault, who nodded. "Roger, that works for us," he replied.

"Great. Gavin says there is a chain restaurant just off the interstate."

"Ten-four."

Two hours later they pulled into the restaurant parking lot. The tables and booths inside were only about half filled, so they chose a table in a corner. They were pleasantly surprised when their server was a young Native woman.

"My name is Linda," she told them politely, her eyes lingering for a second on Gavin's long single braid. A few minutes later she returned with their coffee and water and was ready for their food order.

"Where are you from, Linda," Primault asked.

"Standing Rock," she said. "But my husband and I have lived here for a few years."

"How is it, living here?" Gavin asked.

"It's okay, mostly," she said. "Not many of us skins here, though."

After she left with their food order, Ben Wilson motioned to Singer. "What did she mean by 'skins,'?"

"It's a word for us, what we call ourselves."

"Oh, cool. But not on the order of 'honky' or 'cracker,' is it?"

Primault chuckled. "No."

Half an hour later they finished eating and each of them left generous tips for Linda, amounting to more than the ticket itself. They gathered briefly in the parking lot.

"What's our plan when we get to Medora?" Primault asked Gavin.

"Well, it might be too early yet to get rooms, so maybe we can park your cruiser and drive north though the park and get some idea of the terrain and see what's out there."

"The ranch is not too far outside the park," Wilson pointed out. "If we find an unobtrusive vantage point, I can scope it out with my still camera, using the long lens."

"Works for me," Primault said.

As they walked toward the vehicles, Gavin's phone rang. It was his house line.

"Hello," he said, "This is Gavin."

"*Hau, Tunska, miye yelo* (Hello, Nephew, it's me)."

"*Hau, Leksi. Toniktuka hwo* (Hello, Uncle, how are you)?"

"*Matanyan yelo* (I'm good)," Andrew said. "I came over to your house to have coffee with your brother and Joby, and I saw something. A good sign."

"Really? What did you see?"

"I was filling the water tank for the horses and a hawk came down and landed on the corner of the corral. It was a big one, a female red-tail. She stayed there for a long time. So, I offered some tobacco, and then she took off."

"That is a good sign," Gavin said. "We saw a red-tail female yesterday, too."

"That's good," Andrew said. "They're telling us something. They're telling us that they know where she is, my niece."

"The one we saw yesterday flew away and went northwest from where we were," Gavin said.

"Then follow her."

"We are. We're doing that."

"Good. You'll find her."

Gavin disconnected the call and looked at the others. "Let's go," he said. "We keep following the hawk."

THIRTY-NINE

Katherine walked up the flight of stairs ahead of the man who had come to the room and ordered her to walk out the door. Dark blue carpeting covered the stairs. After a landing the stairs turned right. The man behind her was broad shouldered and of medium height, with intense dark eyes in a clean shaven face, dressed in a dark striped shirt and denim jeans. He spoke with a low, raspy voice. She sensed that he was not in control, but more of an enforcer—likely the one who had brought the food.

Emerging into a wide, short hallway that opened immediately onto a larger room, Katherine saw bright light through windows to the right. Judging from the angle of the sun's rays on the bare wood floor, it was likely sometime after sunrise or just before sunset.

"Straight ahead, to the other side of the room, and then the door on the right," the man instructed. His speech pattern indicated a police background. A long leather sofa flanked by two leather covered high backed chairs filled one side of the large room, arranged to face a high, stone fireplace. A tall, wooden hutch stood against the wall on the opposite side, behind a glistening, grand piano. She suddenly could hear the waltz coming through the vent.

A darker recollection popped into her head as her eyes briefly lingered on the very large, grand piano. *Piano ain't gonna like it.*

An involuntary shiver went up her back. She hoped there was no connection between the remark and the piano, but a chilling sense of apprehension said otherwise. Turning her gaze away from the piano, she hurriedly scanned the room. No curtains over the large windows on either side. Definitely a far cry from the dank basement room where she had spent two nights. But it felt just as restrictive and far from what she expected.

Reaching the door, she stepped through it and into another sumptuously furnished room. Floor to ceiling bookshelves on two adjoining walls were half filled with books. In front of the shelves were two high-backed chairs on either side of a triangle shaped table with a lamp. On the other side of the Persian rug filling the middle of the room was an ornate wooden desk. At it, in a leather-covered executive chair facing the room, sat a man with gloved hands tented in front of blue eyes set in a paler face, topped by dark blond hair. A slight smile—chillingly predatory to Katherine—was on his narrow lips. His Italian shoes, gray slacks, white collarless shirt, and dark blue sports coat were obviously expensive. Far from what Katherine expected. She wondered what happened to the man who had abducted her, and the thin faced man called Tulo.

"Good morning, Miss Hill," the man said, affably. He pointed to the high-backed chairs. "Please, have a seat."

The man knew her name. A chill went through her and she took it as a warning. Crossing over the carpet she sat in a chair.

"First things first," he said, "I trust your accommodations are comfortable?"

Katherine cleared her throat. "Ah, yes."

"Wonderful. Is there anything you need?"

"A ride to the nearest town."

The man chuckled loudly. "Ah, yes. I admire that spirit. It speaks to what I've learned about you, Miss Hill."

A conversation between her abductor and Thin Face flashed through her mind.

There was a disconnect somewhere. "Since you know my name, I can only assume that I was abducted at your behest," she said.

"Oh, no, not at all. That's the unfortunate reality to—to your situation."

"None of it has been remotely fortunate."

The man nodded animatedly. "Of course, of course. For that I do apologize. However, the most unfortunate aspect of your abduction is that it has caused an enormous problem."

"I don't understand."

"I didn't expect you would, Miss Hill. I know your name because a few days ago your photograph was flashed on television screens and on the internet by the South Dakota Department of Criminal Investigation. An environmental attorney employed by a prominent law firm based in Washington DC is newsworthy. And problematic for me."

"How is it problematic for you?"

"Because the man who abducted you did so on selfish impulse and placed both of us, meaning you and me, in a predicament. He could be traced to me."

A warning in her head was growing insistent. Why is he telling me any of this at all?

"And how am I to be affected by this predicament?" she asked.

"An astute question, Miss Hill. The answer is simple, and as you have probably already surmised. I cannot allow your abduction to be traced to me. The man who abducted you has already been—shall we say—handled. He will not make that mistake again I assure you. That leaves you."

She remembered the noise she thought was a gunshot. Warning bells were growing louder as a chill coursed through her. There's a reason this man doesn't want to be connected to the man who kidnapped her. That was the terrifying reality.

"So that means my abduction was outside your usual modus operandi."

"Yes. It was."

The chill in her stomach intensified.

"So, your preference is young Native girls."

"Of course."

"Why?"

He gazed at her for a second, and then flicked an imaginary piece of lint from his slacks. "You know the answer," he said, hollowly. "No one cares, unless of course, one of you grows up to be an attorney in a high-powered law firm. Mainstream America does not care about one half of one percent of the population, especially when it's not white, and hardly a drop in the bucket of the proverbial melting pot. As a group you're nowhere close to the collective margin of awareness in a society more intent on materialism, and with no sense of racial equality."

"It's despicable, what you're doing."

"It's business. If you are student of history you know that the fur trade was once the largest and most profitable economic enterprise on this entire continent. Driven by the lust for wealth, it used Native people as suppliers. I've simply taken that business model in another direction, satisfying another type of lust. Only this time, the desired commodity is not furs."

"It's young, vulnerable humans."

"The commodity for sale is the object of male desire, and when it is available with no strings attached, then we have an economic boom. Miss Hill, sex trafficking has been a reality since human males gained control. There will always be a market for it."

"And you don't care that you destroy lives in the process. What you're doing to Native girls is the worst kind of travesty there is. You apparently have no conscience."

The man smiled, a bit paternalistically. "Conscience is not a currency of capitalism, Miss Hall. Let me assure you that the girls we use are treated well. They are fed well, and they are not physically abused. If they break the rules, their punishment is prolonged isolation."

"They are held against their will and are raped repeatedly!"

"An immutable necessity, just as dairy calves are penned and restricted from moving so their meat will be satisfactorily tender for the human palate."

Katherine suddenly felt like throwing up, but she swallowed it down, tasting bile in her throat. "No matter what you've said, it's evil, what you do!" she hissed. "There was a funeral, a few weeks ago, for a recipient of that immutable necessity. She escaped and nearly made it home, but she died. The coroner determined it to be from a severe beating. Her name was Melvina Old Lodge, and she was fifteen. There was also evidence of sexual abuse."

The man's face turned dark, his eyes narrowed, his jaw clenched. He was fuming, although he kept it under control. "You're grabbing at straws, Miss Hill."

Fear overcame caution, and perhaps good sense as well. But the cold, hard reality was that her fate was sealed. Yet, Katherine saw an opening, a chink in his armor. "Here's a few more straws," she said. "Melvina Old Lodge walked, and I'm convinced now, from the man camp in the oil fields, across the state of South Dakota, and very nearly made it home before she died in a pasture. In her shoe was a list of names on a piece of paper. Twelve names."

A smile appeared, but it was forced, and his eyes darted for a moment. "And you think that, somehow, those names are tied to me?"

"They are. You know they are. I think you should be afraid."

"Frankly I don't care what you think. Our meeting is over."

The man turned and looked toward the door. "Sanders, if you would, please."

The man who had escorted Katherine from the basement appeared in the doorway.

"Take Miss Hill back downstairs and find a fresh change of clothes for her. I think size 2 will do nicely. And her lunch as well."

Katherine could only stare at the man, knowing that she was face to face with a psychopath. It was the only logical reason for the conversation that had just transpired. An involuntary shiver coursed through her chest.

"Yes, sir." Sanders, the enforcer, stepped into the room and approached. Katherine rose and walked past him into the outer room, back straight and eyes forward. She looked out the windows on both sides of the room as she passed through but couldn't see more than a three-rail wooden fence and a large white building. In the basement she stopped in front of the door to the room and saw two heavy metal deadbolt locks, one above and below the doorknob. Both looked new and out of place. She walked through the door after Sanders opened it, then heard the bolts being closed. She fought back a sob.

Her skin crawled with the ugliness of all she had just heard. On shaky legs she went to the bed and sat on the edge. A cold sense of dread settled in her gut. The man in the expensive shoes had told her everything but his name, and that revealed only two possibilities. She would be indefinitely a captive in this room, or she would be killed.

I have to do something; I have to try.

Escape was impossible. The glass bricks in the window were too thick to break, and the openings were too narrow. The only opportunity would be the next time the door opened. The man had said something about fresh clothes, and Sanders would probably deliver them. But when?

She had to get out. The man had told her that he trafficked young Native girls, purposely and arrogantly, and for one reason. He was absolutely certain she would never be able to tell that to anyone else.

Pacing from one side of the room to the other kept panic at bay. She had to do something and the only opportunity was through that door— the next time it opened. The clothes and maybe more food would be delivered. But what could she do? Sanders was a large man and no doubt adept at subduing people. There had to be a way to distract him, or perhaps disable him. She stopped pacing and looked around the room. She needed a weapon.

Her gaze fell on the table lamps. Crossing to a nightstand she picked up the lamp, a ceramic figurine that looked a fish. It had a little weight, but not much; if she could swing it hard enough, it would have some impact. She thought for a moment and put it back and then hurried to the bathroom. There was nothing obvious that could serve as a weapon, except the towel bars on the wall above the stool or on the glass shower doors. The one above the stool was wood, and too short and likely not heavy. The two on the showers appeared to be a lightweight metal of some type. They were a possibility.

She stood for a moment, looking around, prodded by a growing sense of desperation. That door could open any second. She glanced at the small vanity below the sink. Kneeling she opened the doors and saw a paper towel roll, two small scrub pads, and a spray bottle of what she assumed was cleaning solution. Disappointed, she closed the doors, and a split second later opened them again, reaching for the spray bottle. Unscrewing the top, she sniffed, and recoiled from the heavy chemical odor. She hefted the bottle. It was nearly full.

She stood up with the bottle in her hand. Turning the nozzle, she sprayed the medicine cabinet mirror. Leaning forward she took another whiff. It irritated her nose. Lifting the nozzle, she studied it. There were four different spray settings. Stepping to the shower, she squeezed the handle again, checking the spray pattern. Then she turned the nozzle to the next setting. It was more concentrated but still more or less a wide spray. The next two settings were narrower. She tested them both and decided on the third one.

Perfect. She had her weapon. If she sprayed it in Sanders' face and got the solution into his eyes, he would likely be momentarily blinded—just long enough for her to get away from him. She did two more practice sprays.

Now, all she had to do was be ready at the right moment. How that would happen was the next problem.

After hurriedly using the restroom, she carried a nightstand to the hall door, momentarily debating where best to place it. She stood it against the wall between the door sill and the corner of the bathroom wall. In that position she would sit on it and wait, listening. The two heavy deadbolts would take about two seconds, at the most, to slide open. With her ear close to the door, she was certain to hear any scraping noise, she hoped. Assuming Sanders would have something in his hands—clothes or again a box with a plate of food—she would have a second or two, once the door opened, to raise the bottle to the approximate level of Sanders' face and squirt. After she placed the nightstand against the wall, she sat down and practiced standing and pointing the bottle. Satisfied as much as possible, she sat down to wait.

Time was not important. She pushed it out of her mind. In addition to the spray bottle in her hands, patience was now her main weapon. Gavin liked to say that there was no word in Lakota for the western construct of "time." The sun rose and set, days came and went, so did the seasons, but they were to be experienced, to be lived, not measured. A person's age was not measured in years, but by the number of winters one lived.

There was no time, just being. She stared at the narrow brick glass windows on the opposite wall without really seeing them. Her ears were ready, waiting for the slightest noise.

She lost count of the times she did the rotation of flexing her large muscles; first her shoulders, then her biceps and forearms, and then down to her gluteus maximus, and on to her legs. Staying flexible would be necessary, she felt. Indeed, her life depended on it.

Klink!

It was not very loud, but she heard it. A second later she heard it again.

Klink!

Then the doorknob began to turn. In one motion, Katherine stood and lifted the bottle. The door opened. Sanders was pushing it with one hand and holding folded clothes in the other. She squeezed the spray handle as hard and as fast as she could—ssst!—ssst!—ssst!

"Shit!" Sanders' hands were up to his eyes in a split second, the clothes spilling onto the floor. "Damn!"

With her left hand Katherine shoved aside the door, and saw an opening as adrenaline kicked in. She launched a kick into the man's crotch. With a loud grunt, he simultaneously doubled over in pain and dropped to the floor. Without hesitation she jumped over him and turned for the stairs, taking two at a time, sensing she would have only a few seconds before Sanders recovered and followed her, or raised the alarm.

Gaining the top landing, she paused. She knew the front door was not to the right, so she had to guess left. Stepping quickly, she went behind a wall and found herself in a foyer, at the end of it was an entrance with a large wooden door. Breathing hard from the adrenaline rush more than exertion, she hurried to the door. Grabbing the handle she pushed down on the latch and pulled the heavy door open, determination rising with each passing moment.

Glancing back toward the interior of the house, she listened for any noise. Nothing.

She pulled the door open and came nose to nose with the swarthy visage of Thin Face.

FORTY

Medora was already awake and bustling when the men pulled into town. Happening upon a public parking lot, they took two of the last three spots, gathering between the vehicles to talk.

"I've been thinking," Gavin said. "If there's an outdoor or a sporting goods store that sells camping gear, I might gear up and spend the night observing, if that opportunity presents itself."

"That makes sense," Primault replied quickly. "And you won't be doing it without me."

"Or me," Singer added.

"That goes for me, too," Wilson chimed in.

"I appreciate it, gentlemen. But let's cover our bases and find some rooms if there's any to be had. Tourist season is in full swing."

Primault glanced at his watch. "It's early yet. Checkout time is around noon or so, usually. Maybe we should look for that store you want, grab some coffee, and then see if we can get close to those map coordinates."

As with any town that is dependent on the tourist trade, the two largest stores stocked items used by hikers, campers, and backpackers. Fortunately, some of it was genuine. After Ben Wilson reported that all the rooms in the only three hotels were booked, the only other option was camping. After an hour and a half, the cargo bay of the Jeep and the trunk of Primault's cruiser were filled food, water, two two-man tents, and camping gear and equipment. Included in the purchases were light raincoats and camouflage jackets. They took a brief respite in a busy restaurant, over coffees.

"This is an interesting place. Apparently has some history, from the *wasicu* side," Primault said.

"It certainly does. A Frenchman tried to set up a refrigerated meat storage business here. He named the town after his wife, Medora," Gavin said. "And Teddy Roosevelt lived here for a while."

"I guess long enough for them to name a national park after him," Wilson concluded.

Singer glanced around at the nearly packed restaurant. "So, I guess all these people are here to soak up the essence of Teddy," he quipped, grinning derisively.

"Something like that," Gavin said. "A profitable marriage of history and capitalism."

"Which is why the hotels are full," Primault added.

"Yeah. I think we find that campground and set up there," Gavin said. "At least as a base of operations. If we're lucky it has toilets and showers."

Both were available, as it turned out. They arrived only minutes after two adjacent camping sites had been vacated, according to the campground's seasonal manager. They paid the fee for three nights and began setting up.

The two tents did not take long to erect. After all the metal pegs were pounded in place, two pads and two sleeping bags were arranged in each one. Singer volunteered to go back into town for ice for the coolers, to keep the eggs, bacon, and hamburger from spoiling. In the meantime, Primault set up the portable gas stove, fueled by a canister of propane, to experiment with the percolating coffee pot. "This is a first for me," he admitted. "I watched my mom do this."

Rounding out the supplies were four camel packs for water, packets of beef jerky, several containers of vacuum packed MREs—meals-ready-to-eat—and rolls of toilet paper.

Ben Wilson joined Gavin at one of the picnic tables, spreading a map over it. Gavin traced a road that went north through the south unit of Theodore Roosevelt National Park South Unit. "That seems to be the quickest way to the north side," he said.

Wilson tapped his phone and scrolled it intermittently until he saw what he was looking for. "Yeah, the coordinates put that ranch right about here," he said, searching for the area on the map, and then putting his finger on it.

"Okay, probably private land, could be tricky. Unless…" Gavin said, tracing a line on the map. "That looks to be a trail of some sort, I hope. It is south of that ranch. If we're lucky it's a hiking trail."

"And we're hikers, at the very least," Wilson said.

"Initially, all we need to do is get within effective range of your zoom lens," Gavin said. "We need to see who comes and goes, who's moving around."

"Right. A quarter of a mile would be good. An eighth even better."

"Then we'll just make it happen."

Primault joined them. "Coffee's going," he announced. "If you're brave enough, we can try some later, before we head out, and have a snack as well."

Gavin agreed.

Loading the day's supplies and necessary equipment into the Jeep, they left the cruiser behind. Entering the park, they then headed north. Just after noon they found a parking area at a trailhead on a bluff, just inside the park boundary. According to the map, the trail was about three miles long and passed through the watershed adjacent to a broad meadow south of where the ranch was located.

"If I have to, I'll get 'lost' and see how close I can get," Wilson said.

"Okay," Gavin said. "Let's turn our walkie-talkies to channel 8."

On the trail they adopted a comfortable pace, spacing themselves about five yards apart. No other hikers were encountered until two hundreds yard down trail, when two apparently high school-age boys were hurrying back toward the trailhead. After a quarter of a mile, they stopped at two benches, one on either side of the trail.

"I think it's about a mile more until we come parallel with the position of the ranch," Gavin said.

Wilson checked his phone. "Yeah, about that. Then what?"

"Maybe find a high spot and see what's visible," Primault suggested.

"I'll hang with Ben," Gavin said.

"Right. And maybe Jason and I can go farther down the trail see if there are other vantage points we can use," Primault said.

About an hour later, after another pair of hikers going south passed by them and did not look back, Ben and Gavin went off trail and climbed a high ridge north of it. On the wide summit of the ridge, Gavin pointed to a large cluster of tall soap weeds. "That's excellent cover," he said. "No one can see us behind them."

Hunkering down behind the soap weeds, they had a mostly unobstructed line of sight toward the ranch. With the naked eye, the log house was a dark spot and the white barn stood out more, also because it was much larger. Much more detail was visible through the zoom lens of Wilson's still camera.

"There are a few trees around the house," Wilson pointed out. ""It is oriented north and south. There's an entrance on the east side. I'd say the barn, or whatever the larger building is, is forty yards from the house."

"Any movement?"

"Not so far," Wilson said, handing the camera to Gavin.

Gavin observed for two minutes without comment. "No vehicles," he finally said. "No one moving. From what Brad Coleman said, it's probably not an operating ranch. No cattle, or horses."

"Just someone's really isolated and really expensive place. Especially if it has an airstrip. There's no airplane, at least on the side we can see."

"Right," Gavin agreed.

Wilson opened his backpack and took out an expandable tripod. After opening it up and locking in the legs, he raised and adjusted the platform at the appropriate height. "Let me mount it," he said to Gavin. "This way it will be steadier and our arms won't get tired. You take the first shift, for however long you want," he said. "All you need to do is watch the screen."

Twenty some minutes after quietly watching, Gavin noticed a dark vehicle come into the frame, which couldn't be seen with the naked eye. "Movement," he announced. Wilson reached over and pushed the Record button on the camera. "A vehicle came from the south. It's crossing the yard," Gavin continued. "It's parking at the barn. No, wait. I think the driver is getting out… yeah. He or she is at the door…now pulling it up. He's back in the car and it's moving into the barn."

A couple of minutes later, the barn door closed, and there was no further activity. Wilson stopped the recording.

"What do you think?" he asked.

"Well, that car parked in the barn, so maybe that means it's someone who's been there before or stays there. You know, as opposed to a delivery, or something."

"Good point. I'll bet that barn has living quarters."

"That's likely."

A half hour passed, then an hour, with no further movement, in or out, or anyone emerging from the barn.

Another hour later the walkie-talkie came to life. "We found a high point farther up the trail," Primault reported. "So, we took a chance and went up. From here we can see mostly the white building. We couldn't see much else, even with these fifty-power binoculars."

"Roger, that." Gavin replied. "Sounds like you're not much closer than we are. We picked up movement with the zoom lens. A vehicle arrived and is still inside the barn. Nothing else."

"Roger. You want us to stay here?"

Gavin glanced at his watch. "I think we should give it until sundown, and then meet up back at the Jeep and talk about what's next."

"Ten-four. Check with you later."

Gavin passed the camera and tripod over in front of Wilson. "Second shift."

Wilson made an adjustment and placed the camera so that he didn't need to lean too far forward.

Gavin took out his binoculars and brought the house and barn into focus. The image was nowhere as close as it had been in the camera. After a few moments he moved the binoculars to scope the landscape around the ranch.

"Hey!" Wilson said, excitedly. "We've got movement. Someone's walking to the house."

Through the binoculars, Gavin saw two dark figures moving across the open yard.

Wilson described what he was seeing. "They're at the front door. Someone opened it. They're still standing there—now going in."

Gavin kept the binoculars trained on the house. Wilson kept his eyes glued to the camera screen on the front door of the house. There was no further movement. Another twenty minutes passed.

As he lowered the binoculars and leaned back, a sudden movement of air gently swayed the grass at his feet, and with it came a soft voice, murmuring.

Gavin glanced at Wilson. "What? Did you say something?"

Wilson looked over. "What? No, I didn't say anything. Why, did you hear something?"

"Ah, I don't know. I thought I did."

Wilson turned his attention back to the camera screen, pulling back the frame to get a broader view.

Gavin heard a whoosh over his head. Looking up he saw a dark shape swooping down the slope, skimming over the grass and soap weeds, moving directly away from their vantage point. It was a large bird, a hawk. Copper colored feathers glistened in the sun for a moment. Its tail feathers were spread wide. Something told him it was another female.

It soared upward, gaining altitude, maintaining a straight heading. Gavin lifted the binoculars. The hawk was gliding toward the ranch. He managed to find it the circle of the lens, but it wasn't easy to keep in frame. Lowering the glasses, he watched it becoming smaller as it flew closer to the ranch.

FORTY-ONE

Tulo cleared his throat nervously. He knew what had happened to Nomer, so his legs were quivering and he wished he could sit. Luckily, Piano was not holding anyone but Nomer responsible for Nomer's mistake. Absolving himself of any responsibility was Tulo's basic selfish defense. All the swirling thoughts in his head were a scrambled rush for survival, knowing that Piano had no patience for anyone who made stupid mistakes. Sanders was no less patient. Tulo looked at the big man. It was Sanders who dubbed the head man Piano, after Riley had asked about his name.

"Yes, sir," Tulo said. "One of them turned up missing, back about a month ago."

Tulo had a healthy fear of Sanders. So did Riley, standing nervously next to him.

"A fact you neglected to tell me," Sanders said.

"Yes, sir."

"When did you lose her?"

"She was not there when I went to get her, at the camp. The—ah, client finished and left, and I think that she—she walked out the door."

"That's very likely. How spunky of her."

Sanders turned his attention to the man standing next to Tulo. "Now, Mister Riley. You lost two girls. You were overpowered, was your story, I believe."

"Yes, sir. Someone came out of the dark and hit me."

"And rendered you unconscious."

"Yes, sir."

Sanders shook his head from side to side. "Then, you went to pick up two girls last evening and the room was empty. You then checked at the other house and they were all missing as well."

"Right, sir." Riley affirmed. "The locks was busted. Someone broke them, from the outside."

Sanders returned his gaze to Tulo. "This occurred after you collected the woman?"

"Yes, sir. They were still at the house then, three days ago."

"Indeed." Sanders alternated a cold, noncommittal gaze between the two men. "That is very troublesome, gentlemen." He paused and looked vaguely toward the door of the bunkhouse. "It was good you were on hand to prevent the woman from escaping. That was lucky for you. Now, here's what I want you to do. Go to your quarters in the barn and wait. We have a very serious problem, about as serious as it gets. Piano is looking for answers. I will be back to let you know what he decides."

The two men nodded fearfully.

Curled up on the bed, her wrists and ankles bound by heavy, black zip ties, Katherine gazed at the wall. Thankfully her hands were in front, but that was the only positive fact. Everything else was disheartening.

She had immediately recognized Thin Face, but not the other man. They had grabbed her and held on until Sanders limped into the room, his eyes red and watering.

"Bring her here!" he shouted. Reaching out, he grabbed Katherine by the front of her shirt, and jerked her savagely, pulling her out of the grasp of the two men.

Katherine was prepared to duck after she saw Sanders doubling his fist. In the next instant he stopped himself from carrying out whatever he had intended to do. She had a feeling it would have been painful. But Sanders' face, a mask of twisted, red-eyed rage, was hard to forget. In a moment, he had manhandled her back down the stairs and into the room.

Sighing deeply, she fought back a growing feeling of dismay. She was still alive, still breathing. Perhaps, there was still hope.

A loud click and the door opened. Katherine pushed herself up and slid to the edge of the bed, as the blue-eyed man entered and took three steps to the right, stopping at the center of the wall. "Well, Miss Hill," he said coldly. "That was a bit of excitement."

She tried to wipe any expression from her face and stared into his eyes.

"I commend you for trying. But, sadly, all for naught. What you've done, Miss Hill, has forced me to move up a timeline, to alter my plan. Here's what will happen. Tomorrow, at dawn—I've always wanted to say that in a dramatic context—your friend Sanders will fly you out of here, literally. He will load you into his airplane and take you south, eventually arriving over a particular swamp in Louisiana. And over that particular swamp, he will simply drop you out the door. Then, my problem will be solved."

As surreal as the words seemed, she knew he meant every one. She forced herself to keep her gaze on his face as she felt an ice cold wave of fear.

"Nothing to say, no rebuttal, as it were? Unusual, for a lawyer. Nevertheless, please understand, Miss Hill, that although your abduction was not at my behest, the fact that it occurred has led to unfortunate consequences. And there can be no other solution. I'm sorry."

With an empty smile and a nod, the blue-eyed man turned and walked out of the room. His departure accentuated by the clicks of the deadbolts sliding into place. Katherine took deep breaths, fighting back the sobs building up in her throat.

Oh, my dear Gavin. I need you now!

Nearly half a mile away, Gavin searched the sky above the house with the binoculars, looking for the hawk. If she was up there she was much too far away, even for the binoculars. That sudden sound, a murmur, lingered in his awareness. Closing his eyes, he tried to replay it in his memory. It had been no more than a second, maybe two. The voice had been low, but not a whisper.

Shaking his head, he brought himself back to the moment and the issue at hand. A glance at his watch indicated late afternoon. Sunset in three hours. Finding the walkie-talkie he put out a call to Primault.

"Justin here. What's up?"

"I think we should do some planning. Think you two can find us?"

"Ten-four. We're on our way."

Forty minutes later, after a couple of more calls over the walkie-talkie, Primault and Singer arrived, slightly winded by the climb up the gradual slope.

"We saw a couple hikers approaching and we wanted to get out sight before they got close," Primault explained. "I don't think they saw us. What's on your mind?"

"Initially we saw some activity, but not for a while. At the very least we have to know what's there. Someone is there, we know that."

"But not much else," Primault said.

"I have a feeling about that place. But feelings aren't facts. I have to know once and for all. If she's not there, then we move on. You might think this strange, but I think she's there."

"Okay, then what's our plan?"

"I want to go down there," Gavin said. "But we'll have to wait for darkness."

"All of us?"

"I don't think so. You and me. Ben and Jason should hang back. I don't know how wise it would be to leave our vehicle unattended overnight."

"I don't know if you're planning to return here," Wilson said, "to this location at some point, but I have a thought."

"Let's have it."

"The vehicle that we saw go into the barn down there arrived by a road, from the south. Do you suppose there's some logic in Jason and I taking the Jeep and getting in close on that road?"

"You mean close to that house?" Primault asked.

"Yeah."

All eyes turned to Gavin. "You know, that's a good idea. It's easily a half mile hike from here. We need to wait until it's dark, and if you do that it will save us from having to dodge cactus, soap weeds, and snakes twice."

"Damn, since you put it that way," Primault said, "it's a great idea."

"The map we picked up of the park shows all the roads. I'll correlate it with the coordinates," Wilson said. "We'll find the road. Too bad we don't have an address."

"It's owned by something called the Hanrich Group," Gavin said. "That might be helpful."

Primault leaned over and looked at the still camera's screen. "Damn. I can see the front door. Too bad we can't get closer before we lose the light."

Wilson snapped his fingers. "Hey, I almost forgot!" Unzipping a side pocket on his backpack, he took out a plastic case and opened it. This," he said, "is a night vision camera."

"The hell you say!" Primault chortled.

"I do! This will save you from the cactus and the soap weeds. I don't know about the snakes."

"Why?"

"Snakes are cold blooded. This will show anything hot, that has a body temperature, like people and animals."

"No shit!"

"Is it hard to operate?" Singer asked.

"No, not at all. Main concern is battery life." Wilson turned the camera on and waited. "Good. Shows it has a full charge. Should be good for eight hours."

After a thorough tutorial, Wilson turned the camera over to Gavin, who promptly handed it to Primault. "You're more gadget friendly than I am," he said. "I'll follow you."

"Roger that."

Singer stood up and glassed the hiking trail. "I don't see anyone," he reported.

"Maybe Ben and I should take off now. Since we don't have night vision."

"Sure," Primault said. "Chances are the radios won't work. Topography is too uneven. We should be able to use cell phones." He took his out and looked. "Yup, two bars here."

Wilson looked at Gavin. "I can leave the still camera with you, for the zoom function."

"No, once we get close the binoculars will be fine."

"What do you want us to do, once we find the right road to that place?" Singer asked.

"Well, I think we have cell service, so let us know where you are," Gavin said. "As long as you can get to the house quickly if we need you. If that turns out to be a dry hole, then we need to exfiltrate."

"Right. We'll figure it out and find a place to wait," Singer said, confidently. He glassed the hiking trail again. "Clear," he said.

Wilson and Singer grabbed their packs and stood.

"Ah, one more thing," Primault said, looking at Singer. "Do you have your piece?"

Singer nodded.

"Mind lending it to Gavin?"

"No, sir. Not at all."

Primault turned to Gavin. "I don't know what's down there, but if it turns out to be something tricky or dangerous, I'd feel better if you were armed. I have my piece."

Gavin nodded. "I think you're right."

Singer knelt and reached under the inside of his right trouser leg and unstrapped the short holster with a snub-nosed .38 caliber revolver. From the side pocket of his cargo trousers, he pulled out a leather ammunition sleeve with twelve extra rounds. He held out the revolver and the ammunition to Gavin.

"Thank you, Jason."

"Sure. It's dead on up to about forty yards."

Gavin handed the Jeep ignition key to Singer.

"When you get to the vehicle, call my phone," Primault said to Singer.

"I will. Good luck to both of you."

"Yeah," Wilson echoed. "Good luck."

"Thanks. Talk to you in a bit."

After an affirming nod, Singer turned and skirted the soap weeds, Wilson close behind. Both Gavin and Primault watched them for several moments before sitting back down. Primault checked his watch. "When the light starts fading after sundown, might be a good time to start," he suggested. "Hard to see distant objects in the dusk. And that'll give us more time."

Gavin nodded. "Good thinking." He clipped the holstered pistol onto on his belt at the small of his back. It was a right-handed holster, and there he would be able to grab it with his left hand and press the quick release button with his right thumb. He did two practice draws.

"I forgot you are a lefty," Primault said. "Might take you a couple seconds to pull it out."

"No worries. Hopefully I won't need to." He replaced the pistol and pointed toward the ranch in the distance. "One thing I have to say," he said. "If anything goes south, I'd hate to have it affect your job. I can do this alone."

Primault shook his head. "Well, we might be dancing on the razor's edge here," he said, "but neither one of us is going to do anything stupid. And if it does go south, my job will be okay as long as Chief Avery is my boss."

"Okay. I appreciate your help."

"Well, Singer and I are really only doing our jobs, both as cops and as Lakota men. As cops the words 'to protect and to serve' have to be more than a public relations slogan. As Lakota men, we need to protect our women."

"Couldn't have said it better, my friend."

"Yeah. Speaking of Chief Avery, I think I'll see if I can reach him."

Chief Avery answered on the third ring. "Hey, Justin. I was hoping to hear from you."

"Good evening, sir. Just thought I'd catch you up."

"Fire away."

Primault reported the day's events, adding "so we're a couple hours away from going in. Our objective is obviously to see what's there. If it's not what we're looking for, we exfil without anyone knowing we were there, hopefully."

"Okay. I will have my work phone with me at all times. It'll be by my bed with the ringer on high. Don't hesitate to call if you need to."

"Roger that."

Primault disconnected the call and glanced at the sun. "Now we wait." Forty minutes later his phone buzzed. He quickly glanced at the screen and touched the green button.

"Hey, Jason. How was the walk?"

"It was okay, No one around. How about I try you again when we're closer to Medora?"

"Right. Ah, send a text. If it connects I'll text you back."

"Will do."

For several minutes, they sat quietly, listening to bird calls around them. A meadowlark's warbling was clearly distinguishable, as was the bright cry of a redwing blackbird. From nearby the sudden, thumping whir of a pheasant taking flight was unmistakable. A bumble bee buzzed by them and was gone in an instant.

"I don't know how anyone can look at something like this," Primault said, gesturing at the landscape, "and say there's nothing out here. I remember seeing a bumper sticker somewhere. It said 'Wilderness, land of no use.' No one but a white man would think that. Then one comes and builds a ranch, like that one, and thinks it's an improvement."

A slow breeze waved the grass on the slope below them into a lazy dance. The bird calls continued. Overhead an airliner was leaving a condensation trail across the sky, from east to west. Several moments passed.

"Sorry," Primault said, lowering his voice. "Didn't mean to go off on a tangent. I know you have other things on your mind."

"It's okay. I was thinking about that ranch," Gavin said, pointing toward it. "That's where the air charter brought a piano with a helicopter. Katherine scratches the word 'piano' on the wall of that room. On the surface, it's no more than a coincidence, and coincidences aren't hard evidence. Neither are gut feelings. But that coincidence is—well, I just can't ignore it. And this feeling in my gut tells me Katherine is there."

"Well, then the next step is for us to go there." Primault picked up the night vision camera. "And this will help us find a way in the dark."

"There are two other indicators, signs, that conventional thinking would label crazy, or wishful thinking." Gavin reached into his pocket and took out the black prayer flag that had been dropped at his feet during the *lowanpi* ceremony. "This, and the hawk. Taken together, that's as good as evidence, as far as I'm concerned."

Primault nodded. "Then that seals it for me, too."

They walked into the darkness.

FORTY-TWO

Gerard joined Andrew and Joby by the fire pit in the backyard, unfolding the lawn chair he carried, and sat down. He pointed to the fire crackling in the pit. "A fire under the prairie skies doesn't compare to one in a fireplace in my apartment. Not even close," he said.

"I guess that's a good sign," Andrew said, teasing. "Probably means you're not a totally citified Indian."

Gerard chuckled at the jibe. "Probably," he said. "A fire in the open always reminds me of Mom and Dad. They liked to sit by an outside fire and cook over it."

"They sure did, even in the winter," Andrew agreed.

Gerard sighed and pointed at the horses grazing in the pasture north of the house and barn. "Gavin sure has a nice set up here. I know he has a place on the Wind River, but I think he said it's only for hunting. I don't think he'll ever live there. This is home, for him and Katherine."

"You're right. This place is home. They'll never live anywhere else."

"Yeah, it's not the same, though, because they're not here."

"But they'll be back, both of them," Andrew insisted.

"I know you have insights that I don't have. Maybe I've lost touch and I am more citified, as you said. I know my brother hasn't. He seems to walk more on the Lakota side of life. So, I'm trusting in his abilities, his perseverance. I wish there was more I could do to help him. But is there a reason why you seem to be confident that they will be back?"

"Well, you're helping quite a bit by sending your man to help him. I'm like you. I'm trusting in his abilities. But I know he has help from the other side."

"The other side, you mean the Spirits?"

"That's exactly what I'm talking about. I asked them to help him, and to protect Katherine. A female hawk came here one evening. I know they sent her. I offered tobacco and asked her and her relatives to help your brother, to show him where Katherine is. So, he has help from all sides. He just has to accept the signs and believe."

Gerard watched the flames as they flared high. "That's good. I hope I never become too 'citified' to believe in those kinds of things."

"We'll make sure you don't."

"But he has to find her soon. The more time passes it becomes statistically more difficult. Clues become cold, for one thing."

"There is one thing that bothers me, though," Andrew admitted.

"What is that?"

"I've been seeing something, a snake, a white snake."

"A snake? What do you think that means?"

"I'm not sure. It's white, but it looks exactly like a blue racer, which is really fast. And I've seen it a few times, it just comes into my head. I come upon the snake and it takes off, really fast. Then it finds a hole and just disappears."

Gerard glanced at his uncle, bothered by the look of concern on his face.

FORTY-THREE

Will Riley stared at Tulo, refusing to believe what he had just heard yet knowing it was probably true. Tulo, for all his slipperiness and tendency for tall tales, was scared to the bone.

"Yeah, okay, but why would Piano do it himself? You sure it wasn't Sanders?"

"Fuck yeah, it was him, and Nomer's dead. I buried him."

"Oh, shit! You did? Where?"

Tulo waved his thumb toward the door of the small room. "Here, in the barn, in the last horse stall."

"What? You mean there's a dead guy in this barn?"

"Damn straight! Took me a long time to dig that fucking grave."

"Show me."

Tulo's jaw dropped. "Why? Look man, we've been sittin' here on pins and needles, waiting for Piano." He glanced at his watch. "It's been, what, seven hours? It's dark outside now. Sanders is gonna come, any minute now prob'ly. And you want to see a grave?"

"What's Sanders go to do with it? Okay, okay, I'll go myself. Which horse stall? The last one on the right or the left?"

"Ah, Jesus! Okay, come on! I ain't going to turn on the inside lights just for you." In a huff, Tulo grabbed a flashlight from a shelf and stomped out the door. Switching it on, he led the way along a continuous wall until it turned into the front panels of six horse stalls, unused for years. Vehicles were parked on the concrete floor, two minivans, an ATV, and a four-wheel-drive pickup. Near the end the horizontal and vertical stabilizers of an airplane were dimly visible just beyond the flashlight beam.

Tulo stopped at the last stall. Its door was open. "There," he said. "Right there." The flashlight beam revealed the middle of the dirt floor and an obvious disturbance in the topsoil in a roughly oblong shape.

"Holy fuck! And that's where Nomer is?"

"Five feet down. Yeah."

"And Piano plugged him because of that woman?"

"Yeah! Because that poor bastard broke all the rules. Piano's rules. He took that woman for himself. Wanted me to help him hide her."

"So, you ratted him out?"

"Shit, I didn't want Piano to blame me!"

Riley stared at the slightly discolored dirt, the oblong area noticeably raised. "Well, shit, he's dead over a woman."

"Come on, let's go back. Sanders could show up any time."

Tulo hurried through the door and broke into a trot toward the front of the barn, Riley hurrying to keep pace. As their footsteps faded into the darkness, two heads rose cautiously over the wall of the adjacent stall, gazing in the direction of the departing footsteps.

"Damn!" Primault muttered. "The hawk was right."

"I'll say. We're past coincidences now."

"Right. There is someone named 'Piano,' and he apparently killed the man who abducted Katherine. Is that about the size of it?"

"Absolutely."

"So that means Katherine has to be in the house," Primault said. "And there's someone named Sanders as well. With those two that means at least four people."

"Right."

Some minutes earlier, before they overheard the chilling conversation, Gavin and Primault had forced open a small access door and crawled into the barn. Once inside they saw a twin-engine airplane parked just inside the large double doors. After leaving their backpacks next to a stall and starting toward the front of the barn, with the help of the night vision camera, they saw a flashlight come on. There was no time to run back, so they quickly ducked into a stall.

"Shit! The backpacks!" Primault dashed out the door and grabbed both packs, and scooted back in, an instant before the flashlight beam lit up the wall. They pushed up against the inner wall, hiding in the darkness, hardly daring to breath. Primault drew his sidearm. To their shock and astonishment, the two men entered the adjacent stall.

"Those are the two we saw going to the front door of the house this afternoon," Primault said. "They apparently live here or stay here occasionally. They're the flunkies, the worker bees."

"So that probably means the Sanders character is the next level of management, as it were."

"Yeah, I'd say so," Primault agreed. "And he's about to show up."

"Yeah. I think we need to find a hiding place close to their quarters, close enough to listen."

Primault lifted the camera. "Well, let's have a look."

Carefully stepping out the door, they moved along the wall, Primault in the lead with the camera. The image on the screen was a light green with varying shades of dark lines and angles, showing the interior of the spacious barn. They passed the pickup, ATV, two small vans, and a section of solid wall. Carefully opening a door, a peek inside showed stacks of water bottles in cases and over two dozen closed boxes. More boxes were in the next room. Out of curiosity, Gavin opened one.

"Clothing," he whispered. "New, still in plastic."

"I'll bet it's hoodies and sweats," Primault said. "It's how all those girls were dressed."

Primault moved the camera to the other side, smaller boxes came into view. "Those are shoe boxes," he said. He opened one. "Sneakers. The same kind that Melvina wore."

"Evidence," Gavin said.

"For damn sure."

Leaving the room, they continued to advance slowly along the wall, stopping at a wooden ladder attached to the wall. It led to a loft supported by 4x4 posts. Primault scanned the camera up. "Probably for hay," he whispered. "When there were horses in here."

"It probably goes all the way to the front of the barn," Gavin surmised, pointing to several more posts. "Might be a good place to hide and wait."

"Let's do it."

Primault was the first up the ladder. "It's good," he whispered back down. "Empty up here, and it does go all the way to the front."

After Gavin was in the loft, they stepped carefully, moving closer to the front. There were evenly spaced openings in the floor, about a foot square and covered with narrow metal bars. "Vents, I think," Primault said. He stopped near the front. "This is about where the flashlight came on, I think." He pointed to one of the vents. "Let's hunker down there and wait. We're bound to hear something."

After sitting down, Primault turned off the camera to save the battery. A vertical sliver of light instantly appeared in the middle of the front wall, indicating an outside light. "Tall double doors," Gavin said. "When it was a working ranch, they brought hay up that way. I'm guessing small bales."

They sat quietly in the dark, the first opportunity to rest since they had started down from the ridge after dusk fell. Their gamble had paid off. But the ultimate objective was still not a given. At the moment the only choice was to wait.

Anticipation grew by the moment as Gavin tried to visualize the house, about forty yards away. How to approach it would be the next objective. Given that there had been no reaction to their presence security cameras were not likely in use, at least outside of the barn. But it would be wise to assume the house did have them and plan accordingly.

Music wafted up through the vent. Country music, mingling with voices. The music made it difficult to discern words. A door opened below them and a moment later an authoritative knocking. Another door opened and a light came on. They leaned down to the vent to get a glimpse. Hair on top of a head and shoulders were visible. A deep voice spoke.

"Gentlemen," the voice said. "Our employer has come to a decision."

Tulo switched off the CD player as Riley opened the door. Sanders stepped closer without entering. He had two large manila envelopes in his hands.

"Yeah," said Tulo. "What be going down?"

"First things first," Sanders said. "We need to be certain that you did not leave any fingerprints at either of the houses."

"No, sir," Riley said. "We wore gloves, all the time, like we were told."

"Is there the remotest possibility that you could be identified?"

"Don't see how," Tulo said. "We wore ski masks and put hoods on the girls when we hauled them. No way they saw us."

"Good, just making sure," Sanders said. "So, here's the plan. You will be departing, together, in the morning, no later than six a.m. Your destination is Plano, Texas. You will be traveling for about three days. Keep a low profile. Upon your arrival in Plano, you are to check in at the Desert Sands Motel, and then call me and wait for further instructions. You follow, so far?"

"Yeah, yeah," they said, in unison.

"What's going to happen to the operation here?" Riley ventured cautiously.

"We're closing shop for a while. Your job is to hang low and stay out of trouble until I call you."

Tulo glanced nervously at Riley and cleared his throat. "Mr. Sanders, how we supposed to live, you know, pay for stuff?"

Sanders lifted the envelopes to eye level. "In each of these is twenty grand and a cell phone. You will leave your vans here and take the pickup. If I do not hear from you, both of you, in four days telling me that you are in Plano, Texas, there will be hell to pay. You know we have ways of checking on your location."

Momentary elation was quickly dampened by the threat. The two men nodded like schoolboys being scolded.

"When you leave in the morning, take all your effects with you."

They nodded.

"What you gonna do, Mr. Sanders? Will you be leaving, too?"

"I will be departing shortly after you do, in the airplane," Sanders said. "Do you have any questions?"

"Not me."

"Me, neither."

Sanders passed the envelopes to them and stepped back. "Mr. Tulo, Mr. Riley. I will likely see you in the morning. Good night."

The two men stood motionless after Sanders was gone, holding their envelopes. Riley pried up the brass clasps on his and pulled open the flap. Tulo followed suit. "Shit," Riley blurted. "I never seen this much all at once!"

"Fuck me! I'm gonna have me a ribeye tomorrow!" Tulo declared. He glanced at his watch. "It's past ten. About eight hours before we can leave."

"He said no later than six, so we can leave earlier than that, if we want."

"How about now?"

Riley shook his head. "Nah. I'm tired and I got a headache."

"Okay, okay. We can wait."

The door closed and the voices became less distinguishable. The loft was quiet. "Six a.m. is the deadline," Gavin said in a whisper.

"If Sanders is leaving then, that probably means everyone is, including Mr. Piano," Primault said. "Maybe Sanders is flying him out."

"Possibly. It's the fastest way to skip the country. And where does Katherine fit in? Maybe they plan on taking her, Piano and Sanders, I mean."

"That's possible. We need to do something before six."

Gavin pondered for a moment. "I don't think Sanders will likely be coming back to the barn until maybe just before six. We need to take him out. Hopefully, he is the only pilot, and if so, that means no one can leave."

"Right. We have to get these two guys below us out of the way. Tonight."

"Tying them up would be the best," Gavin said. "They're witnesses. They know a lot."

"I don't know if they're armed. Probably not. But the farthest thing from their minds is any kind of trouble. They've got their heads into that twenty grand. We move now, down the ladder, and neutralize them. I have a pair of handcuffs in my pack. There's bound to be rope or something around here."

"I'm ready when you are."

Moving to the ladder, they climbed down, mindful of the muffled conversation coming from what they could only assume was a bunkhouse area. A single light that had apparently been turned on when Sanders arrived now illuminated the front of the barn interior. They drew their weapons and moved silently to the only door. The two men inside were still talking. Primault pointed at the round doorknob, indicating he would turn it. Gavin nodded.

Primault carefully gripped the knob with his left hand and began to twist, turning the knob a fraction of an inch at a time. Nearly thirty seconds later he felt the slide slip out of the latch and nodded at Gavin. Inside the men were still talking. Gavin motioned for him to push the door.

"On three," Primault whispered. "One—two—three." With a firm push, the door swung inward and Primault stepped inside, sidearm raised. He stepped to the side, making room for Gavin to follow. A voice stopped in mid-sentence.

Both men looked up, shock and confusion morphing their faces as two brown-skinned men seemed to materialize out of thin air. Frightened eyes locked on the weapons pointed at them.

"Shit!" squeaked Riley. Tulo was stunned into silence.

"On the floor, face down, now," Primault instructed. "You first." He pointed at Tulo, who wasted no time complying. "Now you." Riley was just as quick.

Primault kept his pistol and his gaze on the two men and spoke to Gavin. "If you watch them I'll grab our packs."

"Got it covered."

Gavin stepped to a chair, slid it over and sat. "Which one of you is Tulo?" he asked.

"I am," said the darker of the two, his voice hoarse.

"We have much to talk about. I hope you're in a conversational mood," Gavin said. "As a matter of fact, it would be in the best interest of your health and well-being if you were."

Wild fear flashed into the man's beady eyes, though he remained silent, choked by a growing sense of dread. Riley, meanwhile, was trying to breathe evenly, his eyes darting about wildly.

"Keep your hands where I can see them," Gavin said, a menacing tone creeping into his voice.

A minute later Primault stepped through the door, both packs in hand. He also had a roll of duct tape and two black hoods. "Found these in a van. I think these items somehow fit the moment," he said, holding up the tape and the hoods. He bent over the dark-haired man first, pulling both arms over his back.

"That is Mr. Tulo," Gavin said coldly.

"Really? Well, well, well, Mr. Tulo. I have plans for you," Primault spat. In the next few seconds, he wrapped tape tightly over the man's wrists. Then the ankles after he removed the man's shoes. Then, none too gently, he lifted him into a sitting position against a couch. The final move was pulling the black hood over the man's head.

"And you have to be Mr. Riley," Primault said, moving over to the other man. The man nodded. A few minutes later, he was also propped against the couch, bound hand and foot, and hooded.

"We know this is how you treated some Native girls," Primault said. "Did you ever hear of 'do unto others?' Somehow I doubt it, so this is your first lesson."

Gavin checked his watch. "It's almost eleven. I think we turn on the voice record function on one of our phones. I think these—whatever they are—have a lot to tell us."

"Absolutely," Primault concurred. "But don't turn anything on just yet." He drew his sidearm and knelt in front of Tulo and pushed the muzzle of the weapon forcefully into Tulo's crotch. Tulo stiffened. "Mr. Tulo, some shred of decency is keeping me from cutting your balls off." Primault's voice became a menacing growl. "I read the autopsy report for a beautiful, brown-skinned girl, Her name was Melvina Old Lodge. She died of severe internal injuries, inflicted by you."

Tulo involuntarily sucked in his breath.

"I know you were the one who beat her. There are no words bad enough to describe what you are. You're nowhere equal to the lowest form of life on this planet. You better hope some judge sentences you to forever and a day in solitary confinement. If it's anything less, I will hurt you. I will hurt you bad. Do you hear me, Mr. Tulo?"

The man's chest heaved in terror and his head inside the black bag nodded emphatically. A dark blot appeared on his trousers under the muzzle of the pistol as Tulo lost control of his bladder.

Just over an hour later, Gavin and Primault stopped recording, stunned by what they had heard. Primault played back a few seconds of it just to be certain. He sat back, shaking his head in astonishment. Gavin's icy stare stayed on the hooded figures for nearly a minute before he turned away.

"Let's move them," Primault decided. "Over there, against the wall."

Grabbing the backs of their collars, they dragged Tulo and Riley across the floor and set them apart from each other.

"Every fiber of my being wants to storm that house, now," Gavin said, taking a seat. "If I was absolutely certain there was no alarm system, that's what I would do."

"And I'd be there beside you," Primault said, looking at his watch. "But we can't afford to be impatient, or reckless. At the moment, several factors are lining up in our favor. Those two say that Katherine is somewhere in the basement. So, once we get inside we know where to look. It's twelve-thirty. In less than six hours Sanders will be here. We take him down and there's only one other person to worry about—Piano."

With a sigh Gavin leaned back in the chair. "You're right. So, I think rest is the best thing we can do for ourselves right now. I'll take the first watch, until about three-thirty."

"Works for me," Primault said. He stepped over a switched-off table lamp near the couch, leaving only another in the corner near the two bound men. He laid down on the couch. "Wake me if I snore," he said.

Gavin chuckled and decided to satisfy his curiosity about where a doorway in the middle of the room led. Standing, he went to the opening, which was the front of a short hallway. At the end of it was a bathroom and on either side were doors. Behind both were small bedrooms. Peeking in only briefly, he returned to the front room.

"There's beds back there," he told Primault.

"No, I'm good," came the reply. "Bad enough we have to breathe the same air as those scumbags. I'm not sleeping in their beds."

"Totally agree," Gavin said, taking the time to look around the front room. It was a kitchen and living area, with a galley arrangement on one end. Walking to the refrigerator, he opened it and saw mostly packaged food, bottled water, and at least two six-packs of beers. He took a water and returned to the chair. After a drink, he placed the .38 on a nearby table and settled in. It suddenly dawned on him that they had not heard from Wilson or Singer. He pulled out his phone and checked for any kind of message. There was nothing, except for a missed call from his land line number. Likely Gerard.

He had been so focused on getting to the barn that he hardly thought of anything else. Poor cell service was the probable reason, he thought, for the lack of communication from Wilson and Singer. In the unlikely case it was just a one-way problem, he decided to send a text.

> *Jason, have secured barn, we*
> *are inside. Katherine locked in log house,*
> *will effect rescue early morning.*
> *Let us know soonest your location.*
> *GLW & JP*

After pressing Send he waited; but there was no indication the message had been sent. Placing the phone next to the revolver, he finally acknowledged the thoughts circling in his head, ready to pounce. Overall, the situation had turned out better than he had expected. *Cetan hena ohinniyan wicabluonihan ktelo* (I will always honor the hawks). However, knowing that Katherine was within fifty yards of where he sat was frustrating. Still, there was comfort in knowing where she was. *Awanmicayankapo* (Protect her for me).

No substantive plans had been made or suggested beyond rescuing Katherine. After hearing Riley and Tulo spill their guts, he knew it couldn't end there. It was astonishing that one man, with only a few subordinates, could successfully run such a ghastly and horrendous operation for so long. Racism and complacency were the enabling factors. But there was enough blame to go around, starting with the Bureau of Indian Affairs and up the federal ladder.

Rescuing Julia Lake and Maggie Henry had been because of a pure stroke of luck. Rescuing ten other Lakota girls was due to persistence and determination and partly to luck. Now there was one more to do. He and Primault had to find a way.

He had run the gamut of fear and anxiety induced projections knowing that in most instances abductions didn't turn out well. Now the odds of a good outcome were tipping in their favor; but recklessness and bad judgement could tip it back the other way. Luckily, those were within his ability to control.

For the moment the thought of a life without Katherine was a distant fear. He visualized her sitting across the table, smiling at him over a cup coffee. He held on to that image until he began to feel fatigue in his shoulders and neck. Standing, he went to the door, opened it, and encountered a void of silence in the barn's interior. A chill went up his back when he remembered that a man was buried in the last stall, though not because of the dead body. The frightening fact was how that man was killed. In cold blood, by the man in whose house Katherine was still a captive.

Back in the room he finished the bottle of water. Primault was asleep, lying on his left side, his sidearm on the chair next to the couch. Gavin paced the room, mainly to loosen his legs, and then did some toe touches. Stretching his back muscles felt good.

He repeated the exercises several more times in the ensuing two hours. By the time his watch was ending he felt fatigue seeping in. At a few minutes past three-thirty he leaned over and touched Primault on the shoulder. He woke immediately, turning a questioning gaze upon Gavin.

"All quiet," Gavin said. "I texted Jason. No reply yet."

"Sketchy cell reception, probably," Primault said, as he stood from the couch. "Your turn."

While Primault used the restroom, Gavin retrieved his phone and the revolver and moved them to the chair near the couch. He couldn't extend his legs fully but it was good to lay down. Moments later, or perhaps minutes, he felt himself drifting off and saw Katherine gazing at him over a cup of coffee. She was smiling.

FORTY-FOUR

Ben Wilson stared at his laptop screen. "I think we finally got something," he said to Jason Singer.

Parked at a scenic overlook for the past hour, Singer patiently watched for traffic, alternating his gaze between the rear view mirrors and the view through the windshield while Wilson focused on the laptop.

"The address?"

"Yeah. 1-1-2-7-8 Bridger Lane. What time is it?"

Singer glanced at the clock on the dash. "Just after midnight."

"Okay. I can find the road to it now, but at this hour our headlights would be obvious once we're close. And—I'm worried we might lose this Wi-Fi connection if we move. Cell reception is still in and out."

"How far to that address?"

"Seven miles. Since there's been no traffic by here for a couple hours, maybe we should just hang here. I'm sure Justin and Gavin have probably tried to connect with us. As a matter of fact, I'll try another text."

Wilson typed out a message on his phone and waited. "Still doesn't do any more than flash Sending," he said dejectedly.

"I think we're okay here," Singer said. "So how did you finally find that address?"

Wilson chuckled. "Well, that person I emailed back in DC works at Wolf Star Security, where I work, Gerard Lone Wolf's company. I asked my friend Darrell to access the title companies in this area and look for the Hanrich Group or Company."

"Damn. So, if we don't hear from Justin or Gavin, it might be a good idea to move in close in the morning. Would be less suspicious that way."

"Sure."

"Then the next question is do we stay here or go back to the campground?"

"Well, we have water and snacks," Wilson said. "And unless we need to do anything more than take a piss, we're okay. If anyone does happen to stop and get nosy, we can say we were photographing stars, or something."

"Sounds like a plan." Singer found the lever on the seat and reclined it. "Sure glad this Jeep's got good legroom. Time for some z's."

"Absolutely. Sweet dreams."

"Haven't heard that in a while. My mom said it all the time."

"Yeah, so did mine. Do you have any sisters?"

"Yup, older. You?"

"No, two older brothers. This situation, with the girls. That's as bad as it gets, it's pure evil."

"No doubt about it."

"I looked it up on the internet, a couple nights ago," Wilson went on. "Slavery, human trafficking, human bondage...it's been happening for thousands of years."

"Hard to figure out why."

Wilson sighed. "Well, not really, according to one historian. I read a paper he wrote. He says that any economy based on some type of currency, like gold, silver, or exotic spices, anything that can be accumulated, the society doing it eventually uses people as commodities or barter."

"Damn. Definitely a black mark against our species."

After a few moments of silence, Wilson closed the laptop and reclined his seat. He turned his head and gazed out at the night sky. *Looks peaceful,* he thought. *But I think it's all a damn lie.*

Silence hung like a shroud for several minutes until Singer's phone chirped. Pulling it from his shirt pocket he looked at the screen. "Hey," he said. "I think it's a text."

"Maybe the gods are favoring us."

Tapping the screen, Singer saw the message appear. "Yeah, it is."

"From who? What does it say?"

> *Jason, have secured the barn,*
> *we are inside. Katherine*
> *locked in log house. Will*
> *effect rescue early morning.*
> *Let us know soonest your location.*
> *G-L-W and J-P.*

They were silent, absorbing the information.

"Okay," Wilson said. "So, they're there, in the barn and they know Katherine is in the house, and they will get her out in the morning."

"That's it."

"So that means we're in a good spot here, until morning. Ah, you should reply and tell them we'll be nearby in the morning and wait to hear from them."

"Right." Singer typed:

> *Great news. We will be mile from ranch*
> *by sunrise, will wait to hear from you.*

After a few moments he shook his head in frustration. "Crap. It isn't sending."

"Okay, well, all we can do is keep trying."

The lamp light kept Katharine awake. She did not know which she feared most: falling asleep or being in the dark. Although she was positioned with her back to the outside wall, and on her left side facing the door, she was acutely aware that she was powerless against anyone who would sooner or later enter the room. There was no way to know the hour, a best guess was around midnight. Hours ago, she faintly heard the piano again. Someone—and she guessed the blue-eyed man—played classical music.

She was grateful she was still able to move around, albeit restricted by the handcuffs and walking restraints around her ankles. Several trips to the bathroom taught her to accommodate for the ankle restraints. Hunger teased her stomach so she tried to suppress it by drinking water. Consequently, more annoyingly short steps to the bathroom.

Drop her in a Louisiana swamp, the blue-eyed man had said. She was almost numb to such an absurd threat—absurd in her world, but in his a chilling reality of punishment and death. She was not given to frequent thoughts of death, but she did lean toward the Lakota philosophy about it. The one truth that never lied. She had heard Uncle Andrew No Horn, and other elders, say that no one ever fought against death and won. One could fight for life and win, however. Understanding that distinction usually didn't happen—those same elders would say—until death is imminent and no longer a distant "someday." Understanding had come. Someday was here.

There was only one way to live it. She would fight for her life, no matter how painful, no matter who came through that door.

FORTY-FIVE

Pale light seeped in around the edges of the wide overhead garage doors on the west end of the barn. Gavin resisted the temptation to open the side door and have a look. He hoped Sanders would arrive sooner rather than later. He and Primault were in position on either side of the side door.

"It's five forty-four," Primault said, weapon in hand. "We take him as soon as he comes through the door. Get him on the ground and cuff him, search him, remove anything he has on him or in his pockets. We restrain his legs, and then we get him to talk."

"What's our plan if he refuses to talk?"

"Initially, we need to know exactly where Katherine is. The other questions can come later. If he's uncooperative, I'm in favor of shooting off his kneecaps. But, since that's not an option, somehow we need to scare the shit out of him."

"I guess we cross that bridge when we come to it."

They waited in silence, listening. A soft click suddenly came from the door. An instant later it swung open into the barn. A man entered, closing the door behind him without looking back, stepping quickly into the interior.

Primault moved up behind him and placed the muzzle of his semi-automatic behind the man's left ear. "Don't move! Hands on your head!"

Stopping, the man contemplated what to do until he saw Gavin move to the front, revolver raised and pointed at the man's head. "I'd do as he says."

Hands came up slowly. Primault pushed his weapon into the man's back. "Move away from the wall."

Surprise etched on his face, the man took two steps.

"That's far enough. On your knees."

The man complied.

"If he twitches, shoot him in the balls," Primault said to Gavin.

Gavin lowered his aim. The man's gaze fixed on the revolver.

Primault pushed the man's baseball cap off his head, quickly snapped a cuff on the man's right wrist, then the left, both hands behind him. "Now, Mr. Sanders," Primault said. "I have an important question. If you don't answer, we'll find out how much pain you can stand."

Sanders nodded.

"Where are you keeping Katherine Hill? We know she's in that log house in the basement. I want the exact location."

Fear crept into the man's eyes. "Ah, middle room, at the bottom of the stairs."

"Door is locked?"

"Yeah, gravity locks."

"Do we need a key?"

"No."

Gavin dropped to one knee and looked the man straight in the eye. "Is she okay? Unharmed?"

"Yeah, she's—she's okay."

"Where is your boss, right now?" Primault asked.

"Mr. Melrose is having breakfast in the kitchen."

"Are you flying him out of here?"

"No. I'm—I was to transport the woman."

"How exactly was that going to happen?"

The man's gaze alternated between Primault and Gavin. "First I was to get the plane ready, and then bring her out."

"Is your boss armed?"

"Yeah, he carries. Glock nine millimeter."

Primault looked at Gavin. "Any thoughts?"

"Well, I don't think we should take the chance that Melrose will happen to look out a window and see two men approaching. Two men he won't recognize." After a moment, he pointed to Sanders, who was dressed in tan jeans and a light brown leather jacket. "He looks to be about your size, the trousers and jacket should fit."

"Right. Okay, so I walk to the house, get the drop on Melrose and disable him."

Ten minutes later Sanders was cuffed to one of the loft support posts, without his trousers, shoes, and jacket. As a final touch Primault put a strip of duct tape over his mouth. He patted the man's cheek. "I'll see you later." he said.

Gavin retrieved Sanders' cap and gave it to Primault. "Just in case Melrose eyeballed Sanders this morning. See you in a bit."

Outside, Primault walked with his hands in the jacket pockets, his right hand grasping the handle of the semi-automatic. The gravel road into the property forked, with the right fork curving to the barn. The other led to the front of the house and seemed to bend around the corner of the yard fence. Between the house and the barn, where the road forked, was a mowed lawn.

Primault looked at the large windows on the house but saw no movement. Keeping a moderate pace, he finally arrived at the front gate, opened it, and followed the brick tile path to the front steps. The door was huge. He suddenly realized he did not ask Sanders if it was locked. He would find that out in a few seconds.

Grabbing the wrought iron handle on the door, he squeezed the latch. It opened. Pulling the cap's bill lower on his face, he pushed the door and stepped inside, grateful that it made no noise.

He was in an entrance with a stair railing on the right. A stairway was visible, leading down. Suddenly, piano music erupted loudly—either a CD player or a radio, he guessed. Moving cautiously, he went to the end of the entrance, pushed against the wall and carefully looked around the corner. A man was at a very large grand piano, head down, playing. That had to be Melrose, and he was facing the entrance. There was no way to approach him without being seen.

"Guess it'll have to be Plan B," Primault whispered.

One option was to enter with his automatic raised and ready and shoot if necessary. He quickly dismissed that thought. Although he was a police officer, he was out of his jurisdiction, and technically trespassing, invading a man's home—a white man's home. If anything went awry, even a slight mishap, the first thing white law enforcement would focus on was that he was Native. The reason he was here would not matter at all.

And the reason he was here was Katherine, in the basement.

The man at the piano continued playing, dramatic and rolling. Classical music, Primault assumed. Sooner or later the man would stop. And then what? Primault quickly looked toward the other part of the house he could see. A hallway to the left, and doors to other rooms. Maybe he didn't need to subdue the man. Maybe he will keep playing and stay at the piano.

He glanced at the stairwell. Katherine was down there, in a room at the bottom of the stairs. Primault made his move.

With the piano music filling his ears, he went down the stairs, thankful they were carpeted, turned left at a landing, and immediately saw the two slide bolts on a door. With his left hand he slid the bolts open, grabbed the knob and turned it. Pushing the door, he stepped into the room and immediately saw Katherine rising from the bed, her wrists in cuffs and restraints around her ankles, and her face a mask of dread anticipation.

Primault lifted the cap off, revealing his face. "Katherine! It's okay! It's Justin!"

Her expression instantaneously changed to surprise, her eyes widening. "Oh, my god! Justin! Oh, my god!"

Stepping forward he helped her stand, as she stared up at him in utter amazement.

"You found me!" Her hands flew to her mouth, and reached and touched his face.

"We did, Gavin is here, too. But we need to leave, now."

"What?"

A flash of anger coursed through him when he realized he couldn't unlock the restraints. Time was of the essence as there was no way to know when Melrose would stop playing.

"Come on, we need to go. Can you walk with those restraints? I don't have a key."

"Yeah! Yeah! Let's go! Did you say Gavin was here?"

"Yeah, he's waiting." He gently guided her to the door. She took quick steps. The music was still playing. "We need to hurry and be quiet."

She nodded and hurried to the door, and out and to the stairs, which she climbed awkwardly.

Primault kept his left hand under her arm and the weapon up and ready in his right. They gained the landing and turned and were at the top seconds later. He pointed toward the front door. Fortunately, the loud piano playing masked the clinking of the ankle restraints. Quickly opening the door, he let her step through and closed it. Dramatic staccato notes could be heard, leading into crashing chords.

"A man named Sanders was coming to get you and take you to that barn," he said. "So, we're going to walk toward it, and we can't look back."

She nodded. After the steps and the brick walkway, they paused at the gate to open and then close it behind them. The barn seemed a mile away.

Primault holstered the weapon and took Katherine's arm to help keep her balance. The ankle restraints allowed no more than an eighteen inch stride. She faltered once and nearly stumbled, but gamely adjusted. Primault was reasonably certain that if Melrose did look out the window, he would see Katherine being taken to the barn, according to plan. That is if Sanders had informed him.

Katherine stumbled again. "Sorry! I'm sorry!"

"You're doing fine."

Primault wanted badly to look back but resisted.

Past the first gravel lane and onto the lawn. "Twenty more yards," Primault said.

Finally, they reached the graveled drive leading to the barn.

"Where are we?" Katherine asked.

"North of Medora, North Dakota."

"What is this place?"

"It was a ranch, at one time."

The last twenty yards took forever.

Gavin had climbed into the loft the second Primault left and was observing through the window on the right of the double doors. He saw Primault enter the front door. For the next seven minutes his anxiety level rose to a boiling point as he kept his eyes on the front of the house. His legs nearly crumpled when the saw the door open again, disbelief and relief swirling when he saw two figures emerge.

It was her! It was Katherine!

As they came across the first graveled lane he was puzzled that her movement seemed unnatural, and then saw the restraints around her ankles and the cuffs around her wrists. Anger exploded in his chest. His gaze locked on Katherine, looking for any sign of injury. She wore the same clothes she had on when he last saw her—blue jeans and a gray shirt.

Tearing his gaze away he looked back to the front door of the house. Melrose was the only other person in the house, and, by some unbelievable stroke of good fortune, he was apparently, as yet, unaware. According to Sanders, Melrose was armed. Gavin reached back and drew the revolver. If Melrose came out the front door, he would be ready.

When they were ten yards from the barn, Gavin hurried back down the ladder, his heart pounding.

"We made it!" Primault twisted the knob, pushed open the door, and reached back to help Katherine. After two steps inside her hands flew to her mouth the instant a tall figure appeared in the dim light of the barn's interior, and then tears blurred her vision.

She reached out, her legs suddenly weak.

Gavin gently grabbed the tips of her fingers, savoring the sensation of feeling them, and lifted her hands and kissed them softly. No words were necessary. She took a step forward as he wrapped his arms around her, pulling her close. She took deep breaths to quell the sobs, savoring the feeling of their bodies touching.

"Promise me something," she said.

"Anything."

"That we'll always have time for each other, no matter what."

"I promise. For you I have all the minutes there are and will ever be."

In a while Gavin reluctantly lowered his arms and then cupped her face in his hands. Wiping away her tears, he smiled. "Are you okay?"

She nodded. "Yeah. I'm a little tired, and I need to pee."

He chuckled. "I don't know if I should ever let you out of my sight again, but there's a bathroom, through that door."

"Ah, first," Primault said. He had been waiting for the right moment to interrupt, holding up a key. "Let's get those damn cuffs off."

They had been unaware that Primault had looked through the items confiscated from Sanders' pockets.

Katherine held out her arms and Primault quickly unlocked the cuffs. Kneeling, he found the key to the ankle restraints and took them off. He smiled as she immediately wrapped her arms around Gavin. In a moment she stepped back.

"Now, show me where the bathroom is."

While Katherine was using the restroom, Primault and Gavin hauled Tulo and Riley out into the barn, dragging them by their ankles. She had noticed them trussed up and against the wall but said nothing.

Gavin paused and turned to Primault. "Thank you, my friend. I can't—"

"Hey, it's good, it's all good. I know how I would have felt if it had been my wife."

"I don't know how I can every repay you."

"It's not about that, not between friends."

After a firm handshake, Primault nodded at their prisoners. "We've got unfinished business," he said.

"Right. This isn't over, not quite yet."

After washing her face and redoing her ponytail, Katherine returned to the front room. Taking a bottle of water from Gavin, she sat down with him on the couch, and immediately laid her head on his shoulder and took his hand in hers. Primault, meanwhile, had locked the side door and returned.

"The first thing that comes to mind," Primault said, taking a chair near the open door, "is that man in the house. What do we do about him?"

"I think we need to apprehend him. He's the head of the snake," Gavin said.

"I don't know his name," Katherine said.

"Melrose, or at least that's what Sanders says," Gavin recalled. "I wouldn't be surprised if it's not his real name."

"What about the others? I think I recognized one of them," Katherine said.

"Probably Sanders. Likely Melrose's right hand man," Gavin told her. "The other two are—they transported the girls to the man camp from the houses in which they were kept. You were in one of them."

Katherine put a hand over her eyes. "This is all so surreal. Which one of them took me?"

"He's apparently buried in the last stall in this barn," Primault said.

Katherine could only shake her head in disbelief. "I'm almost afraid to ask. Who put him there?"

"According to Tulo and Riley, Melrose did."

"Tulo? I've heard that name."

"Yeah," Primault said. "I first heard that name from Julia Lake and Maggie Henry. Tulo's the one who beat Melvina."

Katherine reached up and grabbed Gavin's arm. "This is so sordid, and horrible."

Gavin put his arm around her shoulders and pulled her close. "Okay," he said, gently. "Let's stop right there. There'll be time to talk about it. I'm in favor of getting in that truck out there and leaving. But I think we owe it to Melvina to put an end to this."

"Yes, we do," Katherine agreed. "I'm up for that."

"But we do have good news," Primault said. "A few days ago, we found the houses, two of them, where ten girls were kept locked away. We rescued them. They're all on their way home."

"You did? Oh, my god! That's wonderful! I'm sure their families are overjoyed. Those poor girls! How were they?"

"Hard to say," Gavin said. "They were talking and became more animated as the reality of being free sunk in more and more. They'll have some demons to fight, after what they've been through."

Katherine covered her face and shook her head. "I heard someone pounding the wall in the basement I was in," she said. "It was them, it had to be."

"It was," Gavin said. "We saw your message on the wall. That's how we found this place. Just by pure chance, I saw a photo of a helicopter transporting a crate beneath it. The pilot who flew the chopper said it was a piano, in the crate. So, I asked where he had taken the crate. This is where he brought it."

"I heard someone say the name Piano. The man talking to the one who abducted me. Soon after I was brought here, down in that room, I heard someone playing a piano. Must have been the one you called Melrose. He's pure evil. He told me that my abduction had been a mistake, and he apologized. And then he said I would be dropped over a swamp in Louisiana."

"What does he look like?" Gavin asked.

"Average height, slender, about sixty, maybe. Pale, I mean, really pale, and blondish hair. Cold blue eyes, really creepy."

"I saw him playing the piano," Primault said, "but only for a couple seconds. He did look really pale."

"If he's the guy who's running this—whatever it is," Katherine said, "he needs to go down."

"It's exactly what we have in mind, and I think we question Mr. Sanders," Primault said. "I'd like to talk to the Chief but I'm not sure of the cell phone reception here. I can try. I'm also puzzled we haven't heard from Singer and Wilson." He paused to glance at his watch. "Believe it or not, it's only six thirty seven. On the other hand, maybe we should first storm the house and take down Melrose."

"I yield to your judgment, my friend," Gavin asserted. "Keep in mind that Melrose is armed, and clearly dangerous."

"Here's a thought," Primault said. "Sanders was to fly out of here, and maybe if Melrose realizes nothing is happening, he might come to check."

"Yeah? That might work. One of us can watch from the window in the loft."

Primault nodded in agreement. "Yeah. Surprising him is safer than—well, wait a minute. Maybe I can approach the house again. I'm dressed in Sanders' clothes."

"Well, I know you're good at what you do, but I'm thinking of your wife," Gavin pointed out. "I say we wait and observe, first."

"Wait," Katherine said softly.

Primault smiled. "We'll wait."

A sound came from the front of the barn. Primault quickly held up a hand, as they all fell silent. The sound grew louder, until it was unmistakable. Tires on the gravel outside.

FORTY-SIX

The man at the keyboard finished with the last stirring chords of "Les Miserables." Rising slowly, he looked down longingly at the piano. He was wearing neoprene gloves. "It's been an honor," he said. Stepping back, he gently pushed the stool forward, aligning it over the pedals. Crossing the room, he entered the short hallway and turned right into the master bedroom, as elegantly furnished as the sitting room. Inside the walk-in closet he quickly undressed, removing the gray sweatpants and shirt. Folding each item precisely he opened a middle drawer and placed them inside. From the top of the dresser, he picked up the faded pair of blue jeans to put on, adding a leather belt. Next a plaid western shirt with shades of blue. From the shoe shelf at the back wall, he took a pair of worn out western boots, sat on a stool, and slipped them on. Reaching up to a shelf he took down a battered straw cowboy hat and put it on his head.

Stopping in front of full length mirror, he tucked in the shirt, buckled the belt, and scratched his two-day growth of beard. Pulling down the hat brim, he reached for the handle of a large roller bag and walked out.

He didn't pause or stop, hardly glanced left or right as he walked briskly through the hallway to a door at the far end of the house. Without hesitation he opened it and walked through, shutting it behind him. He touched a switch on a wall and one of the two garage doors slid upward.

Two vehicles were in the garage. To the right a gleaming white Cadillac Escalade, to the left an apparently vintage light green Ford pickup—a 1994 half-ton two-door, desperately in need of a carwash. In the eight-foot long box were a half dozen small square alfalfa bales, haphazardly arranged. Walking to the passenger side of the pickup, he opened the door and lifted in the roller bag. Going to the other side, he climbed into the cab and started the truck.

The quiet, smooth sound of the 390 cubic inch engine belied the truck's appearance. It was brand new, less than a year old. It, along with a new transmission, had been installed at a dealership in Minot. As a matter of fact, whatever non-cosmetic restorations could be done, were done; front to back, top to bottom. Mechanically, it was practically brand new. It had been built for this transitory moment.

The blue-eyed man removed the gloves, put the transmission in gear, and backed out of the garage. Outside, he stopped, rolled down his window, and tossed the garage remote under the descending door after he pushed the Close switch. Backing up, he stopped, turned the wheels to the right, and took a narrow trail west toward a county road. Never once did he look back. Even after the large log house was visible when he turned left onto the county road, he kept his gaze on the road ahead.

A few miles down that same county road, a tan Jeep Rubicon was parked on the grassy shoulder, close to the three-strand barb wire fence. Its two occupants were tired and frustrated.

"I can't understand why the Wi-Fi works and cell phones have no reception," Jason Singer huffed.

"Different systems," Ben Wilson explained. "Cell phones need a tower. Wi-Fi uses a satellite. Medora is behind us, to the south, and we're outside the south unit of the park. Probably isn't a cell tower close enough."

"Well, we do know where the Hanrich place is. We know Justin and Gavin are there. I think we should get close enough to lay eyes on it."

Wilson loosed a tired sigh. "Sure, let's just go."

Singer started the engine and pointed to an approaching pickup. "Maybe whoever that is knows where there's a cell tower. He probably lives out here."

"Can you stop him, somehow?"

"I can try." Singer put the Jeep in gear and rolled it on the gravel and stopped. Opening his window, he poked out his arm and waved. The approaching truck slowed down and stopped, rolling down his window. Pushing back a straw hat, the driver gazed at them with amused eyes.

"Mornin' fellas, Ya lost?"

"No," Singer said. "We know where we are, we're just trying to pick up some cell phone service."

"Wal, out here, it's kinda sketchy. Ain't no tower 'til ya get closer to Medora. Sorry."

"Okay, thanks."

"Ya sure ya ain't lost?"

"No, we're good."

With a nod the driver of the truck with a load of hay bales rolled up his window and drove away.

"Okay," Wilson said, "we can sit here until hell freezes over and we probably won't get in touch with them. We need to get closer."

"Roger that." Singer pressed down on the accelerator, making the rear tires spin before they found traction on the gravel surface. "Always wanted to do that," he said.

After four miles they came to a slight rise and saw the white barn approximately a mile farther and to the right of the road. Wilson rolled down his window and aimed his camera. "Nothing moving," he said. "The text did say something might happen early in the morning. It's six-forty. It's either already happened, or not yet."

"Guess we just wait."

"Well, I don't know. I have a funny feeling about this." Bracing the long lens against the window frame, Wilson zoomed in as close as possible, studying every nook and cranny of both buildings. "There's just nothing happening. It's eery. Looks deserted."

"Yeah, but we know they're there, in the barn."

"There's two garage-type doors, double doors above them, a regular door to the left of the garage doors, two small windows up higher. Just looks like a barn."

"I would hate to think so, but maybe something happened to them."

"No, no, I don't think so," Wilson protested. "I mean, those are two bad ass dudes, you know. I'd hate to meet either of them in a dark alley."

Singer chuckled. "Good point. Let's at least get closer. I mean, worst case scenario, someone might think we're just lost tourists. That old guy in the pickup didn't seem to mind."

"Okay, if this road goes parallel to the place, we'll stop there."

Half a mile later they came to an approach. A road into a pasture angled to the right, leading to the house and barn, while the county road ran about a hundred yards west of it. "Okay, stop here," Wilson instructed, after they pulled even with the house. His camera up and ready, he adjusted the focus and panned the side of the house in view. "That's a damn big log house," he said. "A beautiful place. Windows are all open. I don't see any movement. The lawn is mowed. Other than that, nothing."

Five minutes passed, then seven.

"I say we get a wild hair up our ass and go there," Wilson said.

"Really?"

"Yeah. You're a cop. What does your gut tell you?"

"If they're about to make a move of some kind, we might screw it up for them."

Another five minutes passed. Wilson could not detect any movement in any of the windows. "What time is it?"

"Almost seven." Singer started the engine. "Okay, let's go back to the road into the place, and make a slow approach in."

"Now you're talking!"

When they turned in off the county road, Wilson turned on the video camera and aimed it out the windshield. The Jeep had plenty of power in low gear to slowly move ahead at idle, with Singer touching the accelerator. They stopped thirty yards from the house, where the driveway forked. Left fork went to the front of the yard fence, the right fork led to the barn.

"I'm sure they're in the barn," Singer said, "so I'm going there."

Almost a minute later they reached the barn and stopped.

"Okay," Wilson said, in a low voice. "What do we do now?"

In the loft, Primault ran to the window to peek out, Gavin a step behind. They had all scrambled up the ladder to hide in the loft.

"Son of a bitch!" Primault exclaimed.

"Yeah, that goes for me, too!" Gavin said.

Primault hurried to the ladder and scrambled back down. Gavin looked at Katherine and grinned. "It's our guys," he said. "They drove up, big as life."

"Oh," she said. "Is that good, or bad?"

"Well, we'll see." He sighed. "Let's go back down."

By the time Gavin and Katherine were back down on the ground floor, Primault opened the door and stepped out. "Get in here!" he said, gesturing emphatically. "Hurry!"

Relief and elation quickly turned to worry the second Wilson and Singer saw Primault's stern expression. Getting out of the Jeep they scurried in through the open door, and saw Katherine standing with Gavin.

"You did get her out of the house!" Wilson said.

"What?" Primault said, "Did you know she was in the house, or are you just assuming?"

"We got your text," Singer told them. "But nothing else. Our responses apparently didn't get through."

"How did you did manage to find your way here?" Primault asked, puzzled.

"I got a bit of help from a colleague. He found the address for us."

Jason Singer stepped over to Katherine. "Good to see you, ma'am."

"Thank you, Jason."

"I haven't had the pleasure," Wilson said, stepping up. "I'm Ben Wilson, I work for Gerard. He speaks highly of you, all the time. Says his brother is the luckiest man in the world."

"Thank you, Ben. A pleasure to meet you."

Singer noticed the man cuffed to the post, as well as the other two, sitting on either side of another post. Their hoods had been removed.

Disheveled, they looked like cornered rats. "What's going on there?" Singer asked, pointing to the prisoners.

"Operatives," Primault told them. He pointed to Sanders. "Mr. Fancy Pants there is number two man, near as we can figure. The other two are the transporters, so to speak. That one," he added, pointing at Tulo, "is the one who beat Melvina."

"Really?" Singer said coldly. Walking over, he dropped to one knee in front of Tulo, who dropped his gaze to the floor, trying to avoid the icy glare he could feel. "You should never have crawled out of whatever hole you were born in," Singer growled.

"Whatever you have in mind," Primault said, "get in line. I'm first."

"Yeah? Well, maybe he'll do the world a favor and have a heart attack and die."

Singer turned away after a few seconds, pure loathing etched across his face.

"Well, if Melrose hasn't looked out and seen the Jeep, he must be totally engrossed in something," Primault said.

"I didn't see any kind of movement, in any of the windows," Wilson asserted." We were on the road to the west, so we looked from there. I tell you, the place looks deserted."

"I have a thought, Jason," Primault said. "How about you and I do a fast infiltration. The front door is unlocked. There's got to be a back door."

"There is," Wilson said. "Near the corner, on the other side."

"Okay," Primault said. "I'll take the front, you take the back."

Katherine reached out to touch Primault's arm. "Justin," she began, "before you do anything, can I ask you a question?"

"Certainly."

"Soon after I was brought here, I heard a gunshot, somewhere, perhaps outside the house, but close. I don't know who might have fired the shot. Is the man armed, do you know?"

"Yes, according to Sanders."

"Okay, but that wasn't my question. This is: what if you have to shoot him? Or Jason has to?"

Primault nodded thoughtfully. "Yeah, that entered my mind this morning."

"And?"

"I see what you're getting at. Jason and I are commissioned law enforcement, but out of our jurisdiction."

"And this is a lily white conservative state. We might be in jeopardy of being charged for trespassing just because we're here. If you shoot Melrose, justifiable or not, the first fact an investigating officer will look at is your race. Let's think about that. Let's make that a part of the equation that factors in to whether you infiltrate that house, or not."

"Okay, okay. So, we'll stand down. But we can't just walk away. We've uncovered something totally evil here. Something has to be done."

"Of course, of course," Katherine agreed. "So, maybe in the next hour or so, we just wait, and watch."

"That makes sense," Gavin asserted. "Maybe Melrose will become curious when he hasn't heard that airplane taxiing and taking off."

"And there's the issue of those people over there," Katherine pointed out, gesturing toward the three prisoners. "What are we going to do with them?"

"We need to question Sanders," Primault said. "And at some point I really need to talk to Chief Avery. We should notify law enforcement in whatever counties those houses are, where those girls were imprisoned. The Chief can initiate that. Trouble is the cell service here."

"I have an idea," Wilson said. "I have email with my Wi-Fi. Can that be helpful?"

"Absolutely," Primault said. "I can send the Chief an email, and then find some damn hilltop where I can get more than one bar, so I can call. When was the last time you had cell service?" he asked Wilson.

"In Medora. The farther we got, the sketchier. Some guy, a rancher probably, told us this morning that there's no cell tower close by."

"Really, where was that? Where did you see him?"

"Oh, just down the road here." Wilson replied.

"Really?" Katherine said. "What did he look like?"

"Oh, older guy," Singer said. "Blondish hair, blue eyes."

"Blue eyes? Melrose has very pale blue eyes," Katherine recalled.

"Yeah? So did this guy." Singer recalled. "Probably a local. He was driving a pickup full of hay bales."

"How did you happen to talk to him?" Primault asked.

"I waved him down," Singer said. "Friendly guy."

Primault noticed Katherine's look of consternation. "Something about that guy bothering you, Katherine?"

"I don't know. I suppose there is more than one blue-eyed white guy around here. They do outnumber us, pretty much."

Wilson touched Primault's shoulder. "Ah, my laptop and cameras are in the Jeep. Okay if I step out and grab them?"

"Yeah, go ahead."

Minutes later Wilson activated his Wi-Fi hotspot receiver and logged on to the internet and gave the laptop to Primault.

"There are chairs and a couch in that front room," Gavin said, pointing to the door to the bunk area. "We might as well be comfortable."

A minute later, sitting at a small table, Primault accessed his work email, collected his thoughts, and composed the email to Chief Ben Avery:

> *Chief:*
>
> *Primault here. We are at Hanrich ranch, have rescued Katherine Hill, unharmed.*
>
> *Have apprehended 3 perpetrators. 1 more still loose, likely in a house we have under observation. No cell phone service here, some miles north of Medora, ND, so emailing. Need advice and help. Should we move to apprehend last perpetrator or stand down? I'm worried about legal implications, re: jurisdiction and racial implications. We are Native officers in white counties. Might be construed the wrong way. Perhaps you can contact county sheriffs here? Apprise them of Katherine situation and previous rescue of 10 girls near Pinnacle. Will wait for your reply for 30 minutes and then move to find cell phone reception so we can talk. Justin.*

Primault read the email out loud. "Did I cover it? Is there anything else?"

Receiving nods of concurrence all around, he hit Send. "Okay, now we wait." He turned to Ben Wilson. "Can you set up your camera in the window in the loft?"

"Consider it done."

"Before you do that," Gavin said to Wilson. "May I use your laptop? I would like to send an email."

"Of course."

Gavin took it to the table and gestured for Katherine to join him. "It dawns on me that we should cover all our bets," he said. "In the event that the legal aspect of this situation becomes convoluted, I want to be ready. I'm going to email Gerard, apprise him of the situation, and ask him for recommendations for representation."

"Excellent idea," she affirmed.

After a moment of thought, Gavin brought up his email account, and typed out his message:

> *Gerard, good news and possibly bad news. Katherine is safe and well, rescued this morning. We have apprehended 3 perpetrators who imprisoned the 12 Lakota girls, possibly a 4th. Jurisdiction is obviously an issue. Proper action is to notify local law enforcement. Chief Avery will do that. We don't know what the outcome will be after white law enforcement enters the picture, usual racial attitudes may outweigh facts of this case. We have evidence and testimony on our side. However, in the event we need legal representation, licensed to practice in North Dakota, who would you recommend? At the moment, email is best method of communication. Time is of the essence. Please notify Uncle Andrew and Loren, regarding Katherine. Gavin.*

After Katherine read and nodded her approval, he hit Send. Reaching out, he took her hand. "Listen," he said, "Before the day is over, white cops will come. I think it might be wise for you to leave before then. Get you out of the crosshairs."

She shook her head, a flash of defiance in her eyes. "No," she said, "not on your life. For one thing, I'm a witness, and for another, we're in this together."

He gazed at her lovingly, not so much with renewed respect, but affirmed respect. "I knew there was a reason Grandma Annie called you Soldier Woman. I love you forever and a day."

"I love you forever and a day and one minute longer," she said, pulling his face close for a kiss. "And don't try getting rid of me again. After what I've been through, I'm not leaving your side. As a matter of fact, I'm considering some kind of connective surgery."

"I don't deserve you."

"Yes, you do."

"Good, because I've been in love with you since you were fifteen."

"And don't you ever forget it."

A chair was handed up to Wilson after he had the still camera in place, trained on the house through the loft window. That eliminated the risk of anyone having to look out the window and being spotted. Wilson took up station on the chair and settled in for the duration.

Singer searched the galley kitchen and found coffee and a small coffee maker, and soon had it going. Primault sat at the table with Wilson's laptop. He glanced at Gavin on the couch with Katherine.

"I think now is the time to question Mr. Sanders," he suggested.

"Before you do, may I suggest one thing?" Katherine asked.

'Of course."

"Just keep in mind what we discussed earlier, that, like it or not, we are in the middle of white territory. No matter how noble our cause, some sheriff or lawyer will scrutinize how you handle those perpetrators."

FORTY-SEVEN

Primault instructed Wilson to give a shout if he saw any movement in the house, especially if Melrose approached the barn. He then put his own clothes back on and tossed Sanders jeans and jacket at his feet. "My friend and I," Primault said, pointing to Gavin, "would like a few minutes of your time. So, we're going to unlock your cuffs and escort you to the last stall. An appropriate place, I think. If you do anything but walk in a straight line I will not hesitate to shoot you in the small of your back."

Sanders cleared his throat, and nodded, his eyes full of fearful respect for the two Native men in front of him. His gaze was fixed on the semi-automatic in the hands of the short-haired of the two. The long-haired man was equally threatening though he had no weapon.

After one side of the cuffs were opened and Sanders stepped away from the post, Primault deftly grabbed Sanders' arms and locked the cuffs again. "Walk," he said.

Sanders walked stiffly to the last stall and stopped in the middle of it, directly over Nomer's grave. He didn't move until Primault said "Turn around."

Light coming in from the two side windows in the loft above barely reached the back of the barn, causing an eerie darkness in the stall. The flashlight in Primault's hand came on with a soft click, with Sanders in the center of the beam. "He's all yours," Primault said.

Gavin stepped four feet in front of Sanders, pausing to slip on a pair of leather gloves, staring into Sanders' apprehensive eyes until the gloves were on. Then he pulled out his black handled hunting knife from its sheath on his belt. The blade was wide and eight inches long.

"Mr. Sanders, we have questions for you. Simple questions that require the truth. Anything less will be painful for you." Stepping forward he swiftly pulled down Sanders' boxer briefs with his right hand, and grabbed the man's penis, gripping it as tight as he could and pulling it straight. Sanders gasped, his body tensed. Gavin lowered the knife slowly and placed it under the base of the penis, the spine upward, and pushed it up.

Sanders' eyes and mouth flew open simultaneously in fearful surprise.

"Now, right now, the blade is down." Gavin pulled up harder. Sanders gasped again, his face contorted in fear. "Imagine what would happen if I turned it to the blade," he continued. "It would slice clean through in about a second, and you would bleed out in minutes. That will happen if you don't cooperate or if you give us anything other than the truth. Am I clear, Mr. Sanders?"

"Yah," he croaked, nodding carefully.

"Good." Gavin lowered the knife. "First question; did you lay a hand on Katherine, my fiancée?"

A head-shaking denial was instantaneous, "No."

"Then, you might live to see the sun set." Gavin turned to Primault. "He's all yours."

Gavin stepped to one side and Primault touched Record on his phone. Totally miserable, the man stood with his genitals exposed. "Be glad this isn't video. What is your name?"

"Gorton, Tom Gorton."

"Not Sanders?"

"No. That's how Riley and Tulo know me."

"I see. So is Melrose your boss's real name?"

"No."

"What is it?"

"I don't know."

"Pseudonyms to protect the guilty."

"Yeah."

"So, the man whose name isn't Melrose, what does he do?"

"He gives orders."

Primault's inscrutable gaze stayed on Gorton's face. "Melrose gives you orders, you pass them down to Tulo and Riley. Do Tulo and Riley ever talk to Melrose?"

"No."

"Do they ever see him?"

"No."

"You mean, they live here, in this bunkhouse at this ranch, they come and go from here, but they never lay eyes on Melrose?"

"No, they don't ever see him."

"What do Tulo and Riley do?"

"They, uh, find business and take girls to the men, and take the money."

"Okay. Then they turn the money over to you and you turn it over to Melrose."

"Yeah."

"What does Melrose do with the money?"

"He pays us. He pays me, I pay Riley and Tulo."

"In cash?"

"Yeah."

"What about the rest of the money? What does Melrose do with it?"

"I don't know."

Primault glanced at Gavin, a look of realization crossing his face. Gavin nodded, arriving at the same realization. No real names, only cash transactions, three levels of operation with limited overlap, or none, from one to the other.

"Who pays the bills for this place? Electricity and propane?" Gavin asked.

"Melrose."

"Does he own this place?" Primault continued.

"I don't know."

"Okay, what will happen now? You have no more girls. Why were you leaving? You were to fly out this morning, I'm assuming in that airplane over there. Why?"

Gorton cast a fearful glance for a second at Gavin, took a deep breath and licked his lips. "Uh, Melrose's orders were to take the woman to Louisiana."

"Louisiana? Where, in Louisiana?"

Gorton swallowed, his face turning pale. "A swamp."

"You have one chance to tell us exactly what was to go down."

"I was to drop her out over the swamp."

Primault and Gavin glanced at one another. Primault could only shake his head at the depravity of Gorton's revelation. Gavin turned a cold eye to

Gorton. If they had not arrived when they did, Gorton would be in the air by now to carry out his task.

"So, this morning, you were on your way here to get the plane ready to fly?"

"Yeah."

"What was supposed to happen after Louisiana?"

"My orders were to go to Plano, Texas, and wait to hear from Melrose."

After a long, disgusted stare at Gorton, Primault lowered the phone and stopped the recording. "Put your damn underwear on," he said coldly.

Gorton quickly pulled up his shorts, obviously relieved, but his expression was that of a defeated man. He stood with his eyes down, waiting.

Escorting him to the front, they let him put his trousers on, use the restroom, and take a bottle of water. Tulo and Riley were given the same courtesy, one at a time, and then tied to a post along with Gorton.

Primault called out to Wilson. "Have you seen anything?"

"No, no movement. It's been about an hour."

"Something about that bothers me," Primault admitted. "Especially after what we heard from Gorton."

"What did you learn?" Katherine asked.

"It's a damn shady affair," Primault said. "Melrose is an assumed name. Tulo and Riley have never seen him, can't identify him. Sanders' real name is Gorton. He doesn't know that much about Melrose either, hardly anything."

"A perfect set-up," Katherine concluded, "predicated on the possibility, or probability, that one day it would all come crashing down."

"Exactly," Gavin agreed. "So, when that moment comes Melrose follows a contingency plan. Nothing is left to chance."

"Tulo and Riley told us they were to drive to Plano, Texas," Primault said. "Gorton was to go there as well and wait. That's all they know. I think Melrose planned to contact them, and then eventually start up business elsewhere."

"Or eliminate them," Gavin suggested. "I'm guessing he killed Katherine's abductor."

"Of course!" Primault said. "After that, there's no one who knows anything about this operation. No witnesses. A perfect getaway."

"So, that begs the question," Katherine said. "Is he still in the house?"

"I saw him playing the piano," Primault said. "He was still playing when we walked out."

"And that was, what, two hours ago, more or less?"

"What are you suggesting?" Primault asked.

"That there's a real possibility he's gone."

"How?"

Katherine turned to Singer. "Didn't you tell us you saw a man in a pickup truck, and he had really blue eyes?"

"Yeah," Singer replied. "We talked to him."

"Oh, shit!" Primault exclaimed. "And how long ago was that?"

"Oh, about fifteen minutes before we got here. But he sure looked like a rancher. Old pickup, hay bales in the back."

"Exactly!" Katherine asserted. "All part of his plan."

After a moment of silence, Primault cleared his throat. "Well, there's only one way to find out. Jason, you go in the back door, I'll go in the front."

Primault first tossed a walkie-talkie up to Wilson. "Keep your eyes on that house and let us know the instant you see anything but us moving."

"You got it."

With eyes scanning every window, Primault and Singer walked to the yard gate. "I'll wait thirty seconds for you to get to the back door," Primault said. "Break in if you have to." Singer nodded and veered off to the right, quickly skirting around the corner. Primault moved up to the front door and counted to 30. He opened the door and quietly stepped in. There was a low, almost indistinguishable hum, but silence otherwise. Moving up to the wall leading to the bigger room, he peeked around the corner. He waited, motionless, listening. A movement in a hallway at the end of the room caught his eye. Jason Singer appeared, moving silently.

Primault stepped into the room, raising a finger to his lips, and motioned to the hallway behind him. Singer crossed the room and together they moved a step at a time. A bathroom on the right was empty, so too a bedroom on the left. The last door was directly ahead. They paused in front of it and Primault stepped in first to a large master bedroom. Singer checked a large closet with clothes hanging.

"I think there's a door to a garage, next to where I came in," Singer said.

"Okay, let's look in the basement first."

Two bedrooms, another separate bathroom, a furnace room, and an exercise room were all unoccupied. Returning to the first floor they went to the door Singer indicated and into the two-car garage. A shiny pearl white Cadillac Escalade was parked in it. Primault looked around at the interior for several long seconds. "Do you notice something?" he asked.

"What?"

"No tools, like most garages have. Nothing left strewn around. It's really neat. The guy must have been a clean freak."

"Look there," Singer said pointing to the floor of the vacant side of the garage. "Are those tracks?" Tread marks were barely visible in the dust.

Primault knelt and leaned in close. "Sure are." He pointed toward the door. "There was another vehicle here, and it went out the door."

"That old pickup truck we saw."

"I wouldn't doubt it."

"Son of a bitch! He was three feet away from me."

Primault loosed an exasperated sigh. "Something tells me that if we dusted this house for prints, we would find Gorton's but not Melrose's."

Katherine and Gavin were not surprised to hear Primault's report. "There was probably another vehicle in the garage. It's gone now."

Like Singer, Wilson expressed his frustration. "Damn! That guy who stopped, he was as folksy as hell. Just a good ol' boy. I'm surprised he didn't have a toothpick in his mouth."

"And neither one of us thought to check his license plates," Singer agonized.

"You had no reason to," Primault assured them.

"Well, I think we pause and figure out what our next move is," Gavin said.

After they gathered in the front room of the bunkhouse, Primault checked his email and found a long reply from Chief Avery. After reading it, he looked up at the expectant gazes. "Well, the Chief has been calling people and he's talked to two sheriffs, one in the county we're in and one in the county where the girls were incarcerated. Sheriff Arlo Kinsley and a deputy are on the way here now. The Chief has told them all he knows and he has also talked to the FBI. So, we're about to have visitors."

"Damn," Wilson fretted. "Sounds ominous."

Gavin checked his email and found a reply from Gerard. "Here's what Gerard says: "Cooperate with any law enforcement, answer all questions. You have not harmed anyone or destroyed property, so the worst you can be charged with is trespassing. I have secured representation for all of you, a prominent Montana lawyer, Max Wittfield. Do not hesitate to inform any law enforcement that you have a lawyer. By all means burn and copy the interrogation audio before you turn it over. Keep me apprised."

"I can do that," Wilson said. "I've got all the necessary gadgets. Give me your phone and I'll get on it now."

While Wilson went to work, Primault opened the two garage doors. "I think we should bring chairs out here and wait. If they can see us immediately, that might be a good thing."

Wilson joined them, reporting that he had emailed the audio to his personal email account. "Just in case your phone or my laptop are confiscated," he said.

A long twenty-seven minutes passed before two vehicles turned into the approach and up the driveway, turning right at the fork and toward the barn. In the lead was a pickup with a sedan behind, both with insignia on the door and a light bar on top.

"Well, the good thing is they didn't come with lights flashing," Primault said.

"That doesn't mean they won't step out of their vehicles with guns drawn," Gavin said.

They all watched as the driver's side door to the pickup swung open and a man in a straw hat stepped out.

FORTY-EIGHT

Sheriff Arlo Kinsley's cautious expression remained as he walked toward the open doors, his gaze moving over the four men and one woman sitting in a semi-circle just inside one wide doorway. Four Natives, one white. He was flanked by a youngish looking deputy, also wearing a white straw hat. Although trim, with light brown hair under a narrow face, the bespectacled sheriff was pushing retirement age. Both men were dressed in denim jeans and tan, long sleeve shirts with county sheriff shoulder patches. Both carried semi-automatics in quick draw clips on the right hip.

Kinsley stopped ten feet from the door. "Which one of you is Lieutenant Primault?" he asked in a mellow voice.

Justin Primault stood and walked forward and extended his hand. "I am, Sheriff. Pleased to meet you."

"Likewise," Kinsley replied, returning the handshake. "Had a long conversation about an hour ago with your boss, Chief Avery. He had some—interesting things to tell me."

"I'm glad you could do that. I'm sure you have some questions for us."

"Right. But I'd like to meet your people first if that's okay. This is my deputy, Earl Johnson."

"Of course, pleased to meet you, Deputy Johnson." After shaking hands with the deputy, Primault gestured toward the others. "This is Jason Singer, Ben Wilson, Gavin Lone Wolf, and Katherine Hill."

The sheriff and the deputy stepped forward to shake hands with everyone, both of them removing their hats when taking Katherine's hand. Wilson politely offered two of the empty chairs, then quickly retrieved a wooden bench along a wall and carried it over. Kinsley turned a curious gaze toward the three detainees sitting forlornly. "I imagine those are the people you apprehended?" he asked.

"Correct," Primault confirmed.

After everyone took a seat, with Singer and Wilson on the bench facing everyone else, the sheriff removed his hat, brushed back his hair, and replaced the hat. "Well, folks," he said, "best to start from the beginning, I think. According to Chief Avery, you all are here because you were searching for a lady who had been abducted. I'm assuming that's you, ma'am," he said, nodding to Katherine.

"Yes," she said.

"I'm pleased they were able to find you."

"Thank you."

"And, while you were conducting the search—if I understood the Chief—you all managed to find a passel of missing Native girls."

"That's essentially how it happened," Primault said.

"Okay, then," Kinsley said, looking at his deputy. "Earl, you mind to fire up that little contraption of yours?"

"Sure thing." Deputy Johnson pulled a small voice recorder from his breast pocket and pushed on the switch.

"I assume you are all okay with us recording you?" Kingsley asked.

"By all means," Primault assented.

"If you don't mind, ma'am, ladies first is the polite way to go. If you can tell me what happened to you, I'd be grateful."

A little over an hour later, the sheriff nodded to his deputy as a signal to shut off the recorder. "Well, well, well," he said, pushing up the brim of his hat. "I served six years in the Navy and I heard enough cussing to last me a lifetime, so I ain't cussed since then. But if anything at all would drive me to cuss, it's what you all just told. This here situation with missing Native girls, I'll admit, by god, I'm one of the ones didn't pay much heed. But if that don't break your heart, you don't have a heart."

"I'm glad to hear you say that sir," Primault said.

"Ma'am," the sheriff said, looking directly at Katherine. "So up until just a few hours ago, you were trapped in the basement of that house?"

"Yes."

"My daughter, my only daughter, is likely about your age. I'd just plain shrivel up if something ever happened to her. I can only imagine what your family must have felt. I hope they know you're safe now."

"Yes, my family knows."

"Sheriff," the deputy said, after a moment, "what's next?"

"Well, as of now this place is a crime scene, considering what went on here, and there's a grave in this barn. All those vehicles are evidence, and likely that log house."

"There are two rooms there," Gavin said, pointing, "and stored in them are supplies and clothing for the girls that were imprisoned. Food and water as well. Two refrigerators full of processed meats—hot dogs, luncheon meat—all that is evidence."

"It sure the hell is."

"May I point out other possible evidence sites?" Primault asked.

"Sure."

"Those vans were used to transport girls. Very possibly there is DNA evidence in them, perhaps hair."

"Good point." The sheriff pulled a small notebook out of a shirt pocket, squinting while he wrote in it. "Where you all staying?" he asked.

"At a campground," Primault replied. "Motels were full."

"Yeah, tourist season. Ah, would be good if you could hang around for a day or so. Don't seem likely, but we might need something further."

"Sure, be glad to. My boss wants us to talk to Sheriff Arnold in Benson County, so we'll be in the area. And there's one more thing, Sheriff."

"Yes, sir?"

"We have audio recordings of the three perpetrators, almost an hour long. I'd like to turn them over to you. We questioned them last night and this morning. Some of it will corroborate our statements. The rest of it will likely curl your hair."

"Thank you. Do me a favor and give it to Earl. He's the gadget guy."

By noon a van had come and gone, transporting Gorton, Tulo, and Riley under guard to the county jail. Two more deputies arrived to help further secure the property. Vehicles in the barn were cordoned off with police tape, waiting for state forensics investigators. The county coroner came to supervise the exhumation of the body in the last stall. By the time the grave was open and the body of Nomer was put in a bag, the Jeep Rubicon was on the way into town with a full load of passengers. All of them, especially Katherine, relieved and glad to be away from the place.

After Gavin took Katherine shopping for clothes and other necessities, they all regrouped in a restaurant for a bite to eat. Motel rooms were still scarce, so Gavin bought another pop-up tent, blankets, and a sleeping bag.

Katherine, Gavin noticed, was hyper-alert among the scores of loud and perpetually in motion tourists. "I'm sorry about the hotel situation," he said to her. "But it is a really nice campground, with showers."

"Please don't fret about that, hon," she said. "I've camped in one or two wild places, and a tent isn't the trunk of a car."

Her remark, though half in jest, nonetheless brought a somber silence to the table.

"At the most, it's just another night," Gavin reassured her.

"You know," Primault said, "since we do have other transport, I think it would be fine for you and Katherine to go home, and Ben, for that matter. I think Jason and I can fill in any blanks if they want to talk to us again. Besides, the statement we gave the sheriff is very comprehensive."

"Thank you, Justin, that's very considerate," Katherine said. "I really don't mind. I'm looking forward to a campfire, actually, with a good cup of coffee. Might help me to decompress."

"In that case," Gavin said, "I think we should all have a good, substantial meal. We certainly deserve one. I noticed a convenience store selling firewood, and we'll get everything else we need for a nice evening by a fire. I think it would be good for us all to relax."

Six hours later a fire was crackling in a metal pit. Gavin brewed a pot of coffee on the propane camp stove and had several steaks waiting on ice in the coolers for the evening's fare. The only empty chair at the circle around the fire was Primault's, who was on the other side of a tent while he visited with his wife on the phone.

"So, Katherine," Ben Wilson asked, "what does an environmental lawyer do?"

"Well, to quote my firm's mantra, we 'litigate, educate, and mitigate.' Some of the attorneys in the firm take issues to court, some provide training to companies, corporation, and even governments relative to laws and regulations, and some help to write those laws and regulations. I'm in the last group."

"Damn. Makes my career choice seem a bit—juvenile."

"Oh, I don't know. From what I've heard, your technological skills helped to find and rescue ten girls. I wouldn't label that juvenile."

"Thank you. I'm glad I could."

"In any case, someone has to do it, right?" she said. "Not all of us understand all the instruments of technology we use every day. I'm lucky to know where the On and Off switches are."

"Well, this is very non-technological," Wilson said, pointing to the fire.

"Not really," Gavin differed. "I used a match to start the fire, which is a product of technology. I split the firewood with a hatchet, also a product of technology. A match and a hatchet are simply not as complex as a phone or a computer. And if I had used a primitive bow drill—a tool that was developed thousands of years ago—it's still technology."

"So, you're saying technology has been around for a long time?"

"Right. It's just easier to use now. Before he could use it, primitive man had to first make a bow drill. Likewise, the forerunner of the hatchet, an axe made with a stone blade. The big difference between then and now is that none of us can build a phone or a computer from scratch."

"I guess I never equated the word 'primitive' with technology, but I do see what you're driving at."

Primault concluded the conversation with his wife and joined the circle around the fire.

"How is Sandra doing?" Gavin asked.

"Oh, she's good. Her mom came down from Eagle Butte a couple of days ago."

"I heard your wife was a teacher," Katherine said.

"Yeah, she teaches fourth grade at the Agency Village school, for Kincaid County. Three years now, since right after we moved down there."

Katherine directed her gaze at Jason Singer. "Jason," she said, "are you married, as well?"

"No, I live with my mom, for a couple years now, ever since my dad died."

"Oh, I'm sorry."

"Thanks, my mom and I have always been close. She still works. She cooks at a Head Start Center."

"My dad left us, my mom and me," Katherine said. "I stayed with my mom, until I went away to college. Then she stayed with me for a couple years after I got an apartment off campus. But she didn't want to move to Arizona when I went to law school. So, she moved back home. She died ten years ago."

"Oh, darn. What do we have here?" Wilson said, pointing to a white sedan driving slowly along the graveled campground road. "Looks familiar."

Primault glanced at the car. "I think it might be the deputy," he said. "Johnson, I think."

A minute later the car stopped behind the Jeep and the driver stepped out, confirming Primault's assumption. Deputy Earl Johnson approached, a conciliatory expression on his young face. "Howdy, folks," he said, touching the brim of his hat.

"Deputy Johnson," Primault replied. "What can we do for you?"

"Sheriff Kinsley sends his apologies, but your presence is requested at the courthouse tomorrow. The county attorney would like to talk to you all."

"Of course," Primault replied politely. "Any particular reason?"

"I'm afraid I wasn't privy to that information, sir. Mr. Halloran will be in his office by eight o'clock in the morning."

"Mr. Halloran is the county attorney?"

"That's correct, sir."

"We will be there then."

"Thank you." The deputy touched the brim of his hat again. "Good evening to you all." He turned and walked back to his car.

"Why do you suppose the county attorney wants to talk to us?" Wilson wondered.

"County attorneys are usually the same as district attorneys," Primault pointed out. "Probably just wants information. Hopefully, that's all it is."

"Any reason to believe otherwise?" Katherine asked.

"Well, this is North Dakota," Primault said, somberly. "It's just as racist as South Dakota, and we apprehended the bad guys on a white-owned property, and we're not white. I'd hate to think that it's in any way an issue of race, but we shouldn't dismiss it off-hand either. We will find out in the morning."

Gavin added two more pieces of wood to the fire.

"Damn! How do you all manage to live under that kind of subtle threat always hanging over everything?" Wilson said, obviously perturbed.

Gavin chuckled. "It's a learned survival skill. It's akin to feeling like you're always in enemy territory."

"God damn!" Wilson exclaimed "Fuck Columbus!" Leaning forward in the next second, he looked at Katherine. "I'm sorry, I didn't mean to cuss in front of you."

"It's okay. It's exactly what I think every now and then."

"Sure does put a damper on a nice evening," Wilson grumbled.

"Tell you what," Gavin said. "Tomorrow will come with all its highs and lows, but it isn't here yet. In that cooler over there are the flank steaks we bought. I think we fire up the charcoals, broil those steaks, eat, and enjoy one another's company on this fine evening in the Moon of Berries Ripening." He looked at Wilson. "That's August to you."

FORTY-NINE

Arriving a few minutes before eight, Primault's cruiser and the Jeep pulled into a small parking lot behind the courthouse, a relatively contemporary looking brick building. A young women escorted them to a room with a table and chairs in the county attorney's office. As they all found seats, Katherine lifted a finger to her lips as a subtle warning for everyone to wait quietly.

Twenty minutes later the same young woman returned with a nondescript man dressed in a dark blue suit carrying a long legal pad. His only distinct features were the cold glint in his eyes and the small American flag pinned to his coat lapel. He took a seat on the opposite side of the table. After the young woman handed each of them a business card, she took the chair at the end.

"Good morning, folks," the man began. "I'm Nathan Halloran, the county attorney. Sally has given you my card. Thanks for stopping by. As you've likely surmised, you're here because of your conversation with Sheriff Kinsley yesterday."

After receiving polite nods all around, he cleared his throat and repositioned his tablet on the table. Gavin had a feeling that he looked familiar, although his name was not.

"To start," the man said, "I'd like your names, for the record, if you please, and place of residence."

Halloran finished writing and looked at the young woman, who nodded. Katherine noticed that, although Sally had a note pad in front of her, she was not taking notes. Her pen lay atop the pad.

"Yesterday afternoon I listened to audio recordings of an apparent interrogation of three individuals, three males. Very disturbing," Halloran said, suddenly turning his attention back to the group.

"Katherine, is it Miss or Mrs?"

'I am not married," Katherine replied.

"Very well. Miss Hill, this entire situation seems to be a consequence of your apparently being abducted. Where do you allege this abduction occurred?"

"I was abducted at a truck stop along Interstate 90, south of Pierre, South Dakota."

"I see. When did that occur?"

"Six days ago."

"And you were brought here, to a location north of here?"

"I didn't know where I was being taken. I was told, yesterday, after being rescued, of the exact location."

"Miss Hill, do you have an idea why you were abducted, allegedly?"

Katherine leveled a cool gaze at Halloran for a few seconds. "I did not know at the moment why I was abducted. I do now."

Primault leaned forward. "Mr. Halloran, I don't understand the reason for that question."

"Mr. Primault, I will have questions for you later," Halloran said, dismissively.

"Mr. Halloran," Katherine injected boldly. "To answer your question, I parked near a white van at the truck stop. I heard a woman's voice calling out for help and I reacted. The cry for help came from the van. As I approached the back of the van, I was grabbed by a dark-haired man who placed a cloth over my mouth. I regained consciousness in the back of that van, my wrists and ankles were bound. Yesterday morning I learned that the man who abducted me was part of an organization that abducted young Native girls for sex trafficking. Since you listened to the audio recordings, I'm sure you are aware of that."

"Miss Hill, pardon me for saying so, but you are not a young Native girl."

"That distinction didn't preclude that fact that I was abducted."

A spark of annoyance flashed across Halloran's face and in the next second he turned to Primault, after glancing briefly at Jason Singer. "So," he said, gesturing toward the two officers, "the two of you are members of the Smokey River Tribal Police?"

"Correct," Primault replied evenly.

"How did you become involved in this situation?"

"Our commanding officer, Chief Ben Avery, instructed us to investigate the abduction of Miss Hill and conduct a search for her."

"I see. What are your official capacities."

"I am the criminal investigator for the Smokey River Tribal Police, and this is Patrolman Singer.

"And while conducting that investigation and search, you rented an airplane and carried out air surveillance?"

"I rented the airplane, and I flew it," Gavin said, locking eyes with Halloran.

"You are a licensed pilot?"

"Obviously."

"And what is your official connection to Miss Hill?"

"Katherine is my fiancée, officially."

The spark of annoyance returned to Halloran's face. He glanced across at Gavin and then swept his gaze over everyone seated across the table and settled back on Primault.

"Mr. Singer and Mr. Primault, at any time during your investigation and search, did you carry a firearm?"

"During the ingress of the Hanrich property, I carried a firearm. Patrolman Singer was not part of that action. There was no way to know how many individuals had Miss Hill in captivity, or if they were armed."

Katherine leaned toward Gavin and whispered. "I'm going to put a stop to this right now." He nodded surreptitiously.

"Mr. Halloran, if you wouldn't mind, I have a request."

"And that is?"

Katherine turned to the young woman. "Sally, may I borrow your pen?"

Sally, taken aback by the request, glanced quickly toward Halloran, who, though slightly puzzled, gave an assenting nod. Sally reached into the pocket of her slacks and pulled out a pen, ignoring the one on her writing pad. Katherine took the narrow, ordinary looking pen and turned over the business card on the table in front of her. On it she wrote a name and slid the card across to Halloran.

"Mr. Halloran, that is the name of our attorney."

Halloran gazed at Katherine for a moment before he picked up the card and read the name, his expression visibly changing to one of indecision. He slowly lifted his gaze to Katherine.

"Is there a reason you feel you need an attorney?" he asked.

"Mr. Halloran, you tell us."

Halloran looked down at the card again, briefly tapping it on the table.

"Very well," Katherine said. "We will take that as a 'no' you will not tell us. Let me further state that I am a staff attorney with the firm of Snyder, Beemer, and Holcomb, based in Washington DC, a firm with considerable political connections. My abduction is being investigated by the South Dakota Department of Criminal Investigation, and most probably the Federal Bureau of Investigation. My abduction was a consequence of an elaborate operation which targeted young Native women. Ten Native girls, all minors, were found locked away in the basements of two abandoned farmhouses in Benson County, adjacent to yours. The Smokey River Tribal Police is still in the process of interviewing those young girls, and I'm sure the Federal Bureau of Investigation will be involved as well. As of now, we know those girls were—according to their testimony—sold for sex to men who resided at a camp operated by an oil drilling company near the town of Pinnacle. The girls were imprisoned for months. I am certain that eventually all the sordid facts of the case will be known and publicized. The shocking reality is, Mr. Halloran, this operation was being conducted in this area for years, under the very noses of all levels of law enforcement and other officials in several counties, and I am sure that the investigation will reveal who was culpable."

Halloran's gaze, though it lingered on Katherine, was no longer assertive.

Katherine turned to Sally. "I'm sure your recorder was sensitive enough to pick up my voice, wouldn't you say?"

Sally's face flushed with surprise and embarrassment. She shot a quick glance toward Halloran, who nodded. Sally slowly reached and pushed the clip on the pen, turning off the device.

"Mr. Halloran," Katherine said, rising from her chair. "I will ask our attorney, Mr. Wittfield, to file a request to your office for a copy of the transcript of this meeting."

Halloran kept his seat, sitting stiff and straight, and simply nodded.

Gavin stood, as did the others, and followed Katherine out the door. Their footsteps were loud on the tile floor all the way to the door. No one said a word until they reached the vehicles. Gavin took Katherine gently by the shoulders and pulled her into a long hug.

"Grandma Annie didn't call you Soldier Woman for nothing," he said.

The other men stepped up to shake her hand.

"I think you just put the fear of god in that man," Primault said.

"The first thing I noticed was the recording device the young lady put on her writing pad. I've used them. He didn't tell us the meeting was being recorded. Then I suddenly realized that he was searching for anything, scraping, for any way to bring a charge to discredit us."

"Why?" Primault asked, shaking his head.

'I'm not sure, but it's a defense tactic when one has a weak defense. He had a reason that was compelling to him, and I don't think it was only because he saw himself as the champion of the law in this county. Maybe we'll never know. I suddenly recalled a lecture in law school about misprision."

"What's misprision?" Wilson asked.

"Knowingly concealing a felony."

"Oh, shit," Wilson blurted.

"Right," she said. "A public official, such as Halloran, could be charged with malfeasance."

"Do you think he'll bother us anymore?" Singer asked.

"I don't think so. He knows who our attorney is. He'll at least be careful from now on," Gavin said.

"Well, I don't know about the rest of you," Primault said, "but I want a cup of good coffee. I'll spring for breakfast. How about it?"

"There's an offer I can't refuse," Wilson agreed.

Finding parking places was more of a chore than getting a table in the busy restaurant. Seated at a corner table, they didn't wait long for the aromatic cups of coffee to arrive. Primault lifted his cup in a toast. "To Soldier Woman," he said. "I know who's going to win every argument in your household," he said to Gavin.

"You also know who's smart enough never to start an argument," Gavin replied.

Katherine blushed and smiled. "Gentlemen," she said. "I have yet to thank you for what you did, for searching for and finding me. I knew, without a doubt, that the love of my life would move heaven and earth to find me." She looked tenderly at Gavin and squeezed his hand. "But the three of you—Justin, Jason, Ben—I'm humbled that you took the time away from your own families, your own lives, to help him. I'll never, ever forget that." She lifted her cup in her own toast. "I'm guessing also, there are ten young ladies who feel the same. You're our heroes. So, here's to you."

Emotion filled their eyes, as the three men lifted their cups, overcome by her gracious sincerity. Wordlessly, they all nodded in response. The cacophony of conversations in the restaurant mattered not at all to the five people in the corner as they sipped their coffees and settled into a conversation while waiting for their food; nor did the fact that while some people saw four men and a beautiful woman, others saw four Natives and a white man.

When the moment had passed, Gavin said "I'm thinking, Ben, that you're free to go home."

"I'll check with my supervisor," Wilson said.

"That's not my brother?"

"Gerard is the head of the company. My direct supervisor is Dean Bartlett. He runs the surveillance department."

"I guess I didn't realize how big your operation is."

"There's two departments, surveillance and analytics, and a central office staff. There's close to twenty employees altogether."

"Wow! That's quite an empire my brother is carving out."

"Oh, yeah. We've got a couple of international accounts. I know one in Canada for sure. Gerard is a hard charger, a leader, not a boss, if you know what I mean."

"I'm not surprised," said Gavin.

"Heck, I didn't know he was a Marine when I first went to work. I mean, there were no certificates or diplomas or anything on his office wall. Just family pictures of you, your parents, your sister, and Katherine, and, I think, his wife. Very pretty lady. There were two plaques with verses carved in them. One was a prayer; 'Eternal Father, grant we pray, to all Marines, both night and day, the courage, honor, strength, and skill, their land to serve, Thy law fulfill. Be Thou the shield forevermore, from every peril to the Corps.' That's how I found out he was in the Marine Corps."

"What did the other plaque say?" Singer asked.

"Oh, that one was a verse from the Marine's Hymn: 'If the Army and the Navy, ever get to Heaven's scenes, they will find the streets are guarded, by United States Marines.'"

Everyone shared a chuckle.

"That sounds like him," Gavin said, nodding knowingly. "When he retired, he gave all his medals and commendations to Loren, our older sister, because our parents are no longer here. They're on her wall, in a shadow box."

"I'm curious," Primault said. "How many, commendations and medals?"

"Twenty-six, including a Purple Heart and two Bronze Stars."

Primault and Singer nodded in admiration.

"Well, in any case, check with your supervisor and let us know. We'll take you back to the airport any time," Gavin said.

"Thanks. I'd like to see it through, at least tomorrow, or however long it takes with Sheriff Arnold."

Breakfast arrived on two huge platters carried by two servers. Katherine caught one of the server's attention. "Could I have another cup of coffee, a small cup, and an empty saucer?"

When the server returned with the coffee and saucer, Katherine placed the coffee in the center of the table and then put tiny portions from her plate on the saucer. Gavin added portions from his plate.

"What are you doing?" Wilson asked.

"It's called a Spirit Plate," Katherine explained. "We offer food, in this case for Melvina, and all our loved ones who have gone."

"In that case, allow me," Wilson said, adding portions from his plate.

Singer and Primault did the same.

"Cool thing to do," Wilson said.

"*Mitakuye Oyasın,*" she said. "Now, we can eat."

After breakfast they returned to the campground and broke camp, cramming all the equipment and supplies in the cargo compartment of the Jeep and the trunk of the cruiser. After consulting a map and deciding on a route, they departed.

After a couple of miles, Gavin suddenly remembered where he had seen Halloran. It was one of those moments when an unwanted or unpleasant memory popped into place without warning. "I know where I've seen him before," he said.

"Who?" Katherine said.

"Halloran."

"What do you mean?"

"At the pipeline protests on Standing Rock."

"He was there?"

"He sure was. He was there the day they came after people with dogs."

"I remember reading about that. What was he doing there?"

"I don't know what his capacity might have been, but he was there, and he was dressed in some type of utility uniform, and he wore a vest, a bulletproof vest."

"Are you serious?"

"As a heart attack. I was helping a friend of mine; she couldn't walk very fast. I was keeping her out of the way of all the sudden activity and confusion. Halloran was with the people who had the dogs, off to one side. I remember, clearly."

Katherine shook her head in astonishment. "That is scary. Still, I don't think that had everything to do with his attitude this morning."

"I agree. But he was there with all those other people who did everything to smash those protests. After the dog incident, they came armed to the teeth; they used percussion grenades, pepper spray, tear gas, rubber bullets. He's an Indian Fighter, and probably proud of it."

"My, my, my. They're everywhere."

"Yeah, here's hoping Sheriff Arnold is not one of them."

FIFTY

oren Lone Wolf Hale heard the front door of the bistro scrape open and immediately recognized the petite, stylishly dressed Lakota woman pushing it open, waiting for an older woman to enter with her. She stood to meet them.

Sandra Primault smiled at the statuesque woman waiting near a table. "Loren," she said, holding out her hand. "Good to see you again. This is my mom, Esther Comes Holy. She drove down from Eagle Butte to spend a couple of days with me."

Loren shook the older woman's hand, noting the sparkle in the deep brown eyes, and the lovely facial features she passed on to her daughter, though her hair was shorter and flecked with gray. "I'm happy to meet you, Esther. Did you drive down alone?"

"I did," she said, brightly. "Her dad stayed home with the dogs. We have two Huskies. They keep us going. It's practice while we wait for grandkids."

Sandra smiled demurely and helped her mom move a chair and take a seat. "Melvina's funeral was the last time we had a chance to visit," she said to Loren.

"It was. I hear a lot of people saying that funerals are the only times we get together. I don't know if that's a comment on families or the number of funerals."

"Both, I think," Sandra said. "So, thank you for inviting us to lunch. We're taking a break from cutting and sewing. We're making a star quilt. Well, actually, I'm learning the basics. Mom's been doing it since she was a girl, and I want to learn."

"Good for you," Loren said. "My Grandma Annie made star quilts. I helped her when I was a little girl, and I started out cutting the diamond pieces. I remember her and my Aunt Phoebe setting up the loom in the living room when they stitched the top, lining, and sewed it back together. It was always in a fan shaped pattern, marked out in chalk. But I'm afraid I never acquired the skill they had, or the patience."

"Now they have machines to do the quilting," Esther said. "I'm going to teach Sandy the old way."

"Well, we'll see how it all goes," Sandra mused. "I'm determined to learn, how that all comes together remains to be seen."

A server appeared, a young Native man, and took their order. After he left, Esther Comes Holy looked around at the cozy little cafe with its eclectic collection of wooden tables and chairs. "This wasn't here the last time I visited," she observed. "Is it owned by Natives?"

"It is," Loren said. "It's been open about a year. The noon hour is a busy time for them, so that's why I'm glad you could come a little early. I'm afraid I forgot how far away you are, on the other side of Agency Village."

"No problem," Sandra said. "I had a chance to talk with Justin on the way. I don't usually answer the phone while I'm driving, but this time I did."

"Oh, how is it going up there? I haven't talked to my brother for a while. I was beyond thankful they found Katherine. Gerard said Gavin told him it was your husband that found her."

"It was. He said he found her handcuffed and shackled, and they sneaked out while the man who held her prisoner was playing the piano. How weird is that?"

"It definitely started out that way. I saw a man at the truck stop up on I-90 taking pictures of Katherine," Loren recalled gravely. "She was abducted from that same place."

"Justin's convinced that was that same man that took her, and also some of the girls they rescued. Today they're back in Pinnacle, taking a sheriff to those houses where the girls were imprisoned, and then I think they might be heading home after that. At least, I hope so."

"Well. Katherine is safe, twelve girls are back with their families. I hope your husband knows what a truly wonderful thing he did."

"He was just doing his job, he said. But he did take it very personally when he heard about Katherine. Actually, he's been talking loud and long about missing Native girls and women for a few years now, he and Chief Avery. They're both mystified about why it's not a big issue, and why there's no cooperation among the tribes."

"My Uncle Andrew says it really is us against the world when it comes to the issues we face as Native people," Loren said. "No one cares, so we have to take care of ourselves, the way our people did at one time, and stop thinking like white people."

"That's what my grandpa would say," Esther added. "All of our problems come from trying to live like white people. Lakota people took care of each other before the *wasicus* came. There was no homelessness, no one went hungry. No one was stealing girls."

"Exactly," Loren agreed, "especially with this problem of missing and murdered indigenous women and girls. This is why I wanted to talk to you. I think women need to take the lead. I don't know how, at the moment, but it has to start somewhere, somehow."

"I think you're right," Sandra said. "I mentioned to Justin that we should teach girls all about situational awareness, the same way they teach cops and soldiers."

"Yes, that's one part of it," Loren said. "I had a thought after I met my brother's boss, the new department head of Lakota Studies at SRU. She has a black belt in karate. We need someone like her, a Lakota woman, to teach basic self-defense techniques to girls."

"You should turn girls into warriors, the way boys used to be taught in the old days," Esther said. "My grandma carried a knife all the time, a big knife in a beaded sheath on her belt. She said every woman used to carry a knife. I think knowing how to take care of yourself, how to fight, is a weapon."

"I couldn't have said it better," Loren said. "My Grandma Annie was the same way. She carried a pocketknife in her purse. After my parents died, she talked my Uncle Andrew into teaching me how to shoot a gun. I went hunting with my brothers several times."

The conversation paused after the food was delivered and their coffees refilled. The noon rush appeared to be starting and the cafe was filling up quickly. Esther was surprised that many of the customers were picking up take-out orders. "Everyone is in a hurry these days," she said. "I was in line at a cash machine at a bank in Pierre when I drove down. The car behind me tooted his horn because I wasn't doing my business fast enough. Every-one hurries and doesn't pay attention. That's the problem."

"Sadly, you're right," Loren said. "Which is why I wanted to talk to you, Sandra. We need to teach our girls and young women to do just that, pay attention. My brother Gerard said the same thing you did about situational awareness."

"It's the phones," Esther said. "Everybody has one."

"Exactly," Sandra agreed. "I've had to confiscate phones from fourth graders."

"It can be a distraction at the wrong time," Loren said. "But having a phone can also save a life. We need to teach girls not to use them in certain situations, especially anywhere there are crowds, confusion and noise, and a lot of movement."

"Like malls and parking lots," Sandra said.

"I like what you said, Esther," Loren said, "we need to teach our girls how to be warriors and take care of themselves. As Lakota women we need to reclaim the influence we once had as the first teachers of our children. Men can't do that, and not enough of them care. Your husband is an exception. Whatever plan we develop, men can help and should, but women need to be in charge and do the talking since our target audience is girls."

"Right, and credibility is key, such as the woman you said has a black belt in karate."

"Exactly, and no one has more credibility than, in this case, a victim. We can tell their stories but it will have greater impact if they tell their own."

Sheriff James Arnold sat at the small table in his office and viewed the photographs of the abandoned houses and the rooms where the girls had been imprisoned, and then watched the videos of the girls themselves as they experienced the first taste of freedom in months. As much as he tried to remain impassive and objective, he couldn't help but shake his head in shock and dismay.

Arnold was forty-eight and finishing his second term as county sheriff. He had been a police officer in Billings, Montana, for nearly fifteen years before coming home and running for sheriff. Like all career law enforcement officers, he had seen sights and sounds during those years that tear at one's sense of decency, and some that were hard to believe. The photos and the videos were not graphic, in that they were not dead bodies or blood and gore. But the implications were what tore at one's heart.

"They're all so damn young," he finally said.

"The oldest was seventeen," Primault said. "All kids. Each of them was repeatedly raped by men in the man camps. Do you have daughters, Sheriff?"

Arnold nodded. "Yeah, as a matter of fact, I do."

"I'm sure they're where they should be, and safe," Primault went on. "There were thirteen Native families on four different reservations who didn't know where their daughters were for months and months, some for more than a year. One family buried their daughter. She had escaped and somehow made it almost all the way home, emaciated and severely injured. One of the men who sold and transported them beat her. She died because of that beating, almost a month ago."

Arnold nodded slowly, sitting with his arms crossed. After a deep sigh he turned to look briefly at Katherine. "And you were locked in one of those houses, Miss?"

"Yes, that's right, The first house in the video."

"I'm damn sorry you went through that." He looked toward Primault. "I had a long phone call with Sheriff Kinsley. They're still at that ranch. Forensics folks are going over everything. If you all don't mind showing us where those houses are, we'll secure them so nothing or no one disturbs evidence."

"Be glad to, Sheriff," Primault said.

Arnold pointed at Wilson. "Young man, I wonder if you can make copies of those photographs and videos. I sure would like to have them. Doesn't have to be today, but as quick as you can."

"If you have a blank thumb drive, it will be my pleasure."

"I'm sure we can scare one up for you. Thank you kindly."

In the parking lot, Primault turned to Katherine. "I was just thinking, if you don't want to go to those houses, you and Gavin can meet us in Blaine at the motel."

"No, I want to. I think I need to."

"Okay. But it's okay if you change your mind."

"I understand. Thanks, Justin."

Katherine and Gavin were the last vehicle behind the second deputy's cruiser. Primault and Singer led the way in the tribal cruiser. Ben Wilson was in the back seat of the Jeep, reading email messages until he lost connection on his Wi-Fi hotspot. Closing his laptop in mild frustration, he turned his attention to the passing landscape.

"'Rural' in the east means farms and residences away from towns and cities and along paved roads," he said. "One place after another, the properties are adjacent. I've seen traffic lights at crossroads. Out here the properties are far apart, a lot of open land in between, and most of the roads are graveled or dirt. Sure as hell aren't any traffic lights; even towns don't have them. Sure is a different definition of 'rural.' How long do you think that will last?"

"Probably until corporate farms buy or control most of the land," Gavin said.

"Family farms have been disappearing for decades. Corporations like Green Giant and Anheuser-Busch buy foreclosed land when a farm or ranch goes belly up, or they pay farmers to raise specific crops. That's why there are abandoned places out here. But consider this, before farms and ranches, it was all a pristine environment. No farms, no ranches, just cultures that survived primarily on hunting and gathering. There were a few agrarian societies, but certainly not so many that warranted using and controlling vast amounts of land for crops."

"I think I like that scenario," Wilson said.

"It certainly was easier on the environment," Gavin pointed out. "No pollution, no extinction of indigenous animal species."

"White people have been damn hard on the world," Wilson grumbled.

"Feudalism and capitalism at work," Gavin said.

Katherine only half heard the conversation as she looked out at the prairie beyond the roads. After they turned on to a narrow dirt road overgrown by grass and weeds, a dark building was suddenly visible in the dust raised by the vehicles ahead of the Jeep. There was a tightening in her chest.

Gavin noticed as she subtly clenched her fists and watched closely for any sign of further distress. Primault and Singer, as well as the sheriff and his deputies, stepped out of their vehicles. He decided to let Katherine make the first move, giving a warning glance to Wilson, who seemed to understand the silent message, and nodded.

A few seconds passed before Katherine reached for the door handle and pushed open the door. After she stepped out, Gavin opened his door as well. Wilson followed them out.

Primault had stopped on the road without turning into the narrow, overgrown driveway. He and Singer waited for the sheriff and his two deputies to catch up before they led the way to the basement entrance of the house. Gavin paused by Katherine and reached out to offer his hand. Hand-in-hand they followed the driveway, staying behind the others.

The door to the basement was visible from the direction they were approaching. It was slightly ajar. Gavin felt Katherine's grip tightening as they drew closer. She stopped walking as Primault led the Sheriff and his deputy into the basement. Singer waited.

"Can we wait until they come back out?" she asked.

"Sure," Gavin said.

She looked around at the surrounding landscape, shielding her eyes from the sun. "This is about as out-of-the-way as it gets," she observed.

"Definitely. If you notice, there is no oil drilling anywhere near here, and no pumping rigs. Most of this area is pasture."

"Melrose, or someone, went to great lengths to find this place, and the other house as well. Do you know if there were only two houses they used?"

"No, actually. We narrowed it down to nine and checked them out one by one. After we found the last four girls, we stopped. There's one more we didn't check."

"Maybe we should," she suggested.

At the bottom of the stairs, Primault stepped to one side and pointed to the short hallway. "There are two small rooms," he told Sheriff Arnold. "Katherine was locked in the one on the left. We found six girls in the one on the right."

Nodding, the sheriff moved past Primault with the deputy behind him, both of them switching on small flashlights. Primault followed, watching them, especially their facial expressions as they looked about. To their credit, they touched nothing. Neither of them noticed the words Katherine had scratched on the wall. Crossing over to the next room, they did the same, looking closely and touching nothing. Neither the sheriff nor the deputy made a comment.

After fifteen minutes, Primault, the sheriff, and the deputy came out. "That didn't take them long," Wilson commented.

"Whenever you're ready," Gavin said to Katherine. She took his hand and nodded.

Leading the way, Gavin went down the wooden steps, holding her hand as she followed. She glanced at the car batteries in the small room as Gavin paused and turned on the flashlight function on his phone, illuminating the narrow, short hallway. He took her hand again and waited. After taking a deep breath, she headed for the open door to the left, and entered the room, still gripping Gavin's hand.

Her free hand went to her mouth. Gavin handed the phone to her. Taking it she aimed it at the objects in the room, exposing them slowly. First, the mattress and pile of bed covers, then the box and composting toilet, and the case of water bottles. Slowly she turned the light up to the wall, revealing her writing.

"That was a smart move," Gavin said. He could feel her hand trembling, so he squeezed gently, and waited.

After a moment, she nodded. "I want to see the other room," she said.

They walked out of the room and across into the other. It was much the same, except there were more mattresses and three boxes of food. The odor from the composting toilet was noticeable. "Those poor girls!" she said softly. "I can't imagine being in here for months!"

"They were all very brave," he said. "So were you."

"I was frightened the whole time," she admitted. "Every minute, every second. If all this wasn't evidence, I'd burn the place down."

"I'd say you have every right."

"I'm ready to leave."

Without a sideways glance, she led the way out of the room and out of the basement and stood outside with her back to the house. The sheriff and the deputy were finishing cordoning off the yard with yellow police tape, wrapping it around fence posts and tree branches.

"Wouldn't it be more sensible to lock that door, or the doors in the basement?" Wilson wondered. "If someone happens to come along and see the tape, they may become curious and check it out."

"You may be right, but if you remember, we broke the hasp. That old wood is rotten."

"Well, " Wilson sighed. "The odds are no one will bother it, I guess."

Ten minutes later the vehicles were driving toward the next house, with Primault once again leading the way. Gavin touched Katherine's hand. She turned and gave him a soft pensive smile. "I'm good," she said.

"I just realized I haven't heard if Sheriff Kinsley put out any kind of bulletin on Melrose as a person of interest, at the very least," Gavin said.

"Damn," Wilson said. "Good question. We gave a good description of the man, and the truck even without the license number."

"I'll mention it to Justin," Gavin decided, "maybe he can check with Kinsley. Trouble is, it's been a day a half. The guy could have switched vehicles by now, or is on his way to Plano, Texas, or who knows where."

"I'll never forget his face. His speech pattern and vocabulary indicated a highly educated individual," Katherine pointed out. "He wore gloves both times I saw him, black leather gloves, so he may not have left any fingerprints."

"Damn!" Gavin exclaimed. "He covered his tracks well."

"Sanders, I mean Gorton, didn't wear gloves," Katherine recalled. "I touched the inside doorknob on the room I was in, and a few surfaces in the bathroom, and the door handle at the entrance."

"Do we know if the house, or the barn, will be dusted for prints? Or have been?" Wilson asked.

"Good questions," Gavin admitted. "If you recall, no forensics people had arrived by the time we left."

"Maybe we should have waited," Wilson thought.

"I'd hate to think the situation won't be given utmost priority," Katherine worried.

The conversation ceased as they turned onto a narrow dirt road Gavin recognized. "We're close to the next place," he pointed out.

A few minutes later they turned into an approach with tall posts and the sagging cross member and stopped behind the deputy's vehicle.

"This is even more dilapidated than the first place," Katherine said. "And even farther out of the way."

She was less hesitant to enter the basement and took more time in the room, which was the smallest, and more dank and sour smelling. The concrete floor was pitted and rough. Katherine showed no signs of stress or discomfort, although Gavin watched closely. She asked him to turn on the flashlight function on his phone and deliberately looked at everything; mattresses, blankets, food boxes. "My god, if they were here in cold weather, and they probably were, there's no source of heat. Those poor girls. North Dakota winters are damn cold. How did they survive?"

Gavin, frankly, had not thought of that awful reality. "We need to ask them," he said.

When they exited, Primault was on the phone outside, standing several yards from the house, and Sheriff Arnold and his deputy were finishing with the police tape.

"I was talking to Chief Avery," Primault told them after he finished the call.

"Apparently rumors are starting to fly after a family put their daughter's picture and story on the internet. It's only one family so far, but the family said their daughter had been kidnapped by white men and sexually assaulted. Which is true. But the Chief is worried that if other families do the same, there's a possibility that it would backfire on the investigation."

"Anything's possible," Gavin said. "Is there a way to contact a Native news outlet and give them the story, you know, the basic facts without revealing the identities of the girls? I think this will be blown out of proportion, or dismissed as just sensationalism in any case, but if the facts are printed, it'll hopefully preclude most of the rumors, and establish that it is a credible story."

"Might be the answer," Primault allowed.

"There are two well-known Native-owned newspapers in South Dakota," Gavin said. "Maybe you and the Chief give them the story, a double-exclusive. I think, by and large, those papers are known for their fair coverage of Native issues and stories, and one of them has published editorials on the biased reporting of Native issues by a couple of the television stations."

"The sooner the better," Katherine added. "If one story is already on the internet, the other families have seen it, or will soon, and they might take it as tacit permission to do the same."

"Good advice," Primault said. "I appreciate it. I'll call the Chief back and tell him what you both said."

Katherine and Gavin walked back to the Jeep. "I think I'm ready to go home," she said.

"Then home it is," Gavin said. "Can you stand one more night? The motel is okay, and Blaine is just a typical little town."

"Sure."

"Then we'll take Ben back to the airport and figure out the logistics of when to take the Jeep back."

Sheriff Arnold had a brief conversation with the deputy that was out of earshot, then approached the trio, which now included Ben Wilson. "Folks," he began, "I sure do appreciate you all taking the time this morning." He gestured back at the deputy getting into his truck. "Jerry's got a call to tend to. Possible cattle theft. I'm heading back to the office to give the state forensics folks a call and see when they can come and look these houses over. I've got your contact numbers and so forth so, if there is anything more, I'll be sure to give you a call."

"Thank you, Sheriff," Gavin said, extending his hand. "We'll be glad to answer any further questions, and come back, if necessary."

"Sure thing," the sheriff said, nodding at Katherine and touching the brim of his hat. "Good luck to you, ma'am."

After the sheriff and the deputy were gone, they waited for Primault to finish a long conversation on the phone. "The Chief completely agrees with your suggestion," he said to Gavin and Katherine. "And he wonders if the two of you can put together a statement, a concise summary, he said. Meanwhile, he's going to contact the two newspapers and try to get them on a conference call. He wants them to hear his request at the same time."

Katherine nodded. "Of course, I've written a few news releases. I think Gavin and I can put something together."

Primault glanced toward the departing vehicles, now raising dust trails in the distance. "Did any of you notice their reaction in the rooms? The sheriff and the deputy?"

Wilson shook his head 'no.'

"I didn't," Gavin admitted.

"Me neither," Katherine said.

"Well, I did," Primault said, irritation in his tone. "They didn't ask questions, they didn't comment. I'm sure they're both hard-bitten salty hands, and they've probably seen ugly stuff doing their jobs, but this is a horrific situation. I was expecting something more than blank looks. It just seemed to me they were going through the motions, and no more."

"That doesn't sound good," Wilson said.

"Maybe I'm reading too much into their lack of reaction," said Primault." But, it was not reassuring and has planted a seed of doubt about their commitment to this case."

FIFTY-ONE

Deciding that the press release was critical, Katherine and Gavin spent most of the afternoon composing, rewriting, and editing. By late afternoon they had a two and a half page, concise narrative on Wilson's laptop and showed it to Primault.

After reading it through twice, he nodded approvingly. "Damn, this is impressive," he said. "Let's email this to the Chief right now."

Waiting until mid-evening, they went for supper at the town's only restaurant. Recognizing them, the server came almost immediately with waters and coffee.

Engaging in small talk after they placed their food orders, they waited until the other customers, a woman and two men, paid their ticket and left before bringing up anything about the day's activities. Primault was the first.

"I don't mean to belabor the point," he said, "but I'm still stewing over Sheriff Arnold. This happened—the trafficking of those girls, and that's putting it mildly—in his jurisdiction and on his watch. If that was me, I'd be on it like an evangelical preacher on sin. I'd be asking us questions, especially of you, Katherine." He glanced at his watch. "It's been more than six hours since we showed him those rooms. He knows we're still here, and he hasn't called. If we don't, any of us, get a call by the time we leave in the morning, then—I don't know, I just don't know."

"If those had been ten young white girls, I would be willing to bet there probably would be a small army of detectives and investigators at both those houses," Gavin said.

"And it would be all over the news," Singer pointed out.

"For that matter, we haven't heard from Sheriff Kinsley," Gavin said. "At least we know he called state forensics people."

"I have a thought," Primault said. "The Chief wants Jason and I to write up a report from each of our perspectives. If each one of you three," he said, to Katherine, Gavin, and Wilson, "would be willing to do that, we would have a complete report. That would all be part of the Smokey River Tribal Police department's record of this whole situation, from Melvina Old Lodge to Katherine's rescue, along with the interviews of Mollie Henry and Julia Lake, and all the others we still have to do. It could be a hell of a teaching tool for tribal police departments."

"Not to mention leverage to get tribal social services departments and tribal councils to become more involved with missing and murdered Native women," Gavin concluded.

"I'm willing to write up my part in it," Wilson said.

"Furthermore," Primault continued, "although every case and every situation is different, how we conducted the investigation and search for Katherine and the girls could be a blueprint."

"Another thing," Katherine said. "The girls' stories, and my story, could also be an experiential basis to teach girls and women about the indicators and danger signals to watch for. There's nothing like a first person victim's story. When I visited the Holocaust Museum in DC every one of those personal oral accounts had an impact."

"Best idea so far," Primault declared. "That way something good will come out of the horror those girls went through."

The evening passed and morning came with no further word from Sheriff Arnold. At seven they headed south for Highway 85 and the first eighty-mile leg to I-94, and then east for the final one hundred and thirty miles to Bismarck. Ben Wilson fired up his Wi-Fi hotspot and rescheduled for the earliest flight leaving in the morning for Minneapolis, and then to Washington DC. While Katherine took a turn at driving, Gavin called the car rental agent and arranged to take the Jeep to Pierre and leave it with their rental company at the airport. Once the arrangement was affirmed, he called Gerard to meet them in Pierre with the Chevrolet pickup so they could transport all the camping equipment as well. Just after eleven they entered the outskirts of Bismarck and by noon were sitting down to lunch at the hotel with Ben Wilson. No further word from Sheriff Arnold.

"I got a call from the Chief just before we hit town," Primault said. "He and Sergeant West, the Public Information Officer, had a conference call with both the newspapers we talked about. They agreed to simultaneously publish the story. Two important facts the Chief added to the story are that this is still an on-going investigation, and no names since all the young ladies are minors."

"Wonderful," Katherine said. "That story will put this decades old problem front and center where it belongs."

"Amen to that," Primault agreed. Turning to Ben Wilson, he said "We couldn't have done it without you, Ben."

"I'm glad I could help and honored as well. Thanks for letting me be part of it."

"Well, the tradeoff is when we travel to DC we'll crash at your place," Primault teased.

"Done, and done," Wilson replied, grinning.

An hour later they were saying a fond good-bye to Wilson. Katherine gave him a long, affectionate hug. "Thank you, for your skill and your diligence. I'm still technically with my firm in DC, and I might have occasion to come to town. Not sure exactly when, but I know my future husband will be with me," she said, nodding toward Gavin. "So, lunch is on us."

"Congratulations!" Wilson said, beaming. "I couldn't be happier for you both, and I will look forward to lunch."

Primault handed Wilson a business card. "Stay in touch. Might talk the Chief into bringing you back for some in-service for our IT people."

"Be happy to. I've started on that report you wanted. I'll email it to you when I finish. Just don't expect good grammar or correct punctuation." Wilson reached out a hand to Singer, "Jason, it's been a pleasure and an honor."

"Likewise, Ben."

Primault and Singer wasted no time leaving town.

Before they left Gavin and Katherine bought some mellow CDs to listen to on the ride home. Several miles east on I-94, just before they turned south on Highway 83, the Eagles CD song "I Love to Watch a Woman Dance" came on. Gavin took Katherine's hand and kissed it gently.

"What was that for?" she asked.

"For some reason that song brings to mind when we were on the wall in Saint-Malo," he said.

"Oh, my, yes," she said. "That will always be a special place for me. I think we should go back on the anniversary of our first visit together."

"Excellent idea. We should book the flights now."

"Plenty of time for that. It'll be great," she said, excitement in her voice.

Gavin noticed that the farther they traveled from the area where the captive house was, the more animated she became. He took it as a hopeful sign, a step on the road to recovery. During the night at the campground and again at the motel in Blaine, she had had restless nights. The only solution he had was to put an arm around her as she lay curled facing away from him, which seemed to help.

After several minutes of staring out the window, Katherine reached and touched his right arm. He moved his hand off the wheel and took her hand. "Can I ask you something," she said.

"Sure."

"What happened in Siberia? I mean, Gerard mentioned it to me last year. He said you were seriously wounded. Can you tell me about that?"

"Yeah, be glad to. It was a rather convoluted situation. What I thought was a simple ransom delivery turned into a rescue mission."

"Ransom? As in kidnapping?"

"Yes. I was to deliver a ransom payment and take the victim back to her husband."

"And she was an old girlfriend?"

"Well, I guess, if three dates in college counts as having a girlfriend. Her name was Natalya and she was married to a man named Charles Whitehead, a wealthy executive. He was much older than her. Kidnappings like that happen frequently, but this one was a smokescreen. Whitehead had worked for some government security agency. Some high ranking government official that he knew or worked with made a statement at the wrong time and in the wrong place that had to do with some highly sensitive information at the time. The statement was made to a colleague and inadvertently overheard by a very minor employee named Dennison. He realized what had happened and he tried to hide; then he ran, then disappeared.

"Whitehead was blamed and was reprimanded and demoted, eventually leaving government service, or so I was led to believe. He found me one day, about ten years ago, and told me his wife had been kidnapped, and wanted me to deliver the ransom and bring her back. She was being held in central Siberia.

"To make a long story short, it was all a set up. The kidnapping was engineered by Whitehead to make it look real. Natalya wasn't in on it. Once I arrived in Siberia, Whitehead appeared and told me the real story. Either I kill Dennison, whom they had found in Siberia, or Natalya would be killed."

"Oh, no!"

"I found Natalya, and together we found Dennison, who had changed his name to Gregor Nevchiko to save himself. A whole squad of assassins were sent after us, which we managed to elude. In the end it was Whitehead himself who caught up with us. He was the one who wounded me."

"My goodness! What happened to him?"

Gavin took a deep breath and exhaled slowly. "I—had to—take him out."

Katherine's expression turned to anguish. "Oh, darling, I'm so sorry."

"Well, it was either him, or me. After I recovered, Natalya and I made our way to Japan. Gerard and Uncle Andrew came and brought me home."

"Whatever happened to Natalya?"

"She went back to San Francisco. I haven't heard from her since."

She took his hand in her both of hers. "I'm sorry I asked. I should have just let it lay."

"No, it's okay."

Gerard was waiting in the parking lot of the Pierre regional airport. He gave Katherine a long, tender hug. "It's good to see you, sister," he whispered, tears in his eyes.

"Thank you. It's great to be back."

After they transferred all the camping equipment and supplies from the Jeep to the truck box, Gavin took the Jeep keys to the rental counter in the terminal. Twenty minutes later they pulled into the parking lot of an Italian restaurant at the west edge of town. After they were seated, Gerard looked at a long text from Loren.

"Fair warning," he said to Gavin and Katherine. "Everyone's gathering at your house. Loren, Morgan, Thomas, Uncle Andrew, and Joby. They don't care when we get in, there will be a celebration. Could go well into the night. Hope that's okay."

Katherine smiled. "Oh, of course. That's so sweet."

"Certainly is reason to celebrate, on several levels," Gavin said.

"I'd say," Gerard affirmed. "You rescued eleven people."

"And your man Ben Wilson had a big part in that," Gavin said. "Thank you for loaning him to us. He will always be our friend."

"Happy to hear that," Gerard said. "So, if you don't mind, tell me how it all went down."

By the time the last morsel of dessert was consumed, the story was finished. Katherine and Gavin interspersed their perspectives and Gerard gave them his rapt attention, his face reflecting the twists and turns of their stories.

"I wonder if there's anything we should pick up for the celebration," Katherine said.

"I don't think so," Gerard replied. "Loren said everything was ready."

Half an hour after they left the restaurant, they were a mile from the truck stop where Katherine had been abducted. Gavin leaned forward from the back seat. "There's no reason to stop here," he said, cautiously,

"I—I would like to stop," she said. "I'd like a coffee. They have good coffee here."

She sat quietly as they pulled in and parked near the west entrance. With Gerard leading the way, they entered the store. Katherine paused for a moment and then headed for the coffee counter. They all decided to get a cup and Gerard laid cash down. Katherine walked out leisurely, her to-go cup in hand, looking around at the other customers and travelers in the store. "Small victories," she said, when they returned to the pickup, reaching up to kiss Gavin before she climbed back in the cab. "This coffee will be the best cup I've had in a long time."

As they drove away, both Gerard and Gavin noticed that Katherine took a deep breath and exhaled slowly, then took a sip of coffee. Gavin looked out the window as they turned onto the interstate. The shadows from the fence posts along the highway were getting long. They reminded him of the day he had driven here, the day she had been abducted. The shadows were long then too, and melancholy. Today, they were not. He suddenly remembered something. Leaning forward, he touched Katherine's arm.

"Hon," he said. "Your purse is inside the console."

Without a word, she lifted the cover of the console and took out the purse, opened it and briefly examined the contents. She looked back at him and smiled lovingly. "Another small victory," she said.

Just before nine they turned off the gravel road onto the dirt trail leading to their house, headlights illuminating the way. A mile and a half later they saw the security yard light and the house lit up as well. Andrew and Joby's trucks, Gavin's Jeep Wrangler, and Morgan Hale's crew cab Dodge and Gerard's rental already filled the drive as they pulled up. As they stepped from the truck, the front door opened and Loren burst through, her arms already open wide.

She flew down the steps and swept Katherine up in a hug and wept. "These are happy tears, sister," she said. "I've never been so happy to see anyone in my life!"

Katherine couldn't help but sob. "Thank you. I'm so glad to see you, too."

"But you're going to have to share," said Morgan, touching his wife gently on the shoulder. Loren finally relinquished her hold and wiped her eyes as Morgan gave Katherine a gentle hug. Thomas, Joby, and Andrew were waiting patiently on the deck.

Loren turned her attention to Gavin, holding out her arms again. He stepped forward and embraced his sister. "Well done, little brother, well done," she said. "Didn't I tell you this day would come?"

"Yes, you did. Thanks for believing."

Gerard, meanwhile, was waiting and waved a greeting to Uncle Andrew.

Gavin followed Katherine up the stairs as she took another hug from Thomas. "Welcome home, Auntie," he said.

Joby stepped forward shyly. "I'm glad to see you, Cousin," he said, giving Katherine a brief hug. "It's good to have you home."

Katherine walked to Uncle Andrew, wiping her tears. "Uncle," she said, managing to keep a sob from erupting. "I know you prayed for me. I know you did all you could to bring me home. I'll always be grateful."

Andrew pulled her into a gentle hug. "I did the easy part," he said. "The warrior I sent to look for you had the hard part, but I knew he would find you. I knew he could do it."

She nodded, her head against his chest. In a moment, Gavin stepped up and took his uncle's hand. "*Wopila, Leksi, Taku ecanu kin iyuha* (I'm grateful, Uncle, for everything you did)."

"*Tokasni yelo* (It's alright). The Spirits sent a hawk to guide you, and now they want the black flag back. The one they threw at you in the *Lowanpi*."

Gavin reached into his pocket and pulled out the black streamer.

"Good," Andrew said. "We'll give it back to them at the thanksgiving ceremony."

Loren urged everyone to gather inside. Gavin and Katherine entered hand-in-hand and immediately saw the long banner hanging from the rafters of the cathedral ceiling:

Welcome Home

Soldier Woman

Katherine smiled through her tears.

"There's coffee, and tea," Morgan said. "And fry bread and *wojapi*. Loren made it, so you know it's good."

"You and Uncle have a seat," Thomas told Katherine. "We'll bring whatever you want."

"Oh, in that case, all of the above," she said.

"Same for me," Gavin told his nephew. "Thanks."

Within a few minutes everyone was seated in the living room. Katherine, Gavin, and Andrew on the couch. Loren, Morgan, Thomas, Gerard, and Joby on the chairs across from them. Everyone had bowls of the fruit soup dessert, several pieces of golden fry bread, and a beverage of their choice.

"Oh, Cousin, by the way," Joby said to Gavin. "The day after you left, UPS delivered a big box for you. I didn't open it. I put it by your desk."

Gavin looked at Katherine. "I'm guessing that's the Australian stock saddle we ordered for you. Took long enough."

"Great. You think it will fit Redwing?"

"I'm sure it will. It's the same style as mine, except for a shorter seat, so it will fit."

"Good, can we go riding tomorrow?"

"Absolutely."

Conversation flowed easily, touching on the weather, local happenings, and a rumored Bigfoot sighting in the Black Pipe district. There was no hand wringing or words of pity or concern directed at Katherine. It was enough that she was home and looked well. They knew she would tell her story when she was ready.

"Hey, bro," Gavin said. "How long can you stay?"

"Oh, maybe a couple of more days. Just to soak up all these family vibes."

"Great. How's the knee? I saw you limping a little."

"It's a bit better, but I have a sneaking suspicion I did something to my ACL. I'll have a doctor check it thoroughly when I get back."

"Does that mean surgery?" wondered Morgan.

"I hope not, but I guess I'll go through with it if necessary."

"Hey," Loren said, "keep in mind you will need to come back for a wedding. I'm going to try to talk these two into doing it sooner rather than later."

"Be great if I had some idea before I left," Gerard said, a twinkle in his eye. "Also, do I need to rent a tux?"

"Oh, I don't know," Loren said, winking at Katherine. "I think breech-clouts might be in order for the groom and best man."

"Works for me," Katherine teased.

"I don't know if Armani makes breechclouts," Gavin added, needling his brother.

"Hey," Gerard said, grinning. "Be careful what you wish for."

After the laughter faded, Gerard looked at Gavin and Katherine. "Seriously, let me know when you set the date and I will book my flight, with breechclout in hand, if necessary."

"What day is it today, I mean, what's the date?" Katherine asked.

Thomas tapped his smart watch. "Thursday, September second," he said.

Katherine turned and looked coyly at Gavin. "How about two weeks from this Saturday, which would be the eighteenth?"

An expectant silence quickly filled the room, all eyes turned to Gavin.

"If it can't be any sooner, it's a date."

Gavin and Katherine smiled at the spontaneous applause and light cheering.

"Does that work for you, bro?"

"Certainly. Gives me time to go back to DC, sign some important contracts, and get back here."

Loren stood and waved to get Katherine's attention. "There's something I want to show you. It's in your bedroom," she said.

As the two women left the room, Andrew nodded at Joby, who stood and brought a box and a small flat case out of the spare bedroom. The box he gave to Andrew.

In the bedroom Loren led Katherine to the walk-in closet and pulled out a long white garment bag. "I went up to Pierre the day we heard you were rescued," she said. "I want this to be a gift from my family to you."

She opened the bag and carefully took out the simple but elegant white dress that Katherine had selected. Katherine took the dress and held it to her chest. "I'm sorry, I can't help but cry. I'm so happy to be alive. I'm so happy to be home."

Loren pulled her into a hug. "It's okay, you're entitled. I came into the bedroom to check on my brother the evening of the day you were abducted. He broke down and cried like a baby. I never, ever heard him cry like that, not even when he was a boy."

"He did?"

"Oh, yes. His whole world had fallen apart. But now it's back the way it's supposed to be, the way that the powers that be have ordained it to be. It's all good."

Loren pulled facial tissue out of a box on the nightstand.

After wiping her eyes and her nose, Katherine walked to the full length mirror and gazed at the dress.

Back in the living room, Thomas and Joby were refilling coffee cups. Katherine rejoined Gavin on the couch.

"*Tunjan,*" Andrew said, opening the box he was holding, "Joby and I have gifts for you. First—these." Out of the box he took a pair of moccasins made of elk hide, fully covered with red, black, blue, yellow, and white beads in intricate and angular geometric patterns.

"Oh, my!" Katherine gasped. "Uncle, those are beautiful. Thank you!"

"They sure are," Loren said. "Who made them, Uncle?"

"Esther Red Thunder," Andrew said. "I knew she had a couple pair. I made sure they're the right size. I made an outline from one of your shoes in the closet," he said to Katherine. "They're to remind you of the hard road you just walked, and to keep reminding you how strong you can be as you walk through life as the Lakota woman you are, so you can keep living up to the name Grandma Annie gave you, Soldier Woman."

"Thank you, Uncle, so much!"

Andrew nodded and pointed at Joby. "*Tunska* has something for you, too."

Joby opened the narrow cardboard container and pulled out a single eagle feather, ten inches long and beautifully symmetrical, from the tail of a young golden eagle. "I found this a few years ago when I was out gathering wood by the river," he said. "Auntie Esther did the bead wrap on the quill. I want to give this to you because I know how brave you were."

Katherine took the feather and shook Joby's hand. "Thank you, Cousin. This is awesome, and so special." She turned to Andrew. "Can I wear it in my hair when I get married?"

"You can wear it anytime you choose," he said. "You earned it."

After everyone had an opportunity to examine and admire the moccasins and the feather, Loren pulled rank and called an end to the evening's festivities.

"We can probably party well into the night," she said, "but common sense tells me some of us have work and school tomorrow, and some of us need rest. So, we must call an end to this absolutely wonderful evening. There are more good times ahead."

Andrew lingered long enough to burn sweet grass and smudge. Gerard volunteered to go and check the water tank for the horses, urging Gavin and Katherine to call it a night.

After carefully arranging her new moccasins and the eagle feather atop the dresser, Katherine took Gavin's hand. "I think I would like to do something I've never done," she said, in a soft voice.

"Okay. What would that be?"

"Take a shower together," she said, kissing his hand.

"That would be a first for me, too," he told her.

It was nearly an out-of-body experience, with senses honed by fear as a result of the threat of losing each other. He was always aware of how indescribably beautiful she was, but the pulsating stream of water and the unpretentious innocence of their genuine awe of each other took them to a different dimension. She lathered him with soap from top to bottom and front to back and stood quietly when he did the same for her. The intimacy of those wonderful twenty minutes was spiritual rather than sexual.

Later, within the boundaries of their bed, they yielded to desire and made love for nearly an hour, speaking not a single world. They fell asleep, her back against his chest and his arm around her, and barely moved the night long.

FIFTY-TWO

Sometime after seven, they walked into the kitchen to find Uncle Andrew and Gerard preparing a breakfast of slow-fried potatoes and elk backstrap, adding scrambled eggs as Gavin and Katherine poured themselves coffee.

"*Hihanni lahci* (So early in the morning)," Andrew called out. It was a common traditional greeting that new-age Lakota speakers consistently mistook as the translation for "good morning."

Gavin returned the greeting as he and Katherine seated themselves at the table.

"I was worried you would miss this spectacular morning," Gerard said. "You should have seen the sunrise. I've seen a few since I've been here. Not an event one can see in the city."

"Sleeping in, in our own bed, was a treat," Katherine said. "Especially after such a wonderful evening. And then, you all are making breakfast. That's the best part of the morning. Thank you."

"Oh, our pleasure, totally," Gerard declared. "It was Uncle's idea, actually. We wanted your first day home to start off in the right way. Good food is the first thing."

"And family," Gavin said. "*Pilaunyayapelo* (We thank you)."

"You're welcome," Andrew said. "Joby should be here shortly. He stopped at Esther Red Thunder's to check on her and found out she's not feeling well."

"Oh, dear," Katherine said. "Is it anything serious?"

"I don't know. He'll tell us."

They sat down to eat while the food was still hot, with a plate set for Joby.

"So, are you going to break out that new saddle and go for a ride?" Gerard wanted to know.

"Entirely up to Katherine. But I'm up for it."

"Of course," she said. "Anxious to see that new saddle first."

"Why Australian stock saddles?" Gerard asked his brother.

"Well, for one thing, they don't have that bulbous horn, like western saddles do, and they're much lighter. Easier on a horse, especially if they're carrying a one hundred ninety pound man in addition to a thirty pound saddle. And, I just like them, always have since I first saw one in a movie."

The landline on Gavin's desk rang.

"This is Gavin."

"Hey, Cousin, this is Joby, calling on Auntie Esther's phone. I just called the Community Health Representative and someone is on the way here. It feels like Auntie has a fever. I'll be here until she gets checked out."

"I'm glad you're there. Thanks for taking care of Auntie. How did you know?"

"I just happened to stop by. I'll call again before I leave."

"Good. Talk to you in a little while then."

Gavin returned to the table with a worried frown. "That was Joby," he reported. "He thinks Auntie has a fever and he'll wait there until a CHR gets there and checks Auntie."

"I think the CHR is Susan Burning Breast," Andrew said. "She was a CNA at the hospital for a few years. She'll know what to do for Esther."

Concern for Esther Red Thunder hung like a distant forming cloud.

Twenty minutes later Joby called again. The CHR was driving Esther Red Thunder to the ER at the hospital in Agency Village. Her fever was 102 degrees. "I'll be there shortly, just about to leave now," he said.

Gavin gave the news to everyone. "How old is Auntie Esther?" he asked.

"I think she's seventy-four," Andrew said. "She and her husband used to live north of Cold River, in the Two Kettle area. After he died their daughter moved her into that house. Then two years ago the daughter died, froze to death with her husband. They ran out of gas over there by Black Pipe one night during below zero weather and tried to walk out. So, Esther's been taking care of her grandkids since then."

"I wasn't aware she had custody of her grandkids," Katherine said. "A girl and boy, right?"

"Chris and Nora," Gavin told her. "Nora is older, twelve, I think."

Andrew reheated breakfast for Joby when he finally arrived. "Esther's grandkids are at the neighbor's place, next door," he said. "The CHR said she'll let me know what they find out at the hospital."

"Aren't they in school?" Katherine asked.

"Cold River school district has a four day week," Gavin reminded her.

"I might just go and get them," Andrew said. "Keep them until I know how their grandma is. Or maybe stay with them at their place."

"Let us know if we can help," Katherine said. "Bring them out here, maybe."

"We'll see," Andrew decided. "You two go for your ride. We'll figure something out."

Gavin opened the large box sitting under his desk and lifted out the saddle encased in plastic. It was polished and smelled of new leather.

"It's beautiful!" Katherine exclaimed.

Gavin attached the steel stirrups, much smaller and lighter in weight than stirrups on western saddles. After a couple of adjustments, he carried it to the corral. A few minutes later, both horses were haltered and stood patiently waiting to be saddled. After they were saddled and Gavin and Katherine changed into riding clothes, horses and riders were heading south toward the river.

"It squeaks," Katherine said.

"It will until you break it in. We can rub in some saddle soap, that'll soften the leather a bit."

The day grew warmer as the sun rose higher. After going through a gate, they reached the river and followed it for a few miles. They saw a young white tail buck, likely the same one they had seen weeks earlier, watching them from between two small plum thickets.

"He's not running," Katherine whispered.

"The horses," Gavin told her. "If we were walking by ourselves, he'd be gone in a heartbeat."

A few minutes later they skirted around a porcupine as it ambled across their path, apparently unperturbed by their presence. Later a mother sage hen limped away, one wing hanging down, apparently injured. "Oh, poor thing," Katherine fretted.

"She's fine," Gavin assured her. "She's acting injured to lure us away from her nest. She probably has some young ones hidden somewhere.

Little late in the season for new chicks. It's possible something might have gotten her first clutch, maybe in the spring."

"So, she hatched some more?"

"Yup. Life goes on."

After another mile they turned west away from the river, and climbed a long, gradual slope until they reached the plateau. There they dismounted and led the horses, keeping a leisurely pace to let them rest. The prairie stretched away in all directions in undulating low hills and rises, dotted with occasional thickets or lone trees.

"It's such a totally different environment up here," Katherine observed, "although we're just a few hundred yards from the river. All grassland, barely any trees. I can visualize bison grazing in endless numbers. Or galloping. I'd sure like to see that in real life."

"It's entirely possible," Gavin said. "The tribe has several hundred head west of Agency Village. We can ask Clayton to put in a word to the director of game and fish, they manage the herd."

"Oh, could we? That would be exciting."

Eventually they remounted and turned east and came to the farm and market road that passed by their gate. An hour later they turned in to their approach and followed the road back to the house. Two hundred yards from the house they could see the blades of the wind generator lazily turning in the breeze. As they rode close enough they noticed that Joby's or Andrew's vehicles were not there.

"I hope Esther is okay," Katherine said. "It's been several hours."

"Depends on how busy the ER is," Gavin said.

After arriving home, they unsaddled and brushed down the horses. After graining them they turned them loose in the pen, and then put the saddles away in the barn. Gerard had iced tea ready for them in the kitchen.

"Uncle Andrew called," he told them. "Esther is on her way home. Apparently she argued vehemently with the doctor, didn't want to be hospitalized for observation. So, one of them, either Uncle or Joby, might stay with her and the kids tonight."

"Must not have been anything too serious," Gavin said. "At least I hope so. Can't always depend on that hospital. Glad family looks in on her and the kids."

"And Chief Avery called, about an hour ago. He sounded a bit upset. Wants you to call him as soon as you can."

Gavin raised his eyebrows and then took a sip of tea. "Thanks. Guess I better do that now."

Taking his glass of tea to the desk, he placed the call.

"I've been debriefing Primault and Singer all day," he told Gavin. "About an hour ago I received a call from the chief of the department of criminal investigation in North Dakota. He was apprised of the rescue of Katherine Hill and the girls. But the reason he called me shocked the hell out of me. I still can't believe it."

"What, bad news?"

"Could be the worst. He said the two houses where the girls were imprisoned burned to the ground last night."

Gavin nearly choked on his tea. "What? Both of them?"

"Both of them!"

"How in the friggin' hell? And why, for Christ's sake?"

"I don't know the how, but the chief suspected arson. He was embarrassed and apologetic. As for 'why,' well, I'm leaning toward someone wanting to destroy evidence."

"Holy shit!" Gavin blurted. "That has to be it."

"Yeah and get this. No one knew until this morning. When the forensics people got to one of the places, it had already burned to the ground. So, they called a rural fire department and hurried over to the next place. Same damn thing."

"Who would do that?"

"According to Primault, only two people knew about the houses. The Benson County sheriff and his deputy."

"And whoever else they told," Gavin pointed out.

"Yeah, and we don't know who that would be."

"Well, shit," Gavin spat out angrily. "What does that do, I mean, what's the fallout?"

"No physical evidence to corroborate the girls' stories. All gone up in smoke. That leaves us with the photos and video."

"Yeah, well, the implications are off the scale. There is one other person who knew, in addition to Sheriff Arnold and his deputy. The county attorney in Leighton County. He was grilling us pretty heavily until Katherine shut him down. She told him about the imprisonment of those girls."

"My first inclination is to assume that someone had something to hide," Avery said.

"Right. There's no way those incidents were random. And it happened only hours after we made statements to Sheriff Arnold and showed him the photos and videos."

"Well," the chief said wearily. "I've got a judicial committee meeting to go to. I'll give you a call if I hear any more."

"Okay. This is just unbelievable."

Gavin disconnected the call and went back to the kitchen table to rejoin Gerard and Katherine. "Judging by what we could hear and the look on your face, I'd say the news was not good."

"Downright crappy, as a matter of fact," Gavin said, taking a chair as he told them what happened.

"The probable scenario is that some official knew about those girls," Gerard concluded. "The last thing they expected was for you all to show up and bring it to light. They were looking the other way or were paid to. Classic case of bribery and corruption."

After Andrew No Horn arrived, Gavin repeated the news. Andrew listened quietly, slowly shaking his head. "You know, I saw something, two, maybe three weeks ago. Maybe it has something to do with what you just told me."

"What did you see, *Leksi?*" Gavin asked.

"A snake, going down into a hole."

"A snake?"

"Yeah, a white snake, but it looked just like a blue racer. They're poisonous and fast. I saw a couple blue racers, a long time ago. They were really fast and they went down a hole, just like that, there and gone. The white snake I saw did that. He went through the grass and down a hole."

"Why would it be white, Uncle?" Gerard asked.

"Melrose, he was white," Katherine told them. "He had light blue eyes and pale skin, very pale. The whitest white man I've ever seen. He was the one running the operation."

"But how would that be connected to the houses being burned down?" Gerard asked.

"Well," Gavin said, "that man covered his tracks really well. His underlings didn't know his real name, two of them never ever saw him, and he got away really slick. So, if he made all those contingency plans, then stands to reason he would go so far as planning to destroy evidence. But the fact remains that someone set fire to those houses, and I'm betting that that someone is just as guilty as Melrose."

"And now we will never be able to prove that," Katherine said.

"Who are the chief suspects?" Gerard asked.

"Sheriff James Arnold, his deputy, and county attorney Nathan Halloran," Gavin said.

"Well, two Lakota owned weekly papers are publishing the story, simultaneously," Katherine said. "We have the witness statements, and mine. That's highly credible and isn't based solely on the evidence that was burned. The witness testimonies—the girls' statements, and mine— will reveal that there is a network, organization, call it what you will, that abducted us and sold the girls for sex. Someone has to, needs to, pay attention to those facts. Someone meaning police departments, law enforcement authorities, the Bureau of Indian Affairs, and tribal councils."

"The only thing we can't say or report, without solid credible evidence, is that we suspect certain people of collusion and corruptions, you know, accepting money for their involvement or silence."

"So even though the perpetrators are getting away, never to face justice, we still have a responsibility to reveal what we know," Gavin said.

"Exactly. Thirteen girls," Katherine emphasized, "that we know of for certain, were abducted, imprisoned, and trafficked for sex. One of them was beaten so badly she died of her injuries. We know where they were imprisoned, we know one of the man camps where they were taken to be raped—the girls' interviews may reveal another. That's what we know. Those are the indisputable facts; and that's what we tell the world. Then, we can say—also factually— 'oh, by the way, the houses where they were imprisoned burned to the ground in the same night.'"

"That's very compelling and powerful," Gerard pointed out.

"Right, so although someone destroyed valuable evidence, they did not destroy the truth," Katherine declared.

"There is one bothersome possibility," Gerard said. "Someone guilty or culpable set fire to those houses or hired someone else to do that. What if it doesn't stop there?"

"What do you mean?" Gavin asked.

"Well, maybe that individual, or individuals, might attempt to discredit the witnesses, shoot holes in the story."

"Yes, but that would be difficult for anyone to do without revealing their identity," Katherine reasoned.

"Not necessarily," Gerard countered. "For example, does the nationwide television audience know exactly who is responsible for all the half-truths and blatant lies that are told in political ads every four years?"

"That's an interesting point, I guess," Katherine admitted.

"Furthermore," Gerard pressed, "the victims, the witnesses, are all young Native girls. I'm guessing that any white print or broadcast reporter—or official, for that matter—with any semblance of legitimacy, refuting all or part of their statements, will seem credible to white readers and the white audience."

"That may well happen but it's no reason for us to hesitate," Katherine said.

"I'm not even remotely suggesting that. I'm simply bringing up the very real possibility that their stories will be discredited, attacked by someone."

"Well, we stand by our stories, no matter what," Katherine insisted.

"Of course. There is one other part of that bothersome possibility," Gerard went on.

"And that is?"

"What if those culpable or guilty individuals are crazy enough or scared enough to silence witnesses?"

"You're just full of cheerful thoughts, aren't you?" Gavin said. "What exactly do you mean by 'silence?'"

"Kill them," Andrew said. He had been listening quietly, nodding occasionally. "This country doesn't like anyone who is different or is thought of as 'not as good.' People who are labeled like that are killed by cops pretty regularly. Poor, homeless, mentally ill, brown, Black, Asian—cops kill them without fear of being punished. In their minds, they're cleaning out the riff-raff, the dregs. So, what's this country going to think when they hear those stories? When they hear that white men kidnapped those girls and sold them for sex, and mostly white men who paid for sex? I think it will be like every other time bad things happen to minorities—most people won't care. But someone may be afraid that they will be named as a, ah, a sex trafficker, or taking a bribe, or knowing about it and not doing anything. Those are the ones we have to be afraid of. That's the dark side of this that we can't ignore."

"Are we saying that those girls, and me, are in danger?" Katherine asked.

"Well," Gavin said, sighing, "I wouldn't have thought so if those houses hadn't burned."

"One other thought," Gerard said, "in the interest of not avoiding harsh reality. Over the years, how many missing Native girls and women were found, or turned up?"

"According to statistics," Gavin replied, "not very many."

"If someone is scared enough and worried enough to burn down those houses, what else are they willing to do?" Andrew asked.

"That's the question," Gerard said, "that should motivate pre-emptive measures to safeguard the girls and their testimony."

"Where do we start?" Katherine asked.

"With the police chief, and that young man, Justin," Andrew said immediately. "For a long time, they were shouting into the wind about this problem. They care."

"I have a woman in my company," Gerard said, "who's a risk manager. She worked for an insurance company and trained corporate executives on mitigating risks to their personal safety. If Chief Avery agrees to provide all the salient information, I will ask her—her name is Jody Hernden—to devise a plan to protect those girls, and their families."

"Wonderful. I don't think Ben would have any objections at all. I'll call him," Gavin said, turning to Katherine. "Also, I think we need to include Clayton. How do you feel about inviting him and Veronica for supper, while Gerard is still here? I think he should hear from you."

"Of course."

"I think I'm going to talk to Henry Two Crow," Andrew said. "We need to do everything we can to protect those girls, to put up protection against any bad intentions anyone has against them. I don't know how many of them and their families practice the old ways, you know, go to sweats and ceremonies, but I would like to bring them all together in one ceremony. I want to know what Henry would think of that."

"I think Uncle Henry would agree with you," Gavin said. "That's the best idea I've heard. *Toske ociciyake owakihi kin omakiyaka yo* (Let me know how I can help)."

"*Ohan. Wopila* (Yes. Thank you)."

Katherine reached and took Gavin's hand. "I was just thinking of what Melrose—or whatever his name is—said to me regarding the man who abducted me. He told me the man was 'handled,' because he didn't want anything traced to him—Melrose."

"That's the mindset we have to guard against," Gavin said.

"And one other," Gerard said, somberly. "Complacency. As the saying goes, 'the surest way to allow evil to grow is to do nothing.'"

FIFTY-THREE

"I'm sorry Veronica can't join us," Katherine said to Clayton Lone Hawk, as she walked with him to the corral to join Gavin. "How long will she be away."

"Oh, just a few days. She has a meeting with the board of directors of the foundation she runs, back in Ohio. They'll be finished tomorrow. It's a quarterly meeting, so it's tolerable being apart for four days every three months. She's looking forward to your wedding. Thanks for the invitation."

"Of course. I hope she didn't have to drive to the airport alone," Katherine said.

"Never," Clayton assured her. "I drive her myself, I wait until she's through security, and I'll be there waiting when she comes back."

"She's stunningly beautiful," Katherine said.

"She is that, and it takes one to know one," Clayton replied with a smile.

Katherine blushed as she reached out for Gavin's arm.

"Glad you could come," Gavin said to President Lone Hawk.

"Certainly. Saves me from having to cook for myself."

"Good. *Leksi* should be here soon, he's bringing the food, and Gerard is in the house, sitting with his knee on ice, I think."

On cue, Andrew No Horn's old Ford pickup appeared over the rise and rumbled toward the house, casting long shadows as it crossed in front of the setting sun.

"Chief Avery filled me in on the—what shall I call them—the prison houses," Lone Hawk said. "Seems like something out of a gangster movie. I also had an opportunity to listen to the audio of the two young ladies Lieutenant Primault was able to rescue. I don't know how to describe what I heard. Good god! I have undying respect for those two young ladies, and I so admire their courage."

Lone Hawk looked at Katherine. "That goes for you, too."

"Thanks."

Lone Hawk nodded and paused, gazing across the prairie. "When will we Lakota men remember that our women are the backbone of our nation? Couldn't be too soon for me."

"I agree with you wholeheartedly," Gavin said.

"Well, I directed our social services department to work with Chief Avery," Lone Hawk continued, "and their counterparts in the other tribes, to make arrangements to interview the other ten girls."

"I think that's a wise move," Gavin said. "Katherine has a thought about that."

"Regarding logistics and making it easier for the girls," she said, "it would be better to bring them all together in the same location. Since Chief Avery and Lieutenant Primault have taken the lead in this situation, I think we should bring them here. We can put them up at the casino hotel. But the most important factor would be having them together sharing what will certainly be a difficult experience. I think it would be a psychological boost."

"Of course, absolutely. Let's do it that way," Lone Hawk agreed.

"Justin had two women officers interview the first two young ladies," Katherine said. "I'm sure that eliminated a great deal of hesitancy. So, all the interviews should be done by women. The two officers, certainly, counselors, and social workers. Loren said she would be willing."

"Would they be interviewed individually, meaning each one separately, or as a group?" Lone Hawk asked.

"I think we should leave that up to those young ladies to decide," Katherine suggested.

"Of course, excellent idea," Lone Hawk agreed.

After visiting with Dancer and Redwing for a few minutes, they heard Andrew call them in to eat. "We have two choices," he announced as everyone meandered toward the table. An enticing mixture of smells were emanating from the counter where serving platters were arranged, along with a tall soup kettle. "We have Lakota food and *wasicu* food. The kettle has *taniga wahanpi* (tripe soup). Next to it is a pan of skillet bread, and over here there is roast chicken, baked potatoes, and salad. We covered all the bases."

Taniga was a traditional delicacy, consisting of small pieces of intestines and the stomach wall of bison and cattle, referred to as the "book." The other ingredients in the soup were wild onion and *tinpsila*, a root tuber mislabeled as a wild turnip. The soup was made after fall hunts in the pre-reservation days, and later after Lakota families managed to procure an entire cow or steer for butchering. It was not as popular with recent generations because it was labor intensive to clean the intestines and stomach and gather all the other requisite ingredients. Younger Lakota people, having adapted to non-Lakota cuisine, were not fond of the smell of the soup cooking. Hence entire generations of Lakota turned up their *wasicu* influenced noses at the traditional delicacy. Not so with all who had gathered this evening. No one touched a single piece of roast chicken, baked potato, or one leaf of salad.

"I'm proud of you, bro," Gavin said to Gerard. "I wasn't sure how you'd react when *Leksi* suggested the menu for tonight."

"Well, I did have some at Grandma's funeral," Gerard recalled. "And there is a Mexican restaurant in DC that serves *menudo*, albeit a bit spicier than this. So, I've had a few bowls over the years."

"I prepared this for my new daughters," Clayton said, "with plenty of warning. They gamely tried and did eat a bowl each. But they never asked for it after that. Veronica did say she's willing to try it again. For most people it's definitely an acquired taste."

"Reminds me of helping my mom and all the women when they cleaned the intestines and the stomach, down at the river," Andrew said. "It was usually an all day job. Us kids would help stretch out the intestines. Did you know that a cow's small intestines are about seventy feet long?"

"My goodness," Katherine said. "So how long is a bison's intestine?"

"Over a hundred feet," Andrew replied.

"Did you make the skillet bread, too?" Clayton asked.

"Yup. I used my mom's recipe. Flour, baking powder, and water, but not lard or bacon grease. I used olive oil to grease the skillet."

"Well, thanks for taking us back in time," Clayton said. "We'd all be so much healthier if we went back to eating traditional foods. I guess the *wasicu* lifestyle that a lot of our people live, and fast foods, are too ingrained."

"We wouldn't have a lot of the diseases and illnesses we have now," Andrew pointed out. "No diabetes or cancer, or heart disease."

"Well, we would be a much healthier and happier people if the *wasicus* had never come," Lone Hawk said. "Their ways were forced on us, to be sure, but in the past twenty years or so, when there are more and more opportunities for us to learn our own culture and history, and language, most of us are not taking advantage. Without culture and language, who are we? What are we? We're losing our sense of identity, and when that's gone, we'll truly be 'apples,' red on the outside and white on the inside."

"That's a scary prospect," Gavin said.

"A case in point, if you will, is this situation with the young ladies that were rescued," Lone Hawk continued. "Women and girls were held in high esteem in the old days. Lakota males, by and large, don't think that way any longer. I don't know if that is part of the basis for the complacency regarding missing and murdered indigenous women. But the glaring truth is mostly men are on tribal councils, mostly men run tribal programs. Juxtapose that with this lack of respect for women, maybe that's why there's not more of an effort to deal with the problem of 'Murdered and Missing Indigenous Women.'"

"How do we change that?" Gavin asked.

"Teach our children the old ways," Lone Hawk replied without hesitation. "The best way to do that is by example. Boys need to see their fathers treating their mothers with respect, treating all women with respect."

"Clayton," Katherine said, "in your opinion, is there a tipping point at which the opportunity to reclaim our culture will be gone?"

"I think it's right now," Lone Hawk said. "One step forward and two steps back is not progress. It's losing, it's regression."

"I gave a presentation at the university a couple of years ago," Gavin said. "After a discussion on recovering language, which most there were in favor of, I made an offer to anyone who wanted to learn Lakota to teach them individually or in a group. No one took me up on the offer. So, I agree. We've reached that tipping point."

"Those of us who are still Lakota and know something of the old ways, and the old stories, we can't give up now," Andrew insisted. "We keep doing the ceremonies, we keep speaking the language, teaching our history. If we quit, assimilation wins. This situation with those girls has at least two strong lessons. First, our Lakota young women are courageous and strong. Two, it's up to us as men to protect them, like Justin Primault and that other officer did."

"Geoffrey Brousseaux," Gavin noted.

"*He wowicake yelo, Leksi* (That is the truth, Uncle)," Lone Hawk said.

Conversation turned to other topics and issues. Eventually it circled back around to the issue uppermost in their minds. "So, is there anything else you need me to do, relative to bringing all those young ladies here, to our Rez?"

"I can think of two," Katherine said: "a setting for the interviews, and accommodations."

"I will speak to the manager of the casino hotel," Lone Hawk stated. "Maybe it can also be the place to do the interviews."

"Of course," Gavin affirmed. "Maybe in the concert venue. And as far as the rooms, Katherine and I will pay for them, and meals. That way there'll be no costs to the girls and their families."

"And I'll help with that," Andrew said.

"Thank you, very generous of you, and we'll find a way to reimburse them for travel expenses. Consider it done on my end," Lone Hawk assured them. "Now, on to the really important issue. Where is your wedding to take place?"

"At Grandma Annie's place," Gavin said. "An instructor from the university and his family are living there now, renting it. But we told them that we will be using the grounds from time to time."

"And what type of ceremony will it be? *Wasicu* or traditional?"

"Both," Katherine replied. "We satisfy the legal side, from marriage license to certificate, and then Uncle Andrew will conduct the traditional part to satisfy who we really are."

"*Lila waste ktelo* (It will be very good)," Clayton declared. "And then we celebrate." He raised his coffee cup, "Here's to the old ways, may they live forever."

All the cups were raised in affirmation.

FIFTY-FOUR

Ten days later, on a warm early afternoon in the Moon of Red Leaves, twenty- four people came to witness the marriage of Katherine Kay Hill and Gavin Gabriel Lone Wolf. They were all gathered just north of Grandma Annie Little Turtle's house, under two giant cottonwood trees, their leaves murmuring in the soft breeze.

In that peaceful setting, for the time being the world beyond was kept at bay by the quiet joy of the moment, with hearts and minds reminded that goodness and love sometimes win the day.

The bride wore her calf length, simple but elegant white chiffon dress. Choosing not to wear a veil, her luminescent hair loose and cascading down the back was a dramatic contrast to the dress. From her left temple hung the eagle feather gifted to her by Joby Bone. On her feet were shoes with sculpted heels

Next to her Loren Lone Wolf Hale stood tall and regal as the matron of honor, also in a white dress, the very picture of elegance and grace.

The groom wore a replica of his great-grandfather's hair shirt, made of brain tanned deer hide, two hues shy of paper white. The shirt was an exact copy of the original, down to the number of locks of hair on the sleeves and the color of the dyed porcupine quills on the breast patch, over the shoulders, and down the sleeves. Dark blue slacks and a pair of intricately quilled moccasins completed his ensemble, a perfect blend of old and new. His hair was in his customary long single braid, and a four-banded antelope leg bone choker around his neck. Attached to the crown of his head was the eagle feather given to him by the High Crane family, whose son's murder he had solved.

His best man, Gerard, wore his dress blue uniform, resplendent with miniature medals on the left breast, and silver eagles on the shoulders. He stood ramrod straight and shoulder to shoulder with his brother.

Not long after Dennis Meyerson, a justice of the peace in Redoubt County, concluded the civil ceremony, Andrew No Horn stepped to the front and asked everyone to gather in close behind the wedding party.

Andrew faced the couple and everyone behind them: Morgan and Thomas Hale, Theresa Hale-Thibodeaux and her husband Stephen, Ben and Elizabeth Avery, Justin and Sandra Primault, Jason Singer and his mother, Clara, Clayton and Veronica Lone Hawk, Henry and Ollie Two Crow, Joby Bone, Esther Red Thunder and her grandchildren, Chris and Nora, Ramona Red Star, the secretary in the Lakota Studies Department at SRU, Douglas Eagle Shield, President of the University, and his wife Minerva. Two other people were apart from the group and busy, one a videographer and the other a still photographer.

"In the old days, a young man would court the object of his love and desire, and he had to do it in a certain way. There were rules with no exceptions. He came to the lodge of the young woman's mother with his elk hide courting robe. If the young woman chose she would meet him in the doorway of the lodge. If she chose not to stand with him, then he was expected to accept her decision and go away quietly."

"If the young woman came out, Andrew continued, "she had to stand with one foot in the lodge, in the doorway, and one foot outside. Then the young man would cover them with his robe, and they would whisper to each other under the robe. Of course, whoever was in the lodge was listening, usually the mother and grandmother. If they felt that he was keeping her too long under the robe, they would clear their throats loudly".

"A young man offered a dowry, not to buy her but to gift her family to signify that he understood what she meant to them. If the gifts were accepted, that was their way of saying they gave her to him. From that moment on, in the eyes of her family and the *tiyospaye*, the community, they were husband and wife, and could begin living together."

Andrew paused and gazed directly at Katherine and Gavin for a few moments. He smiled and spoke again. "I remember," he continued, "when you were fifteen, my girl, and you chose my nephew to dance with you in a round dance." He turned his gaze to Gavin. "From that moment on, *Tunska*, your grandma and I knew this day would come." Andrew looked at Katherine. "And, my girl, your mother told me after you took him into the round dance, that he was the one she wanted you to marry."

Both of them nodded and smiled at each other.

"All of us who know you, who love you, your family and friends, are happy this day has come. That's why we are all here, to share your happiness. When two people who are meant to be together find the way to each other, it restores balance to the world. And it makes all our ancestors happy—your mother, your parents, your grandmother—they are all smiling for you on the other side.

"Now, as you requested, say your vows to each other."

Katherine and Gavin turned to face each other. She reached up and wiped the tears rolling down her face. "Gavin, you are the love of my life.

My life and my happiness are complete because I was meant to be your wife. I will walk with you in this life, through the good and the bad, the happy and the sad. I have loved you all of my life and I will love you after my time on earth is done. I give this ring to you as a symbol of my promise."

Taking his left hand, Katherine slowly slipped a wide silver band over Gavin's third finger. After a deep breath, he kissed her hand and held it. "Katherine, you are the love of my life. I have known you all of your life and my love for you grows every day, and it will never end. You are the reason I am happy, and complete. Whatever may come, I am honored to face it with you, and always at your side. I give this ring to you as a symbol of my promise."

With a gentle, loving smile, he lifted her hand and placed a silver band on the third finger, fitting it with the engagement ring. Finally, he bent down, lifted her chin, and kissed her softly.

Cheers, shouts, and applause broke out.

After a few moments, Andrew raised his hands. "I will offer a prayer," he said.

"*Taku skanskan wakan kin he* (All that moves and is sacred), give this woman, *Akicita Winyan* (Soldier Woman) and this man, *Mayaca Iyanke* (Wolf that Runs) the strength and the will to face what life may bring. Whatever is good on their road, help them to accept it with humility and grace. Whatever is difficult, help them to meet it with courage. Give them long life. *Mitakuye Oyasın.*"

More cheers and applause, this time lasting for several minutes. Everyone pressed in for a handshake or a hug, or both. Loren held them both and wept like a baby.

In a few moments, Loren and Morgan, as the hosts, asked everyone to gather under the long canopy that had been erected next to the corrals.

Beneath it was a long table covered with white cloths and set to accommodate all of the guests. At the end was a table with the food in serving bowls and hot dishes. The main course was bison prime rib with wild cranberry sauce and baked sweet potatoes. There was iced tea made from wild peppermint, water, and fruit juices and platters of freshly baked bread. The food had been prepared and catered by Edna and her staff from Edna's Cafe in Cold River, who stood ready to serve.

Before the meal was served, Katherine and Gavin carried a platter of tiny spirit plates of food and followed Andrew to the cemetery and left an offering on each of the graves. When they returned Gavin took off the hair shirt and put on a white collarless ribbon shirt and Katherine put her hair in a ponytail.

The elders, Henry and Ollie, and Esther, with her grandchildren, were seated at the head of the table. After everyone was in place, the bride and the groom, with help from Loren and Morgan, gave small gifts to each person. A white lace kerchief for the women and a pearl-handled pen knife for the men. Chris and Nora received gift certificates to their favorite stores in the Rapid City mall. Then the feasting began.

Conversation filled the air as the photographer and videographer continuously circled the gathering, skillfully fulfilling their tasks as unobtrusively as possible. Henry Two Crow recalled the boyhood adventures and misadventures of the "Lone Wolf twins," as Gerard and Gavin were known in the community, provoking smiles and laughter. Loren told of Annie Little Turtle's boundless pride when Katherine graduated from law school, the first Sicangu Lakota woman to do so. When Veronica Lone Hawk asked Katherine when and where Gavin had proposed to her, the second time, she smiled and replied.

"It was on the coast of France," she said, "We were walking on the wall between the harbor and the city of Saint-Malo, being tourists. It was a beautiful setting, like a picture on a postcard, just as the sun was going down. I will never forget that moment. That was only seven weeks ago."

"From Horse Creek to Saint-Malo," Clayton said. "That's a love story indeed."

A final ritual took place quietly. Ollie Two Crow invited all the women to join her, including Veronica Lone Hawk and Nora, as she took Katherine aside, while the men watched. After they all took turns brushing her hair, Ollie and Esther—the two oldest women present—meticulously and skillfully fashioned two long braids, wrapping the ends in red ribbon, and then placing them down the front over her breasts as a declaration of a proper married woman. Finally, Gavin was invited to paint the part in his wife's hair with vermillion powder, as a sign of a woman greatly loved.

The tables were cleared, folded, and removed to make room for a circle of chairs, and everyone was invited to sit. Loren and Morgan decided to amend western tradition and forego the usual 'best man' and 'maid of honor' speeches. Laughter and conversation were always a part of any social gathering for Lakota people, and this was no exception. Conversations flowed easily, a natural denouement to a momentous day. Loren asked Henry Two Crow to talk about the correlation of the bow and arrow to marriage.

"Some of you know," he began, "the moon gave us the bow and *Hanwi* is female, so that means the bow is female. You can see our bow when the new moon is a thin crescent sliver. Then *Anpetuwi*, the sun, gave us the arrow, so the arrow is male. The arrows of the sun are the rays that shine down through clouds, very straight.

"It's easy to think of the bow with the arrow, the arrow with the bow. But what we should remember is that one cannot fulfill its purpose without the other. The strongest bow is useless without an arrow. The straightest arrow cannot fly on its own.

"So, when a woman and a man come together, they give each other purpose. One cannot be fulfilled without the other."

Three hours later, as they settled into bed, Katherine was still thinking about Henry's story. "I love what Grandpa Henry said, about the bow and arrow."

"It's one of those forgotten cultural metaphors," Gavin said.

Visible in the window was the moon rising over the eastern horizon. Katherine gasped lightly and pointed. "Look! Isn't that lovely?"

The orange half orb rose slowly, revealing more of itself with each passing moment. Soon it freed itself from the horizon and hung in the sky, a shining disc.

"I once saw a moonrise in Scotland," she said. "There was an old castle in the foreground. Someone there, a young woman, was awed by the sight. I thought the castle was an intrusion, a blight on an otherwise ethereal scene."

"You are definitely an old soul," Gavin said, as they gazed at the rising light in the window.

"I have an idea!" Katherine said, sitting up. "Let's go for a ride!"

"What?"

"Let's saddle up the horses and go for a ride!"

Twenty minutes later, after putting on riding clothes, they slipped out of the house, not wanting to disturb Gerard. Luckily the horses were in the pen. After the saddles were on, Gavin went back in the barn and came out with his encased bow and attached quiver bristling with arrows, and his K-Bar knife. He hung the bow and quiver from the front of his saddle and handed the knife to Katherine.

"Put that on your belt."

"Expecting trouble?" Katherine asked, half in jest.

"In the old days, carrying a bow was a symbol that a man was ready to protect his family. A woman always carried a knife. Just seems like good moves to make."

"I love it. What time is it, by the way?" she asked as they mounted.

"I don't know, didn't bring a watch. Doesn't matter."

As the moon rose higher and brightened the land with its soft, cool light, they rode side by side on the prairie that stretched south from the house. A warm breeze caressed their faces. Somewhere above them a nighthawk grunted as he dived after insects. Katherine had not taken out her braids and they dangled across her back as she swayed with Red Wing's eager walk.

"I've never done this," she said, "I've never ridden a horse at night, much less in beautiful moonlight."

"That makes this a special ending to a wonderful day. The kind of day one only dreams about."

"I'm sure you've ridden at night."

"Never in the company of a beautiful woman. I've ridden up in British Columbia, Alaska, Montana while packing in to hunting areas, or out. But the weather was always cold. So, this is a first for me, too."

"Sometimes we don't know what something is or really means until you've lost it. When I saw the moon in the window, I wanted to fly up to it, and play in the stars. You know, like the seven sisters who floated up to get away from the bear. This is the next best thing."

"Yeah. They're right up there," Gavin said, looking up and finding the Pleiades.

Katherine pulled Red Wing to a stop and reached out to take Gavin's hand. "I'm glad you saved me from the bear," she said, tears glistening in her eyes.

He squeezed her hand. "It was never going to be any other way. No matter how long, no matter how far."

She pulled him close, reaching and standing in the stirrups to put her arms around his neck for a long, deep kiss.

They came to a long, gentle slope and followed the shallow gully toward the river, which was a shimmering ribbon of silver below them. With Gavin and Dancer leading the way, they followed a meandering trail to the water's edge. They dismounted and tied the horses to a small oak tree and walked down the narrow bank to the stream.

"It's warm," Gavin said, swishing his hand in the water. "Hey, want to go wading?"

Removing their boots and socks, they rolled up their trouser legs and stepped into the slowly moving current.

"This is nice," she said. "How far out can we go?"

"The surface looks flat all the way across, which means it's probably fairly shallow."

"I'm sure we're not the first ones ever to do this," she said.

"No, we're not. In the old days, before reservations, Grandpa Black Wolf said there was a village site not too far south of where we are. Our ancestors moved up and down this valley, all the time."

"Well, I think I know how they must have felt, to stand here in the warm water of the Smoking Earth River with the moon up there. It's wonderful."

Holding hands, they carefully waded to the other bank and turned around, watching their wavering shadows on the water as they recrossed.

Reaching the bank, they sat in the grass and brushed off the water from their feet and ankles, before putting their socks and boots back on.

"Remember last year when you went to DC and we met for lunch at the Red Oak restaurant?"

"I certainly do."

"You walked me back and up to my office, and then you left."

He smiled and caressed her cheek. "I didn't want to leave."

She returned his smile. "After you walked out of my cubicle I wanted to go after you and tell you not to leave."

"I would have stayed."

Cradling his face in her hands, she pulled him close for another long kiss.

"And the reason I'm telling you that, is—after what I went through, I don't want to be away from you. I guess I don't trust being safe away from you. Is that kind of silly?'

Taking both her hands in his, Gavin gazed into her eyes, which were even more luminous in the moonlight. "No, it's not silly, it's understandable. For as long as you like, we'll never be more than shouting distance apart."

"As long as I don't turn into a clingy wife."

"Are you kidding? Having you cling to me as what I've dreamed of since you were fifteen."

"But I will spare you the chore of having to come to the bathroom with me."

"I can live with that."

"Now, let's go home and make love."

"In that case those horses will need to fly home."

FIFTY-FIVE

Lieutenant Justin Primault and Chief Avery stood at the back of the multi-purpose auditorium at SRU to listen and watch. A mixture of police officers, mental health counselors, social workers, teachers, and interested parents had responded to the invitation to the presentation on teaching women and girls the basics of ensuring their own personal safety. Several rows of chairs were in middle of the floor, all facing the podium at the front. Practically every seat was filled.

The lecture was being delivered by Jody Hernden, the risk manager for Wolf Star Security Assessment, Inc., Gerard's company. Gerard was seated on the first row of bleachers off to the right side with Gavin and Katherine.

Jody Hernden, a tall, slender Black woman had captured the audience with her opening remarks. "At the age of eighteen, I was abducted and raped, repeatedly." She paused as silence permeated the room. "While walking across a university campus, after basketball practice, I was taken by force by two males, thrown into a van, bound hand and foot, and taken to an off campus house. I was, I learned later, the object of a dare made by several friends who had started drinking together that evening."

Gerard turned a shocked expression to Gavin. "I never knew that," he whispered.

"That horrible episode has stayed with me all my life. It's a part of who I am, but I have learned, slowly, at times painfully, not to allow it to control me. I have done everything in my power never to let that happen again. I will share with you today the lessons I learned along the way, so that you can teach it to your young women, to your daughters and granddaughters.

"My boss, Dr. Gerard Lone Wolf, told me about the recent rescue of ten young Lakota girls, and asked me to come here. I immediately agreed. Indigenous women are twice as likely to experience violence in their lives, and 1 out 3 will be sexually abused. Over sixty-five percent of the perpetrators will be non-indigenous. The number of missing and murdered indigenous women and girls is far higher than for any other group. The contributing factors for this exploitation are poverty, homelessness, sexism, racism, and a white legacy of imperialism. But the most astounding fact is that very little is being done to mitigate it."

Heads in the audience were nodding in agreement, especially the women.

"Law enforcement is doing next to nothing, except posting notices when a girl goes missing. It's too late then. Family and child services, anywhere, are not tasked to deal with this issue, which is true for social service programs in general. So, who can do anything about this? It has to start with people who care. Hopefully, that is why you are all here today."

"The steps and answers to mitigate this problem don't have to be complicated," she continued. "In fact, the simpler the better. It starts with awareness."

Herndon pointed out that being alert and aware of our surroundings was absolutely necessary for the survival of early humans. "You didn't go into the tiger's lair. And you could not let down your guard."

Reaching into her pocket and pulling out a cell phone, Herndon called it "arguably the chief contributing factor for distraction. Human predators will use every advantage and opportunity when it comes to abductions. Women and girls make it easier for them when their attention is focused on their phones in crowds or parking lots. Juxtapose the fact that entire generations of girls have not been taught the value of awareness with the fact that this phone is now a pervasive part of our lives, and we have a recipe for disaster. The solution, the only way to prevent trouble and disaster, is to pay attention. It's as simple as that."

By the end of the afternoon Jody Hernden had outlined all the steps to situational awareness—what it was, how to practice it, and how to teach it. Blending a compelling combination of statistics and images in a slide presentation, she had everyone's undivided attention. At the end of the presentation, everyone departed with a comprehensive pamphlet, and a determination to do what they could.

FIFTY-SIX

Chief Avery joined Lieutenant Primault and officers Jason Singer, Geoffrey Brousseaux, Audrey Hinson, and Madonna White Bear in the conference room. "Thanks for coming," he said. "I got a call from the FBI Supervisory Agent in Pierre, who's in contact with his counterpart in Bismarck. They asked for all the information we have relative to the twelve girls and Katherine Hill. I apprised them that we have yet to interview ten of the girls, which will happen next week, hopefully. In the meantime, I would like all of us here, as a group, to develop a case summary, which will serve as the blueprint for the comprehensive report. The difference between the summary and the report will be all the details from each of you, obviously. If you're all ready and willing, I'll bring in Sergeant West and Jenny to take notes and record."

After nods of assent all around, Avery stood and poked his head out the door. "Gabby, Jenny, if you would please."

"Where do we start?" Primault asked, after the public information officer and secretary entered.

"Let's start with Katherine Hill," Avery said, pointing at Singer. "With Sherholt Transportation and Todd Nomer."

Sergeant West placed the microphone in front of Jason Singer as he cleared his throat and slid closer to the table. Primault followed, checking with Broussard to make sure he had relayed everything they observed and experienced. Audrey Hinson and Madonna White Bear were next, revealing some things the men had not yet heard.

"We met the first girls—Julia Lake and Maggie Henry—in Blaine, at the motel," began White Bear. "We transported them to the hospital in Fort Yates and we just talked to them, or just let them talk. We wanted them to become comfortable with us. They took turns riding shotgun. They each were curious about how a cruiser works, the computer, and so on. So, by the time we got to Fort Yates they loosened up a bit. They wanted us to stay with them, in the room, when the doctors checked them out."

"We set up a room to interview them in, using a voice-activated recorder we picked up in Pierre," she continued. "When we started, they were a little hesitant, but we let them take their time, and after a while it seemed like everything broke loose."

Audrey Hinson nodded and added, "Yeah, once they started talking, we didn't have to ask too many questions. It just all came out. They talked about everything."

"They told us that two men would come just about every evening, especially in the warm weather, and take usually two of them at a time to the man camp. Each one was in a trailer for an hour, sometimes with one man and sometimes there were two. One girl in one trailer." Hinson paused and shook her head. "They had to—they were forced to do all kinds of sexual acts. Sometimes it was worse than at other times."

"When the hour was over the handler would pick them up and take them back to the house. Each way they were barefoot and had a hood over their heads. After they were back in the house, the basement, they had to clean themselves. There were two big plastic tubs and two five gallon buckets of water."

"The food was cold meat, lunch meat, and cheese and bread, and several kinds of chips, sometimes fruit. They drank bottled water. There were personal hygiene items like toothbrush, toothpaste, soap, shampoo, hairbrushes, combs, tampons, toilet paper. They used two camp toilets that were switched out once a week."

Hinson paused and glanced at Madonna White Bear, who began speaking again. "Yeah, and they said in the evenings when the men would come to get them, they knocked twice on the door. That was the signal for the girls to get in the corner and stand. Then the men would open the door and come in with a can of mace, ready to spray in case any of the girls caused any trouble. They would point to certain girls and take them. If they brought food or something else, they would just dump it on the floor, and the girls would have to organize it. They said they were afraid, all the time."

"One of the girls we interviewed said Carrie Little Wolf told her she saw Melvina Old Lodge beaten up by the guy they called Tulo. He opened the door and Melvina didn't move fast enough to get out, so he yanked her out. Melvina pulled her hood off, apparently, and retaliated somehow. Carrie heard when he hit her, so she pulled off her hood and saw it. Tulo hit Melvina in the chest and stomach several times. When she fell, he picked her up and took her in the trailer. That was the last time Carrie saw her. Melvina somehow got away that night. Tulo couldn't find her."

Madonna White Bear stopped and covered her face for a few seconds, then massaged her eyes. "If you haven't listened to all the recordings, I think you should, every bit of it. If anyone who listens to them doesn't feel sick and get pissed off, then something's wrong."

"You're right about that," Avery affirmed. "Thanks, Audrey and Madonna. I'm glad the girls trusted you enough to share their stories. I know it wasn't easy to hear."

"Yeah," White Bear said, "but think of how it was to live it, what they went through, I mean."

A heavy silence descended on the room. Six pairs of eyes stared angrily ahead.

Justin Primault took up the story again and described how the group of men decided to mount an aerial search for the girls on the list found in Melvina Old Lodge's shoe, and invited Gavin Lone Wolf to join the search after his fiancée Katherine Hill was abducted; also how Gerard Lone Wolf sent one of his technicians and advanced search equipment to help with their mission. After rescuing the ten girls, they focused on finding Katherine Hill. They concluded she was being held at a large log house near the town of Medora with a big barn and an airstrip. They caught the two handlers and manager of the sex trafficking scheme and rescued Katherine, only to lose track of the head of the operation, who slipped away disguised as a folksy farmhand.

"Thanks, Justin," Avery said. "At any time during that phase of it, did you have to use deadly force?"

"No, we did not."

"Well done," Avery said. "After I received an email from Justin informing me of the situation, I called the county sheriff and apprised him of the circumstances. Sheriff Kinsley then went to the ranch and took over. The perpetrators, three of them, were transported to jail and other authorities, as I understand it, arrived to conduct investigations that are ongoing.

"We also informed Sheriff James Arnold of Benson County because the imprisonment houses were in his jurisdiction. Justin and the others took the sheriff to those houses. The day after all our people arrived back here, I received a call from the director of the state department of criminal investigation informing me that the two houses where the girls were imprisoned had burned to the ground sometime during the night. An investigation into that is ongoing."

Avery paused and nodded to the clerk, Jenny, who switched off the recorder. "This will suffice as a summary," he went on. "I will have it transcribed, look it over and develop follow-up questions to expand it into a comprehensive report. I appreciate all of you taking the time to do this."

"Chief," Audrey Hinson said, "do you think we'll ever learn who set the fires?"

"I doubt it."

"Does that mean that nothing will come out of it, no further investigation?" Madonna White Bear asked.

"That's very likely."

White Bear was incensed. "So, after everything that happened to those poor girls, right under their noses, that sheriff is going to do nothing?"

"We'll have to wait and see."

Sergeant. West raised a hand. "Sir, you know, word is slowly getting out about this rescue of ten girls. I've gotten calls from other departments, I know you have, too. Do you think it will be enough of a motivation to convince the state, the feds, and other tribes to put this issue of missing and murdered indigenous women front and center?"

"I don't know, Gabby. I hope it does. If this doesn't do it, what will?"

FIFTY-SEVEN

Under the firm and patient control of Chief Ben Avery, the plan to bring all of the twelve rescued girls to Smokey River to be interviewed was implemented without significant problems. Over a dozen women, including the two female Smokey River Tribal Police officers, social workers, mental health counselors, and nurses volunteered to do the interviews. The first step in the process was to attend training sessions conducted by a female gynecologist and a female psychologist: one to inform the interviewers of the sexual consequences of the multiple rapes the girls had suffered, and the other to teach them how to ask the questions.

A film and audio crew from Smokey River University, all females, was assigned to record all of the interviews. When offered a choice between audio only and video, all of the young ladies gave their permission to be put on video. A secure temporary studio was set up in the casino's theatre, usually reserved for musical performances. Two days were scheduled for the interviews. The women in charge, Loren Hale, because she was the director nursing at the IHS hospital, and the chief social worker for the tribe Matilda Hilliard, were not surprised when all the girls wanted to be interviewed as a group.

At the end of the first day of interviews, the interviewers were shocked and horrified as the individual stories from the girls unfolded. It was nearly impossible not to react emotionally, but in the end their reactions struck a chord with the girls and was a main reason for them to trust and hold nothing back. As a result, all the questions were asked and the interviews were completed by seven-thirty in the evening.

Loren and Matilda had requested that the casino cafeteria be closed to the public so the girls could dine together in private, with their families. That evening, during the meal, they were informed of Henry Two Crow's invitation to participate in a healing ceremony. All of them accepted.

The next evening nearly twenty vehicles arrived at Andrew No Horn's place, which was large enough for the twelve girls and any of their families who also wanted to participate. The ceremony began at sundown. Katherine and Gavin brought over the food they had prepared for the meal afterwards and found a woman sitting outside the ceremony house.

"Good evening," Katherine said in greeting. "I'm Katherine Hill-Lone Wolf. Are you related to one of the girls?"

"Yes," the woman replied. "I'm Helen Baxter. My daughter is Neva."

"I'm sure there is plenty of room in there, if you want to go in," Katherine said.

"That's okay. I'll just wait," Helen said.

Gavin carried over a box of food and placed it near the door.

"Oh, dear," Helen said, "We didn't bring any dishes, or anything."

"That's okay," Katherine assured her. "We brought everything, bowls, cups, utensils, and napkins."

"Oh, okay. How long do you think the ceremony will take?"

"An hour, maybe two," Gavin said.

"Well, I never been to one, neither has Neva. I don't believe in that sort of thing, but she wanted to do it, probably because all the other girls are. I'm Catholic, myself."

Gavin brought a second box from the truck, and shook his head at Katherine's puzzled expression, assuming she was taken aback by the woman's comment. He had never found it productive to respond to negative attitudes regarding Lakota ceremonies, especially if it came from a Lakota person espousing to be Christian. They were often the harshest and most vocal critics. He didn't want to engage in a debate.

"All those girls were very brave in telling their stories," he said.

"Did you hear them?" she asked.

"Oh, no," he replied. "They will be kept confidential, and not released to the public. I did hear some of the statements by the first two girls who were rescued."

"Well, my daughter hasn't told me everything, I think. Even though I asked her. She didn't want to talk about it. So, I was surprised that she wanted to come for this."

"She's probably more comfortable because of all the other girls. They're all here together."

"Yeah, that's probably it," Helen agreed.

An hour and a half later the ceremony ended, signaled by the door opening, and one of Henry Two Crow's singers exited.

"How did it go?" Gavin asked.

"Good, really good," the man said. "They brought up something after the ceremony was over. They all want to go and visit Melvina Old Lodge's grave tomorrow."

FIFTY-EIGHT

The twelve girls and Katherine gathered at St. Ignatius Catholic Cemetery, where Katherine led them to Melvina's grave. The dirt mound was still bare of grass and covered with flowers. They formed a circle around it, each of them carrying a red rose. They had decided that Carrie Little Wolf, as Melvina's best friend, should read the card they had all written and signed to Melvina. She opened the card and cleared her throat.

Father Dubin had accompanied them to the cemetery, as well as the girls' families, from three different reservations and two off-reservation towns. Also attending were Gavin, Andrew No Horn, Henry Two Crow and Ollie, Chief Ben Avery, Lieutenant Justin Primault and his wife, Loren Hale, Patrolmen Jason Singer and Geoffrey Brousseaux, and all the women who had interviewed the girls, plus two singers. But at a certain point everyone stopped and hung back. Only the twelve girls and Katherine went to the grave. Everyone sensed that only they had the right for this particular moment of farewell.

Thirteen of those souls had shared a harrowing experience. They had endured pain, anguish, constant fear, and unspeakable degradation. They were bonded forever as sisters because of it all, but also because they had persevered. They had won back their lives because in each of them lived a spark of hope that no amount of pain and anguish could extinguish. Katherine, too, had shown courage and resilience, although she had not endured the same fate of the girls. Their spirits, including Melvina's, had triumphed. It was in their blood as Lakota women, passed down from mother to daughter, stretching back countless generations, a bloodline that was the foundation of a nation.

They did one other honor for Melvina. Each of them wore a red ribbon dress.

So, they stood, the thirteen souls still above the ground, holding hands and gazing down at the flower-covered mound, eyes brimming, and tight throats holding back the sobs waiting to break past the courage. One by one they glanced at Carrie Little Wolf, who had the card in her hand.

She cleared her throat again and began to read:

> *Dear Melvina,*
>
> *We are all here because of you. You saved us by living through hell. You earned your place in the Spirit World. We will tell our daughters and granddaughters about you, so you will always live on here in this world and in our hearts. There is no word for 'goodbye' in our real language. So, we will say what our mothers and grandmothers taught us—ake waunni-yankapi kte (we will see you again). We love you, always.*
>
> *Mollie, Sarah, Anna, Julia, Winnifred, Neva, Jenny, Ann, Elizabeth, Billie, Maggie, and Carrie*

No one who heard the words could keep the tears from coming. Father Durbin wept unabashedly. The pent-up emotions erupted as the girls linked hands, beginning with deep sobs that exploded into pure grief, giving voice to the shattered innocence of youth. Twelve young women wept for a sister, but for themselves as well, releasing the anguish that only those who suffered as they had could understand.

Everyone standing behind the young women waited, standing solemnly, or weeping silently and wiping their own tears. After several moments, the emotions subsided and the young women hugged and wiped each other's tears, supported by Katherine who acted as an Auntie for the group.

Andrew No Horn gestured to the two singers who stepped forward with their hand drums and hit the opening beats and lifted their voices into an honoring song, to sing for the red dress in the ground below, and for those in the circle above.

> *Lakota winyan*(Lakota woman)
> *Nagi skapa yo*(Strengthen your spirit)
> *Niye un ca*(You are the one)
> *Wicicagi na*(All the generations)
> *Oyate kihan*(Of the people)
> *Waciniya pelo*(Depend on you)

After the song ended, the women stepped forward one by one and gently placed a red rose on the grave and took a handful of dust to carry with them.

Only Andrew No Horn noticed the red-tailed hawk circling high above the cemetery, dipping, rising, and disappearing on tipped wings.

GLOSSARY

Ate – Lakota word for "Father"

BIA (Bureau of Indian Affairs) – Federal agency within the U.S. Department of the Interior, established in 1824 as part of the War Department to deal with Native tribes; moved to the Interior Department in 1849 as overseer, then later redirected to be (supposedly) an advocate for Native tribes recognized by the federal government

Hau – Hello

Ina – Lakota word for "Mother"

Lakota –The Lakota, **Dakota** and **Nakota** tribes (each of these words means "allies" or "alliance of friends") make up the largest third of the Lakota nation, which consists of seven bands on five reservations

Leksi – Lakota for "Uncle," used in reference to one's mother's brother(s) or male cousins of one's father and mother or as a term of respect for an older man of one's parents' generation not related by blood

Mitakuye Oyasin – All my relatives

Sicangu – Third largest of the seven bands of the Lakota

Tahansi – Cousin

Takoja – Grandson

Tunjan – Niece

Tunska – Nephew

Wasicu – White person

Wasna – A Lakota power food: dried bison, elk, or deer meat pounded into a paste and combined with fat and chokecherries into patties

Wopila – Thanks and Thanksgiving

ABOUT THE AUTHOR

Joseph M. Marshall III

Award-winning Sicangu Oglala Lakota author and historian, Joseph M. Marshall III, PhD, is one of the most prolific Native writers in the United States. Raised by his maternal grandparents in a traditional Native household on the Rosebud Indian Reservation in South Dakota, he has written eighteen historical fiction and nonfiction books and narrated his own audio books. He is best known for award-winners *The Lakota Way, The Journey of Crazy Horse,* and *The Day the World Ended at Little Bighorn.* His work is informed by his background as a Lakota craftsman, who makes his own Native Lakota bows and arrows; a skilled archer; and specialist in wilderness survival. The accounts of real historical figures along with the events that he experienced on the reservation and heard as a child from his grandparents and their generation of oral storytellers figure prominently in his books. His Native name, given to him at age five is *Ohitiya Otanin,* which means "his courage is known."

Marshall's accomplishments include co-founding Sinte Gleska University on the Rosebud Reservation; teaching; public speaking; mentoring of indigenous youth; and serving on the Board of Directors of Lakota Youth Development, Inc. He has been a teacher at the high school level and a professor at several colleges and universities, where he taught Native culture, Lakota language and history. He often lectures and speaks on

Native issues and topics. In 2022 he received the Crazy Horse Memorial® Foundation Educator of the Year Award for his lifelong leadership in education and the impact that he continues to make on Indigenous youth and communities.

Marshall has served as a cultural and historical consultant and technical advisor on films, television series and documentaries. He has also appeared as an actor in two television mini-series *Return to Lonesome Dove* and *Into the West* as well in documentaries and film. In 2023, he received the Owen Wister Award by Western Writers of America for lifetime contributions to Western literature. Previous honorees include Pulitzer Prize winners N. Scott Momaday and Louise Erdrich. Marshall was inducted into the Western Writers Hall of Fame in 2023.

Marshall's "Smokey River Suspense Series" represents his first contemporary fiction. His latest novels are based on current issues facing Lakota people, including crime and the interface between tribal government, the Bureau of Indian Affairs, and the FBI, and the ongoing epidemic of Missing and Murdered Indigenous Women that has largely been ignored by the American public and media. After spending many years in Santa Fe, New Mexico, Marshall has once again returned home.